Fatal Thunder

Larry Bond

A Tom Doherty Associates Book · New York

This is a work of fiction. All of the characters, organizations, and events portrayed in this novel are either products of the author's imagination or are used fictitiously.

FATAL THUNDER

Copyright © 2016 by Larry Bond and Chris Carlson

All rights reserved.

A Forge Book
Published by Tom Doherty Associates
175 Fifth Avenue
New York, NY 10010

www.tor-forge.com

Forge® is a registered trademark of Macmillan Publishing Group, LLC.

ISBN 978-0-7653-7865-1

Our books may be purchased in bulk for promotional, educational, or business use. Please contact your local bookseller or the Macmillan Corporate and Premium Sales Department at 1-800-221-7945, extension 5442, or by e-mail at MacmillanSpecialMarkets@macmillan.com.

First Edition: May 2016
First Mass Market Edition: March 2017

Printed in the United States of America

0 9 8 7 6 5 4 3 2 1

Author's Note

The demands of publishing require that only one name appear on the front cover, but my coauthor, Chris Carlson, had as much to do with the work of creating this book as I did. As a matter of fact, Chris came up with the idea of a fifth book in what was supposed to be a four-book series.

Our ability to stay in synch, to carry virtually the same story in two different minds, is a tremendous advantage, and while I've worked with Chris for more than thirty years now on dozens of joint projects, I do not take it for granted.

We plotted this story out together, edited each other's chapters, and had a lot of fun telling a story about characters that we know very well.

Dramatis Personae

USS *NORTH DAKOTA* (SSN 784)

Commander Jerry Mitchell, Commanding Officer

Lieutenant Commander Bernie Thigpen, Executive Officer

Department Heads

Lieutenant Commander Philip Sobecki, Chief Engineer

Lieutenant Steven Westbrook, Supply Officer ("the Chop")

Lieutenant David Covey, Weapons Officer

Division Officers

- Lieutenant Russell Iverson, Main Propulsion Assistant

Lieutenant Kiyoshi Iwahashi, Damage Control Assistant

Lieutenant (j.g.) Quela Lymburn ("Q"), Assistant Weapons Officer

Lieutenant (j.g.) Stuart Gaffney, Sonar Officer

Senior Chief Sonar Technician Halleck, Sonar Division Chief Petty Officer

AMERICAN CHARACTERS

Lieutenant Commander Gill Adams, Executive Officer, USS *Oklahoma City* (SSN 723)

Gregory Alexander, U.S. Director of National Intelligence

Milt Alvarez, White House Chief of Staff

Rear Admiral Wayne Burroughs, Commander, Submarine Force, U.S. Pacific Fleet

Commander Bruce Dobson, Commanding Officer, USS *Oklahoma City* (SSN 723)

Malcolm Geisler, U.S. Secretary of Defense

Allison Gray, Deputy White House Chief of Staff

Senator Lowell Hardy (D-CT), former captain of USS *Memphis* (SSN 691)

Admiral Bernard Hughes, U.S. Chief of Naval Operations

Captain Glenn Jacobs, Commander, Submarine Squadron (SUBRON) 15 Chief Staff Officer

Andrew Lloyd, U.S. Secretary of State

Evangeline McDowell, President's secretary

Kenneth L. Myles, President of the United States

Commander Scott Nevens, Commanding Officer, USS *North Carolina* (SSN 777)

Commander Ian Pascovich, Commanding Officer, USS *Texas* (SSN 775)

Dr. Joanna Patterson, U.S. National Security Advisor

James Randall, Vice President of the United States

Captain Charles Simonis, SUBRON 15

Commander Richard Walker, SUBRON 15 Operations Officer

Robert Eldridge, U.S. Ambassador to India

PEOPLE'S REPUBLIC OF CHINA CHARACTERS

Admiral Jing Fei, Commander, People's Liberation Army Navy

Lieutenant/Major Li Shen, intelligence officer, People's Liberation Army

General Shi We, Chinese Minister of National Defense

Lieutenant General Tian Ju, Commander, Hong Kong
Garrison

Major General Yeng Gan, Chinese Defense Attaché to
the United States

Xi Ping, Chinese Ambassador to the United States

Captain Zhang Bo, Commander, Hong Kong Garrison
Naval Brigade

RUSSIAN CHARACTERS

Jascha Churkin, former Spetsnaz commando and
Kirichenko's deputy

Captain Yetim Sergievich Gribov, Master of the icebreaker *50 Years of Victory*

Vice Admiral Ivan Loktev, Deputy Commander of the
Russian Northern Fleet

Admiral Yuri Kirichenko, Russian Navy (Ret.), former
Commander of the Russian Northern Fleet

Anton Kulik, former Russian naval officer and technician working on *Chakra*'s overhaul

Captain Mishin, Russian Naval Attaché to the United
States

Evgeni Orlav, former Russian naval officer and technical expert on Russian nuclear weapons

Captain First Rank Aleksey Igorevich Petrov, Russian
Navy (Ret.), former captain of Russian submarine
Severodvinsk

Arkady Vaslev, Russian Ambassador to the United
States

Captain First Rank Viktor Zhikin, Commanding Officer
of the 328th Expeditionary Rescue Squad

Valery Zykov, Russian diplomat and Washington station chief for the Russian Foreign Intelligence
Service

INDIAN CHARACTERS

Vice Admiral Badu Singh Dhankhar, Commander of the Eastern Fleet

Larraj Handa, President of India

Gopan Jadeja, Indian Foreign Minister

Vishnu Kumar, Director of the Central Bureau of Investigation

Captain Mitra, Supervisor of the Visakhapatnam Shipyard

Commander Fali Gandhi, Visakhapatnam Shipyard Weapons Engineer

Shankar Pathak, Indian Prime Minister

Captain Girish Samant, former Commanding Officer of the submarine *Chakra*

Special Director Ijay Thapar, Deputy Director of the Central Bureau of Investigation

INS *CHAKRA*

Commander Maahir Jain, Commanding Officer

Lieutenant Commander Kumar Rakash, First Officer

Lieutenant Jal Kirit, Combat Systems Officer

Lieutenant Harish Kota, Navigator

Chief Petty Officer Patil, senior sonar rating

Fatal Thunder

PROLOGUE

Joanna Patterson saw the major's excited expression and tried to stay calm. Pausing for just a moment, she announced to the small group in her office, "We'll have to continue this later. Kathy will give you a time this afternoon."

There was no discussion. The meeting was over, and the staffers quickly gathered their materials and filed out of her office as Walsh stepped aside. There were a few questioning looks, but nobody spoke.

Major Kevin Walsh, U.S. Army, remained silent, almost motionless, until they'd left, then quickly closed the door. He didn't bother sitting down. "Dr. Patterson, DSP satellites report a nuclear detonation in Kashmir." He glanced at the wall clock. "Detonation was eight minutes ago."

Her heart turned to ice and she asked, "How big?," then shook her head. "No, they don't know that yet. Where, exactly?"

Walsh opened his tablet and passed it to her. It showed the entire Indian subcontinent, with a small red dot over the disputed territory lying between India and Pakistan. She zoomed in until Kashmir filled the screen. "It's in the part of Kashmir controlled by Pakistan," she observed. "And square in between the front lines."

"The detonation was close to Muzaffarabad." Walsh pronounced the city's name smoothly. He spoke Pashto as well as Arabic, one of the reasons she'd picked him for her staff. "Lashkar-e-Taiba's principal base in Kashmir is located fifteen kilometers to the north of that city, tucked into one of those mountain valleys."

Patterson zoomed the map in again. The red dot looked to be a little north and west of the city. "Right on target. Were the Indians that angry about the stalled peace talks?" She felt a flash of anger, then confusion. No, they couldn't be that stupid. Could they?

Walsh explained, "The whole area's mountains and valleys. The terrain should shield the town from the blast and heat flash, but the fallout . . ."

She started to zoom in again, but stopped short and quickly handed the tablet back to Walsh. They'd worry about civilian casualties later. She was the national security advisor, and had things to do. "Is the quick-look report ready for the president?" She was confirming, not asking.

"Yes, ma'am. Captain Cruz is ready to brief him right now, and Commander Ashe is standing by to brief Chief of Staff Alvarez."

"Get them going, now. The president's going to be calling me five minutes after the briefing to ask for my recommendations. Call Cheyenne Mountain back and get an amplifying report on what the satellites saw. Then get ahold of NGA and see if they have any imagery of the blast area. I'll also need an estimate of the yield. Be back here in four minutes."

"Yes'm." Walsh almost ran from the room, and as he left, she called, "Kathy!"

Her secretary, Kathy Fell, knew that tone and hurried in, notepad ready. "Yes, Dr. Patterson."

"Kathy, a nuclear weapon's exploded in Kashmir, and it's going to look like one's gone off around here when the media finds out. That'll be in about fifteen minutes if CNN is on the ball, and I've got to give President Myles my recommendations before that."

Fell's eyes widened a little, but she replied simply, "Yes, ma'am."

"Get all our senior staff in the conference room for a brief and retasking."

"When should they be there?" Fell asked.

"As soon as they're told," Patterson answered. "I'll be there in ten minutes. Schedule an NSC meeting for eleven o'clock. Principals or deputies, but I want someone there, with whatever information they have about the Kashmir bomb, then another meeting for six tonight of the full National Security Council—no deputies at that one."

"Secretary Geisler's in Cleveland," Fell reminded her.

"We'll set up a video link if he can't get back before then," Patterson quickly answered. "The SECDEF is a must. And reschedule anything on my calendar for today and tomorrow that isn't an ultraviolet priority."

"Yes, ma'am," Fell answered, writing as she spoke.

The phone rang, and Fell started to reach for it, but Patterson waved her off. "I've got this one."

Patterson picked up the phone and listened for a moment. "Yes, Mr. President. No, sir, we don't have any details at the moment. We've started working the problem and I'll have an update for you in fifteen minutes. Excuse me for one moment, sir."

Kathy Fell was almost out the door, and Patterson called after her, "Make sure someone is working on the OPREP-3 message, and get someone to start working on the weather patterns right away—all the way out to the western Pacific."

She raised the phone again. "No, sir, I don't know what the Indian government thinks they can accomplish . . ."

8 March 2017
2145 Local Time
USS *North Dakota*
South China Sea

The sudden knock on the stateroom door jolted Jerry Mitchell from his dazed state. Shaking his head and clearing the mental mist, he managed, "Come in."

The door swung open and a mess specialist walked in, a stainless-steel carafe in his hands. "Here's the coffee you asked for, Skipper. Can I get you anything else?"

Jerry swiftly extended his well-tarnished mug toward the sailor; like a destitute street beggar, he desperately needed the empty volume filled. "Thank you, Petty Officer Johnson, but this is all I really need right now."

Johnson filled the mug and set the carafe on the fold-out work desk. Jerry thanked him again as he left, then took a sip and looked up at the clock. He still had another hour of work reviewing the engineering logs before he could call it a day—a long day. No sense procrastinating. His XO would deposit the next batch of paperwork into his in-box by tomorrow afternoon. Jerry was silently grateful that this patrol was far less eventful than the last one.

It had been almost six months since the war between China and the Littoral Alliance had come to an abrupt end. A lot had happened in those six months: President Myles had been reelected, his close friend Joanna Patterson had become the national security advisor, his boat had been formally transferred to Squadron Fifteen, and to top things off, Emily was expecting their first child. Jerry winced as he recalled the unpleasant move from Hawaii to Guam during her first trimester. Cleaning, packing, and teaching didn't mix well with morning sickness—an empirical observation that Emily had reminded him of, and often.

Jerry's family was beyond enthusiastic when they received the news of Emily's pregnancy. His sister Clarice reported that their mother had actually shouted, "Alleluia!

About time!" Their dad began chuckling ominously and muttering, "My little revenge." This sinister comment had prompted Jerry to recall the knuckleheaded antics he'd pulled as a child.

Still, with the move behind them, Emily feeling better and teaching again, and the soon-to-be grandparents waiting with bated breath, happiness and serenity had returned to the Mitchell household.

Jerry sighed, refilled his coffee cup, and got back to work. He'd only made it through the first set of engine room logs when the Dialex phone rang. Grabbing the handset, he answered, "Captain."

"Skipper, this is the XO, sir. Please come to radio immediately. We just received an OPREP-3 Pinnacle Nucflash message."

Jerry shook his head in confusion; he must be more tired than he thought. "Ah, Bernie, would you repeat that, please? Did you say 'Nucflash'?"

"Yes, sir. We just received a no-shit OPREP-3 Pinnacle Nucflash message. It looks like the Indians popped a nuke in Pakistan."

"I'll be right there," Jerry said, barely pausing to hang up the phone. Racing to radio, he wondered why the Indians would do something so stupid. The current Indo-Pakistani War was the last remnant of the larger Sino–Littoral Alliance conflict, but up to this point, the cease-fire was holding. Even with the talks stalled, and despite some verbal saber rattling from senior military officers on both sides, nothing suggested that either nation was ready to start shooting again. And a single nuclear weapon? This just didn't make any sense. It *had* to be some sort of mistake.

As Jerry reached the radio room, Lieutenant Commander Bernie Thigpen handed him a hard copy of the message. "The nuke went off over the Pakistani-controlled portion of Kashmir," he reported. "It was a big one, too. Initial estimates put the yield at one hundred–plus kilotons."

Jerry remained silent as he read the message. The contents failed to answer any of the truly important questions. It was just a basic report announcing the time and place of the event. There was nothing to explain the "why" behind it. He went over the text again, just to be sure, then handed the paper back to his XO, a look of sheer amazement on his face.

"I'm just as flummoxed as you are, Skipper," Thigpen empathized. "Why in the world India would do something so irrational is beyond me. Trying to kickstart peace negotiations with a nuke isn't exactly a winning tactic. Kind of defeats the purpose, don't you think?"

Jerry was still analyzing the news when a dreadful thought jumped into his mind. Alarmed, he turned toward Thigpen and said, "The wind! Which way . . ."

"It's coming from the west-northwest, sir," Thigpen interrupted. "It's a problem for India, Nepal, and parts of China; Emily and the rest of the crew's family members won't be affected by the fallout. At least not this time."

"Always the pessimist," quipped Jerry, his tone betraying his relief.

Thigpen smiled slightly. "No, sir, a realist. We both know this is really bad news, and it's very likely to get worse. Nothing good could possibly come from this."

Shock Wave

9 March 2017
1100 EST
CNN

They'd changed the studio's backdrop to a map of the Kashmir region that slowly morphed into a Google Earth landscape that then zoomed in on the specific area where the detonation had been reported. The network was still waiting for satellite images of the actual explosion site, so the graphics team had marked the spot with a small animated mushroom cloud. Occasionally the background would go to split screen, with one half devoted to the map, and the other showing photos of the Kashmiri countryside, some taken prewar, others since India's invasion of Pakistan six months ago.

CNN had its best national-security correspondent, Jane Bergen, anchoring the desk. She was a known commodity, with dark hair framing a square face and black-rimmed glasses.

"Good morning and welcome to CNN's continuing coverage of the nuclear explosion in Kashmir. It's been just over twenty-four hours since the detonation of what is now agreed was a nuclear weapon of over one hundred kilotons in Kashmir, a disputed territory and the object of so much recent fighting between India and Pakistan. India is at the center of a public firestorm of accusations, but denies any knowledge of or responsibility for the blast.

"Our entire CNN team is covering different aspects of the developing crisis, which is complicating the already difficult and tense peace negotiations between the two warring countries in Geneva, Switzerland.

"Sources in the U.S. intelligence community have confirmed to CNN that the apparent location of the blast is a major base and training camp for Lashkar-e-Taiba, a large Islamic terrorist organization operating in Afghanistan and Pakistan. LeT is responsible for dozens of attacks in India, including the infamous Mumbai hotel siege in 2008 that killed a hundred and sixty-four people and wounded hundreds more. During India's recent participation in the Littoral Alliance war with China, the terrorist group attacked the Indian naval bases at Visakhapatnam and Rambilli, damaging the Indian Navy's nuclear ballistic missile submarine *Arihant*.

"One of India's publicly stated goals in this fourth war with Pakistan is to, quoting India's defense minister, 'remove, once and for all, the threat of Islamic terrorist attacks against India launched from inside Pakistan's borders.'

"Our first guest this hour is Dr. Mark Ulrich, from the Council on Nuclear Weapons. He is an expert on the design and construction of atomic bombs, and has an update for us."

Ulrich was a heavyset man, with an untidy appearance. His hair was mussed, and he needed to straighten his tie. "We've concluded, based on seismographic readings from several different sources, that the weapon was larger than we originally estimated, approximately one hundred and fifty kilotons, about ten times the size of the Hiroshima blast."

"Does this increased size of the blast change the casualty estimate your group published last night?"

Ulrich riffled through the notes in front of him. "Of course, those were early estimates, but the biggest driver is still the lucky fact that the area is sparsely populated, and isolated by high valley walls, which run southeast to northwest."

He zoomed in on the satellite image. "This small village of Nullaa is closest to the camp's location, and has probably been annihilated, since it's just a few kilometers from ground zero, and lies near the floor of the valley, in line with the blast effects. The uneven terrain complicates calculating the effects at any given place, but any structure within, say, three miles will be virtually destroyed, light damage and injuries could happen as far away as ten miles."

The landscape background stopped moving, and two circles appeared on the map three and ten miles from ground zero. Ulrich pointed out almost a dozen villages and hamlets within the affected area. "There will be a lot of broken windows and minor injuries, even in the local capital, Muzaffarabad."

He sighed. "It's a remote area, which is good, because it means few people live there, but because it's so remote, it will be hard to get help in to them."

"And of course, the whole region is a war zone," Bergen added. "Although there's been a cease-fire since October. What about the fallout?" she asked.

The scientist sighed again. "It's obvious from the seismic readings that it was a ground burst, so hundreds of tons of material have been vaporized, irradiated, and lifted to high altitudes. There will be a lot of fallout. The north-northwesterly prevailing winds will carry it across the parts of Kashmir controlled by Pakistan and India, then into western China. Although Xinjiang Province in China is thinly settled, many parts of Kashmir in the path of the fallout are populated and farmed. The Himalayas will prevent the cloud from spreading south into the densely populated parts of India.

"Our meteorologist will have better estimates later today of the fallout's path, based on the current and predicted weather over the next few days."

He shook his head. "Our estimate of casualties from the explosion hasn't changed significantly, because we really have very little demographic information on the region. Our guess, and it's only that, is that several hundred, at most a thousand souls were killed by the initial blast. That includes many who will not be able to receive medical help for their injuries in time. There may be twice that many injured who will recover, but there will be tens of thousands, possibly many more, who will suffer long-term health effects from the fallout-induced radiation."

9 March 2017
2130 Local Time
U.S. Navy Support Facility
Diego Garcia, Indian Ocean

It had been a long flight from Nebraska, but the crew barely had time to eat while the aircraft was refueled. By the time they got back to the flight line, the ground crew had the plane ready for engine start.

They'd brought over thirty people with them to Diego Garcia from their home base in the U.S., but for this flight, there'd be the bare minimum complement—only enough crew to safely operate the aircraft. That was to minimize any exposure while they flew through the fallout cloud.

There was an atmosphere of urgency, but not haste. The sooner they got to the area and collected their samples, the better. Not only were the radioactive remnants of the blast decaying and dispersing by the minute, there were a lot of people who were waiting for answers.

The WC-135 was officially code-named "Constant Phoenix," but the crew just referred to it by the tail number, "67." There were only two of them in the air force. The other bird, back home at Offutt Air Force Base, was "93." A modified C-135, itself derived from the long-obsolete Boeing 707, it carried devices to capture samples of the atmosphere and any fallout particles that might be present.

The big white and gray aircraft, call sign "Windsock," began to taxi. Nearby, two F-15 fighter escorts came to life and fell in at a respectable distance behind. The U.S. already had overflight rights in Pakistan and had obtained permission from India for this mission, but its course would take Windsock into a shaky cease-fire zone, and right up to the edge of Chinese territory.

Windsock's transponder would identify it as a U.S. Air Force plane, and both the Pakistani and Indian air defenses would be notified before Windsock entered their airspace. The mission would not violate anyone's borders, but the Air Force was taking no chances. An E-3 Sentry radar plane and a RC-135 Rivet Joint SIGINT aircraft were already in position to watch and listen for any reaction from Indian or Chinese air defense.

Aerial tankers would orbit off the coast of Pakistan, over the northern Arabian Sea. Windsock would need to refuel during its eleven-hour mission, and the tankers would also keep a flight of four more F-15s on station over the water topped off and ready until Windsock cleared the area and was headed south again.

10 March 2017
1000 Local Time
INS *Circars*, Eastern Naval Command Headquarters
Visakhapatnam, India

Vice Admiral Badu Singh Dhankhar tried to project an air of calm, in both his tone and his words. "No, Captain, we're not going to cancel the operation. We owe it to everyone who's supported us up to this point."

"Admiral, please, it's not just the press. That's bad enough, but the prime minister says there will be a formal inquiry."

"Of course, but we both know that's all for show. Everyone is blaming India for the Kashmir incident, and after all, you are the head of the navy's nuclear weapons program."

Dhankhar sighed and sat down, but not at his desk. Instead, he used a chair next to Captain Kapil Asrani, and poured more tea. Asrani was taller than the admiral, and younger than Dhankhar by fifteen years, but the admiral wore his rank well. His authority and experience were well known. He'd distinguished himself as a junior officer in the Indo-Pakistani War of 1971. Now almost seventy, and commander of India's Eastern Naval Command, he was widely respected and liked, a pillar of the fleet.

He paused, as if in calm contemplation, but internally gauging Asrani's level of agitation. Too much depended on this man. The captain's office was in charge of developing nuclear warheads for India's submarine-launched missiles: the Sagarika ballistic missile that would go aboard *Arihant*, and the Nirbhay cruise missile that could be used by any submarine, and also by aircraft and from ground launchers. Both programs were a long way from being successful, though. The technical challenges were ferocious.

Asrani was smart and well educated, and Dhankhar believed him to be a patriot, but he was also a worrier. The Indian military was in shock over the nuclear explosion in Kashmir, and the entire world was blaming India for it, so it was no surprise that the captain was on edge.

Finally, Dhankhar said, "Tell them your office had nothing to do with the Kashmiri explosion, that the Indian Navy had nothing to do with the explosion, and of course that you had no personal knowledge of the explosion, before the event." Dhankhar smiled reassuringly. "The first two are certainly true, and the last is only partially false."

The captain listened, then nodded—reluctantly, but agreeing. "I've told bigger lies than that in the past months. You're right, Admiral. There's nothing there that leads back to us, and we really don't know exactly what happened in Kashmir. We can safely continue with the project."

"Continue, and finish more quickly," Dhankhar added firmly. He saw Asrani's surprised expression. "There really is nothing in Kashmir that will lead to us, but an investigation's questions and probing might accidentally trip over our project. Also, the explosion's made everyone nervous, and nervous people make mistakes." He directed a piercing look at Asrani, who nodded again.

Dhankhar said, "Orlav's been working long hours, but he can do more. We are well into the project, and there have been no surprises or problems. Everyone knows what needs to be done to finish. I think we can be ready within a month."

The admiral stood and ordered, "Come back to me tomorrow morning with a firm completion date if we abandon the schedule and work at full speed." Dhankhar saw the captain open his mouth to object, but cut him off. "The quicker we finish, the less exposure and the less risk of accidental discovery. By the time the formal investigation is under way, we'll be done."

"Yes, Admiral, I'll give you a detailed answer tomorrow morning," Asrani acknowledged, standing. "But what about *Chakra*'s refit?"

"After you give me our completion date, I'll go to the yard supervisor and tell him that the refit is being cut short because of 'heightened tensions' after the Kashmir explosion. The way everyone's reacting, that's certainly believable. I'll brief Captain Jain myself."

11 March 2017
1100 Local Time
INS *Circars*, Engineering Hall, Ship Building Centre
Visakhapatnam, India

Captain Girish Samant found most of his staff in the conference room, huddled around a television tuned to a news channel. The announcers were babbling about the first eyewitness reports from the area, and displaying aerial photos. "Back to work! This has nothing to do with us!"

Samant's tone was sharp, almost venomous, and the staffers fled. There were two doors into the conference room, and nobody used the door nearest Samant. In fact, nobody even looked directly at the captain.

Scowling, Samant walked quickly over to the television and turned it off, stopping the offensive chatter. He had no patience for people so easily distracted. They had more important things to do. The program office was behind on a number of mandatory reports, and Samant had called in his entire staff to work on Saturday to catch up. Many of the engineers had complained bitterly about his mad insistence on working extra hours just to keep an arbitrary schedule. *This is why it takes India thirty years to design and build a submarine,* he fumed.

Samant remembered the papers in his hand. He'd been trying to find one of the financial analysts, to review the cost estimates for the propulsion system, and his search had discovered not only one office empty, but all of the offices, and that had led the Indian captain here.

The analyst's name was Singh. Samant had to refresh his memory by looking at the report. He'd been in charge of the project for only two days, and was still learning names.

He would have much preferred remaining aboard *Chakra,* but he could see why Vice Admiral Dhankhar had assigned him here. The reassignment had been unexpected. By rights, he should have remained captain of the sub for another six months before being transferred ashore. He wondered if his predecessor had committed some horrendous blunder, or if Dhankhar had just become fed up with the project's lack of progress.

The Advanced Submarine Program was India's second attempt to design and construct a nuclear submarine. The first program had created *Arihant,* now in service. The second boat, *Aridhaman*, was under construction, so it could certainly be considered a success, but the follow-on submarine design was taking much too long. By rights, the new program, building on the experience of the first, should have progressed much more quickly. But it wasn't, as far as he could see.

His mind returned to the meeting with Vice Admiral Dhankhar. It had been straightforward enough—a review of the progress on *Chakra*'s refit, which had drifted into a discussion of the ongoing truce talks and the course of the war with Pakistan.

India had planned to eliminate Pakistan as a threat—remove her nuclear capability and destroy the bases in Pakistani territory that supported the terrorist attacks against India. They'd almost succeeded before the weather had closed in and ended the campaign until the spring.

Whatever the government might claim were the reasons for agreeing to truce talks, Samant and the rest of the military knew that the Indian Army had stopped advancing. Pakistani resistance had stiffened as Chinese support increased and the weather worsened. They were inside Pakistani territory, but not far enough. The enemy army, largely intact, still faced them, and their nuclear weapons were still a threat.

The most common scenario for the Kashmir incident held by Indian military personnel, discounting aliens, was that some of the Pakistani nuclear weapons had fallen into the hands of, or been handed over to, Lashkar-e-Taiba, and that somehow, perhaps in preparing a weapon for a future terrorist attack, someone had crossed the blue and red wires.

Dhankhar and Samant had been discussing the frightening implications of that hypothesis when the admiral had suddenly declared, "The real problem is China."

Samant had immediately agreed, of course. It was universally understood among the military that with China now providing more support to Pakistan, and with the shock of the initial invasion having worn off, a resumption in fighting would find India facing a much more dangerous opponent, and a harder task.

The admiral stated firmly, "If we could prevent the Chinese from backing Pakistan, we could certainly win the military campaign and force the Pakistanis to agree to our terms."

Samant didn't like to disagree with admirals. Dhankhar was right, but wishing for China to go away was a waste of effort. China was helping Pakistan, and would continue to do so. That was a reality that India had to live with. Finally, he replied, "Wouldn't that just widen the war, sir? And this time, India would be fighting alone. We may have missed our chance, sir. Maybe giving the Pakistanis back their territory in return for assurances . . ."

"And we'll be right back where we started, Captain," Dhankhar replied harshly. "I can't accept that, after so much blood and effort, halfway to our goal."

Dhankhar had ended the meeting shortly after that, and two days later, Samant had received orders relieving him of command of *Chakra* and assigning him to be the head of the Advanced Submarine Program, designing India's next nuclear submarine. It was a logical step in his career, if a little premature, but Samant kept asking himself if there was a connection between the two events.

Instead of putting his foot through the television screen, Samant decided to return to his office. He'd find Singh later, after he'd cooled down a little more. He didn't mind letting the people under his command know he could get angry, but angry people could make bad decisions.

And his outburst had sent a clear message. The rest of INS *Circars* might be going insane. They might double the security at the main gate. They might post sentries and institute ID checks at the entrances to every building. They might even close the commissary because they were worried about terrorist attacks, but this office would not follow their example.

Back in his office, he sat down to organize his thoughts. His eyes fell on the large photograph of *Chakra*, hung on the center of the opposite wall, facing his desk. His new office was almost palatial, compared with the closet-sized space he'd lived and worked in aboard the submarine, but he missed it. He missed being in command of one of the most important units in the Indian Navy.

He still worried about her, too. Was all this confusion affecting the refit? He thought of phoning Jain and visiting for a few minutes, but was reluctant to call. He and Jain had never been that close. It had never seemed appropriate to Samant. Jain would be busy enough without getting a call from his former commanding officer. He might even interpret it as meddling.

Better to focus on the task at hand. Lead by example.

He left to find Singh.

11 March 2017
1700 Local Time
Visakhapatnam, India

Aleksey Petrov often ate at Akshaya's, in the restaurant district northeast of the naval base and the dockyard. Many of the other Russians working in Visakhapatnam, or "Vizag," ate there as well. The staff was considerate of foreign sensibilities, toning down the spices below their customary volcanic intensity, and they'd actually tried adding some foreign items to the menu. Luckily, Petrov liked pierogies, and hadn't had the heart to tell the manager they were Polish, not Russian.

Virtually all the Russians in Vizag worked either at the naval base or the dockyard, and often met at Akshaya's, sharing conversation—usually news from home and complaints about the heat and humidity.

Today the talk was all about work. The Russians who worked at the dockyard as technicians or consultants were in an uproar. At noon, Captain Mitra, in charge of the work on *Chakra*, had called everyone into the shipyard and announced that the sub's refit was to be cut short. She had to be ready for sea in four weeks!

" 'By April tenth,' Mitra announced," Ivanov reported, "as if it was that easy! Admiral Dhankhar was there, too, looking as if he was afraid Mitra wouldn't recite his speech properly."

Anton Kulik, an electronics technician and former sonar officer, complained, "It doesn't make sense. I'm still routing the new cabling. Some of the new components aren't even on hand yet. Mitra says anything that can't be finished by April tenth should just be closed up as best we can."

"Why?" Petrov asked. He was just as puzzled as the others, but not as emotionally attached to the refit work. He worked over in the Engineering Hall as a consultant on submarine technology; that is, until this afternoon. Now he was a special advisor to Mitra.

"The heightened tensions after the Kashmir blast require *Chakra* to be operational as soon as possible, according to Mitra." Ivanov sounded angry, as if he'd been insulted. "Was that the best excuse they could come up with?"

"Maybe they're nervous about having both nuclear subs in the dockyard at the same time," Petrov said, shrugging. "It's not a good reason to end the refit early, but it's easier to believe."

"No, that doesn't make any sense," Suslov said, shaking his head. "The entire reason they scheduled the refit was because they knew *Chakra* wouldn't play a big part in the war with Pakistan. That hasn't changed, as far as I can see."

Everyone at the table, Petrov included, nodded agreement. The Indian Navy had definitely wanted *Chakra* to be refitted. Preparations had included over a year of planning, negotiations with Russia and money spent for parts and equipment to be fitted into the sub, more money to prepare the dockyard—it would fill a book. To suddenly abandon the project like this was more than just a bad decision.

Many of the Russians intended to go back to the dockyard after dinner. "It's long hours for me, but not as bad as Orlav," Kulik remarked. "I'm supposed to take his dinner back to him. He's working in the first compartment— maybe an all-nighter."

Petrov had heard of Evgeni Orlav, a weapons technician in his forties. He was an electronics technician working on the torpedo tubes' interface with the fire control system. "What's he working on that's so urgent?" he asked.

Kulik shrugged as he paid his dinner bill. "It's something the Indians have him doing and he won't talk about it at all. He'll complain about his ugly wife and her enormous family all night, but he never talks shop.

"Orlav really works for Dhankhar, not Commander Gandhi. The admiral put him on the refit team, and Orlav makes his progress reports directly to the admiral. He's either in the first compartment working on the gear aboard the sub, or he's in one of the torpedo shops, 'conducting tests' he says."

Kulik lowered his voice. "I think the Indians have a nuclear cruise missile ready to deploy, or at least test, and Orlav's installing the interface."

Petrov nodded. "I didn't think their cruise missile was ready yet. But perhaps the development schedule has been moved up, and that's why they're cutting the refit short," he reasoned.

Kulik was noncommittal. "That's not the type of thing I'd want to hurry. Whatever it is, after Mitra made his announcement, the admiral pulled Orlav aside and they spoke for a while. Orlav wasn't happy. I'm betting Dhankhar told him to get the work done and to sleep after *Chakra*'s finished."

11 March 2017
1900 Local Time
Tbilisi, Georgia

Yuri Kirichenko heard the satellite phone buzz and almost snatched it from the cradle. Only one person had the number for that phone. He turned it on and said, "Jascha Churkin! So, you're alive."

"Just barely. I was in Ghori, just under five kilometers away, but across a small mountain from the blast. The flash and the shock wave were still beyond anything I've ever seen. I may start believing in God again. Most of Ghori was flattened. Since then, I've been traveling south and waiting for the ionization cloud to disperse. This is the first time I've been able to get through."

"And your search for the missing warhead is now moot. What about the thieves?"

"I found them. Faysal is radioactive gas, but I located Jawad at Muzaffarabad, living a most un-Islamic life. He was drunk."

"Jawad? From our escort? The short one?"

"And his friend Faysal, who Jawad said was an 'electronics expert.' The little thug was following us at a distance, and brought the substitute crate. He even had the correct markings on the outside."

"Morons," Kirichenko muttered, "and yet not. This plan was supposed to be foolproof. The warheads were worthless to the militants from Al Badr we hired. I must have explained to them three times that without the initiators, the warheads were just dead metal."

"And you promised them some live warheads from the next batch," Churkin added. "And they were paid handsomely, but you can't rely on simple greed when stupidity is mixed in."

Churkin had been responsible for security. He was a former Russian Navy special forces commando. But in addition to his impressive military skills, the navy had learned of his talent for illegal activities, ranging from bootlegging to blackmail. Kirichenko had encountered Churkin back in the nineties, out of the service and on the edge of the law. The ex-commando's skills had been vital in ensuring first the secrecy of Kirichenko's stolen stockpile, then its recovery, and now its transport across half of Eurasia.

Starting with their recovery from the Kara Sea, Churkin had shepherded the warheads on their long trip from northern Russia, across the Caspian Sea to Turkmenistan, Afghanistan, and then northern Pakistan, into Kashmir, where one of the six weapons had been discovered to be missing. Churkin had been forced to make sure the rest of the shipment was safe before leaving in pursuit of the thieves, but they had vanished into the landscape. By the time he'd found their trail, he was days behind and too late.

Kirichenko decided it was a good thing he hadn't been any closer to his goal. Churkin and Kirichenko were not fast friends, but they were kindred souls working for a common purpose—massive financial reward. His loss would have been inconvenient, at least. Kirichenko privately wondered what Churkin's plan would have been if he'd reached the LeT camp with the warhead inside.

"So why did Jawad steal one of my nuclear warheads? Did this fool Faysal think he could build his own initiator?" Kirichenko asked, almost laughing.

"No, but Faysal knew that Lashkar-e-Taiba had someone who might be able to—someone from the Khan network," Churkin reported in a dark tone.

"Oh." Kirichenko understood the implications instantly. A brilliant Pakistani scientist named A. Q. Khan had first helped build Pakistan's weapon, and then created a nuclear underground network that had provided technology to Iran, Libya, and North Korea—at least. While he'd been under house arrest for a while in Pakistan, he had been freed in 2008. His network had never been dismantled.

Churkin reported, "Those two thieves walked into that Lashkar-e-Taiba camp and were paid ten times the amount for one warhead that you gave Al Badr to transport all six. Jawad was doing his best to drink his way through his half of the money."

"Did he tell anyone else where they had obtained the warhead?" Loss of one of the six weapons was bad enough, but if the shipment had been compromised . . .

"Jawad said they didn't speak to anyone else on the way, not with what they were carrying. It took them some time to reach the LeT camp after they stole the weapon, and if Jawad was telling the truth, they reached it about the same time that the rest of our shipment crossed into Indian territory. Anyone Faysal talked to is now in hell along with him. I've also just confirmed the remaining five have reached the coast."

"And Jawad?" Kirichenko asked.

"Will not talk," Churkin replied. "I solved his drinking problem." Kirichenko could almost hear Churkin smiling.

"Then there's nothing else to be done there. You should get into India as quickly as possible."

"Understood," Churkin replied. "I'll contact you again when I'm across the border."

12 March 2017
0820 Local Time
Director General Naval Projects, Ship Building Centre
Visakhapatnam, India

Samant looked up from the keyboard when he heard the knock. His office door was open, and Maahir Jain, Samant's former first officer and now commander of INS *Chakra*, was standing in the doorway like a child waiting for a parent to notice him.

He couldn't hide his surprise—it was Sunday and he certainly didn't expect anyone to drop by his office—but he also suddenly felt great pleasure at seeing his old executive officer, and he let that show as well.

Samant almost leapt up from behind his desk, coming around to offer his hand. "*Captain* Jain. It's good to see you! Would you like some tea?" Samant pointed toward the teapot and cups but Jain waved him off.

"I cannot stay long," he explained apologetically. "I have an appointment with Vice Admiral Dhankhar at nine." After a moment's hesitation, he continued, "But I wanted to come by and see how you were faring in your new assignment. The men are asking after you, as well."

I'll bet they are, Samant thought. He'd used a "firm, but fair" command style, emphasizing discipline and professional knowledge. He'd driven *Chakra*'s crew hard, and they'd performed, but they always called him "Captain," never "Skipper." It hadn't bothered Samant, who found it hard to make friends. Being a captain wasn't supposed to be a popularity contest.

As they sat, Samant asked, "Why are you meeting the admiral here and not at the headquarters building on INS *Circars*? And on Sunday? Is this about *Chakra*'s progress, or are they going to give you a third stripe, now that you're in command?"

"You haven't heard, then?" Jain was surprised. "About the change in the refit schedule?"

Samant, confused, shook his head. "I've been trying to focus on getting the program back on schedule and ignored all the bedlam. Bad as it is, I don't see how it has much to do with what we're doing."

"They cut our yard period short, Cap—I mean, sir. We're to sail on April tenth."

"What?!" Samant was thunderstruck. He knew exactly what *Chakra*'s status was, as of a week and a half ago. The tenth of next month? *That is insane!* "Why?"

"I don't know, sir. My main concern right now is getting *Chakra* ready for sea. It's not just that the boat's in pieces. I've got people on leave and in training, and if we're going to sea, I'm already behind in arranging for torpedoes and stores . . ."

"But you're not going to ask why they've made the change?" Samant pressed.

"I'll let the officers with stars on their shoulders worry about why. I've got enough on my plate."

That didn't sit right with Samant, but he held his peace. If Jain had asked him to go with him to meet with the admiral and demand an explanation, he would have gone, but Jain didn't ask.

They talked about other things: an upcoming memorial in June for the men lost on *Arihant*, some of whom they'd both known, and the progress, or lack of progress, of the war.

It was time for Jain to leave, and Samant tried to put as much warmth into his farewell as he had into the greeting. He did wish Jain well, even if he was worried about *Chakra*'s fortunes under his command. She wasn't Samant's boat anymore, and he had to get used to that.

2

Chaos

13 March 2017
0845 Local Time
Director General Naval Projects, Ship Building Centre
Visakhapatnam, India

This is absurd! How in God's name do those idiots expect me to do my job! Samant mentally shrieked. He impatiently erased the tangled lines on his production schedule and tried yet another approach. When he pushed his mechanical pencil down on the paper, the thin lead broke—again. And despite his forceful clicking of the eraser, nothing emerged from the narrow point. In utter frustration, Samant flung the mechanical pencil at the wall. *Doesn't anything in this office work as it's supposed to?!* He rubbed his eyes and yawned. He'd been at this fruitless exercise for over three hours. With a resigned sigh, Samant reached the inescapable conclusion that his program would be dead in the water for at least a month, and there was absolutely nothing he could do about it.

Soon after Jain's visit, Samant received an e-mail from Vice Admiral Dhankhar's chief of staff informing him of the temporary transfer of all his senior engineers and program managers to support the greatly accelerated INS *Chakra* refit. With only inexperienced junior engineers and naval architects left in the office, there was little hope of getting any meaningful work done. Those "children" needed adult supervision just to find the bathroom, let alone figure out the engine room layout for India's next class of nuclear submarines. With frustration bubbling up inside him, Samant walked over and poured himself another cup of tea. Sipping the hot Earl Grey, he weighed his very limited set of options. He'd have to carefully word his response to the chief of staff on the impact the transfer would have on his project. It wouldn't pay to be viewed as a complainer this early in his new assignment.

His new, prestigious assignment. Bah! It was more like hell. Two weeks ago, he was the commanding officer of the hottest boat in the Indian Navy; the most successful submarine captain in India's history. He and his crew had done very well during the South China Sea campaign, racking up an impressive score of tankers sunk and Chinese oil refineries charred and gutted. Now, he was driving a paper-laden desk, in charge of an undisciplined group of civil servants that debated every order, all the while fighting a grotesquely inefficient bureaucracy that moved at a glacial pace. On *Chakra*, he was lord and master, but here, he was just one of many medieval nobles struggling to work within the feudal machine that was the Indian Navy. A dubious reward indeed for a job well done. But fate wasn't done taunting him just yet.

The Advanced Submarine Project's offices were on the south side of the building, with a clear view to the naval dockyard across the channel. From this lofty position, he could see *Chakra* as she was being maneuvered by a tug into the dry dock. Grabbing his binoculars from the windowsill, he watched as the crew topside went about their work. He grunted with satisfaction as the men performed their duties flawlessly. Shifting to the bridge, he could see Jain working with the pilot as the submarine inched its way into the dock. Suddenly, a pang of envy flared in Samant. He *should* be on that bridge right now, he should *still* be in command, not Jain. Samant shook his head to clear away the growing jealousy. His former first officer was simply following orders and doing his job—a job that Samant had trained him to do properly. Jain was a competent officer, if a bit too informal with the men at times. Whatever was behind Samant's sudden exile, it wasn't Jain's fault. He wasn't responsible for his captain's transfer.

Samant then recalled his mother's gloomy accusation that his current circumstances were entirely of his own making, a natural result of all the bad karma he had accrued during the war. She said he was reaping the "rewards" for all the death and destruction he had caused. A devout Hindu, she had long disagreed with her son's chosen occupation, claiming it would only bring evil to his life. At times like this, he wondered if there wasn't more to her words.

The sharp ring of the telephone yanked him from his depressed mood. He grabbed the handset, anxious for some work to drive away the nagging thoughts. "Advanced Submarine Project Office, Captain Samant speaking," he answered.

"Girish, it's Aleksey. I won't ask you how your morning is going, I think I already know. Your people just reported in to me."

Samant cracked a thin smile, recognizing the voice on the other end of the line. Shifting to English, he replied, "Well, I hope they can be of more use to you than they have been for me. And don't be afraid to flog them if they get too lazy."

The chuckle from the handset faded quickly, the voice becoming more firm. "Listen, Girish, I have some serious concerns about the changes to *Chakra*'s refit. Do you have a moment later today that I can drop by? I need a competent Indian's perspective on this. The answers I'm getting from my dockyard point of contact don't make any sense whatsoever."

"Of course, Aleksey. My schedule is largely clear this afternoon."

"Excellent! It will be a few hours until we get this boat safely on the blocks. After that I can break free and drive over to your office. Say, thirteen hundred?"

"That will work nicely."

"Good. I'll see you then."

The morning dragged on and on, and besides drinking a lot of tea, Samant's only real accomplishment was the successful crafting of a suitably polite response to the chief of staff's e-mail. He was respectful, but bluntly informed his superior that the program would be unable to accomplish much until his staff returned. However, every effort would be made to keep working those aspects of the schedule that he could with the remaining personnel. Even as he hit the send button, Samant was still struggling to figure out what exactly he could do with all his senior people gone.

At a quarter to one, Samant cleared off his desk in anticipation of his guest. When the clock struck one, Petrov still hadn't arrived and Samant got up and took another look through the binoculars at *Chakra*. She was high and dry in the graving dock. Annoyed, he started pacing. Petrov was usually very punctual.

He recalled the first time he met the former Russian submariner, now a technical consultant. *Chakra* had just returned from her successful war patrol, and had been met on the pier by the Indian Chief of the Naval Staff, Admiral Rajan. After a brief speech welcoming the boat home and praising their efforts during the war, Rajan introduced Samant to Petrov, announcing that *Chakra* would undergo her delayed refit to upgrade her tactical systems and to repair some of the nagging problems still under warranty. Rajan explained that while Petrov wouldn't be in charge of the refit, he was the senior Russian advisor and would be available to assist with any issues involving the new Russian equipment being installed on board the boat.

What started out as a working relationship based on mutual respect soon grew into a full-blown friendship. Petrov recognized Samant as a kindred soul, understanding and appreciating his passion and drive. Samant was equally impressed by Petrov's refreshing professionalism and extensive technical knowledge; he understood not only how the systems worked, but how they should be employed tactically. It wasn't long before Petrov shared with Samant his checkered past as the only commanding officer of the nuclear attack submarine *Severodvinsk*. The Indian captain listened with rapt attention as Petrov described the collision with USS *Seawolf*, *Severodvinsk*'s impact with the ocean floor, crippling her, and how an ingenious young U.S. naval officer by the name of Jerry Mitchell helped to save him and his crew.

Samant launched himself out of his chair upon hearing Mitchell's name, shocking Petrov into silence. Without saying a word, Samant walked over to a coffee table and picked up a large photo album. He hurriedly thumbed through the pages, stopped abruptly, and placed the album on the desk beside the Russian. Pointing to a two-page letter, he asked, "Is this the same man?"

Petrov quickly read the letter, and noted the USS *North Dakota* letterhead; a large smile appeared on his face. "Yes, indeed! So you tangled with my friend Jerry, eh? I'm glad neither one of you were hurt, but I'm also not surprised that your encounters ended in a stalemate. You are both very good submariners."

"He was an absolute pain in my ass!" grumbled the Indian indignantly.

Petrov laughed. "I believe that was his job, Girish."

The grimace on Samant's face slowly lightened to a faint smile. "You should have seen Jain's and my face when we realized that Mitchell had fired nuclear-armed torpedoes. I never ran away from anything so fast in all my life. Well, that and the angry torpedo barking at my hindquarters."

"I have it on good authority, Girish, that Jerry was the

mastermind behind the U.S. strategy," Petrov remarked quietly. "He somehow convinced the president of the United States to use nuclear weapons in a very unconventional way. As I said, he is very good. But just as important, he's an honorable man—like you."

Samant's reminiscing was abruptly interrupted by the buzz of his intercom. "Sir, Mr. Petrov is here to see you."

"Thank you, Miss Gupta. Please send him in."

A moment later, the door swung open and Petrov slowly walked in. He looked tired. "Good to see you, Aleks sahib. Tea?"

"Please," responded Petrov as he plopped down in one of the armchairs. "It's been a long day and it's only half over. I could use a little pick-me-up. My apologies for being tardy, security throughout Vizag has become incredibly tight and I had to undergo a full search before being allowed into the building."

Samant nodded his understanding and offered Petrov a steaming cup. "So, tell me, when did you get drafted to oversee *Chakra*'s refit?"

"Thank you," Petrov replied gratefully. After downing a few sips, he answered, "Captain Mitra called me into his office on Saturday, two days ago, and informed me of my 'promotion' to lead engineer for the refit. He then handed me the maintenance plan and told me they had to shave two months off the schedule. Apparently Vice Admiral Dhankhar wants the boat ready for sea by April tenth."

Samant bowed his head slightly as he drank. "Yes, Jain told me as much. That's nowhere near enough time to get all the work done, even if you could get every technician in the shipyard working on her. What I don't understand is, what's the rush? Why does the admiral want the boat to go to sea so early?"

Petrov paused, a look of concern on his face. "It gets even more bizarre, Girish. I have a single day for sea trials—one day, and most of the testing involves the sonar and weapon systems upgrades."

"That's ridiculous!" Samant scowled. "How can you possibly test the propulsion plant and auxiliary systems repairs in a single day?"

"We can't. A lot of that work will have to be deferred. Captain Mitra was very specific about that; only those repairs that can be completed within the revised schedule will be considered."

Samant shook his head in amazement; none of this made any sense. What were Dhankhar and his staff thinking? Unable to offer any explanation for the radical schedule change, Samant sat silent, thinking and drinking his tea. After a few moments, a visibly uncomfortable Petrov spoke quietly. "I'll understand if you can't tell me, Girish, but I have to ask. Are there any near-term plans to recommence hostilities against Pakistan? Do I need to worry about a submarine that will be going into combat?"

The blunt questions caught Samant completely unawares; Petrov was definitely out of bounds, but he completely understood why the Russian had asked. Initially suspicious, the Indian looked carefully at his friend; then he saw the haunted look in Petrov's eyes. The man desperately wanted to know if the decisions he'd have to make could result in the loss of another submarine. The ghosts of *Severodvinsk* still clung to him.

"Honestly, Aleks, I don't know of any plans to start the fighting again—not that there couldn't be some contingency plans being considered. There are a number of very frustrated senior officers who are unhappy with the peace negotiations. Our friend, Dhankhar, is one of them. But I can't see why this would require *Chakra*'s refit to be accelerated. Besides, Pakistan's navy has been badly mauled. There isn't a whole lot left, and nothing that would require an Akula-class submarine to take care of it."

Samant's answer appeared to ease Petrov's worried

expression, but not entirely. The Russian finished his tea, stood, and faced his host. "Then I have one last question for you, Girish. And I don't mean to be offensive, or seek access to India's state secrets, but it is a rather sensitive subject, so I must beg your pardon in advance."

"Certainly," replied Samant, now deeply curious.

Petrov took a deep breath, bracing himself before speaking. "Is it the Indian Navy's intention to put nuclear weapons on *Chakra*?"

"WHAT!?" shouted a stunned Samant as he leapt to his feet. "How can you even suggest such a thing!"

Petrov remained calm. Samant's reaction was completely justified; the question did sound like an accusation. "Bear with me, Girish. I will explain my reasons in a moment. Now, please, will you answer the question?"

Fuming, Samant struggled to get his anger under control. Friend or not, Petrov's insinuation was insulting. Several tense seconds went by before the Indian captain responded, and even then it was through clenched teeth. "I know of no nuclear weapons that can be fired from *Chakra*'s torpedo tubes. We currently lack the ability to make warheads that small, that's why we've concentrated on ballistic missiles. Even if the Nirbhay cruise missile were ready now for submarine launch, which it isn't, it would probably be conventionally armed. Besides, such a modification would be a gross violation of our agreement with your country."

"Agreed, on both counts. So, why have I been ordered to install the ability for the combat system to pass data to a nuclear-armed weapon?"

The fury on Samant's face dissolved into disbelief. "You must be mistaken, Aleksey. My country doesn't have a suitable weapon."

"Am I? Look here, Girish," said Petrov as he rolled out several detailed schematics of the fire control system.

"Here are the two Omnibus combat system consoles as currently configured on *Chakra*. The weapon data transfer wiring exits the back of the consoles at this point, runs to these junction boxes in the torpedo compartment, and ultimately feeds into the tubes, here. Now, note the changes on this schematic.

"See here? These are new wires that need to be installed, and they run to the existing junction boxes. But note the new panel section on the Omnibus console. The last time you saw them, this section was plated over."

Samant studied the plans carefully and frowned. "This wasn't part of the original refit plan I reviewed eight months ago. I specifically recall requesting the old CRTs be replaced with flat-screen displays and I was told there weren't going to be *any* substantial changes to the fire control system."

"Exactly, Girish, and that's the heart of my problem. These changes are very recent. But more importantly, on Russian Navy submarines, that is where the nuclear weapon control panel is located. It allows the commanding officer to unlock a weapon so it can receive start-up power, launch data, and also satisfies the final control interlock, allowing the warhead to arm."

"You're certain of this, Aleksey?"

"Absolutely, my friend. I have many, many years of experience with this system. Even so, I've tried to come up with a viable alternative explanation. So far, I haven't found one."

"Have you raised this issue with Captain Mitra?"

"Yes, of course. I made a polite inquiry about the modifications this morning. Although, I, ah, didn't mention the part about nuclear weapons," replied Petrov with a cynical grin. "Mitra said the combat system upgrade is for a new indigenous Indian weapon system that will be available in the near future. He said he wasn't at liberty to discuss it with me."

"What new weapon?" Samant grumbled. "The advanced torpedo DRDO has been working on is for European submarine designs. It's completely incompatible with

Russian submarine torpedo tubes. That's why we chose to acquire the improved UGST-M torpedo . . ."

"Which is of Russian design and manufacture," finished Petrov. "And one other thing. It appears that only Russian technicians are making this modification. Unfortunately, the maintenance package our countries agreed to has a vague clause regarding the replacement of torpedo tube interface wiring as needed. I can't say this modification is outside the scope of the contract."

"This . . . this is incredible!" stammered Samant. "Who approved this change?"

"Vice Admiral Bava, Dhankhar's chief of staff, is the only signature on the modified refit documentation."

"No one from the Controller of Warship Production and Acquisition Office signed off on it?"

"Correct," Petrov answered as he rolled up the plans. Samant rubbed his forehead and started pacing, his mind reeling.

Petrov watched as his friend walked behind the desk, a deep scowl on his face.

"Girish," pleaded Petrov, "I would like nothing more than to think this is just a clever kickback scheme to skim off some money from the refit funding, God knows there's been plenty of that in the past. But, given the nature of the modifications and the insanely truncated schedule, it's not at all consistent with simple graft. My gut instinct says something is dreadfully wrong here."

Samant stopped, and nodded slightly. Then, straightening himself, he said, "What do you want me to do, Aleksey?"

Relieved, Petrov moved closer. His speech was more animated. "Your office has two masters, one here in Vizag, the other in Mumbai. If you could make some discreet inquiries to the Directorate of Naval Design and the assistant chief of naval staff submarine acquisitions concerning new submarine torpedo tube launched weapons, I believe we'll be able to either confirm or deny my suspicions. I will do likewise through the Russian naval support liaison office, although I'm not confident I'll get much help."

"Very well, Aleksey. I will make the calls as soon as you leave. When should we try to get together again?"

"Later this evening, at Akshaya's, say twenty hundred hours. We've had dinner there before; so no one will think it unusual. And if I'm wrong, dinner is on me."

13 March 2017
1030 EST
The White House
Washington, D.C.

Joanna Patterson fought to control her excitement as she strode down the hallway to the Oval Office. She had pleaded with the president's chief of staff, Milt Alvarez, for just ten minutes of the president's time. That's all she said she needed to pass on the results of the aerial sampling analysis; after that she'd have the president's undivided attention. The single piece of paper in the folder she carried was a bombshell.

She barely noticed the lone Marine standing guard, and she didn't realize she had entered the outer office until the president's secretary greeted her. "Go right on in, Dr. Patterson. The president is expecting you."

"Thanks, Evangeline. As my husband is fond of saying, stand by for heavy rolls."

"Are you going to ruin my president's schedule—again, Doctor?" remarked McDowell with a smirk.

"Very likely, ma'am . . . Sorry."

A Secret Service agent opened the door and Patterson walked in to find the president, Alvarez, and Secretary of State Andrew Lloyd watching the TV. Alvarez waved her over, pointed to the flat screen, and whispered, "The Indian ambassador to the UN is concluding his speech."

"Oh, lovely. I bet that's going over well," Joanna said

with a wince. Alvarez's pursed lips and the sharp shaking of his head confirmed her cynical prediction.

". . . our war with Pakistan is a righteous one as they attacked us again, without provocation. The Pakistani government's denial that they had nothing to do with the terrorists that struck our naval bases last year is flimsy at best. Their policy of harboring terrorists, arming them, and protecting them from outside retribution clearly shows the Pakistani regime's true intent. And while India chose to respond militarily this time, as is our right, we have scrupulously followed the rules of war as laid out in international conventions.

"Mr. President, members of the General Assembly, let me be absolutely clear on this. India has not resorted to the use of nuclear weapons, nor do we need to. We have consistently upheld our part of the bargain during this ceasefire; the same cannot be said of Pakistan. The fact that the explosion was at a well-known Lashkar-e-Taiba stronghold can only suggest that the Pakistani government has lost its feeble grasp of reality and has begun to arm its homegrown terrorists with nuclear weapons . . ."

"And it goes downhill from here," sighed Myles as he turned off the TV.

"Wow! I fully expected India to deny using a nuclear weapon," Lloyd sneered. "But to accuse Pakistan of giving nukes to terrorists, that takes a lot of moxie!"

"The ambassador certainly played the part well," commented Alvarez. "He almost had me believing India didn't set off the nuke."

"Probably because they didn't," interrupted Joanna. The heads of all three men snapped in her direction, a shocked expression on their faces.

"Dr. Patterson, you're not suggesting . . ." Lloyd spoke hesitantly.

"I'm not suggesting anything, Mr. Secretary. What I'm saying is the data we have so far doesn't support the theory that it was an Indian nuclear device."

Myles sighed deeply again, and with a weary voice said, "Okay, Joanna, just cut to the bottom line."

Patterson placed the folder on the president's desk. "Mr. President, this is the executive summary of the analysis of the airborne samples collected by the WC-135 Constant Phoenix aircraft. The fallout cloud contained traces of both uranium 235 and 238, as well as multiple isotopes of plutonium. However, the ratio of the plutonium isotopes is not consistent with the manufacturing process used by India. Nor is the use of uranium consistent with Indian nuclear weapon design; they have historically used only plutonium."

"Correct me if I'm wrong, Joanna, but plutonium is made in a nuclear reactor and then refined, so isn't all weapons-grade plutonium the same?" Myles asked as he began skimming the report.

"You're correct, sir, plutonium is produced in nuclear reactors. But different reactor types produce different ratios of the various isotopes. Even weapons-grade plutonium still has some of the undesired isotopes in the material," Joanna replied. "The isotope ratios in the airborne samples we collected are not consistent with a heavy-water reactor that India uses to produce their plutonium. The sample, however, is consistent with a graphite-moderated, light-water reactor."

"And who uses that type of reactor to make plutonium?"

"We do, Mr. President . . . as well as Russia and China." Joanna watched as Myles dropped the file, his face pale.

"Oh my God," Lloyd whispered.

"How . . . how accurate are those results, Joanna?" groaned Alvarez.

"Postdetonation forensic analysis is not nearly as accurate as having the nuclear material itself, Milt. I can't say where the plutonium came from, but we can be reasonably confident about the reactor type that produced the material."

"Is there any way to verify the analysis, Joanna?" asked the president.

"Yes, sir. The ground samples collected from areas near the blast site are already in country and are en route to Homeland Security's National Technical Nuclear Forensics Center. We should have the lab results in a couple of days. If they are consistent with the airborne samples, then there will be little room for doubt."

"The question then, lady and gentlemen, is do we say anything right now?" solicited Myles.

"We can't possibly release this preliminary data without verification!" blasted Alvarez. "If the analysis of the ground samples contradicts these results, we'll look like fools."

"I'm very sympathetic to your views, Milt, but the world in general, and Muslim nations in particular, already holds India guilty of nuking Pakistan—there have been demands for strenuous economic sanctions across the globe," Lloyd warned. "And anti-Hindu violence is running rampant worldwide, even in the European Union. If we don't say anything, we will be responsible for the injury or death of innocent people!"

"It can't be helped, Mr. Secretary. We have to be very careful here, because the alternative explanation is even worse," cautioned Alvarez. "Before we go to the world with this information, we need to have our ducks in a very straight line, because once we say India didn't set off the nuke, the only other possible conclusion is that a Pakistani terrorist group possesses nuclear weapons—weapons that quite possibly came from China."

Lloyd groaned and rubbed his forehead. The chief of staff had a very good, but totally distasteful, point. The Pakistani government had repeatedly claimed that the LeT terrorists were operating under probable Chinese influence. If the U.S. were to indirectly corroborate that view, and then suggest that the LeT terror group had nuclear weapons, India might be compelled to conduct a preemptive strike to counter an unprecedented and unacceptable threat. One nuclear blast could become many.

Myles shook his head, depressed. He really didn't need this right now; the U.S. economy was still trying to recover from the Sino–Littoral Alliance War. He then looked over at Patterson and noted she hadn't said a word. "You're being awfully quiet, Joanna. What do you think?"

I'm trying hard not to, she thought to herself. But recognizing that that wasn't a proper answer, she said, "Both Milt's and Secretary Lloyd's views are valid, Mr. President, but neither recommendation is free from the possibility of political backlash against the United States. I'm afraid this is a case of choosing what you believe is the lesser of two evils."

Myles chuckled, his face sporting a tired grin. "That sounds like our good friend, Ray. He always did have a knack of walking a very fine line."

Joanna looked down, blushing. Being favorably compared to her former boss and predecessor was quite an accolade—Raymond Kirkpatrick was a Jedi master in the policy world. "I'll take that as a compliment, Mr. President," she said softly.

"As it was meant to be," responded Myles. Taking another deep breath and rising, he continued, "Okay, Milt, we'll withhold the results of the airborne samples for now. But I want a well-crafted and coordinated press release to go out the minute after Joanna gets back to us with the ground-sample analysis.

"Andrew, I want the State Department to reach out, quietly, to our allies, the Littoral Alliance, and yes, even the Russians and the Chinese. Tell them what we are doing, but not what we've learned. Ask them for their patience as we evaluate the samples."

Both Alvarez and Lloyd replied, "Yes, Mr. President."

"And you, Joanna, I need those ground sample results

as soon as you can possibly get them to me. But, they have to be done right. We can't afford a mistake on this, we have to be extremely confident of our findings."

"Absolutely, sir."

"Good. We'll also need to release the results of the analyses at the same time, we just can't make a claim like this and ask the world simply to believe us. I want a succinct, but very basic report that we can release publicly. Remember a lot of non-tech-savvy politicians are going to read this, so we have to make this easy to understand. Got it?"

The three advisors all nodded and headed for the door.

13 March 2017
1955 Local Time
Visakhapatnam, India

Samant took another swig of his cold Kingfisher lager; he badly needed a morale boost. He'd arrived early so he could have some time to unwind; the day had been one long serving of bad karma. Petrov walked in exactly at eight o'clock, signaled the bartender, and ordered, "A Kalyani Black Label, please."

Samant chuckled as his friend sat down. "Going native on me, Aleksey? I thought you Russians preferred vodka?"

"No, no, Girish, vodka is for cooler climates. In this heat a cold lager is much better."

"Heat? What are you talking about? It was only thirty-one degrees Centigrade today!"

"Where I come from, we cook at those temperatures," Petrov said with a wink. The waitress delivered his beer, and after thanking her, he raised his bottle and said, "Nostrovia!"

"Cheers!" replied Samant as they clinked their bottles.

After ordering dinner, and taking a sip or two of beer, Samant finally broke the ice. "So, what luck did you have?"

Petrov smiled as he spoke. "Actually, better than I

thought. I confirmed with the naval liaison staff that the only new Russian weapon being added to *Chakra*'s arsenal is the UGST-M torpedo, and that the necessary combat system modifications are actually quite minor. Nothing that requires the changes Dhankhar's staff has approved."

Leaning forward, he went on with a hushed voice. "But I also went down to the torpedo compartment and inspected the junction boxes. Tubes one through four, the original fifty-three-centimeter torpedo tubes, *have* the proper boards with the connectors for the new wiring. Tubes five through eight, the converted sixty-five-centimeter torpedo tubes, do not."

Samant looked puzzled. "I don't recall seeing any extra connectors. And I've inspected those junction boxes numerous times."

"I'm not surprised, Girish," Petrov said with another wink. "They're on the back side of the circuit board. You have to know where to look to find them. The boards appear to be original pieces of equipment. I tried to get the liaison staff to track down the serial numbers, but Osinov refused. He claimed he didn't have the personnel or time for such foolishness."

"If the boards were there from the original transfer, why weren't they replaced? All the other equipment capable of supporting nuclear weapons was removed."

"I suspect the shipyard just left them in place, because with everything else gone, it wouldn't matter. They could save a few rubles by not replacing them."

"Did you ask about the extra wiring?" questioned Samant.

"Of course, I told Osinov that the wiring didn't appear to support anything and I asked him why I had to do it given the severely shortened schedule. He told me that if the 'stupid Indians' wanted the extra wiring routed, then by God we'd route the wiring. He wasn't going to have another cabling debacle on his hands like the one with the *Gorshkov* aircraft carrier transfer. Oh, and the wiring work is to be performed by a technician named Evgeni Orlav. Rumor has it he has been working ridiculously long hours in an isolated area of the shipyard, and supposedly reports directly to Dhankhar himself, even though he's assigned to an Indian naval engineer."

The two men paused their discussion as their meals were served. Petrov took a bite while the waitress moved out of earshot. "What did you find out from your masters in Mumbai, Girish?"

Samant waited as he swallowed. "I had a very unsatisfying discussion this afternoon with both the heads of weapons developments at the Directorate of Naval Design and the assistant chief of naval staff submarine acquisitions. Both said basically the same thing, the only nuclear-armed weapons that will go on Indian submarines are ballistic and land-attack cruise missiles. When I asked about torpedoes or ASW missiles with nuclear warheads, they laughed. Apparently DRDO has some plans, but they are many years in the future. And, of course, there are no intentions to augment *Chakra*'s weapons capability with any indigenous Indian ordnance—it's against the contract we have with your nation."

Petrov nodded, then wiped his mouth. He looked around the room, checking to see if anyone was taking an interest in their conversation. "Here's another tidbit for you, Girish. I was told by an Indian engineer that the combat system change was signed by Vice Admiral Bava on March tenth. The engineer was most unhappy with this, as it was a new requirement that interfered with some of his work and he wanted to coordinate scheduling with my technician. Not only does this confirm that a Russian national will do the modification to the combat system, but when this change was approved."

"The tenth of March? That's the very day I was relieved of command!"

"Coincidence?" responded Petrov skeptically. "I think not. Girish, all these events, the new modification, your reassignment, reactions to the Kashmir blast, everything seems connected. And all these connections come together at Vice Admiral Dhankhar's doorstep."

"I agree that is how it appears, Aleksey. But how do we prove such an incredible theory? If Dhankhar is behind all of this, if he has somehow obtained submarine-launched nuclear weapons and is installing them on *Chakra*, he can't be acting alone. He would need support at the most senior levels."

"You said that there were numerous senior officers unhappy with the peace negotiations. Are they *that* unhappy? Do they truly want to crush Pakistan completely?"

Samant paused briefly, considering his answer. "I'd have to say, yes. There were many flag officers on the Integrated Defence Staff that strongly argued against the truce. Some members even resigned in protest over it."

"Then, my friend, I think we have a very big problem," observed Petrov.

"But that gets us right back to how do we prove this? I certainly can't go up my chain of command. If we're correct, I'd be reporting to the very individuals who are behind this plot. For all I know, the minister of defense himself could be involved. He, too, argued against the truce." Samant grimaced.

"I'm afraid my contractor status limits my ability as well," added Petrov. "Osinov almost threw me out of his office this afternoon. He will tolerate no more delays, or complaints. We are to finish the work we've been assigned, and that's all there is to it. If I push this 'crazy' theory, he'll simply fire me and bring someone in who'll do the work with no questions asked."

"Then who can we turn to for help? And it has to be done quietly, otherwise we'll be discovered," grumbled Samant.

Suddenly a smile flashed across Petrov's face. "I think I know just who might be able to assist us. Tell me, Girish, have you ever been to America?"

13 March 2017
2330 Local Time
USS *North Dakota*
South China Sea

Jerry felt the boat take on a moderate down angle as they descended from periscope depth. With the last submarine broadcast of the day on board, the crew could now settle down for a quiet midwatch. As much as Jerry liked to be in the control room during PD evolutions, he had stayed in his stateroom for this one, finishing up the E-5 evaluations that were due in a couple of days. Besides, having the captain always in control sent the wrong message. His crew had to know he trusted them, and that meant leaving them to do their work without him constantly looking over their shoulders.

Settling into his chair, he grabbed his iPad and thumbed through the digital library. The idea of doing some recreational reading before going to bed sounded really good right now. He'd barely kicked back when the Dialex phone rang. Sighing, he picked it up. "Captain," he answered.

"Captain, Officer of the deck," said Lieutenant Junior Grade Quela Lymburn. "The evening broadcast has been downloaded into your in-box. The commo reports nothing earth-shattering, mostly administrative traffic, but we did receive some personal e-mail."

The last part caught Jerry's attention. "Thank you, Q. I'll be turning in shortly, so keep her between the buoys."

"Yessir, good night, sir."

Jerry hung up and immediately logged on to his ship's account. He bypassed the official message traffic and went straight to his e-mail folder. Opening it, he found several messages waiting for him. Most were from Emily, one was from his sister Clarice, and at the bottom of the list was an e-mail from Aleksey Petrov.

"Petrov," he whispered. "I haven't heard from him in quite a while." Curious, Jerry opened Petrov's e-mail first and began reading it. Soon a deep frown formed on his face. He glanced up at the bulkhead clocks. One was set for Washington, D.C., time, and he shook his head. He quickly typed out a three-word response, "Received. Understood. Standby," followed immediately by forwarding the e-mail to his friend and mentor Lowell Hardy.

Placing the two e-mails in the outgoing folder, he logged out and headed to control. Normally, he'd have to wait for the next communication cycle to get these messages out, or get the captain's permission. Since he was the captain, he'd kick the e-mails out now. Sometimes it's good to be the king.

3

Movements

13 March 2017
1310 EST
Hart Senate Office Building
Washington, D.C.

". . . and no, I'm not going to support a resolution on India at this time! We know almost nothing about what the hell is going on over there!" bellowed Senator Lowell Hardy as he burst through the door into his outer office.

"But Senator, both party leaders are in unusual agreement about this issue," croaked Theodore Locklear, Hardy's chief of staff.

"Based on what, Theo? The presumption that India nuked Pakistan? How about a little evidence before we start passing legislation?"

"Sir, I understand your reluctance, but it's a nonbinding resolution. It's really just for show, to demonstrate to the American public the Senate can act in a bipartisan manner."

"Oh that's wonderful! We'll hold hands, sing 'Kumbaya,' and then collectively look stupid! I'm sure that will be very encouraging to the U.S. public . . . not!" Hardy stopped just inside his personal office, turned, and thrust a finger at Locklear's nose. "Do you know what usually happens when one attempts a fast-draw shot from the hip, Theo?"

The chief of staff shook his head; he was used to his

boss's occasional outbursts—a personality quirk left over from his days as a submarine commanding officer. But to Hardy's credit, he had warned Locklear when he interviewed for the chief of staff job that he'd have to patiently listen to the senator when he had to vent, or as Hardy put it, "perform a steam generator bottom blowdown."

"You end up with a bloody hole in your foot!" thundered Hardy in conclusion as he removed his suit coat, tossed it on the easy chair, and ran his fingers through his thinning hair.

"Look, I have no problem acting when there is evidence that something needs to be done. We have no indications, no evidence—just rumor and innuendo, so sitting on one's hands is a perfectly reasonable thing to do."

"Yes, sir," Locklear replied mechanically. Then, with a hint of humor in his voice, he said, "Have you successfully completed your bottom blow, sir?"

Hardy chuckled and slapped Locklear on the shoulder, "Yes . . . yes, I have. Smart-ass."

"Then what would you like me to tell the majority leader?"

"Please let him know that I would be more than happy to support such a resolution . . . after I'm provided with some factual data that indicates India's culpability. You can candy-coat it as much as you'd like, but that is the gist that needs to get across. Now, I'm going to check my e-mail and grab some lunch before my meeting with Senator Kirk at . . . ah . . ."

"Fifteen thirty, sir. His office."

"Right, got it. And, Theo, thanks." Locklear smiled, nodded, then turned and left. Hardy dropped bodily into his chair, and logged on to his Senate e-mail account. He grimaced when he saw the contents of his in-box. Thank God his secretary screened the account and would flag him when she felt he needed to personally deal with an e-mail. There were a few, but nothing that required immediate action. He switched over to his personal account, one used only by family and friends and not easily attributed to him directly; there were considerably fewer messages. But about halfway down the page, he saw an e-mail from Jerry Mitchell. The senator shook his head. Receiving e-mail from an individual on a submarine at sea seemed . . . well, it just seemed wrong!

"The times be a-changin'," Hardy said to himself as he opened the e-mail. At first, he sat relaxed. Then he slowly straightened and leaned forward as he reread the message. "Oh my God . . ."

He punched out a quick e-mail, attached it to Jerry's, and forwarded it to his wife's personal account. He then whipped out his smartphone and sent her a text message:

> Just forwarded you an email from Jerry to your
> personal account. Please read ASAP!
> Love, Me.

13 March 2017
1330 EST
The White House
Washington, D.C.

Joanna Patterson felt her smartphone buzz; only a few people knew that number, all of them important. She looked quickly at the screen and saw Lowell's message. By the time Joanna had finished reading the text, she'd pivoted in midstride and almost ran back to her office. If her husband thought it was important enough to text her at work, it was a big deal. She logged on to her account and read Lowell's e-mail as she sat down.

> Darling,
>
> Please read the last email very carefully. Petrov sent
> Jerry a request for a meeting with a mutual acquain-

tance of theirs. Yes, the email is vague, but this is Alex we're talking about. I believe he has demonstrated sufficient credibility with us in the past that we owe him the benefit of the doubt. I know it'll be a pain for the Navy, but I believe it's in our best interest to accept the invitation. BTW, Petrov is currently in India.

Love,
Lowell

The last sentence caused Joanna's eyebrows to rise. She paged down and quickly read Jerry's e-mail, and then Petrov's. When she saw that an Indian submarine captain wanted to meet with Jerry concerning the most recent events, she practically fell out of her chair. Without even blinking, she shouted out to her secretary, "Kathy, call the CNO's office. I need to speak with Admiral Hughes immediately."

"Yes, ma'am, and what may I tell his staff is the topic?"

"Tell them I need to ask the CNO to do me a favor."

13 March 2017
1600 EST
CNN

They'd obtained commercial satellite photos of the Kashmiri location yesterday. That had fueled one news cycle. From low Earth orbit, the blasted area showed up as a black and gray butterfly shape on the patchy brown and green landscape. The "wings" extended up the mountainsides to the northwest and southeast, while the longer body represented where the blast and heat had been channeled along the valley, running north and south.

The graphics people had arranged to have the outlines of previously existing roads, towns, and villages in the area appear on the image, and then the background would expand, zooming down to explore the shattered landscape. The image quality was good enough to simulate flying over the blast zone at low altitude. As the view swooped over each village or mountain hamlet, the camera would slow, as if searching for survivors. Close in, smoke from fires obscured the view, but even farther out, all that remained were outlines of structures, or a stone foundation. The photo's field of view was too high to distinguish small details, but debris littered the landscape with a mottled gray and brown.

"Good afternoon and welcome to CNN's continuing coverage of the Kashmir crisis. I'm Jane Bergen. It's been just over four days since a nuclear weapon exploded in Kashmir, evidently wiping out a major LeT training camp.

"Our Jim Riviera has just managed to reach Muzaffarabad and is reporting to us live via Skype."

Bergen's image shrank to a thumbnail as Riviera's face, too close to the camera, almost filled the frame. The image quality was poor, marred with flickering horizontal lines and dim lighting, but his voice was clear. "Jane, I reached Muzaffarabad about an hour and a half ago with a government relief column. The Pakistani government's been very helpful in getting me here. It's in their interest to show the world the extent of the damage and destruction caused by the explosion, but it's in stark contrast to their previous policy before the cease-fire."

Bergen asked, "Jim, what have you been able to find out about casualties?"

There was a moment's pause before the correspondent replied, a deep frown on his face. "Communications north of here are still almost nonexistent. It's bad enough here in the capital of the Pakistani-controlled region of Kashmir. Hospitals that were already taxed by civilian war injuries have been slammed with at least three hundred casualties, mostly trauma from flying debris. Closer to ground zero, the death toll is almost one hundred percent.

Very few people with injuries have been reported, and only a handful has arrived here in Muzaffarabad. From satellite imagery and local reports, at least a half a dozen villages have been totally wiped off the face of the Earth."

Bergen's impassive newscaster's mask slipped for a moment, and she appeared shaken by the idea. "And the radiation?"

Riviera shook his head. "There wasn't one piece of radiological monitoring equipment in the convoy I arrived with. They're scouring the city for equipment from local medical labs that can be used to measure the radiation levels, but the population isn't waiting.

"The few survivors, many badly injured, that have come here from the north, have told wild stories and created a palpable wave of fear in the city. What little good information there is on dealing with contaminated food and water has been overwhelmed by rumor and folktales, some too wild to even consider—unless you're very frightened, and that's the only information you have."

"Jim, thank you very much for your reporting. Please stay safe."

Bergen turned to face the camera and explained, "For his own safety, CNN has ordered Jim Riviera to limit his exposure time in Muzaffarabad to twelve hours, so he will leave the city tomorrow sometime after dawn for a location outside the fallout zone. He's brought his own food and water with him, and will consume nothing from the local area. While he is fortunate to have that option, think about the hundreds of thousands of local Kashmiri who do not."

She drew a breath, as if composing herself, then said, "Our next guest is CNN consultant Dr. Stan Bartoz, a fellow at the Institute for Conflict Resolution. He's been covering the peace negotiations in Geneva between the two warring countries since they began last October. For the past three days, he's been wrestling with the same question most of us have: 'Why did the Indians do this?'"

Bartoz was in his seventies, and lean, almost scrawny. Time had left him with a fringe of white hair. Perhaps in compensation, he had a full beard, with only a few black streaks still holding out.

"Dr. Bartoz, have you been able to devise any scenario that could explain India's nuclear bombing of a terrorist base in Kashmir?"

Bartoz smiled. "Actually, I and my colleagues have come up with over a dozen theories about the circumstances of the bombing. For example, the act could have been carried out by a rogue element within the Indian armed forces. The government's denials are genuine—they were as surprised as the rest of the world. Even now, behind the scenes, they're conducting a fierce investigation and hunt for the parties responsible."

"Is that what you believe happened?" asked Bergen, almost eagerly.

With a small shake of his head, Bartoz answered, "Probably not, given the tight controls India has on its nuclear weapons, and the large number of people that would have to be involved to launch even one weapon." Bergen looked disappointed.

"Or it could have been done with the full connivance of the Indian government, if perhaps they had received intelligence information about a threat at this terrorist base so dangerous and immediate that the only way to stop it was with a nuclear attack."

Before Bergen could ask, he continued, "But if that was the case, they'd be arguing self-defense, and presenting the same evidence to the world that had convinced the Indian government to take such drastic action. It might not be a strong defense, but it would be a defense. Of course, the Indian government's defense right now is that they had nothing to do with the explosion."

"Is there any evidence of such a dire threat to India, Doctor?" asked the CNN anchor.

The academic said firmly, "Nothing that we have been able to determine. We haven't found any evidence to justify such an unprecedented action that would be worth the massive blowback the Indian nation and interests are suffering worldwide. Anti-Indian riots in every Muslim country, a wave of arson within India, and fatal attacks against Indian nationals in many 'civilized' countries."

Bergen added, "Our website has a list of countries that have either already instituted economic sanctions or are considering them. There are many more organized boycotts of not only Indian products, but even Bollywood movies and other cultural exports. Even if no new sanctions are enacted, and more are being added every day, the Indian economy is facing the gravest crisis since the country became independent in 1947.

"So, Dr. Bartoz, if we assume India didn't set off the nuclear bomb, who did? Is there any other possible explanation for this calamity?"

The doctor nodded curtly, "Yes, Jane, there is one hypothesis that is also consistent with the limited facts at hand, although, it is an unpleasant one."

"And what would that be?"

"That the Lashkar-e-Taiba terrorist group had somehow, from somewhere, acquired a nuclear weapon and accidentally set it off in their own training camp. Similar events have occurred before with other terrorist groups in the manufacturing of suicide vests. And India was just as oblivious to this acquisition as the rest of us."

Bergen looked amazed; no one had been bold enough to suggest the Pakistani tragedy could have been self-inflicted. "That is a disturbing theory, Doctor. One that has significant implications beyond this disaster."

"As I said, Jane, it's an unpleasant hypothesis at best."

The reporter paused briefly to compose herself before

going back to the interview's question list. "What impact do you think all of this will have on the peace talks?"

"You mean the lack of peace talks. Well, of course the Pakistani delegation left Geneva immediately after they heard the news. Pakistan's nuclear weapons were already dispersed and deployed because of India's invasion last fall. There is a very vocal minority in Pakistan that wants to fire a retaliatory weapon into India, preferably at a large city. Of course, the nuclear exchange that would inevitably follow would destroy Pakistan as a nation, but many are so angry that they are willing to commit national suicide.

"The two countries' armies are rebuilding, and preparing for a new offensive this spring, which is perhaps a month away. With the 'nuclear threshold' crossed by this one weapon, there is deep concern that the next offensive will involve more atomic weapons. The Indians missed their best chance to win this conflict last fall, and will be going all-out. The Pakistanis know that, and from their perspective have already suffered one Indian nuclear attack, so they are literally teetering on the edge."

Bergen looked horrified. "So your greatest concern is that the war between India and Pakistan will become a nuclear war?"

Bartoz replied, "It already is a nuclear war—regardless of who detonated the weapon in Kashmir. It's unfortunate, and indeed ironic, that in trying to remove the threat of Pakistani terror groups and nuclear weapons, the Indians have significantly increased the chance of suffering such an attack." He smiled, but only at the irony, and then sighed. "For almost everyone currently alive, Hiroshima and Nagasaki are just historical events, dimmed by the passage of time. Having seen for themselves the effects of just one such weapon, perhaps both sides will consider the potential consequences and take a step back from the abyss."

13 March 2017
2100 Local Time
Tbilisi, Georgia

Yuri Kirichenko listened to Dhankhar's arguments care-fully. He'd reluctantly agreed with the admiral that the schedule had to be accelerated. The Kashmir blast was drawing far too much attention to all things nuclear in In-dia. The problem was, he couldn't refute the man's logic about the size of his fee, either.

"We paid for six warheads, and you promised six. We received five, so it's only appropriate that we reduce the payment by one-sixth." Dhankhar was stating this as a fact, not a request. His possession of the warheads made it difficult for Kirichenko to negotiate. He could threaten to withdraw Orlav, but the technician would balk at the loss of his payment, and besides, Dhankhar might simply offer to hire him directly.

"Very well. Five-sixths of the original amount, payable when Orlav's work is completed. I'll be there for the fi-nal inspection and transfer of the arming codes. Chur-kin is currently en route to assist in maintaining security." He'd debated telling him about Churkin's movements, but Kirichenko needed to let the Indians know he was doing all he could. They'd already lost one weapon. There could be no more mistakes.

Dhankhar broke the connection, but Kirichenko sat holding the dead phone, lost in thought. The Indians had paid part of their fee up front, of course, but Kirichenko had used almost all of that to cover his expenses, much of it bribes, needed to recover and transport the warheads halfway across Eurasia. And that money was gone. He didn't think he should ask for a one-sixth refund from the Al Badr militants. He needed to preserve his good rela-tions with people who might be his next customers.

The ex-admiral's mind was in two places. While part

was obviously in India, the rest was up north, in the Kara Sea. He had more warheads to recover and sell, and he needed to learn from his mistakes with the first shipment. His profit from the first batch would be thinner than he liked, but he'd use it to recover more of the warheads next time. With increased security, and delivery only. If he hadn't promised Orlav's services adapting the warheads to fit in torpedoes, he'd be out clean and away by now. But then the Indians might not have concluded the deal. Mentally, he shrugged. That was in the past.

Now everything depended on Orlav—in Kirichenko's opinion, a weak reed to lean on, but the only one available.

The Kashmir blast meant he should pick up his pace, as well. The Kara Sea would be stormy and ice-ridden for several more months, but the first time the weather moderated, he'd have his people ready. He might not be able to get them all next time, but definitely more than six.

14 March 2017
0430 Local Time
USS *North Dakota*
South China Sea

The ringing of his stateroom's phone jolted Jerry to consciousness. He groped for the handset in the dark, finding it by the fourth ring. Pulling it to his face, he muttered, "Captain."

"Sorry to disturb you, Skipper. But we just received a flash priority message for us to come to PD and establish a video link with Squadron Fifteen."

"Squadron Fifteen?" he asked groggily. "What time is it?"

"Yes, sir. Commodore Simonis needs to speak to you personally. And it's zero four thirty, sir," replied Lieutenant Kiyoshi Iwahashi, the officer of the deck.

"Huh? Right. That was fast," Jerry grunted while try-ing to focus on his watch.

"Sir?"

"Never mind, Kiyoshi. Has the XO been informed?"

"He's next on my list, sir."

"Very well. I'll be there in a minute."

Jerry placed the handset back in the cradle, turned on the light, and started to put on his blue poopy suit. He heard Thigpen's phone ring, followed by a loud, but whiny, "Are you kidding me?!"

Once dressed, Jerry made his way to the control room. A very disheveled Thigpen followed close behind. As soon as they entered *North Dakota*'s command center, a petty officer brought Jerry a steaming cup of coffee. After thank-ing the young sailor, Jerry walked alongside the officer of the deck and said, "Report, Mr. Iwahashi."

"Yes, sir. We are on course one seven zero, speed five knots, depth one five zero feet. We currently hold six so-nar contacts, all are classified as merchants, and all have very low bearing rates. Combat system TMA indicates none are close; tracks are displayed on the port VLSD. I've completed a baffle-clearing maneuver with no additional contacts. ESM and radio are manned and ready. Request permission to come to periscope depth and establish a link with SUBRON Fifteen."

As soon as Iwahashi had completed his status update, Jerry looked at the large flat-screen display hanging on the control room's forward port side. None of the contacts were headed toward him. They had been tracked for some time and the sonar data said they were all distant. A quick glance at the command workstation confirmed the ship's course, speed, and depth. With everything as it should be, he ordered, "Very well, OOD, bring the ship to periscope depth and establish a link with SUBRON Fifteen."

"Bring the ship to periscope depth and establish a link with SUBRON Fifteen, aye, sir," replied Iwahashi, repeat-ing the order to ensure he heard and understood it correctly.

Turning toward the ship control station, he commanded, "Pilot, make your depth six five feet. Copilot, raise number-one photonics mast."

As the boat took on a slight up angle, Jerry nodded to Thigpen and motioned for them to head to radio. Once inside the small room, the XO leaned over and asked, "Any ideas why the commodore wants us to contact him?"

Jerry shrugged. "If I had to guess, it may have something to do with the Pakistani nuke." He phrased his answer carefully; he didn't like lying outright to his XO.

"Isn't that a little outside of our theater's area of responsibility?"

"True, but India is in our AOR," Jerry replied frankly. "Anyway, I'm sure Captain Simonis will graciously answer all our questions."

"That'll be a first," groaned Thigpen.

"Skipper, number one HDR mast has been raised, and I have a signal," said the radio room watchstander. "The VTC handshake is nearly complete. I should have SUBRON Fifteen up momentarily."

Jerry acknowledged the report and kept his eyes on the display. Seconds later, the test screen was replaced by the Squadron Fifteen conference room. In the foreground were Captain Charles Simonis, the squadron commander, and his chief staff officer, Captain Glenn Jacobs. There was a small group of tired-looking people behind them.

"Good morning, Captain," greeted Simonis. "My apologies for the early call, but I have a situation that was dropped into my lap forty-five minutes ago that we need to discuss."

Simonis's voice had a definite edge to it. He was not a happy camper. Jerry kept his response casual. "Good morning to you too, sir. What can I do to help you?"

The commodore cut straight to the heart of the matter. "Captain, have you had direct contact with Dr. Patterson recently?"

"No, sir. Per your orders, I have not spoken to or e-mailed her without your permission."

"I see. Then could you enlighten me as to why she asked the CNO to expedite getting you to San Diego?"

"San Diego?" Jerry asked carefully, trying hard to look confused. "Commodore, I don't recall ever asking anyone to send me to San Diego. Did Dr. Patterson provide any explanation for her request?"

"No, Captain," shot Simonis tersely. "Nor does the national security advisor to the president really need to, now does she?"

"No, sir. I'm sorry, sir."

Simonis sighed deeply; the man was uncomfortable with any kind of Washington political intrigue. And while he greatly valued Jerry's out-of-the-box thinking and tactical innovations, his close personal ties to the Office of the President of the United States was incredibly annoying. "All right, Captain. Terminate your patrol and return to Guam at best possible speed. I have to get you to San Diego in six days."

14 March 2017
0900 Local Time
Director General Naval Projects, Ship Building Centre
Visakhapatnam, India

Desam was being irritatingly insistent. "Sir, this is a bad time to go to America."

"What else can we do, Dr. Desam? You know American suppliers would be much more reliable than the Russians, and have better quality control. A trip to the U.S. was already part of our R-and-D schedule, and with our senior people gone we must do what we can to keep things moving!"

"I don't know if they'll be a reliable source after next

week, Captain. Did you see what the American Congress wants to do?" Samant's second-in-charge on the Advanced Submarine Project was a civilian, an academic, which meant Dr. Vishal Desam didn't necessarily accept his boss's declarations as the last word to be spoken.

"You watch too much television, Vishal. The American people think we used a nuclear weapon in Kashmir, and their politicians are just pandering to that mood. But more importantly, the current administration has been unusually silent, which means they're still unsure. I already have an approved visa, and we have the travel funds. There is no reason not to make this trip." Samant paused for a moment, marshaling his patience. "We've discussed this long enough. I'm going."

Desam had been working on the project for over ten years, and Samant valued the corporate knowledge his deputy possessed, but he just didn't seem to grasp Samant's authoritarian leadership style.

"But it's not too late to change your mind, sir. We should at least get some more information . . ."

"That's *why* I'm going over there, to get information!" Samant barked sharply. "It shouldn't take a week to prepare for two meetings with potential vendors in America. This is why . . ."

". . . it takes us thirty years to build a submarine." Desam completed the sentence.

Samant's vexation was replaced by amusement, and he smiled. "Just keep what's left of our team focused, and away from the television. I'll be back in about a week."

Defeated, Desam left, and Samant went back to work. The trip to America actually did involve meeting with representatives of two companies that might be useful to his project, and he had to prepare for them, as well as specific guidance for his people before he left the project in Desam's care for a few days.

Both meetings were in the western United States, in the state of California. Sandwiched between them, he'd see

Jerry Mitchell. There was something very wrong and ominous going on, and now the only one he believed he could trust was an American he'd once tried to kill. But Petrov had spoken highly of Mitchell, and reassured Samant that he wouldn't hold a grudge. A strange combination of dread and anticipation arose at the thought of meeting the American submarine captain face-to-face.

Samant's discussion with Petrov had convinced him the trip to America was the best course of action, and once he'd made that kind of decision, he never looked back. But he did find himself constantly looking over his shoulder.

Whatever Dhankhar was planning to do, he'd decided to exclude Samant, but keep him close by. Was that so the admiral could keep an eye on him? Was Desam, his own deputy, making reports to Dhankhar? Someone else in his office? Anyone at all? Once the seeds of suspicion were planted in his mind, they flourished, and their fruit was not clarity, but confusion.

He reviewed his conversation with Desam, looking for possible slipups, or things the engineer had said that hinted that he knew more than he was saying. Samant knew nothing of spycraft, but suddenly it seemed that he couldn't trust anyone.

It was because of Vice Admiral Dhankhar. Before this, Dhankhar had been the one man in the Indian Navy Samant would have trusted implicitly. The admiral was as famous and respected as an officer could properly be.

Samant had served with him before, as a junior officer when Dhankhar was captain of the submarine *Kalvari*, a rattletrap Russian Foxtrot boat that they'd had to keep running with little more than their wits. The submarine had been turned into refrigerators and razor blades long ago, but the memories were fresh, of a dedicated officer and a fine commander. His peers on other boats had envied Samant's posting.

If Dhankhar had turned, then everyone was suspect, and obviously other people had to be involved.

And Vice Admiral Dhankhar was involved in something very wrong, a plan that involved *Chakra* and quite possibly rogue nuclear weapons, and it was secret from most of the navy. Samant fervently hoped that he was wrong, that he'd completely misjudged the situation, but the odds seemed against that.

He had to plan ahead, to find ways to cover for the time he'd spend with Jerry Mitchell. There must be no paper trail, no gaps in his schedule. He couldn't let them know he suspected anything.

14 March 2017
1000 Local Time
Torpedo Shop 2
Naval Shipyard
Visakhapatnam, India

Vice Admiral Dhankhar returned the sentry's salute, then showed the corporal both his base pass and his navy ID card. There'd been a lot of grumbling about the new security measures, but Dhankhar had found that overreaction to the Kashmir incident was a good cover for the increased protection he had added to a few special locations.

Like this torpedo repair facility, for instance. Instead of "Torpedo Shop 2," the building's sign could read "Nuclear Weapons Magazine." A sentry at the door, blissfully unaware of what he was guarding, seemed appropriate after the arrival of the Russian warheads.

Dhankhar punched in the five-digit code and entered the windowless building. Most of the interior was open, and brightly lit. There were a few offices at one end of the long work hall. The walls were lined with workbenches and machine tools, while the rail for an overhead crane ran the length of the work floor.

The admiral's gaze immediately went to the warheads,

in five somewhat battered-looking wooden crates, placed neatly against one wall, each a meter square by two meters long. He'd been present when they arrived, and had assisted Orlav as the technician checked each one. They hadn't installed the initiators yet. That would not be done until each physics package, the actual nuclear device, was removed from its reentry vehicle and installed in a torpedo.

A sound of metal screeching showed Orlav's location, bent over a torpedo's warhead housing on a workbench. The technical challenges involved in adapting the device to a torpedo were relatively simple. Once removed from the reentry vehicle, the physics package was smaller and weighed less than the torpedo's explosive warhead it replaced. In fact, they'd have to add some ballast to make sure the torpedo's center of gravity didn't change.

Instead of the sophisticated fusing of the original weapon, designed to arm it once it was in flight toward a NATO target, the torpedo would have a simple timer. The crew would have no control over the time of detonation. Of course, the new device would have its own safety protocols and redundancies, but Dhankhar's plan envisioned all the weapons detonating at the same time, so a simple timer was the best option.

Orlav had already designed the new timers, and built six—that was before they'd heard about the theft of one of the bombs. That work had gone quickly, compared with what he was doing now.

Captain Third Rank Evgeni Orlav was a nuclear weapons specialist, or had been before his discharge from the Russian Navy as it downsized. He'd worked on reentry vehicles much like these many times on the warhead bus of submarine launched ballistic missiles. He understood the physics package as well as anyone who didn't have to actually design them.

But he was "not a metalworker," as he complained regularly to Dhankhar. He'd lost a lot of time learning how to fabricate the "mount," the framework that would hold each package inside the torpedo. The admiral had insisted that Orlav do the work himself. He would not bring in another individual to help, or even send pieces of the work to someone outside the shop. Too many questions would be asked.

Orlav had been making slow progress before, but with the schedule change, slow progress would not be enough. Longer hours were the only solution.

Dhankhar noticed a sleeping bag in one corner, as well as the remains of several takeout meals. He doubted that the Russian had left the building since their conversation two days ago.

It was several minutes before Orlav paused and looked up from his work. He was startled by the admiral's appearance, but not enough to drop the power tool. Removing his goggles, Orlav said, "It's too soon to give you another progress report, but there aren't any new problems."

Dhankhar nodded. "That's fine. I have the timer data for you."

"Oh. All right." The time the weapons would detonate would be hard-wired into the timers, and then the weapons would be sealed. On the outside, they would look like standard Russian-made UGST-M torpedoes that were used by *Chakra*. Orlav's one lucky break had been that the manuals for the torpedoes were in Russian.

Orlav didn't even know where the Indians were going to use the weapons, nor did he really care. For the sake of *Chakra*'s crew, he hoped the torpedoes had all been fired and the sub was well away from the area. A 150-kiloton subsurface detonation would shatter anything underwater for miles.

"Your boss says Churkin will be here in Vizag soon, to oversee security."

Orlav shrugged. "What does he have to supervise? I live in this workshop now, and you're the first person I've seen in two days. I don't even get to say hello to Kulik anymore. He just gives my meals to the sentry," he groused.

The admiral was used to Orlav's complaining. Besides, it gave Dhankhar a chance to speak Russian again. "I think Churkin's job will be to make sure you don't have any visitors." He added, "Does Churkin have any useful skills? Perhaps he could perform some of the basic mechanical tasks, while you do the finer work."

The technician just shuddered and quickly refused, replying, "I can finish without his help. I'll find ways to be more efficient." After a moment's pause, Orlav asked, "When will we be paid?"

Dhankhar was surprised. "I'm sure you know it's when the work is finished."

"Of course," Orlav replied, "but I meant exactly when? Is that changed because of the new schedule?"

"Ah." Dhankhar explained, "No, that hasn't changed. When you are paid is for your boss to decide."

"And he can't pay me until you pay him, hence my question."

The admiral stated formally, "When you report that the torpedoes are ready to be loaded, Kirichenko and I will inspect your work. If I am satisfied, I will order the funds transferred to his account in whatever one of those Caribbean islands he's using. And you've got your own account, correct?"

"Yes," Orlav answered, smiling. "And after that, the only question is whether I live in Bali or Miami. No more working on things that explode, no more ugly wife and her greedy in-laws, no more Moscow weather."

Dhankhar patted Orlav on the shoulder, and said, "Back to it, then," and turned to leave. The power drill's screech followed him outside.

He didn't like Orlav, or his boss. They were mercenaries, peddlers of death for personal profit. Dhankhar's plan meant killing thousands, maybe tens of thousands of

Chinese, but he'd settled matters within his own conscience months ago. Final victory over India's longtime enemy, and security against both terrorist and nuclear attack from Pakistan, was a worthy goal. The Chinese had chosen to involve themselves, and now they would pay for their poor judgment.

4

Reasoning

15 March 2017
0900 EST
The Oval Office, the White House
Washington, D.C.

Joanna Patterson had gotten used to it. First President Myles, then Secretary of State Lloyd when he arrived a few minutes later, and now Secretary of Defense Geisler, newly arrived, listened to her report, shook his head, and said almost the same thing: "I was hoping for a different result. I suppose this has been verified?"

Glancing over toward Myles and Lloyd and smiling, she replied, "Twice." Although she was the national security advisor, Patterson had been a scientist first, and was perfectly capable of explaining the report—defending it, actually. Politicians were often reluctant to abandon their opinions when confronted with unpalatable facts.

The other two had already heard her spiel, but it wouldn't hurt for them to hear it again. Their fault, really, for not wanting to wait for the SECDEF in the first place. "The ground samples from the blast area still can't tell us exactly which country made the bomb, but they can tell us about the method used to produce the fissionable material in the bomb. The Indians and Pakistanis produce plutonium using the same method, a heavy-water reactor; the plutonium from the Kashmir detonation came from a different type of reactor, a light-water-cooled, graphite-moderated one. Traces of the elements left from the explosion also show the bomb contained both uranium and plutonium. India has only used plutonium in their nuclear weapons, while the Pakistanis have historically gone down the highly enriched uranium route. They have yet to detonate a plutonium weapon.

"The nuclear forensics also confirm it was a thermonuclear explosion—a hydrogen bomb, not an atomic bomb. There were minute traces of lithium deuterate, a substance that creates tritium when under the exposure of high-energy neutrons." That got Geisler's attention. "Neither Pakistan nor India has ever built, to our knowledge, a successful hydrogen bomb. I doubt the Indians would test the first one on Kashmiri territory.

"And the biggest bomb the Indians have ever claimed to have detonated was fifty kilotons—seismic data from that test suggests the yield was far less. Imagery analysis and ground-based mapping of the Kashmir explosion matches the seismic data we already have, this explosion was at least five times larger than anything we've ever seen from either country—a hundred and fifty kilotons."

Patterson watched Geisler as he processed the information. He stated flatly, "This couldn't have been an Indian bomb, or a Pakistani one for that matter. That at least explains why nobody could figure out why the Indians dropped the thing. They didn't." After a moment's pause, he added, "So it's likely from Russia or China. But Russia has nothing to gain by doing so—they don't have a dog in this fight. And while China is supporting both Pakistan and the LeT terrorists, there's nothing to be gained, and much to lose by giving the terrorists nuclear weapons."

Patterson looked over at the president and Secretary Lloyd. Myles was mouthing the words, "Wait for it . . ."

"So the real problem isn't an irrational Indian escalation, it's a loose Russian or Chinese nuclear weapon. Wait a second! Didn't you say, Joanna, that we use the same type of reactors to produce plutonium? I mean, God forbid, could it have been one of our own weapons?"

Patterson raised a finger; she already had the answer to his question. "We have some 150-kiloton warheads, and they're all cruise missile payloads currently in the reserve stockpile. I had STRATCOM conduct an inventory; all W80 and W84 warheads are accounted for. The rest were disassembled years ago under joint U.S. and Russian observation. It's impossible that the weapon came from us."

"Which gets us right back to Russia and China, with the former a more likely source of the weapon as the intelligence community doesn't believe China has a weapon of this yield," concluded Geisler. "But regardless, the bottom line is still the same. At least one, possibly more, nuclear weapons have slipped out of someone's control."

"And into the hands of a powerful terrorist organization, at least until it exploded," Myles completed. He nodded toward the secretary of state. "Andy and I were hoping you would come up with a different conclusion than we did."

"I think I liked the 'irrational India' scenario better," Geisler replied, still absorbing the implications. Patterson thought he looked a little walleyed.

Myles asked, "This particular weapon is no longer a problem, but the obvious question is, do they have any more?"

"As national security advisor, I agree that is the most urgent question, but I can think of plenty more: How did LeT get the weapon in the first place? Where did they plan to use it?"

"We'll make a list," Lloyd interjected. "Joanna, who else can figure this out, that it's not an Indian nuke? The Russians? The Chinese? I'm guessing the Indians can't, or they'd have said something by now as proof of their innocence."

Patterson nodded agreement. "The Indians have the science, but not the assets to collect the samples." She paused, considering. "The Russians can do it, but their aircraft can't get to the area and I haven't seen anything that said they collected ground samples. The Chinese can get all the samples they want, and they have science. But they have no reason to tell anyone."

"Why should they?" Lloyd replied. "They have to be loving India taking the blame for this."

"Which is why we are going to declassify and publish these findings as soon as possible—today, if we can," Myles declared. "Let's get rid of the anti-India hysteria. It's a distraction we can do without."

Geisler shook his head, disagreeing. "With respect, sir, releasing those findings will look like we're defending India. That will hurt our neutral standing at the peace talks."

Lloyd shook his head. "Not really, Malcolm. India doesn't trust us because we've worked with Pakistan to fight terrorism, and we interfered with the Littoral Alliance war. Pakistan doesn't trust us because we've sold weapons to India and we keep hounding them about hunting down their radical kinsmen. Besides, it's the truth, and we could all use a little of that around here."

"And it will silence a lot of those fire-eaters in the House and Senate," Myles added. "Too much heat and not much light to show for all of it."

"It's early," she replied. "I can have an unclass version ready for the five-o'clock daily briefing."

There was a knock on the door and Ms. McDowell, the president's secretary, opened the door as Greg Alexander, the Director of National Intelligence, hurried in. "I'm sorry, sir, I was across town when I received Joanna's message and your summons. What have I missed?"

17 March 2017
1300 EST
The White House
Washington, D.C.

The release of the information on the Kashmir bomb did not calm the media storm; it only transformed it. It was one thing to blame India for a violent, irrational act, but now the shock and fear arising from the detonation had no clear target. The reality of rogue nuclear weapons had raised speculation about the explosion to hysterical levels.

As national security advisor, Joanna Patterson was well briefed on the current terrorist threat. One of the greatest concerns the U.S. national security community had was the possibility of a nuclear weapon falling into the hands of a terrorist group. Now it had happened, and only good fortune had prevented it from being used against an innocent target.

Yet innocents had still suffered, and the Lashkar-e-Taiba still existed. Their camp in Kashmir, although important, was only one of many large and small establishments scattered throughout the region. And there were other terrorist groups, as well. LeT was just the largest and best organized. It didn't comfort Patterson that LeT's intended victim was likely some large Indian city, and not one in the United States. A mushroom cloud over a Mumbai or a Delhi, with the two warring countries already so close to the nuclear threshold, would almost certainly bring on the catastrophe they all feared—a nuclear war between India and Pakistan. And their apocalypse would be the world's disaster.

It wasn't like the U.S. hadn't been aware of the problem. Many terrorist groups had declared their desire and intent to buy—or, if they had to, build—an atomic bomb. *Good luck with that,* Patterson thought. As a scientist, she understood just what was needed to construct even a crude atomic weapon. Buying a nuke was a much more likely and therefore dangerous option.

So while a good part of the U.S. counterterror effort went toward watching the actors, another focused on looking for people who might have provided, or could provide, nuclear weapons.

Her mind flashed to an important time in her life. She'd already been involved in nuclear science, then politics, campaigning for the environment at the national level, when she'd organized an expedition to the Barents and Kara Seas, close to the Russian coast.

She'd come up with the idea of using a U.S. nuclear submarine to survey the waters there for leaks from nuclear waste dumped there by the Soviets. The problem had already been reported, but only partially. With the endurance and resources of a nuclear sub, they could thoroughly document the problem, and present the Russians with hard evidence that would compel them to clean up their mess. It would be both an environmental and a political win.

The newly elected President Huber had signed off on the idea, and given her the submarine *Memphis* for the work. She'd learned a lot, both about submariners and herself. Lowell had been captain of *Memphis*, she remembered fondly.

But they'd found far more than just radioactive waste. A barge deliberately scuttled off the east coast of Novaya Zemlya had contained dozens of nuclear warheads, reentry vehicles for Russian missiles that should not have existed, weapons hid in secret, in violation of the nuclear disarmament treaties, and then presumably dumped after the fall of the Soviet regime.

She and the others aboard *Memphis* had spent hours trying to puzzle out the motives of the ones who had loaded and sunk the barge. It was reasonable that if the warheads had been built "off the books," then the Soviets would be eager to get rid of them as quickly and quietly as possible, to avoid any repercussions that would come with the warheads' discovery.

But it was more complicated than that. While divers were recovering two of the warheads and bringing them back to *Memphis*, they'd discovered an acoustic sensor nearby, planted on the seabed. Somebody in the Russian government was keeping watch over the barge, and had the resources to send surface ships, aircraft, and even a nuclear sub in pursuit.

Memphis had run, and fought for her life. Patterson still

remembered precisely how scared she'd been. In the end, they'd escaped, bringing the warheads home. They'd all been thoroughly debriefed, and of course warned not to discuss the matter, and as far as she knew, the matter had stopped there. Nothing had ever appeared in the public arena. The Russians had never complained about somebody stealing their warheads. The U.S. had never challenged the Russians on them, either. Not much to gain, and it would reveal too much about what the U.S. knew.

As national security advisor, she could now ask the different intelligence agencies if they'd found out anything more about the source of the secret warheads.

And the answer would probably be nothing. The only place they could look for clues about the warheads' origin was inside Russia, and she could imagine no Russian secret more sensitive or closely guarded than this. The mere act of searching risked compromising those involved, and might reveal to the Russians that the U.S. knew about the barge and its frightening contents.

Still, she couldn't ignore the possibility.

21 March 2017
1815 PST
Ortega's Mexican Restaurant
San Diego, California

Jerry had let Samant pick the place. He wanted the Indian to feel comfortable, in a place he'd chosen. And it looked like the guy liked Mexican. Ortega's was a family restaurant, very close to the Marine Corps Recruit Depot. It was a popular place, evidently—almost full at dinnertime with a mix of customers in uniforms and civilian clothes. Jerry was in mufti.

He had a photo of Samant from the dossier he'd gotten months ago, when the Indian submariner had been an opponent, possibly an enemy. He'd reviewed the file again on the plane flight from Guam: The top performer in any situation, the only Indian to graduate from the British "Perisher" submarine command course. One of India's best. Having maneuvered and fought against him, Jerry respected his skill and aggressiveness, but for the life of him, he couldn't imagine why Samant wanted to meet face-to-face.

He was grateful for the photograph; it was a good likeness, and he spotted the Indian officer in a booth. Samant was studying his smartphone as he approached, and Jerry could see what looked like a photo of him.

Samant stood as Jerry approached and offered his hand. His smile seemed a little forced, but Jerry was sure his was the same. He said "Thank you for coming" as they shook hands.

Jerry sat as Samant slid a menu across the table, and a waitress showed up almost immediately. Grateful for the distraction, Jerry ordered. He noticed that the Indian ordered quickly, sure of his choice. "Have you had Mexican food before?"

"Yes," Samant answered quickly. "There are several Mexican restaurants in Vizag, or Visakhapatnam, the city where I live, although this is much better. At my hotel yesterday, someone recommended this place, and I had dinner here last night as well. It's quite good."

He paused for a moment, then picked up something hidden from Jerry's view and placed it on the table, in front of the American. It was a small, flat box, wrapped with silver string. "A small gift, to thank you for agreeing to meet with me."

As Jerry picked it up, Samant added, "And also an apology, for trying to kill you."

Jerry laughed as he untied the string and opened the box. Inside was a flat silver pendant, covered with an intricate, interwoven design. Samant explained, "Aleksey Petrov said your wife is expecting your first child soon. The pendant has a *mehndi* design, normally applied in henna to the hand or foot. It's a Hindu custom to draw designs like this on the expectant mother at the baby shower. This particular design is a charm for a healthy birth."

Jerry was surprised and moved. His mind flashed to Emily, back in Guam. Every calculation had shown that radiation from the Kashmir blast would never reach that far east, but new fathers don't need a reason to worry. Did Samant understand his concern as well? "Emily will love it, I'm sure. Thank you for such a thoughtful gift." He added, smiling, "Apology accepted."

Samant's face echoed the smile, but it still looked forced. He explained, "I find I am still angry at how your submarine frustrated so many of my attacks. I know you were doing your duty, just as I was mine. While logic and reason say it was nothing personal, I don't like to lose."

"No good submarine skipper does, Captain. You were a formidable opponent, and as I recall, I ended up running away with my tail between my legs a couple of times. I'm glad it's over."

Samant scowled. "The problem is, it may not be over. Our war with Pakistan continues, and now the Kashmir explosion reveals a new danger that could be even worse."

"What?" Jerry was confused. "But the news has been good! The samples my government collected prove India could not have made the bomb. Now we are looking for loose nukes, which is still bad, but it's not India's fault, and no obstacle to the peace talks resuming. And my first name is 'Jerry,' by the way."

Samant sighed, leaned forward, and spoke more softly, "Captain Jerry, I believe we are involved in the Kashmir explosion, at least indirectly."

Warned by the Indian's manner, Jerry managed to stifle his immediate response, but after a moment, asked in the same quiet tone, "So your government is using bootleg nuclear . . ."

"No, no, not the government, but perhaps some within my navy, possibly even higher in the military hierarchy. A conspiracy." He described Vice Admiral Dhankhar's strange actions right before, and after, the blast, and his own unexpected early transfer off *Chakra*. Then he added what Petrov had told him about *Chakra*'s refit—including his discovery of the recently ordered modifications to the combat system consoles. He finished with his concerns about Evgeni Orlav, the Russian weapons specialist.

Jerry's mind reeled with the information, if he could call it that. Disjointed facts that made little sense by themselves did not reveal any deeper meaning when connected, except that whatever was going on could not be good.

Their food arrived, and they both ate, with only a few comments about their meals, while Samant gave Jerry space to consider what he'd been told. They were almost halfway through their dinner before Jerry said, "Have you told anyone in your government about your concerns?"

"No." Samant shook his head sharply. "Everyone is suspect, especially those near Vice Admiral Dhankhar. He is a popular and powerful officer and there have to be others, perhaps even more powerful. That's why I'm here, telling you."

"Does Alex plan to tell the Russian government?"

Again, a quick negative. "No, there is so little to tell. There is no smoking gun, only circumstantial evidence, and his country doesn't want any troubles with this refit. Aleksey's supervisor is not open to anything other than staying on schedule. But our conclusion is alarming. The warheads to be used on whatever weapon is being modified may be Russian, and then there is Orlav's name."

"And you feel that whatever is going to happen will be in early April?"

"*Chakra* has orders to sail on the tenth, bound for who knows where." With intensity, he added, "I don't want my boat, my old crew involved in this!"

"I will pass everything you've told me to our intelligence people. But there's little they can do inside India . . ."

"The Kashmiri bomb came from outside India, and both Aleks and I think there are more bombs involved, otherwise why would Dhankhar have everybody working so feverishly?"

Jerry struggled to imagine the possibilities, which were many, and the potential threat, which was frightening. "I don't know what my government can do with this, but I promise I'll make sure they understand the danger."

Samant's face mirrored Jerry's anxiety. "I want someone besides Petrov and myself to know about this. It may come to nothing, but I must do all I can to protect my boat and my country."

Back in his hotel room, Jerry, still jet-lagged from his flight from Guam, forced himself to lie quietly in bed. He'd done everything he could to relax, from a brisk walk to a hot shower, and even a nightcap at the hotel bar, but his mind still whirled. Meeting Samant was enough by itself, but his information—correction: his warning—managed to be both vague and scary at the same time.

The alarm woke him, and Jerry realized he must have finally gotten a little sleep. He was washed, dressed, packed, and out of his room in minutes, headed back to the airport. He was already booked on an early-morning flight to Washington, D.C., where he would report to the CNO's office for debriefing. He wasn't looking forward to another long plane flight, but he wanted to deliver Samant's message. He knew it wouldn't be the end of the problem, but at least it was a start.

22 March 2017
1530 EST
The Pentagon
Arlington, Virginia

On arriving in Washington, Jerry had phoned the CNO's office and been told to report immediately. He'd taken the Metro straight from the airport to the Pentagon and after passing through security, made a beeline for the Navy's head office on the first floor, E-ring.

All the senior U.S. commanders had their offices on the ground floor of the Pentagon, which not only had five sides, but five concentric rings, lettered "A" through "E" from the center to the outside ring. The E-ring offices were the only ones that had windows with a view of anything besides concrete.

The E-ring also had its own security post, because of all the senior officers, and not only did Jerry have to show his armed-forces ID and building pass, but the sentry checked the list for Jerry's name. "Yes, sir," the Marine guard said. "You're expected in Room 1E240." He pointed. "Down there past the first angle, on the left. You can leave your suitcase here if you'd like, sir."

At his destination, another enlisted man, a navy petty officer, was guarding the door, and asked to see Jerry's ID before letting him inside.

It was a conference room, and he almost turned around when he caught a glimpse of the occupants, thinking he must be in the wrong place. Admiral Hughes, the Chief of Naval operations, was there, at the head of the table, but so were Secretary of Defense Geisler and CIA director Foster, sitting across from Joanna Patterson. She was speaking, but stopped and started to rise when she saw Jerry, a smile lighting up her face. She saw his uncertainty, and so did Hughes. He waved and said, "You're in the right place, Commander. Please sit down."

Jerry might be a decorated senior officer, and the captain of a nuclear submarine, but he suddenly felt very small in a room with a large part of his nation's national security command structure present.

Still a little confused, Jerry let Patterson usher him to a seat between her and Admiral Hughes, at one end of the table. Geisler and Foster sat across from him.

As he sat, Admiral Hughes said, "We've got a lot to talk

about, Commander, and I'll get right to the most important question. How's Emily?"

The surprised expression on Jerry's face was enough to make them all burst into laughter, including Jerry, after a moment.

After he'd drawn a breath, he answered, "She's doing fine." That didn't seem to satisfy the high-ranking government officials, who briefly glanced toward Patterson, who wore a stern expression. Jerry amplified, "She's well into the second tri now, and is eating again. She had a checkup while I was at sea, and her e-mail said the doctor was pleased with her weight gain. They scheduled a sonogram for next month."

Patterson sat back, smiling, pleased, and evidently satisfied with his report. "That will do for the moment," she replied. "I'll get all the details at dinner tonight."

Hughes said, "Thank you, Mr. Mitchell. Your news reminds us that the world does indeed keep spinning, and also why we're all here. We need a little perspective in light of recent events. Now, please tell us about your meeting."

Jerry told the four everything he could remember of his conversation with Captain Girish Samant. He was careful to repeat the Indian's words verbatim, or as close as memory allowed, and Jerry had been paying close attention. He even mentioned their seemingly irrelevant dinner conversation about it being Samant's first visit to the United States, and news about their mutual friend Aleksey Petrov.

As he spoke, he watched their expressions change from interest to concern, then outright confusion. Jerry finished, and waited silently for any questions.

"A nuclear conspiracy in India . . ." mused Geisler.

"But with bootleg Russian nuclear weapons," Foster completed. The CIA director turned to Jerry. "Is it your assessment that Samant was sincere? Did anything in his manner or his story ring false?"

Jerry shook his head. "No, sir, although he could be a good actor. This was the first time I've met him in person. But given what I know of him, I'd have to say he seemed genuinely concerned."

Geisler cut in. "That doesn't make sense, Randall. What good would planting a story like that do India? Besides, they owe us big-time right now. We just proved they didn't bomb Kashmir. I can't see them running an op against us right now."

Foster answered, "Maybe it was Samant they were testing."

Patterson said, "That doesn't work either, Doctor. It's still spreading stories about a nuclear conspiracy. And with us as the target for the disinformation? That's the last thing they'd want. But let's assume Jerry's—Commander Mitchell's information is true. First, we had an irrational India bombing Kashmir, then nuclear warheads in the hands of terrorists, and now something in between: A country that already has nuclear weapons now has bootleg Russian bombs?"

"Not a country," Geisler countered. "A conspiracy within the country's military; just a different group of terrorists, in my opinion. And if a sub is involved, then they want to use them someplace a sub can go."

"And because it's the ultimate stealth platform. Pakistan's the obvious target," Hughes said.

"But they already did, sort of," Foster replied. "Was that an intentional attack? If it was a mistake, it makes me wonder how well organized these guys are."

Patterson sat up a little straighter. "We all agree that nothing pops out immediately. We've gotten more pieces to the puzzle, but still no hint as to what the picture might be. For the moment, we will presume that the information Mr. Mitchell has provided is correct. Dr. Foster, Secretary Geisler, I know your people are already working hard on this, but here are some new leads to run down."

Geisler added, "We must also be very discreet with our

investigation. Even with so few facts, or maybe because there are so few facts, if this became public, it would become an uncontrollable mess. We'd probably never get to the truth." Everyone nodded complete agreement.

Patterson turned to Hughes. "Admiral, if you're done with the commander, Senator Hardy and I would like to conduct a more extensive debrief this evening." Smiling, she added, "There's a new restaurant in Georgetown we want to show Jerry."

"Of course, Doctor." As they stood to go, the three men each shook Jerry's hand, thanking him for his report. Admiral Hughes added, "I'm looking forward to seeing you here in Washington soon. I have several billets in mind that you might find interesting."

Jerry forced himself to smile, and tried to make some sort of noncommittal reply, but the CNO cut him off. "Don't try to lie about looking forward to shore duty, mister." He grinned. "But we need people like you here, and you'll just have to endure it like the rest of us."

"Aye, aye, sir."

Jerry left, following Patterson, and after collecting his bag at the security station, they headed for the Mall entrance, where her car was waiting. As they got in, he heard her tell the driver, "Back to my office, please."

He was a little confused. In her e-mail, Patterson had insisted that he stay with her and Hardy at their place in Georgetown, after dinner. As they pulled away, she explained, "Slight change in plans, Jerry. I'd like to show you something, and ask your opinion."

She filled the drive to the White House with questions— not only about Emily, but about Guam, where he'd moved her after his boat was transferred there, and even about Commodore Simonis, his squadron commander, and the other submarine captains in Submarine Squadron Fifteen.

She seemed to be hurrying as they passed through the gate and more security on the way to her office in the West

Wing of the White House. Jerry focused on answering her question about the repairs to his new quarters in Guam, while telling himself that the White House was just another government office building.

It was late afternoon, almost evening, but there were still many people working. She greeted everyone by name, but rushed on without introducing Jerry to anyone, not even her secretary Kathy, who started to offer her boss a handful of message slips, but stopped when Patterson said, "No visitors until I say so, and please contact Lowell. Ask him to come here." Kathy nodded, and reached for the phone.

Jerry followed her into her office. It was spacious, and as Jerry had expected, tastefully furnished. "Make sure the door is locked behind you," she asked, and Jerry made sure the door had latched before turning a substantial-looking deadbolt.

She was rummaging in a safe built into her desk, and pulled out a fat folder with brightly colored security markings. She handed it to him and pointed to a chair as she sat down. "Remember that?" she asked.

Jerry looked at the label on the file, and was so surprised he sat down a little harder than he normally did. The chair took the hit without ill effect, and he hardly noticed the impact.

In the middle of the warning labels and prohibitions, the tab on the folder had a single word: "Rainfall." It was intended to be meaningless to anyone who wasn't supposed to know anything about it, but Jerry knew all about it.

He opened the file, and paged through material he hadn't seen or thought about in many years. There was the track of USS *Memphis* in the Kara Sea, pages of testimony from the officers and crew, and eight-by-ten photos of the two nuclear warheads they'd removed from a barge that had been deliberately sunk by someone who'd wanted to hide not just two bombs, but dozens of them, weapons that weren't supposed to even exist. It was a thick file, with photos of them all, looking more like mug shots, including one of Emily, Patterson's assistant on that mission. She'd worn her hair shorter back then.

He probably paused for too long on Emily's photo, because Patterson said, "There's an exploitation report all the way in the back, by Sandia Labs."

He found it, a spiral-bound booklet with Sandia's blue thunderbird logo on the cover. Even the title was classified as Top Secret/Sensitive Information: "Analysis of Russian Nuclear Warheads Recovered by USS *Memphis,* March, 2005."

Some of it was familiar to him. *Memphis*'s XO, Bob Bair, had actually identified the bombs from markings on the cases. They were reentry vehicles for the SS-20 Saber intermediate-range ballistic missile. The Russian name was "RT-21 Pioneer." The analysis confirmed that, and other obvious facts, before getting very, very technical. There was a section on the casing, with photographs, and he realized that they were disassembling the warhead, taking photos as they went. He wondered how they'd dealt with the anti-tamper devices. Half of him wished he'd been there to watch, and the other half was very glad he hadn't.

After that were sections on fusing . . .

"Find the section on 'fissile material,'" Patterson instructed.

It was marked by a tab, and Jerry opened the booklet to that page, which showed a color photo of polished dull-colored metal surrounded by an intricate framework. It was an actual piece of the bomb's core, exposed during the disassembly.

"The next page has an analysis of the material," she prompted.

He found it quickly enough. It was even marked with a sticky note with the word "Mixed." After a description of how the material had been removed and analyzed, it listed the chemical composition of the metal: isotopes of uranium and plutonium, lithium, traces of chemicals that had been used in the extraction process. Jerry understood it well enough. It was the same physics he'd studied learning how to run a reactor—just applied to a different purpose.

Patterson leaned forward and offered Jerry another document, with its own colorful security markings. "Here's the report on the air and soil samples from the Kashmir explosion. Look at the table on page fifteen."

Jerry studied the table in question. It listed the substances in the samples, and the two key elements, uranium and plutonium, both present, and in exactly the same proportions. But it was the yellow sticky note that drove it home; the plutonium isotope ratios were identical to the ones of the material in the Russian reentry vehicle.

He sat back in his chair, trying to fit this into what he already knew. "We were still at sea when I saw the news reports about the blast not being from an Indian weapon. That meant rogue nukes, and of course I thought about the ones we found, but this proves it."

"It's from the barge, or one just like it," Patterson replied.

"I'd bet on the barge," Jerry answered, "but I don't know if it's much help to know where the weapon came from."

Patterson nodded. "You're right. In fact, the only thing it really tells us is that we're probably dealing with more than one loose nuke. Master Chief Reynolds said there were dozens on that barge."

Jerry shivered at the thought. It had been years since they'd discovered the thing. Had whoever put them there gone back for some of them? All of them?

"Knowing, or having a strong suspicion we know, where the bomb came from gives us another lead to run down."

"Straight into Russia," Jerry completed.

Patterson's desk phone buzzed, and Kathy Fell's voice came over the speaker. "Senator Hardy's here."

As she said "Thank you" to her secretary, Patterson nodded to Jerry, who got up and unlocked the door. As he opened it, he quickly stepped to one side, and Senator Lowell Hardy (D-CT), Commander, USN, retired, stepped inside. Jerry closed and locked the door again as Hardy gave his wife a small hug and a peck on the cheek. She was as tall as Hardy, which meant they both were taller than Jerry, but he was used to that. Hardy had always been a big man, although with his retirement from the navy, some parts had gotten even bigger, and he fought a continual battle with his middle.

Hardy had been Jerry's first skipper, aboard *Memphis*, and while their relationship had not started out well, Jerry now regarded the retired submarine captain as one of his closest friends and a mentor.

He greeted Jerry warmly. "It's good to see you, Jerry. I'll get the lowdown on Emily and the house later. I assume since you wanted me here instead of the house . . ." He saw the security markings on the documents Joanna offered him, and immediately sat down. Jerry took another chair to the side.

Patterson reprised Jerry's report at the Pentagon, and then her discovery about the likely identity of the Kashmir bomb. He skimmed the sampling report as she talked. "I hadn't seen the classified version of this yet," he remarked after she finished. "I wouldn't have thought to compare this with the analysis of the warheads we recovered."

She accepted the compliment with a small smile, but her expression changed to concern. "If you agree that the barge is the most likely source for the Kashmiri warhead, then the next logical step is to tell someone. As soon as Jerry started talking at the Pentagon, I suspected the connection, but I couldn't mention it then, because Admiral Hughes isn't briefed in, and I had to double-check to make sure that Geisler and Foster were both on the list." She tapped the folder for emphasis.

The "Rainfall" incident had been "deeply compart-mented," which meant that if you didn't need to know about it, you didn't even know that it existed. Revelation of the recovery of two nuclear warheads from a sunken barge in Russian waters, even if limited to the classified community, would create as many problems as it tried to solve. There was also the unwelcome fact that nothing stayed classified in Washington forever. They'd managed to keep Rainfall secret by ruthlessly limiting the number of individuals on the "need to know" list. If the list grew longer, the risk of public disclosure would become very real.

Hardy chewed on the idea for a moment, then observed, "Knowing where the bomb comes from simplifies the search tremendously. And everyone needs to know that there is a very real chance that more than one weapon is involved." He stood, and then started pacing. Her office was big enough that he could go a fair distance in one di-rection before turning, and he made two full circuits be-fore continuing to speak.

"You're going to have to take this out of its box, so the community can start investigating. No choice." He paused for a moment. "Politically, this is one secret that doesn't embarrass anybody, except the Russians. There will be hell to pay if they find out. At least we'd be revealing it at a time of our own choosing. That lets us have a response pre-pared in case it does go public."

Patterson put the documents back in her desk safe as she spoke. "I'll be briefing the president on both of these to-morrow morning." She turned to face Hardy. "Lowell. I have to have recommendations for President Myles when he hears about this. What do you think I should advise him to do?"

"I think you already know the answer, Joanna. Brief anyone who's working on the Kashmir explosion into Rainfall, and keep looking for something that will corrob-orate or explain what Jerry's reported. There's a lot to do before we understand what's going on. I'll bet our bio on this Vice Admiral Dhankhar isn't even current."

She nodded. "That's what I thought, but it's nice to have a reality check." She stood up, and reached for her purse. "If we head straight for the restaurant, we can still make our reservation."

5

Cascade

23 March 2017
0830 EST
The Oval Office, the White House
Washington, D.C.

"Don't even think of saying no to me, Senator. You've already done that once, when you turned down that ambassador's posting." President Myles saw Hardy look toward Patterson. "And don't blame your wife for this one. Andy Lloyd came up with this, and I agreed."

Senator Hardy started to say something, then closed his mouth. After a thoughtful pause, he replied, "Mr. President, it's not that I'm refusing to do it. I just don't know that I'm the best person to be communicating what will undoubtedly be a very unpleasant message, and I certainly can't predict how the Russians will react." His tone mixed unhappiness with uncertainty.

They were seated in the Oval Office, on two couches facing each other. President Myles and Secretary of State Lloyd were on one, Patterson and Hardy on the other. There was a low table with a coffee service between them. Nobody had touched it.

Lloyd spoke up. "Senator, I'm still trying to grasp that we've had two Russian nuclear bombs in our possession for years, and that many more have been lying hidden on the seabed. And that's on top of a possible conspiracy by part of the Indian military to use some of said weapons."

"Too many questions, not enough answers," Myles remarked.

Lloyd nodded emphatically. "Exactly. Any more clues and we won't even be sure of our own names. We need answers, and I believe we don't have a lot of time."

"Until early April, at least, if Petrov and Samant are correct," Patterson replied.

"I disagree," Lloyd countered. "If there is a conspiracy, and they've changed the schedule once, they could do it again. And there has been one detonation already. We don't know if it was deliberate or accidental, but the risk of a second explosion heaven knows where can't be ignored. Even if it's not on U.S. soil, it could still affect our interests in a dozen different ways, none of them good."

Myles explained, "Until Dr. Patterson briefed me yesterday, I was willing to go with the simplest theory—that somehow a Chinese weapon had been given or fallen into LeT's clutches, and they suffered an epic fail while preparing it for use. The intelligence community seems to be leaning that way."

Hardy sniffed. "Based on nothing but supposition."

"But it was consistent with all the facts," Myles replied, "or it was until Dr. Patterson shows up with not one, but two revelations. That was before we called you here.

"I hadn't forgotten about the barge you found, but the match between the two reports can't be ignored. The information that Commander Mitchell provided, that's another matter. It's largely based on rumor and speculation." He raised one hand as Hardy tried to reply. "But we'll run it down, as best we can. Our intelligence coverage in India is thin, at best. But Andy and I agreed that the connection between the Kashmir explosion and the barge is much stronger, and takes precedence."

"Your wife just recommended that we needed to tell people about the barge if we were going to get anywhere," Secretary Lloyd explained. "And I realized we had to tell the Russians. That's when we called you."

Lloyd added, "And there's another consideration. I understand why the previous administration did not want to tell the Russians about this when we first discovered the hidden weapons. But since then, we haven't been able to find out anything else, and now we have evidence that at least some of those bombs are no longer on the seabed. If we sit on this any longer, and another bomb goes off anywhere, we will bear some of the responsibility. We need the Russians to understand the urgency of the issue, that's why I thought it would be best to have the captain of the U.S. submarine that actually took the weapons explain it to them. It's all about credibility, Senator."

"So we tell the Russians about the barge." Hardy stated flatly. "The problem is, as soon as we say when and where, they'll link it to the loss of their sub."

"It can't be avoided," Myles replied. "And the official position of the U.S. government is that their submarine was lost while making an unprovoked attack on one of our vessels. And you did not fire a single weapon in your defense. *Gepard* was sunk by one of her own torpedoes, decoyed away from *Memphis*.

"If they want to kick up a fuss, first they have to explain about the barge and its contents, and why *Gepard* was attacking one of our subs in international waters. And we can do that privately, or publicly."

"I can't predict, or even guess, how the Russians will react, Mr. President." Patterson's expression showed her worry.

Myles was more optimistic. "One of the reasons I picked you as my national security advisor was because you've dealt with the Russians successfully. You persuaded them to work with us when *Severodvinsk* was crippled on the Arctic seabed."

Lloyd said, "I think they'll react every way we can imagine. Anger, embarrassment, denial, and fear. They may even demand we return the warheads."

"Which I would happily do," Myles added. "It costs a

pretty penny to keep those things secure. There might even be a few reporters around for the handover." He turned to face Hardy directly. "So I will ask you again: Will you meet with the Russians and tell them about the barge?"

"I'll set it up in a secure room at the State Department building," Lloyd added hopefully. His tone became more serious. "They need to know about this."

Hardy looked over at his wife. She looked as worried as he did, but nodded silently.

23 March 2017
1630 EST
State Department, Harry S. Truman Building
Washington, D.C.

Ambassador Arkady Vaslev didn't know what to expect when his car arrived at the State Department building, but it certainly wasn't Secretary Lloyd's chief of staff, Ron Davis, waiting for them at the main entrance. "Ambassador Vaslev, Captain Mishin, Mr. Zykov, thank you for coming on such short notice."

Vaslev shook his offered hand, and replied carefully, "Your request was most urgent, but not very informative. It is hard to prepare for a meeting when you don't know what it is about."

The summons arriving that morning had requested an immediate meeting on an "urgent and critical matter." It had asked not only for the ambassador's presence, but also that the naval attaché and the deputy cultural attaché attend.

Requesting Mishin's presence implied a naval or maritime topic, but while Valery Zykov might hold the title of "deputy cultural attaché," he was actually the station chief for the Foreign Intelligence Service, the SVR, Russia's overseas intelligence arm. Vaslev had long suspected that American intelligence had deduced Zykov's true role, but to have them ask for his presence by name confirmed that fact. Why did they want a known intelligence operative at the meeting?

Davis, a career diplomat, chatted amiably as he passed them through security and down the hall to a secure conference room, if the armed guard at the door was any indication. He snapped to attention as the group came into view.

The room was a small briefing theater, with the seats facing a large screen on one wall. A tall, heavily built man with thinning gray hair stood to one side. Davis introduced him as Senator Lowell Hardy, of Connecticut, a retired submarine captain. "He has information vital to both our governments to share with you."

The Russians were offered chairs in the front row. As Vaslev moved to take his seat, motion to the side caught his eye, and he noticed two people sitting down in the back; he immediately recognized them as Secretary of State Lloyd and Vice President Randall.

They hadn't been introduced, but had simply come in after the Russians and silently taken their seats. The implication was clear. This matter was of the highest importance.

The moment all three Russians were sitting, Hardy took the podium and the lights dimmed. Vaslev noticed that Davis was assisting Hardy, and there were no other assistants or aides in the room.

Hardy's voice was strong, and he appeared to speak a little slowly, perhaps in deference to his audience. "In 2005, I was the commanding officer of USS *Memphis*, a *Los Angeles*–class nuclear submarine homeported in New London." A photo of the sub flashed onto the screen, a record shot that would be more familiar to Mishin and Zykov than to the ambassador.

The photo was replaced by a map of the Barents and Kara Seas. "In May 2005, we left on a patrol that took us into the Kara Sea." A dotted red line appeared on the map, showing the sub's path. "Our orders were to survey several areas off the east coast of Novaya Zemlya for radioactive waste dumped in those waters by the Soviet and Russian governments, and measure the levels of contamination."

Vaslev bristled a little at the idea of an American submarine so close to the Russian coast. It happened all the time, but nobody in Russia liked Yankee subs spying on them. This "radioactive survey" sounded like a typical cover story. But why go to all this trouble to tell such a fairy tale?

"In the areas we'd been assigned to search, we used remotely operated submersibles to locate and photograph debris, and to measure the levels of radiation." The map was replaced by underwater photos of junk, most of it barely recognizable as machinery or waste containers. "We will provide you with a copy of the survey's findings."

So it wasn't a cover story; but now irritation at the sub's presence mixed with concern. Radioactive material had been dumped indiscriminately during the Soviet era, and to a lesser extent, afterward. Bellona and other environmental groups had complained about the issue for years, but had never been able to provide such detailed information.

This could be troublesome, but hardly rose to the level of vital national interest. And "urgent"? This happened years ago . . .

Hardy was describing the search with the ROVs. ". . . end of our mission, one of the last sites to survey was in Techeniye Guba." The map came back on the screen, and Vaslev followed the sub's track to the marked location. He looked closer, and remarked carefully, "It appears that the site is within twelve miles of our coast." The edge of Russia's territorial waters was also marked on the map.

Hardy frowned, but answered, "We did send the ROVs inside the twelve-mile limit, but *Memphis* remained outside. Our only intention was to photograph whatever was there and take radiation samples. You will be interested in what we found," he added mysteriously.

Several photographs, taken at close range, of the barge were accompanied by an artist's sketch of the entire object. It was a medium-sized barge, intact, resting on its bottom on the seabed. "We took water and soil samples, of course, and that's when everything changed."

Hardy reached into the podium and took out a document, which he offered to Vaslev. "This contains the gamma-ray spectrum analysis we collected near the barge. The many others we'd taken up to that point are listed in the official study I've already mentioned. They showed cesium, strontium, cobalt—typical components of spent fuel or radioactive waste. This sample had had a particularly dominant isotope of one element: plutonium 239, in concentrations consistent with a nuclear weapon."

Hardy paused to let that sink in. "Photographs taken by the remote vehicle showed the inside of the barge filled with cases. They did not look like waste drums. On my own authority, I brought *Memphis* in closer to the site. We sent out divers who entered the barge and opened one of the cases. This is what they found inside."

Vaslev, still reeling from the idea of American divers operating covertly inside Russian territorial waters, saw a photograph, in poor lighting, of a cone-shaped object. A diver to one side let him judge the size: almost two meters long and slightly less than a meter across at the base. The poor-quality image was replaced by another, presumably of the same object, out of the water in normal lighting. It was dull green or black, and detail photos of the base showed white Cyrillic lettering.

"*Stoy!*" Vaslev shouted, so upset that he had to deliberately recall the English word, and finally repeated, "Stop!" He looked over at his two colleagues. Their expressions were unreadable. They were both looking over to him, perhaps for guidance. He gestured for them to remain silent, and gathered his thoughts.

Vaslev stood, and said, "The enormity of this act is almost overwhelming. The American navy entered Russian waters and stole this object . . ."

Hardy interrupted, "Actually we took two, this one, and another still in its case. Aren't you even interested in what they are?"

"They are obviously property of the Russian government," Vaslev answered immediately. After a moment's pause, he added, "This confession, years after the fact, does not alter the seriousness of this violation of our territory . . ."

"We didn't ask you here to confess anything, Mr. Ambassador." Secretary Lloyd's voice overrode Vaslev's speech. "You haven't even asked what Soviet state property we stole. We recovered two reentry vehicles for a Russian RT-21 Pioneer missile, each fitted with a 150-kiloton thermonuclear warhead. The RT-21s were medium-range ballistic missiles that were supposed to have all been withdrawn under the INF treaty in 1987. Observers watched the destruction of the missiles and the disassembly of all the warheads, at least all those reported under the treaty. Can you explain where these came from?"

Vaslev, surprised by Lloyd's speech and then its sternly delivered content, appeared genuinely confused, but said, "I have no information about this barge or alleged warheads. These are serious charges. My country has always lived up to the letter of every international treaty, and . . ."

Lloyd's tone sharpened. "Mr. Ambassador, I'm not interested in the party line. We are ready to hold a press conference and wheel both bombs out in front of whoever wants to see them. I'm sure the media would be very interested in this."

Vaslev held up his hands. "What can I say, Secretary Lloyd? Again, I have no knowledge of this. I'll of course contact my government as soon as I return to the embassy."

"You can also tell your government that the exterior of the barge has some marine growth, but hadn't been in the water more than ten years. Was your government deliberately concealing nuclear warheads, in violation of the INF treaty, since at least the mid-nineties?"

Vaslev sat. After a brief pause the ambassador ventured, "The ocean is not typically used for storing anything. Since you found these objects in the same area as radioactive items that had been discarded, perhaps these were also discarded." Vaslev was warming up to the idea. "These may be warheads that are flawed, or defective and were dumped by the old government."

Hardy shook his head. "Our examination of the two devices showed them to be fully functional, ready for installation on the warhead bus of a ballistic missile. And you forget the marine growth . . ."

Vaslev waved his hand to brush the argument aside. "Seaweed is not proof of anything."

Hardy nodded to Davis, who pressed a key, and a new image appeared on the screen. "Then how about an acoustic sensor, fixed to the seabed near the barge, and placed at the same time? Somebody was keeping watch on those nuclear weapons."

The ambassador glanced over to Mishin, who was studying the image carefully. He looked at Vaslev and nodded his head slightly. He recognized it. In Russian, he reported, "It is a standard type of fixed acoustic sensor."

The implications and consequences of this discovery were beginning to take shape in Vaslev's mind. But he needed to think . . .

"Why are you telling us this now, after so many years?" It was an honest question, the first the ambassador had asked. It was intended to buy time, but he was curious.

Hardy replied quickly, "Because there is a high probability that the weapon detonated in Kashmir came from this source."

Vaslev's thoughts struggled to follow several tracks at once. Foremost was protecting Russian interests. Second was trying to understand the Americans' intent. Consideration of the actual facts being presented came third and last. But the American's statement brought everything to a sudden halt.

Stunned, the ambassador blinked, then blinked again. Almost automatically, with reflexes trained by years of diplomatic service, he asked, "What proof do you have of this?"

Hardy handed the Russians two documents. "The first one is an analysis of the fallout and soil samples from the Kashmir explosion. It's more detailed than the one released to the public last week. The second is our analysis of the reentry vehicles' fissile material. The isotope ratios of the plutonium in all three cases are identical. The measured size of the explosion also matched the warheads' rated yield—one hundred and fifty kilotons."

Vaslev studied the tables on the marked pages. His spoken English was good, but he sometimes had trouble with the Roman alphabet. Now the words might as well have been printed in Martian. But numbers were the same in both languages, and so were the chemical symbols for uranium and plutonium.

Lloyd, still standing nearby, waited until Vaslev had looked at both analyses and handed them to Mishin, then sat down next to the ambassador. "Mr. Ambassador, as the representative of the United States, I am speaking to the representative of the Russian Federation. There is or was a large cache of nuclear warheads in your northern waters. Whether they were put there at the orders of your highest leaders, or by some faction within your government, one of those weapons has now exploded, causing exactly the type of destruction its designers intended.

"The United States is deeply concerned that the Russian government has lost control of these weapons, indeed if they ever had control. They present a grave danger, not just to Russia, but the entire world. We will give you every scrap of information we have about them, but the trail leads back inside Russia, and your country must take the lead in tracking them down."

Vaslev sighed, not in surrender, but in the realization that Russia was indeed in grave, perhaps mortal danger. He truly did not know anything about the barge the Americans described. That was no surprise in a country that still told one only what was needed to do one's work, and sometimes not even that. And who knew what secrets had been fed into the communist regime's shredders before they lost power?

Others would make sure the Americans' information was authentic, but for the moment, he would assume they were telling the truth. He couldn't imagine this was some sort of deception.

"All right," Vaslev announced, "I will pass all this information on to my superiors with the strongest possible endorsement. What they will do with it, or what actions they will take, I cannot say."

"We would hope that in the spirit of cooperation, and given our openness in supplying such detailed information to your government, we can continue to work together to quickly resolve this, before there is another catastrophe." Lloyd's words were couched in diplomatic terminology, but his request was sincere.

"I can make no guarantees about that, either. Those decisions will be made by others."

"You should also tell your government, that given the great urgency and the great danger of this situation, if their investigations are not successful, we will quickly broaden our investigation to include other governments, and possibly even the public. Everyone in the world is in danger until these weapons are found and the persons involved are stopped. One could argue that the world needs to be told."

It was a credible threat. The Americans had already revealed what they knew to their adversary. Telling their friends or the public would cost them little. Vaslev wondered which revelation would cause Russia greater problems: that the Soviet regime apparently violated a nuclear treaty, that the Russian government had covered it up, or that it had now lost control of at least one of the weapons.

And who had them now? He shivered at the thought of the Chechens or some Muslim group, and there were many inside Russia, possessing such a weapon. And there were nationalists in Georgia and some of the "Stans" who would love to strike at their Russian neighbor.

"There is one more piece of information for you, a possible lead for your investigators."

"Lead?" Vaslev asked, puzzled by the word.

"Clue," Lloyd explained. "A name: Evgeni Orlav. A Russian national. This individual is working in India as part of the refit of the Indian submarine *Chakra*."

"And the nature of his involvement?" Vaslev asked.

Lloyd sighed. "We don't know. But information from a source in the shipyard says his actions have been suspicious since the Kashmir explosion."

The ambassador looked over at Zykov, who was taking notes. The official looked up and asked, "May we interview this source?"

"No," said Lloyd firmly. "Not now. Possibly later."

So the Americans still wanted to keep some things secret. Still, intelligence shouldn't have any trouble locating this man and putting him under surveillance.

Captain Mishin spoke up. "I have a question. With the ambassador's permission, it is a matter related to the barge."

Vaslev nodded.

"Could you please put the map back up on the screen?"

Davis typed for a moment, and the waters of northern Russia reappeared.

Mishin studied it for a moment before nodding slightly, as if satisfied. His expression became very solemn. "In the spring of 2005, I was a junior officer assigned to staff duty in Murmansk, at the Northern Fleet headquarters. There was an incident in that same area, a pursuit of what was reported as a foreign submarine in our waters. I remember coming on duty to find our fleet actively pursuing a submarine contact as it tried to escape. It was general mobilization," he recalled. "We were on a war footing."

He'd been speaking to the entire group, but now he turned to face Hardy directly, confronting him. "Was that submarine USS *Memphis*?"

Hardy replied, "We arrived at our patrol area on May twenty-third, and discovered the barge on June eleventh."

Mishin's face hardened. "The dates agree. One of the units pursuing the foreign submarine—*Memphis*," he corrected himself, "was the submarine *Gepard*. After she reported detecting a distant hydroacoustic contact, on June fourteenth, she was never heard from again."

The naval officer stood and walked to the screen. He picked up a pointer and tapped the chart. "The next day, we discovered debris here, and her wreckage, containing the seventy-three men who served on her, was located later that month.

"Her loss was a tremendous blow to the fleet, as well as to the wives and mothers whose men never returned. It's long been suspected that she was sunk in battle. Is that what happened?"

Vaslev was surprised by Mishin's intensity, but it was understandable. *Gepard* had been the newest submarine in the fleet in 2005, and her loss, following that of *Kursk*, had dealt a huge blow to the Russian submarine arm's morale.

Hardy said, "I can provide a more detailed account later, if you wish and my government allows it." Hardy walked over and stood near Mishin, facing the naval officer. "Late on the fourteenth, we'd crossed the sixty-eighth parallel heading north. *Memphis* had been damaged by depth charges dropped on us during the pursuit, so we were not as quiet as we might have been. *Gepard* was waiting, in front of us, and fired two torpedoes only moments after we detected her presence. I maneuvered and dropped countermeasures, and managed to avoid those weapons. We both continued to maneuver, quite violently, and more countermeasures were dropped, by both submarines. She fired again, another pair of torpedoes, but I was able to evade them with the use of a mobile decoy.

"She went active and launched a third salvo of two torpedoes. Because of our maneuvers and the number of countermeasures in the water, I believe the guidance wires on her torpedoes may have been broken. The third pair of weapons was also decoyed away from me, but *Gepard*'s radical maneuvering put her in the path of the torpedoes. My sonarmen heard their seekers shift to a range-gating scale, followed by an explosion and breaking-up noises."

Vaslev asked Mishin in Russian, "What does 'range-gating scale' mean?"

The Russian submariner explained, "He means that the torpedoes—our weapons—detected *Gepard* and began pinging more rapidly. All acoustic homing torpedoes do that when they attack. It gives them more precise bearing and range information."

"So she was sunk by her own torpedoes? Is such a thing possible?"

Still answering in Russian, Mishin said, "Normally, no. There are circuits in torpedoes specifically designed to prevent that from happening. But in a close-range, maneuvering situation, with the guidance wires cut . . ." He shrugged.

Vaslev couldn't believe that a Russian submarine had been lost to its own weapons. Switching to English, he asked Hardy, "Did you fire at *Gepard*?"

Hardy quickly replied with a shake of his head, "Absolutely not, Mr. Ambassador. One of my decoys was launched in that direction, but I didn't launch a torpedo."

"Even after you were fired on."

"Truth be told, because of the damage my boat had received, I was incapable of firing back, even if I wanted to. Besides, we were in international waters, Mr. Ambassador. I could understand why the Russian units fired on us when we were close to your coast. The American term would be 'hot pursuit.' But *Gepard*'s attack, that far away, shocked us, and it is only our good fortune that we weren't sunk."

"And *Gepard*'s misfortune." Vaslev replied acidly.

Mishin leaned over and spoke in Russian a little more softly than last time. "When they investigated the wreck of *Gepard*, they found pieces of Russian USET-80 torpedoes outside the hull, on the seafloor. The inner hull near the first compartment, where the torpedoes were stored, was flooded, but largely intact."

"Couldn't those torpedoes be the ones found outside of *Gepard*?"

"No, sir. Those would be intact. In this case, the weapons were in pieces. The largest were of the propulsion section, and is consistent with a warhead that had detonated. As much as I want to blame the Americans for her loss, they may not be at fault."

Mishin shifted to English and said, "For all this time, the families of those seventy-three men have grieved, ignorant of the reasons behind her loss. It's hard to accept that it was simply 'bad luck.' "

"Although I've omitted many details, my summary is complete. *Memphis* made no attempt to sink your submarine, only to escape. My crew and I have always regretted being involved in any way, even unwillingly, in *Gepard*'s loss. They were our adversaries, but also submariners, and we understood the risks they took."

Lloyd spoke up. "*Gepard*'s captain fired not just one, or two, but three salvoes of torpedoes at *Memphis* in rapid succession. Did he act on his own? Does a Russian submarine commander have that kind of authority?" He was looking straight at Vaslev, but Mishin answered the question.

"After the incident, Admiral Yuri Kirichenko, the Northern Fleet commander, was court-martialed for ordering the pursuit, and was judged responsible for *Gepard*'s loss."

The ambassador felt a flash of irritation with his naval attaché, but understood his desire to protect the reputation of a fellow submarine officer. And it wasn't classified information. The findings of the court had been given a lot of coverage in the press. "Captain First Rank Mishin is correct," he said.

"Based on the actions of your navy, we had to assume that the warheads had been deliberately hidden by the Russian government, and decided not to make the matter public, or bring it to the attention of Russian officials, without finding out more information. To date, our investigations have been completely unsuccessful, because every clue we have led straight into Russia."

Vaslev reasoned, "So if there had never been an explosion in Kashmir, you never would have told us."

"Never is a long time, Mr. Ambassador, but no, we would not be having this meeting now."

The ambassador sighed. "This will be a long report to Moscow. Courtesy requires me to thank you for sharing this information with us, but only time will tell if I should be grateful."

Lloyd said, "I'd like to arrange a time for a follow-up meeting, so that we can learn what you have found out. That will likely assist our investigations."

Vaslev sounded uncertain. "Perhaps in a week or so . . ."

"There could be another explosion at any time, Mr. Ambassador. I was thinking more like forty-eight hours."

"Please, Mr. Secretary. I am sure that after they read my report, I will be recalled for consultations. Once I get them to understand that this is not a joke, it will trigger vigorous debate, and then investigations. Certainly my government will make no major decision until they have a better understanding of the situation."

Lloyd pressed his point. "We cannot know what is happening right now. I must insist that any information you discover be shared with my government immediately. We are willing to keep this matter private for the time being, but only as long as it assists your investigation."

The meeting ended, and the ambassador shook hands with Lloyd; then Ron Davis handed Vaslev a bundle of documents. A little to one side, Hardy shook hands with Mishin, and they exchanged a few words. Lloyd was curious, but wouldn't ask. If there was anything Hardy needed to share, the senator would tell them.

Vice President Randall left immediately after that, thanking the other three for their good work.

Before Hardy left, Lloyd asked him, "Ready for that ambassadorship yet?"

The submariner quickly shook his head. "Irate voters are enough for me. But why did you invite Zykov? Mishin made sense, considering the topic. But why the SVR station chief?"

"Because Vaslev and the political leadership may know nothing about the barge," Lloyd answered. "The three of them represented the major power blocks in Russia: political, military, and intelligence." Lloyd shrugged. "All three now know what we know. One of those groups has to know something. And in the meantime, we can work with what we have: the name 'Evgeni Orlav.'"

6

Rude Awakenings

25 March 2017
0845 Local Time
Icebreaker *50 Years of Victory*
Murmansk, Russia

The captain paced impatiently on the starboard bridge wing, waiting for the "important officials" the Rosatom main office said were coming. The morning air was crisp, with a light fog on the water, but the sun looked like it would burn through the morning haze in no time. *Not a bad day to go to sea,* he thought. He just wanted to know why he had to drop everything and prepare his icebreaker for immediate departure. The engineers were working frantically to bring the ship's two reactors critical, and the main office had already arranged for the provisions *Victory* would need. Whatever it was, it must be damn important to get Rosatom moving that fast.

His sharp eyes caught the black car as it raced down the pier access road. The car braked hard, coming to an abrupt stop by the ship. His first mate, Timur Markov, opened the door, and two Russian naval officers emerged. Without waiting for Markov, they walked quickly toward the gangplank. "Hmmm," the captain said softly. "A vice admiral and a senior captain, and in such a rush, this could be most interesting."

Victory's master went back into the bridge and prepared

to receive his guests. On the chart table were a carafe of hot tea, cups, and a small platter with some biscuits— good, everything was in order. Straightening his sweater, he waited by the ship's wheel. It was only a couple of minutes later when the door popped open; Markov directed the two naval officers onto the bridge and introduced them to his master.

"Captain, this is Vice Admiral Ivan Loktev, Deputy Commander of the Russian Northern Fleet, and Captain First Rank Viktor Zhikin, Commanding Officer of the 328th Expeditionary Rescue Squad. Admiral, Captain, Captain Yefim Sergievich Gribov, master of the icebreaker *50 Years of Victory*."

"Admiral, Captain, welcome to *Victory*. May I offer you some tea? Biscuits?"

"Thank you, Comrade Captain," replied Loktev hastily. "Perhaps later, but time is of primary importance. What is the status of your preparations for getting under way?"

Gribov wasn't surprised by the admiral's response, particularly after Gribov heard that the head of the Northern Fleet's rescue divers was with him. "Admiral, my chief engineer is almost done with the reactor startup checklist. We should be ready to answer all bells within five or six hours. Provisions have already been ordered by Rosatom, and once they arrive my crew can have them loaded in a few hours. All I need to know is how many passengers I'm embarking, and where we are going."

Loktev's strained expression eased a little. Motioning to Zhikin, the captain broke out a chart and spread it on the table. Pointing to a spot on the northeast side of Novaya Zemlya, Loktev said, "We need to get Captain Zhikin's divers to Techeniye Guba as quickly as possible."

Gribov looked at the chart briefly and nodded. "Not a problem, Admiral. The ice this time of year in the Kara Sea is perhaps fifteen to eighteen centimeters thick. *Victory* can easily plow through that. The hull is rated for ice two and a half meters thick."

"How fast can you get there?" The admiral's face frowned again.

"My maximum speed is just over twenty-one knots, but that is only in open water. Even in thin ice, I have to slow down." Gribov grabbed a pair of dividers and measured the distance. After calculating the time in his head, he said, "If all goes well, two days."

The admiral nodded approvingly. "Excellent, Captain! You will be taking Captain Zhikin and twelve of his divers to these coordinates," explained Loktev as he handed a sheet of paper to Gribov. "Myself and two of my staff will be accompanying them, as well as six Spetsnaz commandos."

"Spetsnaz?!" Gribov exclaimed. "Admiral, just what are my crew and I getting into here?"

"That is a state secret that you don't need to know, Captain," growled Loktev. "Your job is to get Zhikin and his divers to Techeniye Guba. He'll take care of the rest."

26 March 2017
1400 Local Time
United Services Club
Mumbai, India

It felt good to finally relax. Dhankhar sipped his gin and tonic as he looked out across the club's grounds to the Arabian Sea. The wind was coming off the water; its coolness refreshed the body, while the heady salty air invigorated the senses. The United Services Club was the perfect place to hold their meeting. It was an elite country club. Only serving and retired officers and a few prominent civilians could be members. Foreigners had to receive special permission, well in advance, to even step through the main gate. The club itself was located in the Colaba area of Mumbai. Situated at the far end of the peninsula, the club was deep within the Navy Nagar, or navy preserve, jointly run and policed by India's armed forces. No one would consider it unusual for the country's seniormost military officers to congregate at the exclusive club for a round of golf and cocktails. Now, with the eighteen holes behind them, they could get to the business part of their gathering.

"Come, Badu," said Admiral Jal Rajan softly as he placed a hand on Dhankhar's shoulder. "We are ready to begin the meeting."

Dhankhar gave out a deep sigh, reluctant to leave his private tranquillity. "It's so peaceful, Jal. I have so longed for this."

"I know, my friend. And all of India will eventually enjoy a peace such as this, but only after our work is through. Now, come. You have the lead-off presentation."

"Aye, sir," Dhankhar replied, then downed the rest of his drink.

He strode into the conference room filled with a veritable Who's Who of the Indian military. Admiral Rajan took his seat at the head table to the left of General Nirmal Joshi, Chief of Staff of the Army, and Chairman of the Chiefs of Staff Committee. To Joshi's right sat Air Chief Marshal Danvir Suri, Chief of Staff of the Air Force, and Lieutenant General Bipin Raina, Chief of the Integrated Defence Staff. These four were the most powerful men in the Indian armed forces, and the driving force behind Operation Vajra.

Named after the thunderbolt wielded by Indra, the Hindu king of the gods, and the god of weather and war, the nuclear strike against China was designed to finish the wounded dragon economically and politically. Although badly bruised by the war with the Littoral Alliance, China still possessed considerable military and economic power. Given time, she would recover. In the meantime, the Chinese waged a proxy war against India by providing substantial aid to Pakistan's military, as well as the Islamic terrorist groups in the northern tribal region.

Following the U.S.-brokered truce between the Littoral Alliance and China, India suddenly found itself constrained militarily, unable to attack Chinese targets directly. China, on the other hand, was now free to pour resources into the shadow war it had started. As Pakistan's resistance increased, buoyed by Chinese weapons and supplies, India's offensive ground to a halt. With casualties rising, the Indian president agreed to peace negotiations and sent a team off to Geneva, despite the Chiefs of Staff Committee's strong reservations. After months of heated discussions, there was still no resolution in sight, and the army began moving forward with its planned spring offensive.

Then in early January, the Indian minister of defense suggested in a press conference that a return to the status quo antebellum, Pakistan's primary demand, was not outside the realm of possibility. Furious that their government would even consider abandoning captured territory before the main objectives for the war had been achieved, and after a river of Indian blood had been spilled, senior officers seriously considered a military coup. It was Dhankhar who suggested that the "center of gravity" of the conflict wasn't the Indian government, or even Pakistan—it was China's support to the Pakistanis. Without that support, the war would quickly be resolved in India's favor. Dhankhar then volunteered that he had been in contact with someone who could provide the tools they would need to win, and knew how those weapons could be deployed secretly. The swift strike against China's battered economy would be completely anonymous, and lethal. If the four men at the head table were the heart of Operation Vajra, Badu Singh Dhankhar was the brain.

"Gentlemen, would you please take your seats?" asked Joshi. As the stragglers shuffled over to their chairs, the general motioned for Dhankhar to come forward.

"First of all, I want to thank you all for coming," Joshi continued. "I know this was an unexpected trip, but given the circumstances it couldn't be helped. I would also like to thank our host, Vice Admiral Mehra, Chief of the Western Naval Command. You've done well, Pradeep, in arranging these wonderful accommodations on such short notice, but don't think for a moment that this will excuse you from paying off your wagers on the golf game."

The collection of men laughed while Mehra feigned disappointment. "Next, we'll get a status update on Operation Vajra from Vice Admiral Dhankhar. Badu, the floor is yours."

"Thank you, sir." Dhankhar bowed toward the army chief of staff. "Gentlemen, soon after the unfortunate incident in Pakistan's northern tribal region a little over two weeks ago, I spoke with General Joshi, Admiral Rajan, and Air Chief Marshal Suri, recommending that we speed up the timetable for executing Vajra.

"Initially, I was concerned with all the extra noses probing for the source of the Kashmiri weapon that someone might accidentally stumble across our facility. And, indeed, we did have a close call. Fortunately, two of our civilian colleagues with the Intelligence Bureau and the Central Bureau of Investigation provided sufficient warning to clear the workshop before the investigation team arrived. Assistant Deputy Director Singh and Special Director Thapar, I wish to publicly thank you for your critical services."

The military officers present applauded heartily as the two civilians nodded their appreciation. Raising his hand, Dhankhar quieted his audience. "However, we are not out of the woods just yet. Even though the Americans' analysis has categorically demonstrated the nuclear blast was not from an Indian weapon, which did have the beneficial result of terminating the internal investigation, the entire world is now looking for a possible Russian or Chinese source of rogue nuclear weapons. And this, gentlemen, represents an even greater threat to us, as there is a very short line connecting the Russian arms dealer to this august gathering."

The crowd's murmurings echoed the mixed feelings they all felt about the U.S. administration's press release. On the one hand, India was no longer being held accountable for the "despicable act." But on the other, a multinational effort had been launched to track down the source of the weapon, or weapons, obtained by the Pakistani terrorists. An internal Indian investigation was troubling enough, but it could be handled, and influenced. An international investigation sponsored by the major nuclear powers, and endorsed by Delhi, would be much more difficult to control.

"Therefore, it has been decided to keep to the accelerated schedule. In that vein, I'm pleased to report that the physics packages of the five remaining weapons have been removed from their parent reentry vehicles and the remnants were disposed of at sea. The modifications to the torpedoes are proceeding a little slower than I'd like, but with one less weapon to work on, the job should be done by about the eighth of April.

"INS *Chakra* is currently in the graving dock at the Vizag naval dockyard, and work to upgrade the fire control system to support the modified torpedoes and install the improved towed array sonar is well under way. Minor repairs to propulsion and secondary systems will also be done, but on a not-to-interfere basis. While the completion of these repairs is not a necessity for the mission, they do need to be done eventually, and doing them now not only enables us to make good use of limited dry-dock resources, but assists in the cover story. All modifications and repairs are on track to support the revised 10 April departure date.

"*Chakra* will then proceed at her best tactical speed to the initial target area, with the last weapon deployed on or about April twenty-seventh. Three days later, five of China's busiest ports will be obliterated. This will reduce her export capability by at least half, along with the destruction of several major oil refineries and China's two largest financial centers. The resulting economic shock will finish what the Littoral Alliance war started, and quite possibly hasten the fall of the communist government, which is under considerable stress. With China in the throes of civil unrest and chaos, her support to Pakistan will be significantly reduced, if not terminated completely. Then we can finish the job we started last year." The sudden applause forced Dhankhar to pause. As soon as it died down, he continued.

"Finally, you'll be pleased to hear that I've successfully renegotiated the final cost of acquiring and modifying five weapons instead of six, and that a refund to your private accounts will be forthcoming. Are there any questions?"

An air force flag officer raised his hand and rose when acknowledged by Dhankhar. "Badu, has there been any additional discussion on saving one or two of these weapons to strike Pakistan directly? We could severely degrade their nuclear retaliatory strike capability with two well-positioned weapons."

Dhankhar sighed quietly; he'd heard this argument before, many times. "Yes, Uttam, it was briefly discussed and rejected for the same reasons as before. The use of these nuclear weapons must be anonymous, something we would very likely lose if we launched them at Pakistani nuclear targets. Our attack would not possess the element of stealth, and a severely degraded retaliatory strike capability still represents a significant threat. We cannot afford to have them destroy even one of our cities with a parting shot."

The air force general persisted. "But Badu, thanks to the Pakistani terrorists blowing themselves up, we have an opportunity here to mask our attack behind their incompetence."

"To what benefit, Uttam?" said General Joshi from the head table. "We all witnessed the scrutiny the world gave us when we were wrongly accused of the Kashmiri explosion. Even if we did improvise a delivery method for the devices, it would leave too many clues. The United States did some fine detective work to prove the weapon wasn't of Indian origin. Do you honestly believe we could hide a direct attack against Pakistan from all those prying eyes?

"Yes, the LeT terrorists and their Pakistani handlers have a love/hate relationship. But no one would buy the terrorists blowing up Pakistani nuclear strike assets. It's just too hard to believe, and those prying eyes would once again turn our way. No, Badu is correct. We must use these Russian weapons secretly and efficiently—and that means Chinese targets. This topic is now closed, gentlemen. Thank you, Badu, for your report."

Dhankhar bowed and started walking back to his seat. He avoided looking in the air force general's direction; the man had objected to Operation Vajra's Chinese focus from the very beginning. Rumor had it that he was envious of the navy's central role, but only the navy had a stealthy platform in the Akula-class submarine. And stealth was absolutely crucial to their ability to pull this gambit off. Dhankhar heard Joshi announce the next agenda item, a review of the central thrust of the spring offensive, but the admiral wasn't particularly interested. That job was for the army and the air force. Unconcerned, he let his thoughts meander back to the targets and the effect a 150-kiloton warhead would have on them.

27 March 2017
1700 Local Time
Icebreaker *50 Years of Victory*
Techeniye Guba
Novaya Zemlya, Russia

Vice Admiral Loktev paced impatiently on the icebreaker's helicopter deck; the divers had been down for almost half an hour and he was chomping at the bit to know what they had found. Silently he hoped the Americans' claim was wrong; the alternative would be humiliating beyond words.

"Comrade Admiral," shouted a deckhand. "The divers are coming up."

Loktev acknowledged the report and walked to the rope ladder hanging over *Victory*'s port side. The broken ice chunks, crushed by the ship's massive hull, were being pushed aside by men with long poles to keep a small area clear for the divers to surface through. Soon air bubbles could be seen breaking the dark icy film, and a moment later a man emerged, then another. The divers first swam toward and then crawled on to the ice floe. After removing their fins, masks, and air tanks, they walked to the ladder and hurriedly scurried up. Zhikin had barely reached the deck when Loktev swooped in, demanding a report.

"The Americans' claims are right, Comrade Admiral." Zhikin spoke through shivering blue lips. "The barge is exactly where they said it would be, and their description matches what I saw below."

"And the contents?" pressed Loktev.

Zhikin gladly took a towel offered by one of his men and started walking toward the watertight door and warmth; if the admiral wanted to talk, he could follow him. "There were numerous containers within the barge, each about two meters in length and one meter in diameter. Their appearance is consistent with the description of Pioneer missile reentry vehicle storage canisters, but we won't know for sure until we get one on board and open it."

The chilled diver grabbed the door's handle and yanked on it, and a gush of beautifully warm air engulfed him. Once inside, Loktev removed his *ushanka* and heavy winter mittens, while Zhikin peeled back the dry suit's hood, disconnected the gloves, and removed the liners. He traded his gear with a waiting lieutenant who stood by with two cups of steaming tea. The hot liquid going down his throat felt amazing. After making sure the lieutenant was out of earshot, Zhikin turned to the admiral and whispered, "The barge is not your normal dry cargo type, sir. It was specifically modified with ballast tanks, fore and aft; there are standard submarine salvage connections on both ends. Comrade Admiral, this barge was designed to be surfaced and retrieved."

"Any identifying markings? A serial number?"

"None that I could see, but we only looked over the barge's exterior. There could be markings, or maybe a nameplate, on the inside, but I wouldn't get my hopes up."

"How many containers?" Loktev asked.

"There are thirty-five storage cradles in the top layer. I can't be sure how deep they go because the barge has settled some, but I'd guess two, perhaps as many as three layers. If the lower ones are the same, then we are looking at a potential total of seventy to one hundred and five canisters."

"My God! That many? This is . . . this is inconceivable," groaned a shaken Loktev.

Zhikin nodded slightly as he took another sip of tea. The admiral's shock was completely understandable—the diver's report had given the older man quite a jolt—but Zhikin had worse news to deliver. "Unfortunately, sir, that's just the beginning. We found eight empty storage cradles in the top layer. If the Americans have been truthful to us, and they only took two, then someone has come back since then and retrieved six more. And judging by the small amount of silt in several of the cradles, this was done recently."

Loktev's face paled. Stunned, he leaned slowly against the bulkhead for support. He looked back at the diver, his mouth hanging open, speechless.

"One more thing, Comrade Admiral," added Zhikin slowly. "There was a submarine communications cable near the barge. I followed it out and found an MGK-608

Sever module one hundred meters away, out toward deeper water."

Loktev's expression changed to one of confusion. "Is it the one the Americans said they found?"

Zhikin shook his head. "No, sir. According to their report, that one should be much farther away, and to the southwest. This is a different module."

"Someone must have laid the Sever modules to guard the barge," Loktev concluded. "But who?"

"I have no idea, sir. But I did get a good look at the module's nameplate," remarked Zhikin as he pulled an underwater writing slate from his suit's breast pocket. "Here is the module's serial number. With any luck you might be able to trace who authorized its installation, and when. I'm sorry, but that is the best I can do for now."

The admiral smiled thinly and slapped Zhikin on the shoulder. "You have done well, Viktor Ivanovich. We'll solve this mystery together. Now, what do you recommend we do next?"

"I have two dive teams ready to go down as we speak, one to retrieve one of the canisters, and the other to do an in-depth inspection of the barge; to gather basic dimensional data and ascertain how deep it sits in the silt. If we begin immediately, we can find out if the canisters hold reentry vehicles within the hour. Then we'll have a better idea of the recovery effort."

"Will you retrieve the canisters one at a time?"

Zhikin shook his head vehemently. "No, sir, it's too risky and would take far too long. Besides, I'm not sure we can even get at the layers underneath without dismantling the upper structure. No, since this barge was designed to resurface, then that's what I recommend we do. *Victory* should have the necessary hoses to hook up to the salvage connections; if not, they can be transported by helicopter in a matter of hours. If all goes well, we can blow the ballast tanks dry and have the barge on the surface by tomorrow."

"Excellent, Captain!" Loktev exclaimed. "We'll proceed as you suggest. Get your men in the water, and let me know the moment they have recovered one of the canisters. I'll be on the bridge trying to figure out how I'm going to report this to Northern Fleet headquarters and Moscow. I must construct my message carefully. I'm not sure I would believe it myself if one of my aides were to place it in front of me. This is a political catastrophe of unimaginable proportions."

Nodding slowly, Zhikin smiled and said, "Comrade Admiral, I do not envy you. I suspect I have the easier of the two tasks."

28 March 2017
1130 Local Time
Naval Shipyard
Visakhapatnam, India

Petrov was in the graving dock when his cell phone buzzed. Irritated, he looked and saw he had received a text from his Russian supervisor summoning him to the liaison office immediately. "I don't have time for such nonsense," he mumbled to himself. But there was no point in arguing, Igor Osinov was as impatient as he was arrogant and Petrov would only lose more time if he tried to debate the matter with him. Signaling to one of his assistants, Petrov pointed to several deep scars on some of the anechoic coating tiles below the stern pod that would need replacing. Once confident that the man knew what had to be done next, Petrov walked to his car and drove over to the support office by the Russian hostel near the naval base's main gate.

The drive did little to soothe his aggravation, and Petrov strode angrily into Osinov's office demanding, "What is it this time, Igor? You know I don't have the time . . ."

He stopped in midsentence. Osinov wasn't alone; there

were two men with him, one Indian and the other probably a Russian. There was a fearful expression on Osinov's face.

"Please close the door, Aleksey," ordered Osinov; his voice was shaky. Petrov did so, turned, and approached his boss as he gestured to the well-dressed Caucasian.

"Aleksey Igorevich Petrov, this is Foreign Intelligence Service Officer Leonid Nikolayevich Ruchkin from the embassy in New Delhi, he's here to ask you a few questions."

Petrov's eyes darted to the SVR agent; the young man had a friendly demeanor and extended his hand. "I know how much of an inconvenience this is, Captain Petrov, so I will attempt to be brief."

"It's been a long time since I was addressed by my rank," replied Petrov as he shook Ruchkin's hand.

"But it's still appropriate, is it not? You did retire honorably, despite the unfortunate incident. Please, be seated, Captain."

Nodding politely, Petrov took his seat, while Ruchkin pointed toward the Indian. "This is my colleague, Field Agent Tungish Sharma of the Indian Intelligence Bureau. He'll be observing our discussion."

"Captain," greeted Sharma. Petrov reciprocated, but his nerves were on edge. Something wasn't quite right here; he felt something nagging at him.

Ruchkin wasted no time and launched into his interview. "Captain, in your opinion, is there anything unusual about the refit of INS *Chakra*?"

Petrov's reaction was one of amazement. If he had been nervous before, there were now alarm bells going off. The presence of the Indian intelligence agent complicated the situation greatly, and with Samant's warning ringing in Petrov's mind, he decided to play it straight.

"Unusual, Agent Ruchkin? The whole damn refit is unusual!"

"How so?"

"The customer cut our time by two-thirds, completely

rewrote the refit's work schedule, and made a mess of it!" vented Petrov. He only hoped his anger would mask his nervousness. "The schedule is so disjointed that there have been times when I had multiple teams trying to make repairs on colocated systems at the same time. If you haven't been in a submarine, space is at a premium. I don't have the room for all those people to do their work safely. Especially if hot work is involved."

The SVR agent's eyes glanced toward the Indian, who was writing furiously. "Have you been given an explanation for these changes, Captain?"

"Of course not," snapped Petrov. "I can only assume it has something to do with the Kashmiri incident, but I don't see how. All I know is that my Indian Navy point of contact, Captain Mitra, has given me precious little time to get a lot of work done."

"Do any of the repairs seem out of place to you?" asked Ruchkin pointedly.

Struggling to not show the growing anxiety he was feeling, Petrov paused to think the question over. He wanted to tell the SVR agent about his and Samant's suspicions, but that would expose his friend to Sharma; and every fiber of his being screamed this would be a really bad idea. Petrov prayed to God his expression looked pensive. "No . . . No, not really," he lied. "All the work items are valid. If anything there is an overemphasis on tactical systems that I believe is not prudent. There are a number of persistent, but not critical, engineering issues that could use more attention—in my opinion."

Ruchkin momentarily stopped the interview as he wrote some notes. Petrov glanced over at Osinov, who was literally shielding his eyes to prevent contact with the SVR agent. There was no doubt in Petrov's mind that his supervisor would have a piece of his rear end later.

"So, Captain," resumed Ruchkin. "How did you become the lead engineer for this refit? The position is not in your contract."

"You're correct, Agent Ruchkin, my original assignment was as a submarine technology liaison with the Indian Navy to assist in planning modifications and upgrades for their Russian-produced submarines—which includes INS *Chakra*. I also provided some consulting to India's design teams for their next nuclear submarine, mostly in the propulsion plant area. Captain Mitra essentially drafted me to be the lead engineer because I have the technical and tactical experience on Project 971 submarines. I was a *starpom*, ah, excuse me, first officer, on K-157 *Vepr*. My understanding was the radical reduction of the refit schedule required someone with more experience be assigned to oversee the refit. I just happened to be handy."

"I see. Well, Captain, I do appreciate the candor you provided in your answers. It's not often I find someone willing to speak their mind so freely. Wouldn't you agree, Mr. Osinov?"

"What? Oh, yes, absolutely, Agent Ruchkin." Petrov tried hard not to smirk. He would still get an ass chewing over this, but nothing official would come of it.

"One last thing, Captain," said Ruchkin as he pulled a piece of paper from his pocket. "Do you recognize this man?"

Petrov took the photo and studied it carefully. The picture was an official photograph of a middle-aged man in a Russian naval uniform. He looked a little old to be a captain third rank, but it was not uncommon in the Russian Navy for some officers to advance more slowly, particularly in the noncommand specialty fields. "No. I don't believe I've seen this man before."

Ruchkin's eyes narrowed. "Are you sure, Captain? He is a Russian national assigned to the refit project."

Petrov saw the Indian agent's eyes widen a bit. He began moving slowly, attempting to get a better view of the photograph. "I'm sorry, Agent Ruchkin. But if this man is working on *Chakra*, I haven't seen him. But I must remind you I've only been in the job for about three weeks. I

Fatal Thunder | 121

haven't met every one of my countrymen working on this boat. In fact, I've intentionally limited myself to contact with my assistants, as there is just so much work to do."

"Understandable. Well, then, perhaps you've heard his name: Evgeni Orlav?"

Petrov tried to keep his eyes on Ruchkin, but Sharma seemed visibly annoyed. Was the Russian SVR agent venturing off a previously agreed track? Or was Ruchkin trying to catch him in a well-laid trap? Again, Petrov's instinct was to play it safe. "Oh, yes, I have heard the name. He's a torpedo specialist, or so I'm told, but he doesn't report to me. Mr. Orlav does most of his work off-hull, and his immediate supervisor is an Indian naval engineer, Commander Fali Gandhi, I believe."

"Don't you find that odd that you haven't seen him?" pressed Ruchkin.

Petrov shook his head. "No, not particularly. According to the contract he's to inspect and test the new UGST-M torpedoes that were recently purchased by India, and to run tests on *Chakra*'s combat system to ensure the system can pass tactical information to the new weapons. Most of his work would keep him off-hull and in one of the weapons repair shops."

"Pardon me, Captain, but why isn't something so important as a submarine's main weaponry of more concern to you? Isn't it one of the key requirements in the new refit schedule?"

The snide remarks angered Petrov, and he let it show. The SVR agent was intentionally goading him. "Agent Ruchkin, as I have said before, I have many things that need to be done before the sea trials in a little over a week. I must carefully pick the work elements that would benefit the most from my limited time. Mr. Orlav's job is not overly complex, but it is very time-consuming. The contract specifications are especially strict, requiring each torpedo be stripped down and thoroughly checked, and then pass three complete diagnostic tests before the weapon will be accepted. This takes time, a lot of time, time I do not have. If the Indian engineer was not satisfied with Orlav's work, I'd hear about it, and then I would get involved. I have heard nothing from the Indians about Orlav's performance."

Ruchkin nodded, a smile once again on his face. "Thank you, Captain. I won't keep you from your duties any longer. I wish you good luck in completing the refit. It sounds like you're a very busy man. But I would appreciate it if you would keep Mr. Orlav in mind as you go about your work. Here's my card. Feel free to call me at any time."

Petrov took the card and quickly bid Ruchkin and Sharma farewell; he wanted to get out of sight before he lost his composure. Fighting to walk at a casual pace, he made a beeline to his car, and calmly started to drive away. It was only after he was out of sight of the liaison office that his hands started to shake.

28 March 2017
1500 Local Time
INS *Circars*, Eastern Naval Command Headquarters
Visakhapatnam, India

The problem with taking even a short break was that the paperwork didn't stop flowing while one was away. The pile had continued to build relentlessly, and a mass of correspondence and reports awaited Dhankhar when he returned. He'd breathed a heavy sigh at the sight of the imposing mound, hung up his jacket, and dug into the backlog. The admiral had managed to plow his way through most of the stack on his desk when an aide knocked on his door.

"Begging your pardon, sir. I know you didn't want to be disturbed, but a Mr. Bapat from the United Services Club is on the phone. He insists that he needs to speak to you. It concerns your last visit."

Dhankhar's initial irritation at the intrusion was replaced by curiosity. The combination of the man's name and the club was a prearranged code that a member of the Vajra group wanted to speak with him. "Very well, please forward the call."

As soon as the phone rang, Dhankhar grabbed it. "Vice Admiral Dhankhar here; how may I help you, Mr. Bapat?"

"Good afternoon, Admiral, this is Shiv Singh. I need to speak to you on a secure line." Dhankhar immediately recognized the voice of the assistant deputy director in the Indian Intelligence Bureau.

"One moment please," replied Dhankhar as he opened the top drawer of his desk and took out a smart card with an embedded microprocessor. He inserted the card into his phone and punched in his ID number. Moments later the phone's display read SECURE.

"Shiv, the call is now secure. What's the problem?"

"Admiral, one of our agents just reported in that he accompanied a Russian Foreign Intelligence Service officer this morning as he interrogated a Russian engineer involved with *Chakra*'s refit. The SVR agent was most interested in knowing if there was anything unusual or odd about it."

Dhankhar sat up straight. Singh now had his undivided attention. "Go on."

"The engineer is a retired Russian naval officer, his name is Aleksey Petrov. According to the report he's a former submariner, my agent said the SVR officer addressed him as 'captain.' I looked up his visa information; he's an engineering consultant here to facilitate planning future upgrades to Russian-built submarines. Apparently, Captain Mitra of the naval dockyard brought this Russian on to expedite *Chakra*'s refit."

"That was a most unfortunate decision by Mitra," growled Dhankhar quietly. "A senior Russian naval officer with submarine experience could be a significant risk to our plan. What did this Petrov tell the SVR agent?"

Singh ran down the list of questions and responses about *Chakra*'s refit during the meeting. It was clear that Petrov thought that the refit's priorities were skewed and there was a lot of work to do in very little time. Singh then concluded with some of the agent's personal observations. "He noted that Mr. Petrov seemed particularly whiny about conflicting work requirements and safety issues, and that he was visibly angry about those aspects of the refit."

"All that means is that Petrov is a competent engineer and manager. His concerns about the refit have been echoed by many of my own people," remarked Dhankhar. "They aren't pleased with the changes I've made as well. Any indication Petrov is aware of the true nature of *Chakra*'s modifications?"

"No, sir. Nothing leaps out from the report; he seems to be mostly concerned with managing the entire confused effort—very much a big-picture man. Although, our agent was not happy with the SVR officer when he went beyond the prearranged plan. He showed Petrov a picture of a Russian national, who apparently is supporting the refit. Petrov didn't recognize the photo, but he was familiar with the name: Evgeni Orlav."

At the mention of Orlav's name, Dhankhar's blood ran cold. The SVR agent's presence demonstrated that the Russians suspected something, but what? Did they know about their plan? Had they somehow managed to track down Kirichenko or one of his minions? For the first time, Dhankhar felt fear. This couldn't be just a coincidence, could it? The Indian admiral struggled to keep his cool as he asked, "What did Petrov say?"

"That he hadn't seen Orlav, nor was it likely he would given his duties. Petrov didn't seem concerned about the man because he hadn't heard any complaints from Orlav's Indian supervisor. Petrov claimed he didn't have the time to deal with issues that didn't require his attention. However, the SVR officer did ask Petrov to keep his eyes open.

There was an implicit request by the SVR agent to contact him if he came upon anything."

"I see," replied Dhankhar quietly. "Thank you, Shiv, for
this information. I'd appreciate a copy of the official report as soon as it is completed. Oh, and please alert the
four councilmen of this incident. They should be aware as
well."

"Yes, sir. I will do so immediately. Good-bye, Admiral."

As Dhankhar put his smart card away, he realized his
hands were cool and clammy. His heart was beating at a
rapid pace. The possibility of discovery when they were
so close to completing their task was unnerving and unacceptable. Their goal was vital, but the situation was hazy
and unclear. The Russians were asking dangerous questions, but the casual manner of the interrogation suggested
they didn't really know what was going on. Could it just
be a coincidence after all? He really didn't know much
about Kirichenko and his people. An overreaction now
could be just as deadly as doing nothing at all.

Dhankhar looked at his watch and then picked up his
cell phone. It was time he made another call.

7

Investigators

29 March 2017
1215 Local Time
INS *Chakra*
Naval Shipyard
Visakhapatnam, India

Petrov sat with Anton Kulik, one of the technicians working on the sonar system upgrade. Today he'd been installing new signal-processing boards for the main hull array. Since the sonar cabinets were located in the first compartment, Kulik was one of the few team members who actually interacted with Orlav, as he sometimes worked in the torpedo room, located on the deck above.

"When he's there at all," Kulik explained as they ate their lunch. They were in *Chakra*'s mess deck. Because of the refit, the galley itself was closed, but the Russians had made sure the air conditioning aboard the boat still worked. Even in March, the air outside was a sticky eighty-five degrees Fahrenheit. The mess was sized to feed forty men, so there was plenty of room for the small group of Russian technicians to eat their "tiffins," boxed lunches bought from vendors or restaurants on the way to work. The British had started the practice in the colonial era and invented the word, but it had become a habit for many Indian workers, and the Russians had quickly adopted the practice. Curried vegetables, rice, and flatbread made a satisfying lunch, especially since most of the Russians either were bachelors or had left their wives back in Russia.

"I've brought Orlav a takeout dinner every night for two weeks now." Working in the same compartment, they were on speaking terms, but Kulik said that Orlav wasn't really close with any of his countrymen.

"He's been working that hard? And nobody's helping him?"

"We're all busy," Kulik replied, "but at the last planning meeting Shvetov asked Captain Mitra about Orlav's progress and his deadline. By rights, Orlav should be reporting to Shvetov, or at least Commander Gandhi. Shvetov is the team leader, after all, but Mitra told Shvetov that Orlav wasn't his concern, and that his work was a 'separate project.' That's got to be their new missile, the Sagarika."

"Sagarika is a ballistic missile," Petrov answered. "You can't fire it from a torpedo tube."

"Then they're using their new Nirbhay cruise missile, or perhaps one of the missile types we've supplied to them, like the Klub, and gluing a nuclear warhead on the front. The Klub is fired like a torpedo." Kulik brightened. "That makes sense. We have to give them technical help on so many other things, so they hired Orlav to do that. What have you found out?"

The question caught Petrov off guard. "Me? What have I found out?"

"Come on! You've been pumping me about Orlav the entire meal." Kulik shrugged. "I don't mind, but fair's fair. You have to tell me what you've discovered." He noticed Petrov's hesitation. "It's all right. I know you're curious about what he's working on. So am I. Everyone on the team is, although we may be the only two who have actually figured it out," he added with a conspiratorial air.

Petrov hadn't realized his inquiries had been that transparent. That worried him a little bit, but meanwhile Kulik was waiting for an answer.

"I am curious," Petrov admitted. "I guess I'm a little concerned about what it means if you're right." That was at least half true.

"I'll tell you what it means," Kulik answered confidently. "Karachi? BOOM. Hyderabad? BOOM. Quetta? BOOM."

"If the Indians were to use nuclear weapons, the Pakistanis would as well," Petrov argued.

"Don't I know it!" Kulik agreed. "And Vizag would be a great target—a major naval base, and catch *Arihant* while she's still being repaired. Since the bomb went off in Kashmir, everyone's been on edge, with good reason. Something's going to happen, and it won't be good. The instant we're done here, I'm on the first plane going anywhere west. Not east. I don't want to be caught in the fallout pattern."

After finishing their meal, they both returned to their work, and even though he was busy, Petrov kept running the conversation over in his head. He'd learned nothing new. What occupied his mind was that his interest in Orlav had been so obvious. He'd tried to be subtle, but obviously failed miserably.

The problem was that before his lunch with Kulik, he'd spent the morning trying to find out what he could about Orlav, first from Captain Mitra, in charge of the project, then at the personnel office, and of course he'd looked around the torpedo shop where the technician spent almost all his time.

The shop was a large, windowless building, and if the keypad lock wasn't enough of a deterrent, the armed soldier out front kept him from even lingering in the area. Of course, short of peeking in a nonexistent window, Petrov didn't have a clue what he could have done or learned. He decided he was a better engineer than a spy.

Girish Samant agreed. "You are indeed a very lousy spy," he declared as they ate dinner together that night.

They were not eating at Akshaya's, but a smaller place, away from the shipyard. The Mirakapi had good food, but Petrov had to ask for extra rice to kill the fire from the tandoori chicken he'd ordered.

"And what would you have done?" Petrov retorted. He felt a flash of irritation, but he realized part of it was his competitive nature, one of the things he and Samant had in common.

"The same," the Indian answered quickly, with a smile. "Until now, I think we were both proud of our lack of guile. Unfortunately, there is no time to learn as we go. If Russian intelligence wanted you to play detective, they should have given you the handbook."

"Written in invisible ink, no doubt," grumbled Petrov.

"We will find other ways to gather the information we need."

29 March 2017
2000 Local Time
INS *Circars*, Eastern Naval Command Headquarters
Visakhapatnam, India

Dhankhar listened with frustration. It had been more difficult than usual to get ahold of Kirichenko, and after finally catching him; it was hard to read the man's reactions over the phone. He never replied quickly, rarely expressed surprise, or anger, or any strong emotion. Dhankhar couldn't tell by the sound of Kirichenko's voice how he was taking the news of someone asking questions about Orlav.

"Would Petrov have any other reason to ask questions about Orlav beyond the SVR agent's request?"

Even though he was on the phone, Dhankhar automatically shook his head. "No. Certainly it has nothing to do with his assignment assisting in *Chakra*'s refit," the admiral replied. "Captain Mitra was quite sure, and reported that Petrov asked about Orlav in several different places this morning."

"Why would the SVR care about Orlav?" Kirichenko asked. "Has he done anything to attract attention to himself?"

"I don't know," Dhankhar admitted. "But Petrov is following through on the agent's request, or he is at least trying. Mitra got his personnel file when he was assigned to assist with *Chakra*. He's a retired submarine captain, and now an engineer and naval constructor. No obvious ties to intelligence or law enforcement agencies."

"I know of him," Kirichenko said. "He was captain of *Severodvinsk*, but lost her on his first patrol in a collision with an American submarine. Nineteen men were killed. The investigation found him to be at fault and he was allowed to retire."

"Is he trying to redeem himself, then?"

"Possibly. We certainly can't let him find out anything more." Kirichenko asked, "Has Orlav talked to anyone?"

"No, he works alone in the torpedo shop, and goes back to his apartment every few days to shower and change clothes."

"Move him out of his apartment. Find quarters for him on the base; keep him away from the other Russians." Dhankhar felt a flash of irritation at the peremptory order, but then remembered that Kirichenko had also been an admiral, before he left his navy. "Are you sure he never leaves the shipyard?"

"As far as I know. The only places he goes are the torpedo shop, *Chakra*, and occasionally his apartment, just outside the north gate."

"That we know of," Kirichenko replied. "He's weak-willed, prone to drink and other distractions. That's why he was kicked out of the Russian Navy. If he's somehow managed to sneak off and gotten into trouble, it not only affects our schedule, it jeopardizes the security of the entire plan."

"I don't have enough people to watch him all day," the admiral protested. "I'll be able to constrain his movements if he stays in the shop, but I can't assign more guards to watch him inside the building. I've been able to boost security at the gates after the Kashmiri explosion. That wasn't hard, but beefing up security inside the base requires that I either bring more people into the project, or a long explanation. Both bring unwanted attention to Mr. Orlav and the torpedo shop—attention we can ill afford."

"Then do what you can. Visit him at unusual times for the next couple of days. After that, Churkin will be there and he can watch Orlav. Everything depends on that *zadnitsa*." Dhankhar's Russian was good enough to include slang. Kirichenko was not being complimentary.

"Agreed." Dhankhar didn't like what Kirichenko was saying, but it was true.

"What about Mitra? I'm assuming you haven't told him, have you?" The Russian's tone was accusatory.

"Certainly not," Dhankhar replied with a righteous tone. "Nothing beyond what I told him at the start. Orlav is working on a secret weapons project authorized by the Defense Ministry. I needed Mitra's cooperation to secure the torpedo shop, the guards, supplies, as well as having Orlav reporting only to me, while keeping the lead artificer at arm's length."

"Good." Kirichenko asked, "Is Petrov important to finishing *Chakra*'s refit on time?"

Dhankhar tried to remember what Mitra had said the Russian was doing aboard the sub. "Nothing special, supervisory work, mostly. He's very good at organizing things, and he's solved a lot of problems brought on by the truncated refit schedule. But the critical path is the delivery of several items of electronic equipment from Russia. He can't help with that. Why do you ask?"

"It's not important," Kirichenko replied quickly. "Hopefully, his playing detective is not interfering with his work."

30 March 2017
0900 EST
Embassy of the Russian Federation
Washington, D.C.

Hardy took Joanna with him this time. She had been un-happy at being excluded from the first meeting, and the presence of the national security advisor would remind the Russians of the importance of this issue to the U.S. The senator still wasn't completely sure that the Russian government was taking this seriously.

Ambassador Vaslev was waiting for them after they went through security, and they immediately went down one level below ground to what Hardy assumed was a secure conference room. The Russian flag in one corner and the picture of the Russian president on the wall triggered some old Cold War reflexes, but the Russians were trying to be hospitable. Tea had been laid out, as well as pads and pens for notes. The Americans left their phones and other recording devices at security, of course.

The only other person in the room was Colonel Valery Zykov, the SVR station chief. When Vaslev had entered with his two guests in tow, Zykov spoke into a microphone and a flat-screen display on one wall had come to life.

The screen showed three men sitting at a table. Two were in naval uniforms, the other was dressed in civilian clothes. He recognized one of them, Captain Mishin, the naval attaché that he'd briefed a week ago.

Mishin spoke. His English was heavily accented, but understandable. He explained, "After our meeting with you, I flew back to personally brief my superiors. They have made me action officer for this matter, along with Major Tumansky of the FSB." He was gesturing toward the man in civilian clothes.

"Immediately after I passed your information to the navy, they sent an expedition to verify your story. In spite of some bad weather, an icebreaker was able to reach the location. We did find a barge exactly where you said it would be, as well as the seabed acoustic devices you said detected your submarine."

He gestured to the other naval officer next to him. "Captain First Rank Zhikin is in charge of the 328th Expeditionary Rescue Squad, and along with others from his unit, dove down to the barge to investigate. He returned from the area just yesterday."

Although the same rank as Mishin, Zhikin looked older, or possibly just more weathered. He spoke Russian, while Mishin translated. "They found one barge, with three MGK-608 series fixed acoustic sensors around it. Inside the barge, they found many cases identical to the ones in the photographs you provided. They recovered one of the cases, and after taking precautions, opened it. They found a—" Mishin paused for a moment as if gathering his strength. "—nuclear device, just as you described."

Hardy was watching the diver's face and could see he was remembering the shock and surprise at the discovery of the case's contents. Mishin nodded to someone off-screen, and the three men were replaced by a series of underwater photos. The divers had set up lights to illuminate the interior of the barge. He could see rows of cases, then realized there was a second layer, and a chill ran race-tracks up and down his back at the thought of that many weapons hidden away for who knows what purpose.

Mishin and the other two Russians reappeared on the screen, and seemed to be waiting for some sort of response from the Americans. Patterson said, "Congratulations on finding and recovering the warheads. Can the Russian government provide assurances to the United States that the weapons are now secure?"

The two naval officers had a quick exchange, and Mishin answered, "I will not presume to speak for my government, but the cases are still being recovered. Captain Zhikin's divers are finishing their preparations as we speak."

She looked puzzled. "Preparations?"

Through Mishin, Zhikin explained, "The barge had settled into the silt and we had to do a little excavating before we could attempt to raise it. It has been modified with a ballast system similar to that of a submarine. Hoses have been attached to fittings and high-pressure air will displace the water, and the barge will rise to the surface. They're waiting for a tug and armed escort from Severomorsk. They should arrive tomorrow."

"That sounds like a lot of work. Wouldn't it be easier to have the divers just bring up the cases?"

When Mishin translated her question, Zhikin shook his head sharply and spoke. "Far too many dives, even if they bring up two at a time."

Patterson's expression matched the worry in her tone. "Exactly how many warheads did you find aboard the barge?"

Vaslev cut in. "That is not important. What matters is how many have been taken. I will say on behalf of the Russian Federation that the warheads from the barge are under our control, and under the terms of the INF treaty, will be destroyed as soon as feasible."

"It *is* important," she insisted. "According to that same treaty, the destruction must be done in the presence of observers. Since the treaty also requires reporting the number of warheads to be destroyed, withholding the number found would be in violation of the treaty, and destroying them without observers present would be a cause for grave concern. The number also tells us something about whoever put them there."

Mishin and Vaslev exchanged looks, and Vaslev nodded. The Russians were not willing to be viewed as breaking the treaty, not under these circumstances, and she was right. Besides, the Americans would find out eventually. Mishin replied, "There appeared to be sixty-two aboard the barge. If the cases that were taken were the same as

the ones we found, then the barge could have held seventy."
Mishin looked very unhappy.

Hardy's mind whirled at the thought of so many weapons at risk. *No wonder they didn't want to say how many were involved.*

"So hopefully, there's no more than six taken, and one's been accounted for, although that's small comfort to the people in Kashmir," Patterson observed.

The ambassador said carefully, "The Russian Federation is making every effort to locate and recover the missing warheads. Major Tumansky is our liaison with the FSB, and the president has ordered every law enforcement agency in Russia to assist in the investigation. In the last week, what has the United States discovered?"

Hardy answered. "That Evgeni Orlav, identified as a former Russian naval officer, has never entered or passed through U.S. territory or contacted any of our embassies."

Vaslev shrugged. "That's all?"

"All we had was that name," Hardy replied. "And like so many other clues, it led straight into Russia. But we have also been working from a different angle. We keep a careful watch on terrorist communications, especially anything that might relate to nuclear matters."

"Of course," Vaslev agreed.

"Normally, with so many terrorist groups worldwide, our ability to watch everyone is very thin. But the explosion in Kashmir gave us a time and a location. We managed to find a communication regarding a Pakistani scientist, a Dr. Tareen. We know he taught nuclear physics at Islamabad at the same time that A. Q. Khan was there. The communication was from one Lashkar-e-Taiba group to another in Kashmir the day before the explosion."

The ambassador still wasn't impressed. "LeT's involvement was decisively revealed by the blast itself. We will pass your information on Dr. Tareen on to our investigators, but I suspect the only way to locate him now would be with a Geiger counter."

"What about the clues from the barge?" Hardy pressed. "The warheads, the barge itself, the acoustic buoys all give you places to start looking."

Mishin answered that one. "Yes. Captain Zhikin's men took extensive photographs of the barge and the acoustic sensor modules." He looked over to the man in civilian clothes. "Major Tumansky is a specialist in crimes within the defense industry. He has been given broad investigative powers by the president."

Although relatively young, Tumansky was nearly bald, which only emphasized his broad Slavic features. His English was perfect, to the point where his accent was not Russian, but to Hardy sounded almost Southern. "The serial numbers on the warheads match, and are in the same sequence, as the two you stole twelve years ago. The barge is of a standard type, used for the transport of dry cargo. Over one hundred were manufactured in a factory on the Dvina River. Many are still in use. Before this one was deliberately sunk, all identifying numbers were ground or burned off. Wherever the divers scraped away the marine growth, the barge is still in its original red primer."

He scowled. "Forensic techniques can be used to recover the information from the surfaces where the information was erased, but not while it is underwater. After the barge is raised, we will make another examination.

"Inquiries at the factory revealed that production of this type of barge ended seven years ago. Their records were poorly maintained and are incomplete. We have assigned men to find and account for all the barges where the factory does have information, and a more thorough investigation, including interrogation of the factory personnel, is in progress.

"The acoustic sensors are still operational, and are part of a defensive barrier that lines our northern coast." The investigator looked over to Mishin.

Mishin explained, "The chain is monitored from a facility in Severomorsk. We immediately discovered that the location of the sensors, as provided by you and verified by us, is different from where the Northern Fleet headquarters believed them to be. The three surround the barge in a loose circle, instead of forming the northern end of the barrier, spaced much wider apart, and located well to the south."

Hardy noticed how the Russians were suddenly vague about the spacing and position of the sensors, but that defensive acoustic barrier was not part of the problem, as far as he could tell. But there still was a useful clue. He spoke up. "Your units seemed to have no trouble finding us, so somebody had to know where those sensors actually were located."

Mishin nodded agreement, but said, "Records of the incident—from the time of detection until the loss of *Gepard*—were classified after the court-martial of Admiral Yuri Kirichenko."

"I remember hearing about that. He was commander of the Northern Fleet. Why exactly was he court-martialed?" Patterson asked.

Mishin replied, "The official charge was 'violating standing fleet orders and using poor judgment.'"

"So pursuing *Memphis* violated your rules of engagement."

"Not at first," Mishin answered, "but once an intruder was some tens of kilometers from our coast, and was definitely moving away, standing orders were to track him, but not attack it again. Instead, against the advice of his chief of staff and other senior officers, when *Memphis* left the coastal defense zone, the admiral did not recall the pursuing units. Instead, he mobilized more Northern Fleet ships and aircraft.

"Testimony from officers present, and I can corroborate this from my own experience, is that he was fiercely determined to sink the American sub—*Memphis*—no matter what it took." Mishin rubbed his temples, as if the memory was stressful.

"Sonars in the pursuing ships heard the sound when *Gepard*'s torpedoes exploded. At first, it was hoped that meant the American sub had been sunk, but when some time had passed and our submarine failed to report, which was standard practice, Admiral Ventofsky, Commander in Chief of the Russian Navy, ordered the prosecution ended. Even then, Kirichenko did not seem ready to stop, and Ventofsky finally ordered Kirichenko's chief of staff to take command and organize the search and rescue effort for *Gepard*."

Hardy said, "I can only express my deep regret at the loss of your submarine. We did our very best to avoid combat. Our only desire was to leave."

"After intruding into places you had no business going," Mishin replied. "Your actions may have been justified, but the Russian Navy has always defended its home waters with vigor, and we will continue to do so." Mishin looked directly at Patterson as he spoke, and Hardy noticed Vaslev smiling. *That message has been successfully delivered.*

Hardy bristled and began to speak, but Patterson laid a hand on his arm and he remained silent.

Tumansky continued the narration. "At the court-martial, Kirichenko said that his only motive was to defend Russian territory and punish the intruder—you, but his actions went far beyond what was required. He even invented a story about a spy that the intruding sub had picked up to justify continuing the attacks. His explanation was incredible, but was accepted at the trial because his motivations were essentially irrelevant. The charges were based on his actions, not his reasoning. Now, with this new knowledge, we can see what he was so desperate to protect.

"Once we knew what to look for, we could see that Kirichenko knew where those misplaced acoustic sensors actually were. While his staff took charge of the pursuit, Kirichenko himself gave many of the tactical orders. His initial commands to the fleet sent them well north of the intruder's reported location. Since your submarine was fleeing north, the exact spacing did not attract attention, especially since our units successfully detected you. Reconstructing it now, using the sensors' true position, we can see that he was following standard fleet doctrine for the prosecution of a *Los Angeles*–class nuclear submarine, beginning at the sensors' true location."

"So the commander of the Northern Fleet was involved in the scheme." Patterson sounded surprised, even incredulous.

Mishin was defiant. "Admiral Yuri Kirichenko has always been seen as an able commander who made a reckless, and deadly, mistake. Over three decades of faithful service saved him from demotion and possibly a fine or even prison. At the time, it was thought nothing would have been gained by criminal punishment. Instead, he was allowed to retire immediately, without a pension."

"And where is the former admiral now?" Patterson asked.

Tumansky explained, "That is what my investigators are trying to find out. After the court-martial, he moved into a small house near the Severomorsk naval base. For a while, he kept in touch with a few friends and associates. He didn't have any family. Eventually, contacts with those he knew became less frequent, and finally rare. A member of his staff stopped by his house one day, about half a year after the court-martial, to find it vacant. He left no word with anyone we've spoken to. We're tracing his bank records and other documentation, but that all ended about the same time."

"In other words, he's vanished," Patterson concluded.

"While doing his best to not leave any tracks," Tumansky agreed. "But we have many other paths to follow. He

didn't load and hide the barge by himself, and there are
many questions regarding the warheads. Their manufacture was so highly classified that there may be only a few
people now who knew they even existed. Are these seventy all that were made? Who ordered their production?"

Tumansky sighed. "It's easy for me to believe that these
warheads were manufactured in secret. Even with the end
of the Soviet regime, Russia's defense industry is compart-
mentalized and divided to an absurd degree, all in the
name of secrecy. In my seventeen years as a chief investigator, I've only dealt with a handful of security violations
but hundreds of cases of graft and malfeasance.

"Because of that secrecy, only a few records were kept
and most of them are now missing. Our investigation has
only started, but so far nobody in the government or military claims to have any knowledge of these weapons. But
somehow Kirichenko knew." Tumansky sounded frustrated, but added, "Once I find that link, we'll use it to
track down Kirichenko and the rest of his helpers."

Patterson asked, "I'd like to get complete information
on the good admiral, please. Photos, fingerprints, and his
contacts of course."

Both Vaslev and the Russians in Moscow looked puzzled, and asked, "Why?"

"So that we can see if he ever came to the U.S., of
course. He's had twelve years to go anywhere he wanted.
For all we know, he's been living in Cincinnati. Also, we
can reexamine our intelligence to see if the admiral has
appeared, probably under another name, somewhere else.
Now that we have someone to look for, if he or his group
have been peddling stolen Russian nuclear weapons, we
may find their trail."

Even as Patterson asked for the file, Tumansky scowled,
then had a rapid-fire dialogue with Mishin—in Russian.
Vaslev also chimed in, after she finished making her request.

Vaslev answered for them. "We can give you the basic

information on him immediately, but the file will have to be reviewed by the Director of the FSB . . ."

"And sanitized, I imagine," she interrupted with a critical tone.

Vaslev shrugged. "Surely you understand, the file contains sensitive information, and might reveal techniques . . ."

She almost laughed. "What information could possibly be more sensitive than a renegade Russian admiral selling bootleg Russian nuclear weapons? Ambassador, gentlemen, the quicker we get the file, and the more information it contains, the better chance we have of stopping them before there's another—and possibly worse—catastrophe."

The ambassador didn't respond immediately, and she added, "Whatever is in the file will have limited distribution to those directly involved in this investigation. It is in the United States' interest to keep this matter quiet, for the time being." There was an edge to her voice, and she kept Vaslev centered in her gaze.

In Russian, Mishin spoke first, then Tumansky, addressing Vaslev. Hardy couldn't understand Russian, but their tone indicated she'd managed to convince them. Vaslev finally nodded, and then said, "All right, Dr. Patterson, on my authority, you will have the file this afternoon."

8

Arrivals

Evgeni Orlav was delighted with his luck. Instead of sleeping on a cot in the torpedo shop, or traveling back to his run-down apartment, he'd spent the night in luxury, on the orders of Vice Admiral Dhankhar.

Not that he'd been very polite about it, Orlav remembered. Dhankhar had shown up late last night at the shop. Orlav had been in the middle of test-fitting one of the mounts inside a torpedo body when the admiral had come in, standing silently until the technician had put down his tools.

"When you're ready to stop work for the night, tell the sentry outside. He'll have a driver take you to your new quarters, here on the base."

Orlav had been surprised, and started to ask a question, but the Indian cut him off, adding, "All your personal effects have been moved out of your apartment and brought here. Now there is no need for you to leave the base."

Dhankhar had been almost scowling as he spoke, and when he finished, Orlav simply said, "All right, I understand," and Dhankhar had left.

Orlav didn't like Dhankhar, and knew it was mutual. He

was the kind of officer that had always caused problems for Orlav back in his navy days—stiff-necked martinets who believed their rank actually meant something. All they thought about were rules and duty, and believed everyone else should be the same way. They'd made life so miserable for him he'd actually missed his wife and her family. At least his in-laws wouldn't give him grief for taking a drink now and then.

The mount had fit properly, and feeling satisfied with himself, Orlav had decided to break for the night. It was almost midnight, and he was curious, and a little concerned about where he was going to sleep. He didn't trust Dhankhar in the slightest. Well, if his new lodgings were that bad, he still had the cot here at the shop.

Stepping outside, Orlav told the sentry he was finished, and within a few minutes a jeep appeared and parked nearby. The driver said it was just a couple of kilometers away. Even this late, the night air was warm and thick with humidity. Holding out a hand as they drove, Orlav could feel moisture collecting on his fingers.

Truth be told, he wouldn't miss his "apartment" in town. Right, more like a prison cell. It was just one room, with barely enough floor space for a bed and a table. The toilet and shower were communal, just down the hall, and the entire building reeked of curry and sweat. Even with what the management called air conditioning, everything was sticky with moisture.

He'd picked it because many of the other Russians also lived there and commuted together. They lived there because it was cheap, and it let them send more money home to Russia. He needed the "cheap" part, and as for sending money home . . .

The character of the base changed quickly from an industrial appearance to residential as the shipyard's shops were replaced by neat one- and two-story barracks and office buildings. At that hour, there was little traffic, but the soldier was dutifully obeying the fifteen-kilometers-per-hour speed limit, which gave Orlav time to take in the sights.

He was surprised when they stopped in front of a white-painted brick bungalow. It sat near one end of a row of similar houses, all with neat gardens and red tile roofs. He'd been in the service long enough, and been on enough military bases, to recognize that the quarters were meant for senior officers. A brick walkway ended in steps that led up to a screened-in porch. A small nameplate said it was number forty-seven, but the space for the occupant's name was empty.

The driver said, "The admiral says you will live here until your work is finished."

Nodding his understanding, Orlav got out of the jeep, a little surprised but accepting. The screen door opened with what sounded like a deafening screech in the late-night quiet, and he stepped through to the shadowed front door. A polished brass knocker gleamed in the faint light from the street.

The door was unlocked, and after finding the light switch, Orlav found himself in a sitting room, not only completely furnished, but also tastefully decorated. He stopped in the doorway, hand still on the knob, transfixed. This was not only better than his apartment, it was better than his home in Moscow, and much better than the place he'd grown up in Rybinsk, with ten people and three generations in a three-room apartment.

He could see a small kitchen in an alcove to his left. An open door to the right beckoned, and he went through to find a bedroom, as nicely appointed as the rest of the house. The bed was already made up, as in a fine hotel.

This is how I want to live, Orlav thought, with an intensity that almost surprised him. *Someday soon, I'll be able to have a house like this, with enough money so I don't have to scrape to get a meal.*

A set of keys lay on the bed, next to a folded note. It

was in Dhankhar's handwriting. The admiral's spoken Russian was fair, but his Cyrillic lettering was like that of a child, each letter carefully drawn. "This house will let you get proper rest while staying close to your work. Do not leave the base until you are finished."

Orlav crumpled the note, and after a quick search, tossed it in a nearby wastebasket. He liked this place. He would keep it neat.

The search also revealed two battered suitcases and a couple of boxes sitting in a corner of the bedroom, his belongings from the apartment. He wondered who had moved him out. How had they gotten the key to his apartment? Although he didn't know any details, it was clear that the admiral's conspiracy extended into every arm of the Indian government, including law enforcement. Maybe one of Dhankhar's confederates had shown up and flashed a badge.

It took him only a few minutes to unpack, and he hurried a little. The bed reminded him of his fatigue, and promised a much better night's rest than he'd had in a long time.

He fell asleep wondering if they'd gotten his security deposit back.

He'd awakened after the best sleep he'd had in months, certainly since starting this job. The rumbling of his stomach reminded him that he was hungry. There was no food in the house, of course, but he always ate breakfast at the shop, while he set up for the day's work. He'd even obtained a small refrigerator and a plug-in teapot. As he dressed, he wondered if he should bring those things back to the bungalow, and have a proper breakfast here in the morning. But that might take longer.

It was great to have such a nice place to live, and to think about such mundane things.

Remembering to take his key, he had stepped outside and turned to lock the door when a harsh Russian voice came out of nowhere. "So you're finally up. No wonder you're not finished yet."

Startled, Orlav dropped the key and quickly knelt, fumbling to pick it up. At the same time, he looked around for the source of the voice. To his right, sitting in a wicker chair on the screened-in porch, was Jascha Churkin.

Churkin seemed pleased with the surprise he'd given Orlav, and said, "Good morning." His pleasant tone did not make Orlav feel any better.

Where Orlav was thin, almost scrawny, Churkin was built like a wrestler or a weight lifter. They were about the same height, but the ex-commando outweighed him by fifteen kilos, and none of it was fat. His black hair was cut very short, and dark eyes gave life to a face that had seen more than a few fights. When Churkin smiled, which he was doing now, Orlav could see a few gold teeth, and also a few gaps.

Kirichenko had found Churkin on the wrong side of the law, and had spent a fair amount of bribe money to get Churkin out of jail before he could be sentenced to an impressive number of years in a Georgian prison. Churkin was an ex-Spetsnaz "reconnaissance diver," skilled in many types of combat as well as underwater work, and a veteran of both the Chechen and Georgian wars. Among other skills, he spoke fluent Arabic.

Finding someone like Churkin had been vital to Kirichenko's plans. Under his direction, the commando had personally dived on the barge to bring up the warheads, with the admiral waiting on the boat above. Churkin guarded the warheads on their long trip across a lawless landscape while Kirichenko dickered, bribed, and organized each leg of their trip. Throughout it all, Churkin had been as reliable as a stone monument, because Kirichenko knew the one thing that could hold his loyalty: money.

Seeing him just a few feet away, so suddenly, Orlav suppressed a chill. Churkin was not only Kirichenko's right-hand man, he was also his executioner, if need be. The ex-admiral had made it plain to Orlav that if he didn't perform well, or if he was stupid enough to try and leave, Churkin would happily hunt him down and slit his throat. Eventually.

"Tell me about Aleksey Petrov," Churkin ordered.

Orlav was still fumbling on the floor for the key, and as he picked it up and stood, he turned to face Churkin. "I don't know the man." The question puzzled him, and he searched his memory.

After a moment, he added, "I saw him for the first time last week, when Captain Mitra called us all together and told us we were going to have help with the work. He was the only Russian. The rest were Indians from different departments in the shipyard."

He held up his hands. "That's all I know. Maybe you should speak to some of the others."

"I already have," Churkin replied quickly. "Yesterday. Now I'm talking to you. Has Petrov spoken to you?"

"No."

"Have you seen him nearby while you did your work?"

"No. Never. I think I've passed him on the sub a couple of times, but that can't mean anything."

Churkin announced, "He's been asking questions about you."

"What?" A flash of fear ran through him. If they had been discovered . . .

"Aren't you supposed to be on your way to the torpedo shop?"

"Oh. Yes." Orlav realized he was still holding the key, and turned back to lock the door. He carefully put the key in his right pocket.

Churkin stood, and when Orlav looked at him, a little bewildered, finally said impatiently, "So let's go."

Orlav turned and quickly went down the steps and the brick path, then turned right to head for the torpedo shop. The route was simple, and would only take fifteen minutes to walk. Churkin followed easily, and matched Orlav's pace.

"So Aleksey Petrov's been asking questions about what you're working on, why you don't report to Gandhi or Shvetov, and so on. I'll ask you again. Are you sure you haven't said something to Petrov to arouse his curiosity?"

Orlav answered firmly, "Definitely not."

"To anyone else?"

"No!" Orlav insisted. "Of course not!" When he could see that Churkin was unconvinced, he added, "I work alone, I eat alone. The only person I say more than 'Hello' to is Anton Kulik, and that's when I ask him to bring me my meals. Maybe the isolation is what attracted Petrov's attention."

"Perhaps," Churkin admitted, "but I have to find out if anyone else is involved with him, and how much they know. I'm taking over security down here—especially your security until you finish the project." While Churkin was aware that an SVR agent was the probable source of Petrov's questions, Churkin had been expressly forbidden to tell Orlav. The whiny technician was already a bundle of nerves and it wouldn't take much to get him to panic. But Kirichenko also needed to know if Orlav had done something stupid to attract attention to himself. Churkin was satisfied with Orlav's answers and would report his impressions to the boss.

Orlav continued walking in dejected silence. The thought of the ex-Spetsnaz thug hanging around, watching his every movement, did not make Orlav feel any more secure. As if he needed another incentive to finish quickly.

A block or two from the torpedo shop, Churkin suddenly turned and walked down another street. He didn't even say good-bye, although Orlav was happy to see him go.

In addition to all the depressing thoughts whirling in his head, Orlav was disappointed by Churkin's visit. The Russian engineer had been looking forward to the morning walk from his new quarters, a chance to organize his thoughts for the day's labor. Instead, Mr. Buzzkill had not

nly ruined the tranquillity of the moment, but managed
o increase his paranoia. A great start to the day.

Forget Petrov. He just wanted to keep clear of Churkin.

1 March 2017
330 Local Time
istrict Central Library
isakhapatnam, India

irichenko had insisted on meeting in a completely ran-
om location. Dhankhar hated what seemed like pointless
loak-and-dagger games, but then he remembered that
irichenko had been underground for over a decade, and
at he was peddling nuclear weapons he'd stolen from his
wn government. The man had every right to be paranoid.

The admiral hadn't found out where they would meet
ntil just half an hour before the appointed time, when
irichenko had phoned him and simply said, without pre-
mble, "The public library on High School Road."

High School Road was a major thoroughfare that led
est away from the water into the city. He'd driven by the
lace more times than he could count. "I know it," he'd re-
lied, and the Russian had hung up without another word.

They always made this business glamorous and excit-
g in the movies, but Dhankhar just checked out with his
ag secretary for the day and drove out the front gate. The
reets were still busy with the evening rush hour, but the
brary was only a few miles away. Fifteen minutes early,
e pulled into a bank parking lot a short distance from the
brary.

He started to walk in a direction away from his desti-
ation, intending to circle the block, to check for anyone
llowing him, then stopped, laughed, and headed straight
r the library.

Dhankhar had no way of telling if he was indeed being
llowed, and even if he was, there was nothing he could

do about it. Abort the meeting, he supposed, but that woul
be pointless. A tail, especially by the authorities, woul
mean that they'd already been discovered, and that Vaj
was doomed. He chose to believe that for the moment the
plan was still secret.

He'd never seen the Russian, and wasn't sure that h
could recognize his voice. Kirichenko always kept the cal
as short as possible, and Dhankhar could not be sure, bu
suspected that he used some device to alter his voice.

On the other hand, Dhankhar's photo was easily avai
able on the Internet. He had an aide who made sure that
was included with all the base press releases. He'd ju
have to wait until Kirichenko approached him.

He walked up the steps seven minutes before the 7:00 P.M
meeting time and tried to act like he needed a book. Th
library's reading area was busy, a mix of schoolchildre
and adults at almost every table. He didn't see anyon
immediately that looked like an ex-Russian admiral, an
climbed the steps to the second floor.

This was the reference section, and much less populate
He slowly walked past the rows of bookcases, looking f
he wasn't sure who, but certain he hadn't seen him.

A voice in Russian behind him almost made him jum
"Good evening, Admiral. Please follow me." He turned
see a heavily built man with close-cropped black hair a
ready walking away, and Dhankhar quickly followed hi
to one side of the second floor. A row of audio listenin
booths lined one wall, and his guide led the admiral to on
end. Inside, a gray-haired man with sharp features nodde
and stood.

Dhankhar opened the door and stepped inside, while h
guide, and presumably Kirichenko's associate, lounge
outside but nearby. Skimming quietly through a book, a
if he could actually read Hindi, he would make sur
Dhankhar and Kirichenko were not disturbed.

Kirichenko didn't bother with pleasantries. "My co
league Mr. Churkin," he said, indicating the man outsid

heir door, "has been investigating Mr. Aleksey Petrov for
s. Have you learned anything new since our last conver-
ation?"

"I've seen him working on *Chakra* and in the shipyard.
t's hard to hear what he's talking about without getting
oo close to him, but he seems to be intent on his tasks.
He hasn't gotten near Orlav or the torpedo shop."

"That is good, but Churkin can now take over the secu-
ity for Orlav and your project. That will let you focus on
naking sure the refit is completed on schedule."

"Ended is more like it. There was so much work that had
o be abandoned. If this project wasn't so important . . ."

"The only thing that matters, as far as I can see, is
hat *Chakra* is seaworthy and can fire torpedoes. My job
vill be to keep Orlav on task and on time. Churkin has
apers identifying him as a representative of a Russian
rms company, the Morteplotekhnika Research and De-
ign Institute. They manufacture the engines for the
UGST-M torpedo, so that should answer any questions
bout his comings and goings. Can you arrange for an
fficial base pass and whatever other authorizations he
eeds?"

"Of course," Dhankhar nodded. "They'll be at the
ecurity office near the front gate by noon tomorrow."

"Good." Kirichenko stood, and seemed almost eager to
eave. "That should be it, then. If you see Churkin, don't
peak to him, or acknowledge his presence, unless it is ab-
olutely necessary. You've never met."

"I understand," Dhankhar answered. He started to stand
s well, but Kirichenko motioned to him to remain sitting.
I'd appreciate it if you'd remain here for a few minutes
fter we leave."

"All right," Dhankhar answered, willing enough. The
wo Russians disappeared quickly.

It was a sensible request, he thought. They should en-
er and leave separately, so any surveillance would not see
hem together. But of course, if they were already under

surveillance, it could be too late. *The real reason he aske*
me to remain, he realized, *is that if I'm arrested, I can*
tell anyone where they went after leaving here.

1 April 2017
1935 Local Time
INS *Circars*
Visakhapatnam, India

Churkin had decided to act quickly, at Kirichenko's urg
ing. Not that he disagreed. Petrov was trouble waiting t
happen, and the sooner he was gone, the better. Kirichenk
had provided him with the address of the Russian Hoste
where Petrov lived and the locations of his office and hi
workstation in the shipyard. Normally, Churkin woul
observe someone for a few days before taking any action
but in this situation, time was critical.

Petrov lived alone in the apartment. Churkin could easil
break in and wait for him. There might even be some
thing valuable there, which he would be happy to take. Th
police would classify it as a robbery gone bad—the un
fortunate victim surprised the intruder.

But Churkin didn't like it. Although he'd wear gloves
even in this heat, there was no way he could avoid leavin
trace evidence behind. Also, he didn't know enough abou
the people living nearby. He might be seen breaking in
and once inside, he had no way to know what was going
on outside the apartment.

Churkin also didn't like sitting and waiting. It was pas
sive, and required patience. He'd never liked waiting. An
he couldn't be sure when Petrov would return. What if h
went out drinking after work?

The real problem was taking his eyes off the target
Churkin had access to the base, and could certainly fin
Petrov at work, not that he'd do anything there. But onc
he'd found the man, it was against Churkin's instincts t

ose sight of him, even if it was intentional, even if it was o set up an ambush.

Simpler was always better, in Churkin's experience.

He'd been given photos of Petrov from his personnel ile, and had no trouble finding him as he came off *Chakra* n midmorning. He was taller than Churkin, but not by nuch, and the ex-commando saw nothing that would make iim a difficult target. According to Kirichenko, he was n ex-submariner, and now a consultant. *This should be asy.*

By himself, it was difficult tracking someone's movenents without being noticed, but the engineer kept it simle. He spent the workday either on the submarine or in is office. Petrov worked late, and it was well after dark efore he headed for the main gate. *All the better,* Churin thought. He wasn't terribly worried about being seen, ut the darkness had a comfortable feeling for him. He was n his element.

Unexpectedly, Petrov boarded a local bus. Churkin got n as well, using the other door. The vehicle was nearly ull at that hour, and it was simple to keep out of Petrov's ight while keeping track of when he left the bus.

Petrov got off in a small shopping district. *Better and etter,* thought Churkin. An assault and robbery here vould appear completely random.

Lights from the street and the storefronts gave a fair mount of illumination, but there were plenty of shadows. There were other people on the sidewalks, and traffic, but he streets weren't crowded. Best of all, he didn't see a sinle policeman or any other sign of law enforcement.

Churkin felt his excitement building. He wanted to renain calm. He wouldn't need adrenaline for this job, but is target had only minutes to live, and Churkin loved hese moments. As he walked, he slipped on a pair of lightolored gloves, made of the thinnest material he could find. His hands would start sweating soon, but he would be lone before that was a problem. He was actively hunting

now, waiting for the foot traffic to thin out, marking es
cape routes . . .

There. Ahead of Petrov, a recessed storefront created
wide alcove, deep enough for the inset corner to be almos
completely shadowed. Churkin was ten or twelve meter
behind Petrov. He could build up a little speed to catch up
and then use that momentum to shove his target into a cor
ner. They'd be hidden from anyone up ahead, and it woul
be over in seconds.

His steps quickened, and he pulled a cloth around hi
neck up to cover his nose and mouth. Petrov was still walk
ing, facing away, completely unsuspecting. Pinned in a dar
corner, he'd never see the man who killed him.

Churkin had closed more than half the distance, and
was still picking up speed. With only the briefest thoughts
he reached back for the knife he'd concealed under hi
loose-fitting shirt. The sheath hung just beneath his nec
and shoulders, handle facing up and easy to grab. He'
spent time yesterday modifying the sheath and practicing
drawing the knife quickly.

He had to conceal it along his back because of its length
He'd gone into several shops yesterday looking for
double-edged blade at least sixteen centimeters long, hi
minimum. He'd finally found a nice one, almost as long
as his hand and sharply pointed. He'd had others like i
before, and experience told him what to look for. It wa
more properly a dagger, and so narrow it could almost be
called a stiletto. It was perfect.

Churkin's left hand was out in front, raised to catch
Petrov behind the shoulder blades and propel him into th
darkest part of the corner. His right hand, with the knife
was down near his waist. Experience had taught him how
to come in low, just above the waist, and stab up. The long
blade would pierce the heart.

A young couple stepped out of the store, just ahead o
Churkin. He automatically angled a little left, and saw he

would clear the two, but they both looked directly at him, and saw the knife in his hand.

He ignored the couple. They were no threat to him. But the man shouted, and used one arm to shove his wife or girlfriend back behind him. She was screaming, and Petrov started to turn toward the noise. Churkin angled more to the left, still trying to aim for his back, but Petrov was turning too quickly, so after half a step, Churkin changed his plans, raising the knife slightly. He'd catch Petrov in front, in the belly, still under the rib cage, and just as lethal.

Petrov not only saw the couple making so much noise, he spotted someone charging toward him at a full run. He didn't see the knife at first, but automatically tried to move out of the way, backing up and moving sideways, away from the storefront. More confused and surprised than afraid, he raised his hands to fend off his—attacker?

Still two meters away, Churkin cursed his luck. Petrov was bringing his arms up. It was not a trained defensive move, but it meant there was almost no chance of a quick kill, not against someone who was aware of his assailant. He could see Petrov's eyes widening; he'd finally seen Churkin's knife. Petrov called out, "Knife!," but it was in Russian.

Then he surprised Churkin. Instead of bracing to meet the attack, he turned and fled down the street. Churkin, already at speed, tried to grab him by the shoulder, or just Petrov's shirt collar, but missed by inches.

Spurred by fear, Petrov flew down the street, still shouting, first in Russian, then also in English, for help, not that his situation needed any explanation. Churkin kept pace with him for almost half a block, but both men were in good physical condition, and Petrov had a slight edge in height, and that longer stride helped him open the distance, first from inches to a foot, and then more.

Other passersby had seen the pair now, running full tilt down the sidewalk, and Churkin realized that even if he caught up with Petrov, his murder would be neither quick nor quiet. Keeping up speed, he turned right down a cross street with less traffic, and then left into an alley that he could see ran the length of the block. By the time he'd reached the other end and emerged, the neck scarf and gloves were off and the knife was back in its sheath. The loose-fitting shirt, bright-colored, was gone to reveal a similar, darker one underneath. He slowed his pace, and looked behind him for any sign of pursuit.

Then he tried to figure out what to do next. *Kirichenko will not be happy.*

Petrov ran for another half block before he realized that he was no longer being chased. Winded, he leaned against a storefront. His surprise at the sudden and completely un-expected attack magnified his fear. He reached up to brush his hair back and discovered his hand was shaking. If not for being braced against the building, his entire body might be doing the same thing.

A few pedestrians who had seen the chase approached him cautiously. He certainly didn't think he looked very threatening, and a middle-aged man asked in English, "Are you all right?"

"I think so," Petrov answered, but then stood up straighter and flexed his arms and legs. Nothing hurt. "I am fine."

"Who was that?" a woman asked, but he just shook his head. "I don't know."

Another man said, "I saw him run down a side street," and pointed.

The woman said authoritatively, "You should call the police."

"I will," Petrov replied, and reached for his cell phone.

No longer needed, the pedestrians dispersed, returning to their errands, but occasionally glancing back at the for-eigner.

At the interview in Osinov's office three days earlier, Ruchkin had given him a card. Petrov fished it out of his wallet and dialed the number. It rang three times before a recorded voice repeated the number and asked the caller to leave a message. Wonderful.

Should he call the local police? It seemed pointless to Petrov. If it was just a random robbery attempt, there was little the police could do. A mask had hidden most of his attacker's face, but what little Petrov saw hinted that he might have been a foreigner—European or perhaps even Russian.

And why would a foreigner pick another foreigner to rob on a busy street in the early evening? He didn't like the answer, and called another number.

They'd met on a busy street corner, and gone into a nearby bar, chosen because it was close and half-filled with customers. They both hoped a public place would be the safest choice. It catered to sports fans, and large-screen TVs at opposite ends of the room were showing cricket and football matches, with the attendant cheers and groans from the patrons. Samant ordered Kingfisher beers for both of them and they found an empty table.

Samant didn't really say anything until Petrov had finished telling his story a second time. With repetition, his second account had less emotion, and a little more detail. Even so, there was little to work with.

"Now I understand how you feel," Petrov remarked.

"If you mean that you are now as paranoid as I am, good." Samant shivered. "I am very glad they missed their chance with you, but now we must both be on guard. I should have expected they would become violent. After all, what's one life when you're selling weapons that can kill tens of thousands?"

"I don't think they know about you, yet. I was the one asking about Orlav, and then I was attacked," Petrov explained.

"I'll take precautions anyway," Samant replied. "And so will you," he insisted.

Petrov nodded. "I tried to call the SVR—that intelligence agent that questioned me the other day. I haven't been able to reach him. I haven't told the local police."

"Good!" Samant replied. "Even if they believed your suspicions and were willing to investigate, Vice Admiral Dhankhar has enough political influence to deflect their questions completely. And it would confirm his suspicions."

"I will e-mail Jerry, or perhaps you should."

"I will," Samant replied firmly. "We can't know how closely they're watching you."

"I just hope the Americans can do something. I wasn't expecting immediate results, but it would be good to know they are acting."

"If they can, I believe they will," Samant reassured him. "This is as much a threat to the USA as anyone." He sighed. "And now, more than before, we have to make sure that someone besides us knows."

9

Fatal Encounter

1 April 2017
1600 Local Time
The White House
Washington, D.C.

"E-mail will be the death of me yet," muttered Joanna Patterson as she scrolled down the three screens of waiting correspondence. It had already been a very long Saturday, and she hadn't had an opportunity to sneak away and thin out the herd. Fortunately, none appeared to be an April Fools' joke—she'd already announced that she would personally have the first transgressor shipped to Siberia. Even the president didn't want to challenge her on that one. Her husband, Lowell, proved himself even wiser by sending a dozen red roses instead. "Peace on Earth begins at home," said the card.

She scanned the titles as she moved down the list, looking for any obvious "Me First!" messages. Joanna saw Jerry's e-mail two-thirds of the way down on the third screen. The subject line wasn't reassuring—"Hostile Intent Demonstrated." She clicked on the e-mail and began reading; the contents were even less encouraging.

Just received an urgent email from Samant. Someone tried to attack Petrov this evening. The assailant appeared to be a Caucasian, not Indian. Petrov believes he was a Russian. Alex has reported the attempted assault to the Russian embassy, but not the local military police. Samant believes it would attract too much attention. If this wasn't a random act of violence, then someone is worried that Alex knows something. Is there anything we can do to help?

Joanna scrolled down and read Samant's brief message. It held little additional detail, but the Indian was convinced the attack confirmed his and Petrov's suspicions. She sighed and shook her head. Yes. The attack, if indeed it wasn't just a botched mugging, would be an indication, but still it wasn't proof. She needed hard evidence if she was to advocate getting the U.S. involved. Joanna typed out a quick reply asking Jerry to relay her request. She was about to tell him to keep her apprised when she saw Jerry's closing line; he was going to be unavailable for the next few days and e-mail contact would be spotty. That could only mean his boat would be at sea. "Damn it," she whispered. "Talk about really bad timing."

Briefly, she considered asking the CNO to keep *North Dakota* tied up to the pier for a few more days, or perhaps even a week, but rejected the idea. Admiral Hughes had already done her a huge favor in getting Jerry to San Diego on short notice, and while he might be understanding about another request, it would be seen for what it was—micromanaging a navy asset. Certainly Captain Simonis, the squadron commander, would be very annoyed with more "rudder orders from Washington." And then there was Lowell's stern counsel after their meeting with Jerry, "Don't try to drag Jerry onto your staff. He's a submarine commanding officer, and he has a boat to run."

Sighing deeply, she told Jerry to pass on her e-mail address to Samant and Petrov. Joanna promised she'd do what she could to help them, but repeated the need for firm evidence. She clicked the send button, then reached over for her secure phone. Time to call SECSTATE Lloyd and Randall Foster to see just what the U.S. could, and could not, do to assist the two men in India.

2 April 2017
0900 Local Time
Naval Dockyard
Visakhapatnam, India

The sights and sounds of the shipyard were unexpectedly refreshing. As soon as Samant walked onto the graving dock, he looked up at his old submarine. INS *Chakra* sat majestically in the dock on large wooden blocks; there were sparks flying about her sail that made it look like she even had a crown. *Chakra* looked absolutely huge from the floor of the dock; it never failed to amaze him how deceptively small even a large submarine looked when most of the hull was concealed under water. A loud beep, followed by someone shouting at him, forced Samant to scurry to get out of the way of a forklift carrying a pallet of replacement parts. There were people everywhere as the workmen toiled to get *Chakra* ready for sea. Sea trials began in five days.

Up ahead, Samant saw Jain inspecting the main sonar dome with one of the foremen. The composite structure surrounding the submarine's main hull array, and the coating around it, was still dripping wet. Two men with pressure washers stood at a distance, waiting. Jain saw Samant approaching and waved. After reaching for a clipboard, Jain signed a form and gave the workers a thumbs-up. He then jogged over to Samant, stopped short, snapped to attention, and rendered a smart salute. After Samant had returned the honor, he extended his hand. Jain hesitated, then accepted the offer. He seemed a bit flustered.

"How goes the refit, Maahir?" Samant asked while waving to the surrounding activity.

"I hate being in the shipyard, sir. I can't wait to get back to sea so I can get some rest," shouted Jain. He looked uneasy.

Samant nodded sympathetically. "I completely understand, shipyard periods can be very stressful. I always found the noise to be irritating."

Jain smiled slightly while pointing to his earplugs. "These help, a little. What can I do for you, sir?"

Samant then noticed that Jain was still at attention; his former first officer was behaving as if he were still in the job. The Indian captain sighed. This wasn't how he wanted their relationship to be now. Finally, he said, "At ease, Maahir." The younger man visibly relaxed. Moving closer, Samant spoke with an informal, almost fatherly tone. "Listen, Maahir, you are now the commanding officer of a nuclear submarine, that's a very exclusive club, and we almost have a quorum right here with just the two of us. I'm not your CO anymore, and we're not even in the same chain of command. Yes, I'm still a senior officer, but we're now colleagues, and I'd appreciate it if you would see it that way as well."

Jain looked down, surprised and confused. It took him a moment, but when he lifted his head, he was smiling. "Thank you, sir. I would be honored." Samant nodded and gave Jain a friendly slap on the shoulder.

"So, Captain, what brings you to this den of chaos?" asked Jain, more upbeat.

Samant chuckled and shook his head. "I had to get away from my office. The work has been most frustrating as of late."

Jain looked incredulous. "But, you're on shore duty now. Why are you coming in on a Sunday? The weather is glorious, you should be on the golf course!"

Samant looked rueful and depressed. "It's very bad, Maahir. The project office is so damn dysfunctional. I've been in every weekend since I was assigned, trying to make some sense of what had been done, and what still needs doing. I'm still not entirely sure what my predecessor did during the two years he was in the post. I've managed to get things moving again, but it's been slow going. I'm not sure what my people hope for more: our being successful or me suffering a heart attack!"

Jain roared with laughter. Samant found he liked the sound. "I see that the great Captain Samant hasn't changed his stripes!"

"True," Samant said with a grin and a shrug. "But I see you have." He reached over and brushed some dust off one of Jain's new epaulettes. "Congratulations, Commander."

"Thank you, sir. But I owe this promotion to your *gentle* tutelage." Jain smiled sheepishly.

"Gentle? As I recall, I flogged your ass on a regular basis!" teased Samant.

"Yes, sir, you did. Fortunately, the trousers hide the calluses." Both men laughed heartily, and Samant took another friendly swipe at Jain. It felt good to be back with his old boat.

"Would you like to take a quick tour, sir?" inquired Jain. "I know the crew would appreciate seeing you again. You have been missed. Besides, you look a little homesick." The smart-ass grin on his face utterly failed to hide the delight Jain felt at razzing his former captain.

Samant rolled his eyes. "Maahir, you'd make a lousy poker player. And while your observation *may* be correct, you are to repeat it to no one. I do have my reputation to consider."

"Of course, sir, not a word to any living soul." The twinkle in Jain's eye said otherwise. "I'll inform the sentry that you'll be up shortly."

"You're a cruel man, Captain," Samant grumbled playfully. "But, thank you."

"My pleasure, sir," replied Jain. "Oh, and one more thing. Don't expect it to be very tidy on board. These shipyard workers are absolute pigs!"

It was now Samant's turn to chuckle; he knew exactly

how Jain felt. Still, it was a little surreal hearing his own words coming from his former first officer. A feeling of satisfaction came over Samant when he returned Jain's departing salute. As the young captain ran off to his next appointment, Samant turned and walked toward the dock's wing-wall ladder. He forced himself to walk slowly, holding the excitement he felt inside.

The sentry post was manned by one of the crew's junior officers and a petty officer. Both were happy to see their old captain, and after a casual check of his ID card, Samant was allowed on board. Climbing down the ladder into central post, he was suddenly overwhelmed by memories, as well as the smell of burnt welding flux and ozone. The space was very crowded, noisy, and hot. Trying to stay out of the workers' way, he scooted over to the Omnibus combat system consoles. Looking down at the operator's panel, he saw that the cover plate in the upper left-hand corner on both consoles had been removed and a number of wires now protruded from the openings. It was the exact same panel section that Petrov had shown him earlier.

Samant leisurely surveyed the area, as if trying to relive some past event. He noticed that everyone else was focusing on the ship control and engineer's stations on the other side of the central post. Slowly, he took his smartphone from his pocket, and after making sure the flash was disabled, quickly took a number of photos of the alterations to the consoles. Pausing briefly to check the results, he repocketed the phone and made his way to the first compartment.

There were far fewer people in the torpedo room, and after chatting with a number of his former crewmen for a few minutes, he went forward to look at the tubes. Acting as if he were doing a routine inspection, Samant went over them as he had done numerous times before. In the background, he could hear some of his men snickering. If they wanted to think their old captain was taking a walk down memory lane, that was fine by him. He opened the wiring junction box for tubes one and three, and feeling behind the circuit board, found the connectors that Petrov had told him about. Samant also noted that there were wires attached to those connectors. Grunting his approval, he finished his normal inspection and proceeded to visit the remaining compartments. Partly because Samant wanted to be true to the story he was creating, and partly because he wanted to see more of his crew. Jain was right; he was homesick.

Refreshed, Samant left the graving dock and headed down the street toward the submarine artificer's shop. The tour of *Chakra* was an unexpected but welcomed opportunity, but his primary reason for coming to the shipyard was to find out what he could about the new Russian UGST-M torpedoes. Walking down the narrow street between the workshops, he was surprised by just how crowded it was. For a Sunday, the activity throughout this part of the shipyard was very heavy, almost frantic. Dhankhar must have put the fear of the gods into everyone involved with *Chakra*'s refit. As he strode into the main weapons shop, Samant immediately picked out the loud voice of the chief weapons officer shouting orders to his men. Commander Fali Gandhi was a ragged-looking, gray-haired engineer in charge of all submarine tactical weapons. A vicious purist, he would have nothing to do with those "abominations of DRDO"—ballistic missiles.

Many years Samant's senior, Gandhi was nonetheless junior to him in rank. The grizzled, outspoken engineer had often come into conflict with senior officers, and his lack of decorum had adversely affected his chances of promotion. And yet, no one would dream of replacing him . . . he was that good, and Samant held a deep respect for the man's abilities. Every weapon Samant took into battle performed exactly as it should, not one failure during his entire patrol. Gandhi had personally assured him that every weapon had been thoroughly checked and had passed muster. He was also quick to accept responsibility if any of the weapons failed to run properly. Aiming them correctly was Samant's job.

"Commander Gandhi!" shouted Samant. "May I have a word with you, please?"

The older man spun about. A huge grin flashed on his face. "Ah, Captain Samant! What brings you to my workshop on this beautiful Sunday morning? Don't have anything else better to do?"

Samant just shook his head; for the second time that morning he'd been implicitly accused of having misplaced priorities. "Why is it that everyone assumes that one's personal work habits have to change when they are on shore duty?"

Gandhi smiled broadly. "Because, my good Captain, they usually do. Your predecessor, Captain Palan, certainly had no problems taking up residency at the East Point Golf Club."

"I don't play golf," snipped Samant.

"Ooh, that's heresy, Captain."

"Do you play, Fali?" Samant shot back smugly.

"No, sir, I don't have the patience for the game. I find it aggravating to hit a ball, lose it, only to hit it and lose it again."

"That makes two of us. Now can I ask you some torpedo questions?"

"Ah, my favorite topic. But let's go to my office, it's too damn noisy out here."

Samant followed the engineer to the back of the workshop, to a small glass-enclosed space with a single desk, a chair, and numerous filing cabinets. Precariously stacked manuals and drawings lay on almost every available horizontal surface. Gandhi wasn't very apologetic. "Please forgive the clutter, but this is a workshop, not a fancy corporate office. Tea, sir?"

"No, thank you," replied Samant as he looked for a place

to sit. Gandhi noted this and simply reached over and swept a stack of manuals off the chair.

"Your questions, sir?"

"I understand you have received some UGST-M torpedoes, I was wondering about your first impressions."

Gandhi leaned on the desk, thinking. "Well, Captain, it started out very rough, five of the first twelve failed their diagnostic tests; that was mid-February. Our admiral was none too happy about that and he yanked the Russians hard to fix the problem. So far it seems to be working. I should have twenty-four weapons ready for *Chakra* by her departure date.

"As for the weapon itself, it's got a little more range than the UGSTs we have now. The seeker is supposedly better, but I can't confirm that until I get some in-water test runs. When that will occur has yet to be determined. Why do you ask?"

Samant leaned forward, rubbing his hands. "I'm working on the next class of nuclear submarines and I can't get a straight answer from DRDO on our torpedo procurement plans."

"There's a surprise!" grumbled Gandhi. "They're still trying to re-create the German SUT torpedo thirty-plus years after the Germans produced it! DRDO's foolishness is why we are in negotiations to buy the German Sea Hake."

"I agree, but I need to look at all our options, which means I need to consider Russian weapons as well."

"Of course. But you do realize, sir, that the Russian torpedoes are considerably longer than NATO standard weapons? That will cause your designers a lot of grief, I would think."

"Yes, Fali, I'm well aware of that. And while I don't think it's likely, I still need to have a rough design of a torpedo room to accommodate a weapon of this size. The powers that be will have to make the decision."

Gandhi nodded his understanding. "So what do you need from me, sir?"

"How about some good information on the UGST-M?" Samant smiled. "I can't have my designers working off of sales brochure data. Also, I'd like to get a quick understanding of the acceptance process, just in case I need to add extra time to the acquisition timeline."

The old engineer smiled, waved his hand, gesturing for Samant to come to the desk. Gandhi pointed at a large open logbook. "Here are the records for the first shipment of UGST-M torpedoes; there are thirty-six in all. These seven have failed testing and need to go back to Mother Russia. This next set of nineteen weapons has completed the new testing protocol and has been accepted. These five are currently in the testing process with the Russian contractor. This last five . . ."

"Petrov?" asked Samant innocently.

"No, no, he's in charge of the work on the boat itself. He has nothing to do with weapons. No, a fellow named Orlav does the torpedo work. I almost never see him now; he's kind of a hermit over in Torpedo Shop Two. I check in on him every now and then."

"I take it he's a busy chap."

"Very," grunted Gandhi. "Vice Admiral Dhankhar's revised torpedo acceptance criteria are extensive and they take a lot of time to complete. The Russians are under the gun to have twenty-four weapons ready, they have eight days left." A devilish smirk popped on his face. "The 'Old Man' isn't giving them a millimeter of wiggle room, he's holding them to the letter of the contract."

Gandhi then pulled out the writing shelf on his desk, closed the logbook and shifted it over. Underneath was a thick binder. "This, my dear Captain, is a technical manual for the UGST-M torpedo. You may borrow this for however long you may need it."

Samant eagerly grabbed the manual, but soon frowned. He opened it, and then let out an exasperated sigh.

"Something wrong, sir?" asked Gandhi. There was a hint of sarcasm in his voice.

"I don't suppose you have this manual in Hindi? Or even English, Commander?" snarled an irritated Samant.

"But I thought you could read Russian, sir?"

"Yes, I can, with some effort. But my designers do not, and I'm not about to read them bedtime stories so they can do their work!"

The engineer started laughing, and even Samant had to reluctantly smile. Gandhi was willing to help; he just had to have a little fun at Samant's expense. "Wait a moment, sir. I think I can find something that'll work for you. Just stay here, I'll be right back."

"Thank you, Fali." Samant grimaced.

Still chuckling, Gandhi left his office. As soon as he was out of sight, Samant quickly reopened the logbook to the UGST-M entries and removed his smartphone. After checking to see if anyone was watching, he took photos of the serial numbers and the arrival and transfer dates to Shop Number Two of the five torpedoes still being worked on. He then noticed a new note card taped to the writing shelf. It had a list of five-number sets and what was probably part of a building number. Thinking that they could be access codes, he took a photo, just in case, and put his phone away. Samant then closed the logbook, pulling it over so it covered the note card, and opened the Russian-language tech manual. Gandhi returned less than a minute later.

"Here you go, Captain. The diagrams aren't as good as the Russian version, but the text is far more readable."

"Thank you, Fali, I'm sure this will be fine. What my designers need are the numbers; the diagrams are an added benefit. I'll have my people copy the necessary data immediately and I'll have this back to you later this week."

Gandhi waved his hand. "Take your time, sir. We have a few more in the shop to support the work I still need to do."

Samant thanked the engineer again, shook his hand, and departed with the technical manual. Walking quickly, he made his way back to his office; he had to download the photos from his phone and make copies for Petrov. Samant's spirit was buoyed; he thought for sure that he now had some of the evidence the Americans had been asking for.

2 April 2017
2200 Local Time
Russian Hostel
INS *Circars*
Visakhapatnam, India

Petrov turned into the parking lot of the Russian Hostel very late. The hydraulic system testing had taken much longer than anticipated, and by the time he'd returned to his temporary home, all the parking spots were full. Frustrated, he headed down the street to the overflow lot two blocks away. Still nervous from the attempted attack the night before, Petrov carefully scanned the streets and buildings as he drove slowly by. He hoped he'd be safer on the base than out and around the busy streets beyond the gates, but he couldn't be sure of that.

As he pulled into the parking space, Petrov killed the lights immediately, but took his time shutting off the engine and getting out of the car. He needed time for his eyes to become night-adapted. The lighting for the next three hundred meters or so was fairly dim, with only an occasional streetlight providing some illumination. He locked the car and started walking, but instead of using the sidewalk, Petrov walked in the street, his right hand tightly grasping a can of Mace spray.

He forced himself to keep his pace casual. If he looked confident, perhaps that would deter a would-be attacker. Besides, walking slowly meant he made less noise, and that gave him a better chance of hearing someone approaching him. It didn't take long to pass by the first intersection, although to Petrov it seemed like an unbearably slow process. Soon he was more than halfway to the hostel, and he started to think that maybe he was just imagining things, his nerves rattled by the stress he was under.

Suddenly, there was the sound of gravel crunching underfoot behind him and to his left. As he turned, there was a hard jab on his left rib cage; he heard the fabric of his overalls being ripped. The blow pushed him toward the building to his right; struggling to keep his footing, Petrov pivoted and tried to run, but his assailant grabbed his left shoulder and spun him about. The man's face was hidden in the shadows, and he was totally silent. Petrov could barely hear him breathing. He struck again, this time landing a solid thrust to Petrov's rib cage by his heart. The pain was intense and Petrov thought he heard a cracking sound, but the protective stab vest held and the blade was deflected.

Surprised, the assailant hesitated, momentarily confused that his victim hadn't fallen to the ground. Petrov took advantage of the delay, raised the can of Mace and blasted the contents into the attacker's eyes just a few inches away. The man only grunted in agony, but the shock caused him to lift his hands, allowing Petrov to break loose. Despite the pain, the attacker doggedly continued his assault. But with his eyesight impaired, and in the darkness, his attacks became undisciplined—wild, slashing wherever he thought his target might be. Petrov was able to dodge or deflect these less-precise thrusts, and after a particularly wide swing, he turned again to try and escape. Unfortunately, the man got hold of Petrov's left arm and bodily yanked him closer. And even though Petrov was about the same size as his attacker, the latter was far stronger, and Petrov just couldn't get away.

As he was spun around, Petrov tried to use momentum

to his advantage, and threw a vicious right hook at the man's face. The blow connected on his assailant's jaw, but it seemed to have little effect. Once again, the man only grunted. But between the assailant's forceful yank and Petrov's swing, the Russian engineer's left foot slipped out from underneath him. Both men were already badly off balance and fell, with Petrov slamming into the asphalt on his left side. The badly bruised areas of his rib cage screamed their displeasure as he bounced. The attacker, being above him at the start of the fall, flew over Petrov and hit the curb. Petrov heard a dull thwack, like a coconut hitting a hard surface, followed by a raspy gurgling sound.

Staggering to his feet, Petrov had no intention of seeing if his attacker was alive, and he took off down the street toward the hostel's entrance. He slowed to a fast walk as he rounded the corner into the light and slowly pushed the lobby door open. The night manager was busy looking at his computer screen and hardly noticed a thing as Petrov walked to the stairwell. Once inside his room, Petrov locked and bolted the door. His heart was beating like a scared rabbit's and he found himself struggling to breathe normally; his body shook uncontrollably.

Slowly, painfully, he took off his shredded overalls and the protective vest. There were deep gouges in two of the left panels, and he had two huge bruises on his left chest and side. Petrov then opened the refrigerator and grabbed the bottle of vodka. Sitting down on his bed, he took several deep swigs and tried to make sense of what had just happened. That someone wanted him dead was beyond doubt, but who? His assailant wasn't an Indian; the man was white and large. Petrov suspected he was a Russian, or possibly Eastern European, but that didn't answer the fundamental question of who wanted him dead. Could it have been the SVR agent, Ruchkin? He certainly would've been trained in hand-to-hand fighting. Petrov desperately tried to remember how big Ruchkin had been, and whether or not that vague memory matched the shadowy image of his attacker. Nothing made sense.

He fished his cell phone from his pocket and hit the speed dial for Samant. The phone rang several times before a sleepy voice answered in Hindi, "Hello?"

"Girish, it's me, Aleksey, I was just attacked near the Russian Hostel. I think it was the same man that tried yesterday."

Petrov heard bedding being pulled rapidly aside. "Are you all right, Aleks?"

"I've got some ugly bruises, but otherwise in one piece. And thank you. The protective vest you gave me saved my life." Petrov paused as he took another sip. "Girish, I think I may have killed a man tonight."

"What!? How!?"

Petrov gave a quick summation of the attack, how well the vest worked, the Mace, and the lucky fall that allowed him to escape, and possibly killed his assailant. ". . . it sounded like his head hit something very hard, and then there was a nasty gurgling sound. I didn't stay to see how badly he was hurt, or if he was even alive. I just ran for my life."

"By the gods, you are a fortunate man!" said Samant, sounding shocked. "Where are you now?"

"I'm in my room at the Russian Hostel. Do you think I'm safe here?"

"I don't know what to think anymore, Aleks, but it's clear they know where to find you. And your attacker was able to get on the base." Samant paused briefly as he considered their options. The situation was beginning to spiral out of control. Finally, he broke the silence and said, "I'm coming over now to pick you up. You should be safer here in my flat. Pack all the things you wore tonight into a bag, and don't forget the Mace spray. I'll be there in twenty minutes."

3 April 2017
0830 Local Time
INS *Circars*, Eastern Naval Command Headquarters
Visakhapatnam, India

An angry sigh hissed past Dhankhar's lips as he paged through the security report. Two bodies had been found within the base's perimeter earlier that morning. Both were white males, probably Russian, and both had serious knife wounds to the chest. One was found over by the graving dock, facedown in a shallow basin, the other by the Russian Hostel. Neither body had any identification, but the second one had nearly fifteen thousand rupees in his pocket. There were photos of the dead men's faces attached to the back of the report. One man had a particularly horrid gash on his forehead. Shaking his head in frustration, he whispered a single word, "Kirichenko!"

The admiral grabbed his cell phone and punched up the Russian's number, grumbling that the man had better answer this time. Remarkably, Dhankhar heard Kirichenko's voice after the third ring. "Yes."

"Mr. Kirichenko, this is Vice Admiral Dhankhar. Just what manner of mischief are you raising on my naval base?"

"I'm afraid I don't understand, Admiral, has there been some trouble?"

"Trouble?" Dhankhar asked incredulously. "I would call the discovery of two dead men, very likely Russian nationals, within the base perimeter trouble. Is this the work of your man, Churkin?"

"Quite possibly," replied Kirichenko coolly. "Jascha told me yesterday that he had been following a Russian national that was poking his nose into places where he shouldn't. Do you have any identifying information on these men? Photos perhaps?"

Dhankhar was amazed at how calm Kirichenko's voice was; the news was nothing more than a trivial incident to him, a matter of course in his business marketing death. "Yes, there are photos of the two individuals. Stand by while I send them to you."

The admiral pulled up the electronic copy of the report, deleted all the text and sent the photos to Kirichenko's anonymous e-mail account. "There, you should have them shortly. According to the security report, both men probably died from a single knife wound to the chest."

"Well, that certainly sounds like Churkin," admitted Kirichenko. "He prefers using a blade over any type of firearm. Ah, there is the e-mail."

There was a brief silence over the phone as Kirichenko looked over the photographs. After a few seconds, Dhankhar heard him take a deep breath, followed by a hushed, "Well, that represents an unfortunate complication."

"What? What is it?"

"The second photo is Churkin," replied Kirichenko flatly.

"Churkin? How is this possible? Wasn't he a commando?"

"Yes, Spetsnaz, and quite skilled at hand-to-hand combat. He was convinced that Petrov was getting too close to our operation, asking too many questions. Jascha was planning on taking him out, making it look like a mugging."

"Could this Petrov have defeated Churkin?"

"Ridiculous!" Kirichenko exclaimed. There was a hint of insult in his voice. "Captain Petrov was a submariner, not a special operations soldier. There is nothing that I know of in his past that even suggests he had anything but a rudimentary knowledge of self-defense. It's far more likely Churkin misidentified someone he thought was Petrov who possessed the skills to kill him."

"What about the other man?" questioned Dhankhar. "The photo doesn't match Petrov's security badge picture."

"I don't know who it is. But it would be prudent to run the photo through your database of Russian nationals working on *Chakra*'s refit."

Dhankhar bristled at the obvious suggestion. "I'm sure the naval police are working on that as we speak. I'll be sure to keep you apprised of their findings. What do we do about Petrov?"

Kirichenko sighed. "If you can find a way to arrest him, or even detain him, that would be helpful. Unfortunately, I can't think of a good reason to justify his arrest without drawing unwanted attention to Churkin. He had access to the naval base under an alias that was approved by your office."

"I can revoke Petrov's access to the base. Claim he's under investigation for fraud or some other petty crime."

"Which would only have the effect of confirming some of his suspicions and pushing him to blather what he knows to the Russian embassy. No, he hasn't said anything because he's either unsure of what he knows, or he lacks enough proof to get anyone to listen to him. It would be better if you just overload his schedule with administrative meetings and reports—keep him busy. How soon before *Chakra* leaves the graving dock?"

"We are to float her out in two days," responded Dhankhar.

"You may want to think about moving your deployment date up a bit," Kirichenko suggested. "You may be running out of time."

"I'll consider your recommendation, but I find it hard to believe that you are all that concerned about my mission. I think you're just worried about being paid, Mr. Kirichenko."

"That too, Admiral. But it's considered bad business practice to leave behind unhappy customers. I have a contract to keep, and you have my word that I shall fulfill all the requirements."

"Very well, then. Besides moving up the departure date, what do you suggest we do now?"

"Keep on course, and see if Orlav can speed things up a bit. I was planning on coming out to the base tomorrow to check in on his work. But given these recent events, I'll be there this afternoon."

After hanging up, Dhankhar sat quietly contemplating his options—there weren't many. While his scheme hadn't been exposed, yet, the chances of this happening were growing, all because of a curious Russian. But his problems weren't due to just a single Russian. No, this whole debacle was because Kirichenko and his people were sloppy. First, they lost control of a nuclear weapon that the fools in Pakistan accidentally set off, and now Kirichenko's right-hand man, a Spetsnaz commando, lay dead in the base morgue.

Every misstep caused more eyes to look his way, and yet Operation Vajra depended on absolute stealth. Dhankhar finally admitted to himself that he needed outside assistance if he was to successfully contain this latest disaster. He also had to find a way to rein in this Petrov, who appeared to suspect what was going on. Perhaps Churkin was correct. Petrov was getting too close and in the name of stealth, he had to disappear, one way or another.

Dhankhar grabbed his cell phone again and looked up the number to the Vajra contact at the Central Bureau of Investigation. He hit the call button and waited impatiently while the phone rang.

"Deputy Director Thapar," answered the voice.

"Ijay, Badu Dhankhar, I have a serious situation at Vizag and I need your assistance."

3 April 2017
1100 Local Time
Torpedo Shop 2
Naval Shipyard
Visakhapatnam, India

Dhankhar marched past the sentry, slowing just enough to return the guard's salute. After punching in the five-digit access code, the admiral yanked on the door and went inside. It was dark in the workshop, but he could see Orlav working under bright lights at the far end. As Dhankhar approached, it was clear that Orlav hadn't left the building since that first night after he'd been restricted to the base. The man was disheveled and looked like he hadn't showered in a few days. Orlav saw the Indian admiral enter and didn't even bother to wait for his routine question.

"I'm just about finished with this weapon, Admiral. I have a few things left to install, then I can program the date and that'll be it. I still have those two weapons to modify, but I don't see any problems having all five torpedoes ready by April tenth."

"Very good, Mr. Orlav. I'm pleased to hear your task is progressing well."

Orlav smiled slightly, then looked down into the torpedo's innards, away from Dhankhar's gaze. "Sir, I would really like to get a good night's sleep in my own bed, and a shower. It's getting tiresome being cooped up here in the workshop every day. And I still need to do the final control console installation on board *Chakra*."

"I understand your discomfort, Mr. Orlav. But your safety is of greater importance to me. Churkin is dead," announced Dhankhar bluntly.

Stunned, Orlav dropped the screwdriver he was holding and staggered away from the torpedo. "D . . . dead!? How!?"

"He was stabbed. His body was found this morning over by the Russian Hostel. We have no idea who killed him, so I think it's best that you stay here for the time being. However, I'm concerned about the combat system consoles. How much time do you need to finish the installation?"

Orlav was still wide-eyed, his face radiating fear; it took him a couple of seconds to respond. "I . . . I need about two, maybe three hours to install the keypads and then conduct circuit checks in the torpedo compartment."

Dhankhar nodded. "Very well, I'll have a guard escort you to *Chakra* during the night shift so you can complete your work; there are fewer people on board during that shift. Then afterwards, perhaps we can swing by your bungalow long enough for you to take a shower."

"Thank you, sir," quavered Orlav.

"You are almost done, Mr. Orlav. In another week, you'll be somewhere in South America or the Caribbean enjoying the fruits of your labors." Dhankhar smiled and patted Orlav on the shoulder. "It's just a little longer. By the way, Kirichenko will be paying you a visit later. Good day, Mr. Orlav."

Dhankhar didn't even wait for Orlav's reply and walked quickly to the door. After making sure the lock had engaged, the admiral turned to the sentry, pulled a photograph from his pocket, and handed it to the petty officer. "From this point forward, only myself and Kirichenko may enter this workshop. No one else is allowed access, is that clear?"

"Absolutely, Admiral," replied the sailor.

"Very good. Oh, if anyone is particularly obstinate and refuses to comply with your warnings, shoot them."

Orlav sat dazed and sweating in a near panic. Churkin had been killed. He couldn't imagine anyone beating the former Spetsnaz commando in a fight—he'd seen him in more than a few barroom brawls. The man could be totally vicious. The Russian engineer struggled with the news of his colleague's death. It wasn't that Orlav liked Churkin; on the contrary, he hated the man. But he also feared him. Churkin was a thug—pure muscle, incapable of doing anything but providing security or convincing someone to pay their bills. Kirichenko had found him useful, but that didn't matter anymore because Churkin was dead.

Shuffling back to the weapon, Orlav tried to get back to work, but his mind just wasn't on the job. He made slow progress, mumbling to himself over and over again that he couldn't believe Churkin was dead. Then, as he was installing one of the last cover plates, a stray thought wandered into his mind: If someone *had* killed Churkin, then that could only mean they were on to them—and that he could be next! Horror filled Orlav as he realized that the only thing standing between him and a trained assassin was the young guard out front.

In total dismay, Orlav threw the ratchet set on the floor and ran over to his makeshift bed. He grabbed the overnight bag he'd brought and started stuffing his personal gear into it; he'd leave nothing behind that could be linked to him. Then he remembered that he'd touched all the tools. Frantically, he finished stuffing the bag and was just about to begin wiping off the tools when a stern voice shot out of the darkness.

"And just where do you think you're going?"

Orlav stood, shaking, as Kirichenko came into the light. "Yur . . . Yuri, we need to get out of here! It's no longer safe!"

"And you think that by running away this will make the situation better? Really, Evgeni, you need to calm down and start thinking this insane course of action through."

"Insane! Yuri! Someone *killed* Churkin! Who but another assassin could have done that!" screamed Orlav.

"Possibly, but do you honestly believe you'll be safer running away from this base? Where would you go? And by doing so, you'd not only have this unknown assassin, but also Dhankhar looking for you with very evil intentions. No, my friend, your chances of survival would be essentially zero. Now, put the bag down and finish your work."

"Yuri, it isn't worth it. They aren't paying us enough to do this work, under these conditions," whimpered Orlav. The man was about to break.

"You need to take a longer view, Evgeni. We have many more weapons to sell, and we have several good leads.

owever, if it will make you feel better, I won't offer your rvices as a modification specialist. The buyer takes re- ipt of the weapons as they are, no repackaging.

"Oh, and as far as payment is concerned, you're forget- ig that Churkin's failure means he won't be collecting s portion. I'm sure a fifty percent increase going into ur pockets will compensate you for these extraordinary rcumstances."

Orlav's eyes widened. He hadn't even thought about at. The allure of that extra cash was just too enticing. He opped the bag and headed back to the workbench.

10

Lawbreakers

4 April 2017
0100 Local Time
Naval Shipyard
Visakhapatnam, India

It had rained earlier, and Petrov had hoped it would gi[ve]
them some cover, but it stopped at half past midnight, lea[v]ing air that seemed even more humid and sticky than b[e]fore. He fought the urge to creep or slip from shadow [to]
shadow, and also the feeling that they were being foolis[h.]

Samant had it right, Petrov decided. Choose your pa[th]
and don't look back. The Indian was slightly in the lea[d]
as the two walked toward the torpedo shop where Orla[v]
had been working. Petrov was following Samant's lea[d]
mentally as well as physically. They needed hard inform[a]tion, and this was the only place to get it.

Petrov had called in sick that day, complaining of s[e]vere cramps and a long night that had left him feelin[g]
"cleaned out and miserable." The Indian clerk that took t[he]
call joked that he might have eaten something a little t[oo]
hot for his weak Russian stomach. Petrov remarked that [it]
had less to do with too much spice and more about que[s]tionable sanitation. Either way, he wouldn't be in till lat[e]
in the day, if at all. He did, however, leave specific instru[c]tions for the duty foreman to phone him if Orlav showe[d]
up on *Chakra*. He got the call a little after midnight.

The sentry, a corporal, had been relieved an hour ea[rly]

er, and was still wide awake. If he was surprised at seeing a senior naval officer in the yard at that hour, he hid it well. But *Circars* was a busy place, and work never stopped, specially now.

As Samant approached, the corporal said formally, "Good evening, sir. State your business." He'd moved his rifle from slung to port arms, certainly not pointing at anyone, but ready for use. He never got the chance. As the soldier finished his challenge, Samant quickly brought up the can of Mace and sprayed him full in the face.

The corporal had been exercising proper trigger discipline, and Samant's other hand grabbed his forefinger, and pulled his hand away from the trigger and, incidentally, the grip stock. Petrov, stepping up from behind Samant, grabbed the barrel near the muzzle and twisted the weapon out of the sentry's grasp.

Choking, eyes burning with pain, the soldier could barely breathe, much less resist the two. His knees buckled, and he would have fallen to the ground if Samant had not pushed him back against the wall.

As Samant supported the soldier's limp form, Petrov slung the rifle and pulled out a large plastic cable tie and bound the guard's hands. A short strip of duct tape would keep him quiet. With the soldier secured, Samant pulled out his smartphone and pulled up his photo library.

"This is why those obnoxious security officers keep nagging us not to write down passwords," he whispered softly in Russian, a cynical smile on his face. "Someone might see them and copy them." He then quickly punched in the five-digit code for Building 2 with his gloved hands. It didn't work the first time, and the lock's display flashed twice. Forcing himself to slow down, Samant pressed the sequence again, and they both heard a satisfying, but surprisingly loud, "clack" as the door unlocked and opened.

Samant and Petrov dragged the limply struggling soldier inside, and Petrov dashed back around the corner to retrieve the bag with their gear.

As the heavy door closed behind them, Petrov found and hit the light switch. In bright illumination, their world expanded from a few nearby shadows to a large workshop. He could see benches, tools, and the bodies of disassembled torpedoes, but he fought the urge to investigate. Their first order of business was their prisoner.

Neither of them had said much since approaching the sentry, and Samant now reminded Petrov with one word, "Chair." He spoke in Russian. They'd agreed to use Russian as much as possible, in the hope that the soldier didn't speak the language.

Samant quickly bound the guard's feet with another cable tie, while Petrov brought over a battered metal chair. Together they hoisted the corporal onto it in a sitting position. A few bungee cords and some more duct tape held him upright, as well as in the chair, and Petrov looped a couple of the bungee cords from the chair to a nearby pipe.

Petrov, also wearing gloves, pulled the man's head back and, still speaking Russian, said, "Hold still, I'm going to wash your face off." This was a test to see if the sentry understood Russian. He showed no reaction, coughing and shaking his head as if trying to clear his eyes.

Samant pulled out a water bottle, rinsed the sentry's face and eyes, still tightly shut. He pulled the tape back carefully and then held the bottle to the guard's mouth. Samant ordered, "Rinse your mouth and spit," in Hindi. He let the soldier take a pull from the bottle, then quickly stepped to one side as the corporal spat it out toward Samant's earlier position.

"You will be better soon," he said, again in Hindi, and added as he replaced the tape, "Your eyesight will also return." As a final touch, Petrov pulled a cloth bag out of the duffel, and placed it over the soldier's head.

With their victim secured and safe, Petrov joined Samant as the two stood and surveyed the interior of the building. Samant had been inside this workshop many times before, and was familiar with its layout. Petrov had seen similar spaces in Russia, and the UGST-M torpedoes made it feel almost like home.

"I see only two torpedoes," Petrov observed in Russian.

"No surprises there, the modifications are probably done on the others and they're locked up somewhere," Samant replied. "I'll start with the workbench."

"And I'll take a closer look at the torpedoes."

The two UGST-M torpedoes sat disassembled in their dollies. They were massive machines, over twenty-three feet long and weighing over two tons. Moving at fifty knots, they'd do considerable damage to a vessel without the warhead, but the 650 pounds of high explosive they carried would cripple all but the largest vessels.

The warhead wasn't in the nose, though. That first two feet of the torpedo was separated from the rest of the weapon and was reserved for the sonar homing system in the flattened nose, and the weapon's computer. The acoustic seeker could listen passively for the right combination of sounds, or send out active pings to search for a contact. The computer was programmed to dig out the tiniest of echoes from a noisy environment littered with countermeasures and decoys. It was smart enough that the torpedo could be described as a killer robot with fins.

The warhead section was missing on the two torpedoes. An empty space almost five feet long showed where the warhead module had been removed. The monofuel propellant tanks, power supply, and propulsion system were all joined together in the larger section that was behind the empty space. Petrov quickly found the nameplate data on the two torpedoes and took photographs with a digital camera. The serial numbers matched two of the weapons that Samant had obtained from the base's torpedo shop.

Petrov then spotted five wooden packing crates lined up along one wall, painted dull gray with large white warnings stenciled in Cyrillic—"Corrosive." The crates were empty but the wooden supports inside suggested a single large object that was conical in shape. He took several more photos of the crate's interior and exterior before returning to the torpedoes themselves.

The two torpedo warhead sections sat on the work bench. One of the sections was still empty, but the other had been fitted with a metal framework, bright with machining or scorched black from welding. It was crude work, and Petrov saw Samant examining similar components on a large workbench against the wall. The Indian picked up a half-finished framework and walked over to Petrov.

Silently, the Russian pointed into the torpedo, and Samant held it in the cavity, nodding. "This is how they will mount the device," he said softly. Petrov had his camera out, and took photos of the warhead sections, and especially the metal framework.

Petrov didn't have a clue as to what the guts of a nuclear warhead would look like, but he didn't see anything that was the right size and shape to fit in the modified torpedo warhead section. They'd accomplished much in the first five minutes, but now they spent another fifteen quickly checking every part of the work area. They even searched the corner that Orlav had used as a living area, not that he'd hide a nuclear bomb under his cot.

Finally, Samant pointed to the overhead crane. One spur of the rail ran from where the crates had been opened. Pointing silently, Samant then traced the rails straight to a very solid-looking door ten feet high and eight feet wide. "Storage for the completed torpedoes?" Petrov asked. Samant nodded. If the nukes were anywhere, they were in there.

Just on the remote chance it might work, Samant tried the same code that had opened the door to the shop, without success, then reversed it, tried adding and subtracting one, while Petrov took more photos and looked at his watch.

During the afternoon, they'd planned their break-in meticulously, as only a pair of submariners could. They'd both agreed that if they couldn't get what they needed in half an hour, they wouldn't get it at all. According to Petrov's watch, they had about five minutes left. He tapped Samant on the shoulder and shook his head. The Indian shrugged and sighed, then headed back over to the workbench, rummaging for more clues.

Petrov took the other end, looking through a litter of tools, metal parts, and electronic components. Notes and sheets of paper were tacked up here and there, and he carefully arranged and photographed each one. A folder, half buried under a stack of electronics boxes, attracted his attention. Opening it, he immediately recognized a drawing of the junction box in *Chakra*'s torpedo room. "This is important. Help me with these."

Samant came over and angled a work light to point at the folder, then pulled each sheet of paper out of the way when Petrov said he was ready. They were running late, if his watch was right.

"Done," Petrov announced softly. He had just started to put the camera away when he noted a separate piece of folded-up paper tucked underneath the schematics. Petrov removed the crinkled paper and slowly opened it. Flattening it out and turning it around, the men leaned over to look at its contents—and no sooner had they begun reading than both drew a sharp breath. The paper held a list: Hong Kong, Shanghai, Dalian, Qingdao, and half a dozen more. All of them were Chinese ports, but this was a collection of the top ten busiest ports, the heart of China's export economy.

Samant shook his head in awe. "The man is insane!" he whispered. "He's not planning on attacking Pakistan, he's going after China!"

Petrov stood overwhelmed as well, his mouth hanging open. He hadn't had a clue that Dhankhar was planning anything so bold. The implications were staggering.

Samant waved his hands frantically at the paper. "Take a picture! Take a picture!" he exclaimed in a hushed voice.

Petrov took a dozen, just to be safe. He then looked at his watch and saw that they had long overstayed their welcome. He pointed repeatedly at his wrist; Samant nodded and began refolding the paper and carefully putting it exactly where they'd found it.

While Samant put the folder back under the electronic boxes, Petrov took one last look around the room for anything useful. He was frustrated that they weren't able to find and photograph the devices themselves, but the evidence was overwhelming that they were here, almost certainly in that locked vault. He and Samant had discussed the idea of sabotage. If they could damage the nukes, they'd at least delay the plotters, who were obviously on a tight schedule.

Theoretically, if they removed the right component, or bent the correct widget, they'd render the nuclear device unusable. But neither was expert enough to know exactly what to do. They both knew enough about nuclear weapons to know that they were fitted with anti-tamper circuits, and contained several kilograms of high explosive, used to start the nuclear reaction. If they fiddled with the wrong widget, they could trigger what was called a "low-order detonation"—no nuclear reaction, but a conventional explosion that would scatter bits of radioactive and toxic uranium and plutonium over a sizable part of the base, mixed with the two of them.

Their captive was silent, but was breathing, and occasionally testing his bonds. He'd be released when his relief discovered him at 0400. With a nod from Samant, Petrov opened the door and pretended to look like he was checking for rain before stepping out.

The coast was clear, no sign of anyone nearby. Samant followed. He turned the lights off so they didn't draw attention to the building. The hooded prisoner wouldn't know the difference.

Once out of the building, they set a brisk pace, and headed straight for the gate, five or six blocks away. After retrieving the camera from the duffel, Petrov tossed the bag into a trash dumpster. Next, he took the memory chip out of the camera and replaced it with an empty one.

Meanwhile, Samant used his cell phone to call the number Patterson had given him in their e-mail exchange yesterday. It was late afternoon in Washington, and he heard her answer on the second ring. "This is Patterson."

"We have the proof. We will be at Cyberpatnam, the Internet café I mentioned in the e-mail."

"I have the address. Stay there and keep a low profile. Someone will come for you. Call me back in an hour if they don't."

"Understood."

The gate to the shipyard faced Port Main Road, and was four lanes wide. At this hour, there were only two uniformed soldiers on duty, both lounging near the guard shack in the center of the street. The two burglars waited for what seemed like years until a car turned in to the gate. With the guards distracted and their night vision degraded, Petrov and Samant forced themselves to walk at a normal pace across the short distance to the pedestrian exit. Then they were outside on the street. Petrov's watch said 0155.

Samant's Maruti sedan was parked in a small lot outside the shipyard, and Petrov only partly relaxed once they were moving. The police might be looking for this car, and if they'd had any distance to go, he would have worried more. But Cyberpatnam was just two miles to the east, back toward the business district. They'd already covered half the distance to the place, especially the way Samant was driving.

The area right around the shipyard was industrial, and there was little traffic at that time of night except for an occasional truck. At the halfway mark, they reached Convent Junction, a traffic circle and a major crossroads. The cross street, Port Gymkhana Club Road, neatly divided the industrial and business districts. Past that point, the roadside was lined with stores and offices, and the streets were still quite busy. Petrov was a little relieved, both for the anonymity of a crowd, and that traffic was actually moving freely. Daytime traffic in Vizag could be glacial.

As his tension eased, stray thoughts popped into Petrov's mind. "I wish we could have done something to slow them down."

"I managed to cause them some trouble," Samant replied smugly as he drove.

"But the warheads were locked away."

"Orlav won't be able to do any work for a while, though." Petrov could see him smiling broadly even in the dim light. "I cut the cords on all his power tools and took them with us in the duffel."

Petrov laughed, imagining Orlav's face when he saw Samant's handiwork.

They had to park about a block away, but the nighttime crowds didn't slow them at all. The café offered food as well as coffee and tea, and they paid for the drinks and snacks with a minimum of fuss; they also purchased some rental time on one of the café's machines.

While Samant logged on, Petrov reinserted the valuable memory card and connected his camera to a USB port on the computer. They'd talked about what to do with the images for hours, and finally worked out a procedure: First they'd log onto a cloud file storage service account they'd established that afternoon; then they uploaded not only Petrov's photographs but the ones Samant had taken earlier aboard *Chakra* and at the weapons depot. While the images were being uploaded, Samant drafted an e-mail to Jerry Mitchell and Joanna Patterson from a recently created e-mail address with the link to the account.

At Patterson's express request, they did not send the pictures to the media or any official agency. Both Petrov and Samant had resisted at first, arguing for as wide a distribution as possible. She had pointed out, however, that Dhankhar and the others were still free to act, and Kirichenko, the man who had peddled the bombs, was still on the loose. The sound and fury that would follow from the disclosure of the plot to the public, or even to other government agencies, would only complicate their search for all the plotters. Patterson then appealed to their submariner nature, arguing that "running silent" was the best course of action—for now.

She also promised Samant that his government would be officially notified very soon, in a way Dhankhar could not interfere or control, and reassured Petrov that the Russian government would be fully informed. In the end, the two men agreed. After all, if the Americans didn't come through, they'd still have the cloud storage sites, and the memory card.

After the first e-mail was sent, Petrov relaxed a little. The information was out there. He and Samant had done what they needed to do. He still kept looking at his watch, though, and had turned his chair so he could see the street. Samant was already uploading the photos on to a second, different cloud service.

Petrov didn't know what to expect. The only thing he could be sure of was that whoever came through the door, it wouldn't be the man who had tried to kill him twice. Samant had wondered aloud earlier if there might be someone new hunting for him now. In the movies, the second opponent was always much more dangerous than the first. And what if they sent more than one? After all, they didn't know the size of the conspiracy. Those thoughts had not been helpful.

They were uploading the photos for a third time, to a cloud storage service in Germany, when two Caucasian men walked in. One was in his mid-thirties, and blond. The other was a little younger, with dark crew-cut hair. Both were dressed in jeans and casual shirts, but the younger man wore a jacket, in spite of the heat. They were obviously looking for someone. The younger man paused just inside the door, placing himself where he could see both the interior of the café and the street. The older man, after only a moment's hesitation, headed toward Petrov and Samant.

Samant, focused on the keyboard, hadn't seen them, and Petrov tapped him gently on one arm. "Company." His tone carried a warning.

"I need two more minutes. Keep him occupied," Samant said bluntly.

Petrov was determined to do just that, but couldn't do more than stand and position himself between the approaching stranger and the seated Samant. The stranger didn't appear threatening, and had both hands in sight. He wouldn't try anything here, in a public place, would he?

The stranger, still looking directly at Petrov, reached around to his back. Petrov braced himself for some sort of attack. Lacking anything else, he slid a nearby chair in front of him. Of course, if the stranger had a gun . . .

There was a dark object in his hand, and while Petrov was still trying to recognize it, the stranger stopped, a good six feet away from Petrov and his defensive furniture.

"My name is Paul McFadden. I'm from the U.S. Consulate in Hyderabad." He opened the object and offered it to Petrov. It was his identification, and Petrov had heard enough American-accented English to recognize it when it was spoken. Almost collapsing into the chair with relief, Petrov took the credentials with his left hand and offered his right. Mr. McFadden was assigned to the political-economic section of the consulate.

As they shook hands, McFadden said, "We have a car outside, and a long way to go." Samant was standing up behind him, and handed Petrov the camera. McFadden turned and headed toward the door, with Petrov and Samant close behind. McFadden hadn't introduced his companion, who waited until the other three had passed, eyes on the café, before going outside himself.

McFadden headed toward a well-used SUV, a dark green Tavera illegally parked in front of the café. A third man was waiting by the driver's-side door. He was older, and also had the short haircut of a military man. He waited outside the car, scanning the street, until McFadden reached the door. By the time the others had belted in, they were moving. McFadden took his cell out, and after pressing a key, waited a moment, and then said, "We have them. We're moving now."

Sitting in the backseat, Petrov smiled and reached over to shake Samant's hand. The Indian wasn't smiling, though, and Petrov knew that his feelings were very different. Petrov had sought safety in a foreign land suddenly turned hostile. But however justified, Samant was collaborating with a foreign country against his own military. His future was uncertain, as was India's, especially if the conspiracy succeeded. Samant might not be the type to regret his choices, but they came with an uncertain cost.

After a short conversation, McFadden put the cell phone away. "Once we're out of town, the traffic will be light, and we should make good time. We should arrive at the consulate a little before noon. You should both try to get some sleep."

"Can you please confirm that Dr. Patterson got our e-mails?"

"Yes, she told my boss that the files were being downloaded right now."

The last bit of tension left him, and fatigue washed over Petrov. It would be a ten-hour drive to Hyderabad, and he thought he might sleep through all of it.

3 April 2017
1915 EST
The White House
Washington, D.C.

Cursing her lack of forethought, Patterson had commandeered a secure conference room after looking at the first few photos, bumping a legislative planning session, and probably whatever came after it. She'd had Allison Gray move operations down there, while her secretary Kathy started calling people.

President Myles walked in, unexpected and unannounced; the sudden quiet near the door caught her attention. She started to stand, along with everybody else in the room, but Myles motioned for them to sit down. "Back to work!" he said with a stern tone, but he was smiling.

Everyone else sat down, but Patterson broke off her conversation with the State Department rep and came over to where Myles was standing. "Mr. President, we're preparing a briefing for you now . . ."

"If this information is as hot as it seems, minutes may count," Myles answered. "I don't need a polished briefing. From what you told me before, the information is definite."

She nodded enthusiastically. "Refreshingly so. I've spent the past hour calling in people from agencies all over the government. I'm asking them to find something that might suggest that these *aren't* nuclear weapons."

She gestured, sweeping her arm wide to include the entire room. "I've got people from the CIA and DIA, of course, but also state, energy, and defense." She pointed to one corner, where a young man and woman were arguing over a laptop keyboard. "Those two are from the NSA and Homeland Security. Now that we've downloaded the photographs," she paused, "several times, I might add, those two are in charge of deleting the accounts from the cloud and making sure nobody else has downloaded the photos."

"What about the two men who took these?"

She glanced at the wall clock. "They're still driving from Vizag to our consulate in Hyderabad. They won't get there until about noon local time."

"And they are out of any danger? And our people with them?"

"Aside from the hazards of traffic in India," she answered, smiling.

"Good," Myles replied. "Now, show me the photos."

"Sir," she protested, "we need to put these in context . . ."

"Which will take hours, or more likely days. Just show me what you got."

She offered him a chair, sat down next to him, and pulled over her laptop so it sat between them. She led off, "There are fifty-seven photos in all, taken on board the Indian submarine *Chakra*, in the naval base's main torpedo depot, and in the building where the torpedoes are being converted."

It took longer than she'd like, almost twenty-five minutes. After the first fifteen minutes, he caught her glancing at the clock, and said, "I had Evangeline clear my schedule this evening."

She frowned. "Won't that attract some attention?"

"It may," he admitted, looking around the room, "but I don't know how much longer we'll be able to keep this under wraps. Are all these people now briefed into the compartment?"

Making a face, she answered, "Briefed, yes. We're still catching up on the paperwork."

"Good enough," responded Myles. "Please continue."

Patterson picked up where she had left off and highlighted the critical points in each photograph that supported Samant and Petrov's theory. As she worked her way down to the last six pictures, she paused. "The last photos are the most disturbing, Mr. President, and are the key to Vice Admiral Dhankhar's plot."

"That bad, eh?"

"Yes, sir, that bad," replied Patterson as she clicked to the next picture. Myles gazed at the image; within seconds the expression on his face transformed from curiosity to depression. He let out a long despairing sigh.

"He's out of his mind!" Myles whispered. "Does he truly believe he can get away with nuking China?"

"If he could have kept it completely under wraps, how would the Chinese know who to blame? The forensic analysis would have shown them to be nuclear weapons from Russia or us, and given the Kashmiri explosion, everything would point to Russia. Would China attack Russia in response based on such scant evidence? Highly unlikely given the fact that Russia's own retaliatory strike would obliterate China.

"No, sir, it is a very nicely packaged conspiracy. Nothing would explicitly point to India."

"What are we talking about here as far as damage potential is concerned?"

"A detailed assessment is being worked on, but basically everything within four or five miles of ground zero will likely be leveled. The damage radius will be even greater, and given this is essentially a ground burst, the radioactive fallout could cover thousands of square miles."

Myles sat stunned. "So what you're saying is five of China's busiest export ports would be eliminated, a very large chunk of her shipping capacity destroyed, along with considerable collateral damage. This would almost certainly cause her economy to collapse—the political upheaval would constitute a dire threat to the Communist Party's hold on power."

"Yes, Mr. President, that appears to be Dhankhar's goal."

President Myles stood, and then began pacing, rubbing his face with his hands. Finally, he took a deep breath, turned back toward Patterson, and asked, "So, where do we stand?"

"In addition to the damage assessment, I have the Navy working on possible avenues of approach to the targets, how fast *Chakra* could go without being easily detected. We also need to try and whittle down the target set. They only have five weapons; there are ten targets on the list. And finally—" She pointed over to another corner. "—Anne Shields from communications is already working on several draft responses for you: What if we catch them in time, what if we catch them but it's not in time . . ."

Myles nodded. "So you've covered all the bases. What are your recommendations? I'll understand if they're a little on the rough side."

"We have to get Petrov and Samant out of there. And we have to tell the Indians. Right away. Now. We know where the weapons are, and they need to go get them. Gloves off. Surround the base, send in troops. Arrest Dhankhar and Orlav, and this Kirichenko fellow if we can find him, and start squeezing them for answers."

"Very reasonable," he agreed. "I'll phone Andy Lloyd after we're done here."

"Sir, I'm glad you're willing to move so quickly on this, but there's a lot of analysis . . ."

"And you've got everyone started nicely. Let them do their jobs. Your task now is to convince the Indians, just like you convinced the Russians, that there are bootleg nukes on one of their naval bases, that there's a nuclear conspiracy in the highest levels of their military, and that if *Chakra* sails with those weapons aboard, there's going to be hell to pay."

4 April 2017
1330 Local Time
Hotel Novotel
Visakhapatnam, India

This time they were meeting on ground of Dhankhar's choosing. Already on the defensive over Churkin's death, the Russian had agreed without argument to the admiral's peremptory summons. Besides, with Churkin gone, Kirichenko had no one to canvass the meeting place before he arrived or watch for eavesdroppers. If Dhankhar thought it was safe, that would have to do. If Dhankhar had set a trap for him, there was little he could do to avoid it.

The admiral waited in the lobby, reading the morning's

copy of the *Hindu*, which in spite of its name was published in English. He was tempted to order a gin and tonic, but settled for tea.

Kirichenko was on time, thankfully. Dhankhar didn't want to waste a lot of time on this. *Chakra*'s mission was actually supposed to trigger a chain of events, and as her sailing date neared, he needed to prepare for those actions. He refused to consider the idea that the plan they had all worked and risked so much for might never happen.

As the Russian approached, the admiral motioned toward the elevator. Dhankhar selected the top floor and the Infinity restaurant. He remained silent as the elevator ascended. When the doors opened, Kirichenko immediately felt better about the venue. The restaurant was a glass-enclosed space on top of the hotel that offered a phenomenal view of the Bay of Bengal. There were many tables open, as the lunch rush had just ended, and Dhankhar chose one close to the glass wall and well away from the remaining diners.

After Kirichenko sat, Dhankhar said simply, "The torpedo shop was broken into last night."

"Wh—" Kirichenko managed to suppress his initial outburst, but the alarm and surprise showed on his face.

"Two men. They Maced the sentry and tied him up, then rummaged through the place. They sabotaged all the power tools as well. Orlav's spending precious hours this morning scrounging replacements from all over the shipyard."

Kirichenko listened uncomprehendingly, still digesting the news. Dhankhar could almost see the wheels turning as the information sank in. "If they saw what was in there . . ."

"Which they most certainly did, and quite likely photographed everything! Thank heaven the devices were in the secure storage vault. It was probably Petrov, with an Indian accomplice according to the guard; the man was in an Indian naval uniform—a captain. They probably tried to get into the vault, but evidently didn't have the code. They *did* have the code for the door to the shop itself. They are resourceful," he admitted.

Kirichenko said unbelievingly, "Discovery . . ."

"Discovery is the disaster we have all feared, and their actions were no doubt precipitated by your subordinate. As a security operative, Churkin was less than effective. In fact, our security became decidedly worse since his arrival. Did you know the other body found in the basin was the SVR agent, Ruchkin? I've been able to suppress the release of this information on the grounds that we can't alert the criminal. But I can't keep this hidden for very long, perhaps a week. I've also called in some favors from sympathetic friends. I have CBI looking for Petrov and his associate on presumed charges, but if they are as clever as they seem, it's probably too late." Dhankhar's scowl deepened.

He gestured toward the newspaper and turned it so Kirichenko could see the front page. "In fact, I was just checking the front page of the *Hindu* for any articles about us. It would be quite the scoop!" His anger, so carefully controlled, finally surfaced, and he whipped the newspaper at the Russian, aiming for his face.

Kirichenko easily blocked the attack, but not the fury behind it. Dhankhar's tirade had given him time to process the news and understand their very grave situation. His first fear wasn't arrest or incarceration. There were few ties between him and the Indian conspiracy, and he was always ready for a quick escape.

But he couldn't abandon the project. Without Dhankhar's payment, he was out of business. His small network of informants and helpers depended on steady payments, or it would evaporate—or, worse, turn against him. He'd hoped to keep Churkin's share of the money and put it to good use, but then he'd had to use half of it to keep that idiot Orlav in line. He'd done so much already, and was ready to do anything to get paid. He'd take care of Petrov and his accomplice himself.

Kirichenko asked, "Where are they now?"

"Out of sight, and well beyond your capabilities," Dhankhar answered. "Don't even think of attacking them again," he warned sternly. "All you've done is trip over your own feet."

"We have to do something!" Kirichenko countered. He spoke softly, but Dhankhar heard fear mixed with his intensity.

"What you are going to do is assist Orlav. This latest catastrophe has slowed him down, and put us all on borrowed time. I don't care whether it's wiring circuits or making coffee, get in that shop and do whatever you need to help him finish. I've spent most of the morning speaking to Mitra and others at the shipyard. They'll have *Chakra* ready to sail at ten hundred hours on the seventh. I will come to the shop at zero seven hundred hours. I'll expect to see five completed torpedoes, ready for loading. And no more prorating. Unless I see five, you won't get a single kopek. That's the only language you seem to understand—money."

Dhankhar sat back in his chair. Kirichenko was silent for a moment, but when he began to speak, the admiral cut him off sharply. "We are finished. Get out."

Retrieving the newspaper, he barely noticed when Kirichenko left.

Alarm Raised

Petrov kept gazing out the window as the SUV slowly arced off of National Highway 9. The traffic had been unexpectedly heavy since early morning and their progress had been agonizingly slow; they were already two hours late. Now the traffic was getting even more congested and the frustrated driver decided to take an alternate route to the consulate. Stiff and achy, the Russian shifted his body gently, trying to find a more comfortable position. His bruised left side was not pleased with being strapped in a car for twelve hours and it was protesting. As he leaned against the doorjamb, his eyes caught sight of a huge medieval-looking building. It seemed out of place; its size and ancient European architecture was in stark contrast to the modern buildings that surrounded it.

"That's Amrutha Castle," Samant volunteered quietly. "It's a hotel, and a reasonable one at that. The regular rooms are a little on the small side, but that shouldn't bother an old submariner like you." A thin fatigued smile was on his face.

"Well, it certainly looks impressive," said Petrov. A sudden yawn interrupted his next words. Yielding to it, he stretched himself carefully before asking, "Did you have a good nap?"

Samant shook his head, extending his back as much as he could with his seat belt on. "Not really. I dozed in and out over the last six hours or so. This isn't the most comfortable of vehicles to sleep in, and I couldn't stop thinking about the chaos our visit will cause. Dhankhar must surely know who broke into the torpedo shop by now. He'll be livid, of course, but he will also be afraid. That makes him even more dangerous."

"We took the best shot with what we had, Girish," Petrov replied firmly. "And it was as good as we could have hoped for. I think you're just impatient at having to wait so long to see the results of our shot. Torpedoes are a lot quicker at telling you if they hit or missed their target."

Samant grinned. "I suppose you are right. But disengaging as we did also means we are out of contact with our target, and that concerns me."

"Gentlemen, pardon the interruption," interjected McFadden, "but we are almost there. The consulate is just on the other side of Hussain Sagar Lake, and we should arrive in about ten minutes."

Without thinking, Petrov turned his head a little too quickly, and a jolt of pain shot up his left side. "That's good to hear, Mr. McFadden," he gasped. "I think I've had just about enough of this."

McFadden nodded. "Understood, sir. We'll have a doctor take a look at your injuries as soon as we can. The Consul General, Mr. Erik Olson, would like to meet with you first and fill you in on the president's intentions."

"Has Dr. Patterson said anything more about the photos we sent her?" asked Samant.

"No, Captain. The last message I received from her said they had successfully downloaded all the files. The pictures were clear, the content excellent, and that they'd be working all night putting together the case to present to the Indian government. That was . . ." McFadden glanced at his smartphone, noting the time of Patterson's e-mail. ". . . six o'clock our time this morning."

"That's eight hours ago!" grumbled Samant. "I would certainly hope more has been done since then!"

"I'm confident of that, sir, but Dr. Patterson gave explicit orders that there would be no further discussions on this issue until you and Captain Petrov were safely within the consulate. That's why we are meeting with the consul general as soon as we arrive."

Samant grunted his understanding and leaned back into his seat. Edgy with impatience, he struggled to keep his mind occupied for the last few minutes and looked out onto the man-made lake. As soon as he did, he found himself staring directly at the eighteen-meter sculpture of Gautama Buddha atop a small island just offshore. The serene face of the "enlightened one" had a calming effect on Samant, and although he was not particularly religious, he took it as a good omen. Silently, he offered up a short prayer for a favorable outcome to the "whole bloody mess."

The SUV looped around the north side of the lake and then veered off the highway onto a busy side street. A half mile later the driver took an abrupt hard left onto a quieter avenue. Petrov saw McFadden look behind him to the security guard. The man was watching out the back window; a thumbs-up gesture signaled the all-clear. After another quick turn to the right, McFadden checked again and then spoke into his radio. Up ahead, Petrov saw a large gate begin to open. Barely slowing to check for oncoming traffic, the driver burst across the street and into the covered security checkpoint. As the vehicle screeched to a stop, the large reinforced gate closed behind them.

"Welcome to the U.S. Consulate General in Hyderabad, gentlemen," said McFadden as he showed the Marine guard his identification. After a quick inspection of the vehicle, the inner gate was opened and the SUV drove up to the main entrance of Paigah Palace. Petrov took in the striking view as they swung around the driveway. The castle was a large two-story building with an extravagant portico supported by three tall semicircular arches. The architecture was definitely European; he'd seen buildings with similar facades in St. Petersburg.

As soon as the SUV came to a stop, Petrov unbuckled himself and swung open the door. Cautiously ducking the doorframe, he slowly extracted himself from the abusive vehicle, and just as carefully began walking over to Samant and McFadden. It hurt to walk, but it was a good hurt. His body delighted in finally being able to stretch out fully. A small group of people, led by a rather hefty man, was exiting the palace and quickly approached them.

"Captain Samant, Captain Petrov, welcome to the United States Consulate in Hyderabad. I'm Erik Olson, Consul General." The large man offered each of them his hand in turn, then motioned to the front door. "This way, please."

Filing into the building, they walked down an ornate grand hallway toward the main conference room. Samant was impressed by the decor, but he couldn't miss the stacks of sealed boxes and loose packing materials. Passing by several very busy offices, he found it curious that he didn't see a single Indian employee. He knew diplomatic missions usually hired locals to help with the administrative, cooking, and cleaning duties. As they were ushered into the conference room, Olson pointed toward a table with some refreshments.

"Please, help yourself to tea, coffee, or water. I hope sandwiches and salad are acceptable. I'm afraid our food service is a bit limited this week."

Petrov and Samant both eagerly grabbed something to eat. They'd stopped a couple of times during the trip to Hyderabad, but that was only for fuel and other absolutely necessary human functions. Snacks were, of course, available, but both wanted a more substantial meal.

Samant loaded up a full plate and picked up a cup of tea. Carefully carrying his lunch to the conference table, looking toward the consul general, he asked, "Mr. Olson, I couldn't help but notice all the boxes in the hallway and offices. Are you moving?"

"Yes, Captain. You may not be aware, but the United States has only leased Paigah Palace while a new consulate compound was constructed in Gachibowli—fifteen kilometers to the west as the crow flies. We begin moving in later this week. Needless to say, it has been utter chaos here. But the secure video teleconference system is still hooked up and we'll be able to link you in when Secretary Lloyd briefs President Handa on the information you've obtained."

"And when will that be?" asked Petrov as he sat down with his meal.

"We really don't know, Captain," Olson replied sheepishly. "You see, the ambassador is having a difficult time reaching either President Handa or Foreign Secretary Jadeja."

Both Samant and Petrov stopped eating and looked at Olson with confusion and concern. Neither could understand why it would be so difficult to reach the Indian president or his foreign minister.

Seeing their stunned expressions, Olson quickly explained, "They are both taking some personal time to celebrate the Festival of Ram Navami tomorrow with their families, and are currently out of the capital. The Indian government is largely shut down for the next few days."

Samant let out an exasperated sigh and rubbed his face with both hands. How could he have zoned out so completely as to overlook such an important Hindu holiday? No wonder he hadn't seen any of his countrymen in the consulate. They had all been let go early to be with their families. In the back of his mind, he could hear his mother lecturing him . . . again.

"I don't understand," said Petrov, still perplexed.

"Ram Navami is the culmination of a nine-day period called Navratri," Samant injected. "It commemorates the birth of Lord Rama, one of the most revered deities in Hinduism. Since this day also marks Rama's marriage to his wife Sita, the holiday period places great emphasis on the family."

"And as President Handa and Foreign Secretary Jadeja are conservative Hindus, they take religious festivals such as this very seriously," Olson said. "It's unlikely we'll have the briefing today, and unfortunately, tomorrow may not be much better. The ambassador is over at the Ministry of External Affairs as we speak pushing for an audience, but one cannot drag a head of state to a meeting if he doesn't want to come." Olson shrugged his shoulders.

Petrov was awestruck, Samant quietly resigned. They'd risked so much to get the information to the Americans, and now the Indian president was going to put off even listening to the evidence because of a holiday! It's not that Petrov had anything against religious or national holidays—he loved the Christmas season—but given that the very future of India was at stake, religious holiday or not, an elected leader needed to put the well-being of the nation ahead of his own personal desires. Fueled by fatigue, his anger slowly bubbled to the surface. Dropping into his old ways, Petrov spoke with the voice of an irritated, seasoned navy captain.

"Then Mr. Olson, I strongly recommend that more direct language be used to convey the urgency of the situation. I realize that diplomatic conversation tends to be more polite, but every hour we delay gives our adversaries time to finish their preparations. And God help us if *Chakra* sails before we can stop them."

The intensity in Petrov's eyes reinforced the sternness of his voice. Olson's surprised expression showed that he had gotten the message loud and clear. "Yes, Captain, I'll forward your recommendation immediately, emphasizing the time factor."

"Good. When can we speak to Dr. Patterson?"

"Once we knew there wouldn't be a meeting with President Handa today, she went home to sleep. Her e-mail said she'd be back in the office by about six thirty A.M. Washington time; that's still a couple of hours from now," Olson responded.

Petrov nodded with frustration. The time zones were an unfortunate fact of life. There was nothing that they could do right now, but the thought of just sitting around waiting, wasting time, was maddening.

"In the meantime, we have prepared rooms for you. I'm sure you could use some rest. I don't know about you, but I find it impossible to sleep soundly in a car," said Olson, motioning to one of his staff.

The young woman that came forward was petite in size, but athletic in appearance. Her dark eyes, fair complexion, and fiery-red hair were an unusual but attractive combination, at least as far as Samant was concerned. "This is my administrative assistant, Ms. Shereen Massoud, she'll show you to your rooms and will answer any questions you may have about the consulate's facilities. I'll be sure to let you know when Dr. Patterson is available."

Olson then excused himself; he said he needed to pass Petrov's recommendation up his chain of command. Massoud politely greeted the guests, then sat down as they finished eating. Petrov brooded silently as he mindlessly chewed on his sandwich, still struggling with the disappointing news. Samant was gloomy, but he wasn't as affected as his Russian friend. He'd seen important tasks move slowly before. Recognizing that they were being rude, Samant politely exchanged small talk with the young woman while he finished his meal.

"How long have you been stationed in India?" he asked.

"A little over two years," Massoud replied. "It's been a great tour, and I've learned a lot, but I am looking forward to getting back home."

"Homesick, are we?"

"Sort of, sir." Massoud looked a little uncomfortable. "Sure, I miss my family, but, honestly, I'm not a big fan of the spicy food. And it's hard to find a good hamburger in a country where the cow is considered sacred. However, your country has a killer lemonade."

"Ah, so you like Panaka?" Samant chuckled as he referred to the lemon-based drink made with jaggery and pepper.

"Hell, yeah!" exclaimed Massoud. Immediately regretting her outburst, she rushed her hand to her mouth. Blushing, she apologized, "Excuse me, I mean, yes, sir."

Samant laughed out loud, and even Petrov had to smile over the young lady's enthusiastic response. With their meal finished, Massoud showed the two men their rooms. Samant was duly impressed with the suite; it was almost as big as his apartment in Vizag. While inspecting the bathroom he spied the shower—the very thought of hot water washing over him was seductive. He sat on the bed and slowly removed his shoes; he then lay down and stretched his weary body out fully on the mattress. *I'll just rest here for a minute,* Samant thought. He didn't make it to the shower.

5 April 2017
1145 EST
White House Situation Room
Washington, D.C.

Frustration, exasperation, vexation . . . Patterson mentally ran down the list of synonyms for her feelings as she paced impatiently around the conference table. She just couldn't comprehend how a national leader could be so blasé about something so serious. Did he just not get it? Lloyd was sympathetic, but his explanation earlier that morning did nothing to make her feel any better.

"President Handa *is* making a compromise, Joanna," argued Lloyd. "We'll brief him today, but it will be after sunset, his time, so he can complete most of his religious obligations. The fact that he's agreed to listen to us at all today is a major concession."

"Potentially a very costly one, Mr. Secretary. I'm quite certain Admiral Dhankhar has made very good use of the thirty hours this delay has cost us!"

Ten minutes before noon the secure VTC links between the three locations were synchronized and the audio and video channels checked. Patterson could see Olson, Samant, and Petrov on the left-hand screen. On the right-hand screen were the deputy chief of mission and the naval attaché. Ambassador Robert Eldridge had gone to greet President Handa at the embassy's main entrance. The ambassador had warned Secretary Lloyd that the Indian president was irritated with the "ill-timed summons," and that only the promised presence of President Myles at the meeting had convinced the Indian to cut short his holiday.

The Indians were still grateful to the Americans for clearing them as the source of the Kashmir explosion. The ambassador had used that to his advantage to convince the Indian leadership that they really needed to come to the U.S. embassy and listen to what those "same Americans" had to say. The kindest Indian reaction had been "This better be important." Lloyd reassured Eldridge that the information the U.S. government was going to provide would be worth the diplomatic capital expended.

Patterson looked again at her notes. She knew the content by heart, but the flow of the briefing had been modified and she wanted to make sure she stayed on script. Myles had insisted that she present the information to the Indian president. A scientist, not a diplomat, had to be the messenger. The president also wanted to keep Petrov and Samant offscreen at first. Their presence had "shock value" for President Myles, and he wanted to use that shock to drive home their difficult message to Handa. It was critical that they apply the blow at the right time; thus, Samant and Petrov would not be brought on until after the evidence had been presented.

With five minutes to go, President Myles walked into the situation room and greeted his staff. He then dismissed everyone not participating in the VTC. Only four people would be in view during the virtual meeting. Myles didn't want to overwhelm the Indian contingent by sheer force of numbers. A couple of minutes later, the naval attaché gestured to the screen and said, "Stand by."

Myles signaled for everyone to stand. The secretaries of defense and state flanked the president, while Joanna stood offset behind Lloyd.

"Attention on deck!" sang out the navy captain.

Joanna watched as Eldridge appeared on the screen, followed by four Indians. Handa was tall for an Indian, and easily stood out from the rest of his countrymen. His face was weathered, with deep furrows on his forehead, and while he had most of his hair, it was snowy white and cropped short. The tightly clipped white goatee complemented his sharp facial features, giving him an air of authority. He carefully positioned himself in the center of the table and gave the traditional Indian greeting of "Namaste" with a slight bow. Joanna noticed the restrained frown and pursed lips. The man was not happy.

Myles reciprocated by putting the palms of his hands together, bowing, and repeating the word "Namaste." Then, speaking carefully, he greeted the Indian head of state.

"President Handa, I very much appreciate your presence here this evening, and I regret having to take you away from your family during this special holiday. I know it is a considerable sacrifice on your part, but I would not insist on this video conference if the matter were not of the utmost urgency and importance."

The Indian took a deep breath, pausing to keep his emotions in check. "President Myles, I must admit that I'm not in a particularly pleasant mood. The observance of the Festival of Ram Navami challenges us to focus our attention on our family—being together, fasting and praying, is vital to our future happiness and prosperity. And to break with those sacred activities prematurely is . . . most annoying.

"Ambassador Eldridge has been steadfast is his urgings that I come to the U.S. embassy to hear your concerns about this so-called nuclear crisis. I'm not accustomed to being summoned by a foreign government in my own country, nor do I appreciate being instructed as to whom can accompany me."

Joanna fought hard not to wince; the Indian president had good reason to be upset. Both his deeply held religious beliefs and his pride had been badly bruised. She wondered just what Eldridge had said to the elder statesman.

"Mr. President, I completely understand your irritation, and it is I, not Ambassador Eldridge, you need to direct your anger toward. He was just following the strict orders I gave him. And it is I who owes you a most sincere apology for my actions. As for the 'summons,' it was unavoidable. The information we are prepared to give you is highly classified, and our nations' secure communications systems are not compatible. In time we could have worked this out, but we do not have the luxury of time.

"Furthermore, as this information implicates that some senior Indian military officers are behind the conspiracy, I could only disclose it to the *civilian* leadership of the Republic of India."

Myles paused briefly to let his last statement sink in. "President Handa, we Americans have a reputation, deservedly, for being excessively blunt. But I would much rather risk a diplomatic faux pas than allow significant pain and suffering to occur to a nation that I consider to be a friend."

Handa nodded slightly, accepting Myles's explanation for the highly inconvenient meeting. Pointing to the men with him, Handa made a quick introduction. "You know, of course, my Prime Minister, Shankar Pathak, and my Foreign Secretary, Gopan Jadeja." Both men bowed their greetings.

"To the left of Foreign Secretary Jadeja is Mr. Vishnu Kumar, the Director of the Central Bureau of Investigation, the highest law enforcement agency in India. Given the vague reference to a potential 'military conspiracy' in Ambassador Eldridge's messages, I thought it wise to include Mr. Kumar in the discussion. Now, please, tell us about this information that concerns you so deeply."

Touché, Mr. President, thought Patterson, as she let out a sigh of relief. The thin smile on Handa's face showed his tenseness had eased some. Myles, also smiling, quickly introduced Lloyd, Geisler, and Patterson, and then motioned for everyone to be seated. Joanna walked up to the podium, brought up her title slide, and formally introduced herself. She wasted no time in getting to the point.

"President Handa, it is typical in U.S. policy briefings to provide 'the bottom line up front,' followed by the supporting evidence. Therefore, I must ask for you and your compatriots' indulgence. Our message is not a pleasant one."

She hit the button to pull up the BLUF slide and spoke quickly; the fuse was now lit.

"We have multiple collaborating sources that indicate elements of the Indian Navy are planning to attack five of China's largest ports with nuclear weapons similar to the one that exploded in Kashmir last month. The weapons are to be delivered by torpedoes launched from the Project 971U submarine, INS *Chakra*. We know the mastermind behind this planned attack is Vice Admiral Badu Singh Dhankhar, although it is likely other flag officers . . ."

That was as far as she got before the Indian officials at the U.S. embassy exploded in a cacophony of noise. They could not believe what they had just read and heard. It was impossible for Joanna to go on over the indignant shouting.

What little the Americans could pick out told them that the Indians not only refused to accept the idea, they were insulted at the very thought. Myles motioned for Joanna to stop; understandably, President Handa and the others were upset and needed to blow off some steam before she could go on.

In Hyderabad, Samant covered his eyes and groaned as he watched the turmoil unfold. The reaction was pretty much what he expected, but that didn't make it any easier. He prayed that Handa and the others wouldn't slam their minds shut to the evidence.

Petrov saw his friend's pained reaction and spoke quietly. "I've known Joanna Patterson for over ten years now, and she can be very . . . direct. But, I'm alive today because of that directness. She knows what she's doing, Girish."

"I'll take your word for it, Aleks," Samant whispered. "I just hope President Handa doesn't have a heart attack!"

The Indian president finally managed to rein in his subordinates and turned, seething, to the camera. "President Myles, this is an outrage! Admiral Dhankhar is a noble officer and is highly respected by my office and his colleagues! To levy such an accusation is unmitigated slander . . ."

Myles rose to his feet. He raised his voice. "Mr. President! Please let Dr. Patterson present the considerable evidence that supports it. You'll see there is no possible alternative!"

Handa closed his eyes and took several deep breaths. He knew the American president was not the kind of man to shout at meetings. Struggling to control his anger, he slowly sat back down and said carefully, "Very well, proceed."

"Dr. Patterson, please continue," commanded Myles.

Joanna pulled up the next slide with a photo of a barge surfaced in ice-laden waters and started to describe the source of the nuclear weapons. She explained how she was part of a submarine mission that discovered the barge off the Russian island of Novaya Zemlya in June 2005, and of the subsequent recovery of two nuclear warheads for Soviet SS-21 intermediate-range ballistic missiles. It was the analysis of the nuclear material from these warheads that allowed the United States to claim with high confidence that the Kashmir explosion could not have come from an Indian weapon.

She then told them of their meeting with the Russian ambassador, where the United States admitted their less-than-legal activities and asked for their help in recovering the weapons. The Russians did so promptly, but reported that another six weapons had already been removed from the barge, and recently. The Russians also said that a disgraced admiral by the name of Kirichenko was undoubtedly the individual who knew about the barge's location and likely recovered the weapons and had offered them on the black arms market. Kirichenko's whereabouts had been unknown for years.

Her next slide showed a diagram highlighting the significant changes to *Chakra*'s refit. She emphasized the abruptly shortened time period and the change in focus that concentrated the work on sonar, fire control, and torpedo upgrades. The vast majority of the engineering-related repair items were suddenly deferred, repairs that India had already purchased expensive parts for. None of these changes made any sense; all had been approved by Dhankhar's staff, and all occurred *after* the Kashmir explosion. Next came slide after slide of close-up, detailed photos taken on board *Chakra* and in the base workshops. She didn't bother to point out the obvious that the photos came from secure areas within the naval shipyard at Visakhapatnam.

Petrov and Samant watched the Indians' reactions closely. All were angry, but as the photographs of *Chakra* appeared, different officials showed confusion, disbelief, and surprise.

Patterson spent some time describing the modifications to the fire control, torpedo tubes, and torpedoes. "All this work was to be performed by a single Russian national, a Mr. Evgeni Orlav, who worked alone in an isolated workshop. And based on rumors from numerous Russian and Indian shipyard workers and supervisors, he reported directly, and only, to Admiral Dhankhar.

"The Russians later volunteered information that Orlav was a retired naval engineering officer who specialized in the care and maintenance of ballistic missile reentry vehicles—to include the 'physics package.' With the loss of one warhead to the LeT terrorists, who accidentally detonated it, the five remaining warheads were removed from their reentry vehicle casing and reassembled into five UGST-M torpedoes, two of which were visibly identified at the shop where Orlav did the majority of his work." There were muted exclamations at the photographs of the torpedo shop interior and the torpedoes, as well as the ominous shape on the workbench.

One of her last slides showed the picture of the crumpled piece of paper with the list of Chinese ports. A total of ten were on that paper; all were major ports that supported China's export economy, her petroleum infrastructure, and/or her financial markets. An accompanying table showed the historical throughput capacity of each of the ports in terms of standardized containers and barrels of oil. The numbers were staggering.

The last slide was summary recap. The targets were major Chinese ports; the weapons were rogue Russian nuclear weapons, placed in torpedoes by a Russian technician, and delivered by INS *Chakra*. The unexplainable changes in *Chakra*'s schedule refit were made immediately after the Kashmir explosion, and everything associated with the changes came from Vice Admiral Dhankhar's office.

Joanna theorized that Dhankhar might have been motivated by the stagnation of the Indian offensive and the ongoing peace negotiations. She cited some of the admiral's own public statements expressing his concern about the direct military aid Pakistan was receiving from China. She closed by warning that should Dhankhar successfully destroy several major Chinese ports, the retribution against India would be catastrophic. The plot was no longer a secret. Too many people in Russia and the United States now knew about it. It would be unwise to think that China wouldn't eventually learn the truth.

Joanna turned off the screen feed and sat down. The situation room was absolutely silent. The Indians looked completely amazed. No one spoke for at least a minute. Finally, Myles rose. "There you have it, Mr. President. You're now in possession of the same information that we've been working with. I trust you now understand why we had to have this meeting."

Handa remained silent, running his right hand over his goatee. He was struggling with the revelation presented by Patterson. Myles then saw the director of the Central Bureau of Investigation lean over and whisper to the Indian president. The older man nodded, and Kumar faced the camera.

"President Myles, what you've shared with us is very disturbing. But I must ask, how did you get many of those photos? If I understand Dr. Patterson correctly, they could only have been taken within our shipyard at Visakhapatnam."

"You're correct, Mr. Kumar. They were provided to us by a confidential source."

Kumar's face visibly tightened; his voice became hard. "I see. So what you're saying is that you have a spy in our shipyard!"

"No, sir," Myles countered firmly. "The photos were provided by individuals who had already reached the same conclusions and sought outside help, not to hurt India, but to save her!"

"Very commendable, if true!" hissed Kumar.

Handa raised his hand, silencing the director. "President

Myles, I accept that you believe this information to be factual, and that you have shared it out of a genuine concern for the well-being of India. And for that I thank you, and I also forgive you for demanding that we meet this evening."

"But?" asked Myles.

"The information you've provided does seem to implicate Vice Admiral Dhankhar, but it is totally at odds with my personal experiences with the man. Yes, he's been a critic of our peace negotiations with Pakistan, but he is a loyal and faithful officer who has followed orders in the past. He has done *nothing* that would cause me to distrust him."

"I see. So you believe this information was manufactured? To possibly discredit Admiral Dhankhar?"

"Since I do not know who supplied you this information, I cannot rule out the possibility that it is a smear campaign to ruin Dhankhar's excellent reputation," Handa protested. "He has served me and my predecessors well, Mr. President."

"What do I have to do to get you to believe us?"

Handa hesitated, considering Myles's question. Kumar leaned over again and whispered to his president. Facing the camera, Handa said, "We'd need to have direct access to your sources."

Joanna suppressed a smirk; President Myles had nailed it perfectly, and was ready to reel them in.

Without flinching, Myles exclaimed, "Done! Milt, please bring up the consulate in Hyderabad."

The VTC screen suddenly cut in half with Petrov and Samant now visible on the left-hand side. Myles launched immediately into the introduction. "President Handa, may I present Captain First Rank Aleksey Igorevich Petrov, Russian Navy, retired, and now chief technical advisor to the Indian Navy on INS *Chakra*'s refit. And I believe you are already acquainted with Captain Girish Samant, the previous commanding officer of INS *Chakra*."

The four Indians sat stunned; a single feather could have knocked all of them over. Upon seeing Samant, Handa began trembling, and his voice was unsteady, quavering; his tone sounded more like a plea than a question. "Cap . . . Captain Samant, is what the Americans have told us true?"

Samant wavered momentarily. He regretted the pain he was about to cause his nation's leader, but the Indian captain had already made his decision. There was nothing left to do but carry on. "Yes, Mr. President, everything that Dr. Patterson has said is correct. It was Captain Petrov and I that discovered Dhankhar's dark secret. Dr. Patterson helped to provide the missing pieces that enabled us to collectively put the entire puzzle together."

Handa slumped back into his chair, his hands cradling his head. The prime minister and foreign secretary were equally dumbfounded and remained silent. Director Kumar recovered first and asked the only obvious question.

"Captain Samant, are you confident of your findings? Is there no other credible alternative explanation?"

Petrov looked at Samant, the Indian nodded his approval. "Mr. Director," began Petrov, "I have considerable experience with Project 971 submarines. I was a first officer on one of our boats and I have detailed technical knowledge of the Omnibus combat system. There is only one reason for a panel in that position on the console: to pass firing data and unlocking codes to a nuclear-armed weapon.

"*Chakra* wasn't equipped with those panels when my country leased her to you. But the refit plan I had to execute required running new data communication wiring from the console to the torpedo tube junction boxes. Orlav was to install and test the panels, and he worked directly for Vice Admiral Dhankhar."

"Director Kumar," interrupted Samant. "Both Captain Petrov and I looked into every other possible weapon, both Russian and Indian. The only new weapon we're ready to field is this new Russian torpedo, and even if there were a new Indian weapon, which there isn't right now, it would be incompatible with the Russian combat system. I'm sorry, but we were unable to find a credible alternative explanation.

"We went to the Americans because we needed an informed outsider to confirm or deny our theory. I couldn't report our suspicions up the navy chain of command, or indeed the Defense Ministry, as we had no idea how widespread this conspiracy had become. Admiral Dhankhar could not possibly do this on his own—we believed he had to have help from above."

President Handa lifted his head from his hands; his face looked drained. Myles and everyone else could see that he'd been presented with an unexpected nightmare. Everyone waited as he processed the news and considered the many dangers.

Finally, Handa asked, "Have you told the Chinese? How much do they know?"

"No," Myles replied quickly. "We have no indication that the Chinese know about this yet, and we haven't told them a thing. We believed it would be better for all concerned that you resolve the matter internally—if the first thing the Chinese hear is that you stopped a plot and the conspirators were in custody, then the danger would have passed."

Visibly relieved, Handa replied, "Yes, tensions with China are high enough right now. I agree, and appreciate, the opportunity to settle this matter within India's borders." He gave a slight nod toward the camera. "We will act quickly to stop these criminals before they ruin us all."

Myles added, "Although the weapons were made in Russia, my advisors are confident that if the plot had been carried out, China would still see India as the perpetrator, with a likely retaliation in kind." Even though Myles's words were carefully phrased, many in the room visibly shuddered at them—at the idea of Chinese missiles destroying Indian cities.

Speaking softly, the Indian president asked, "President Myles, what do you want me to do?"

"Apprehend Dhankhar, Orlav, and Kirichenko as soon as possible, and open a public investigation. For our part, I'll have Secretary Lloyd and the State Department work with your people on a statement of U.S. support to be issued after you announce the arrest of Dhankhar and his associates, and that *Chakra* is still in port and firmly under Indian Navy control."

5 April 2017
2330 Local Time
Flag Officers' Quarters
INS *Circars*
Visakhapatnam, India

The ringing of his cell phone pulled Dhankhar from his book. Irritated at the intrusion, he looked at the caller ID screen. No name was displayed, but he recognized the number. Sighing, he answered, "Admiral Dhankhar."

"Badu, it's Ijay Thapar." Dhankhar heard the familiar voice of the deputy director for the Central Bureau of Investigation, but something wasn't quite right. The man's voice seemed to waver.

"Ijay, it's late. What can I . . ."

"Badu, President Handa is aware of Vajra," interrupted Thapar.

Dhankhar froze, dazed. This was his worst nightmare. "How?" he asked.

"The Americans briefed him at their embassy a couple of hours ago. They know everything, Badu." The voice started to sound panicky.

"Easy, Ijay. Tell me what you know."

"The American president's staff told Handa about a sunken barge the weapons came from. The Russian government had been informed and they've recovered the arge. The Russians said six weapons were missing and that a man named Kirichenko likely took them." The name sent shivers up Dhankhar's spine. He'd never shared Kirichenko's name with any members of the group, and they hadn't asked. If they had his name . . .

But Thapar wasn't finished. "The Americans know about a technician named Orlav, and that he's modifying the new Russian torpedoes to carry the devices. Badu, they had detailed photographs from *Chakra* and the base. And somehow they found the list of potential targets."

Dhankhar's hands had started to tremble at the sound of Kirichenko's and Orlav's names, but it was the mentioning of the target list that got his heart beating wildly. The Americans had indeed learned a great deal of Operation Vajra. Forcing himself to calm down, the admiral half asked, half asserted, "Ijay, was it Petrov?"

"Yes, Badu. He's at the U.S. consulate in Hyderabad. But he wasn't alone."

"What? Who betrayed us?" Rage now crept into Dhankhar's voice.

"Girish Samant."

"No, that's not possible," whimpered Dhankhar, crushed.

"I'm afraid so. He backed up Petrov's testimony. Badu, you were specifically accused by name."

The admiral didn't know what to think or say. His intricate plan was falling apart before him. Thapar waited only a moment before continuing. "The council members have been advised. All electronic and hard copy documents concerning Vajra will be erased or shredded and burned. After this call, all special cell phones will be destroyed and the accounts deleted. Financial transaction records will also be erased. There will be no linkage between you and the rest of the assembly."

Dhankhar grew cold; his colleagues were abandoning him.

"The other members have not been informed of this

tragedy, but the execute order has just been sent to preclude them from doing anything untoward and drawing attention," Thapar explained. As part of the security protocol, none of the assembly members were to contact another once the execute order was issued. There would be no formal communication until the council sent word that it was safe.

"Were there any instructions for me?" asked Dhankhar.

"Yes. Get *Chakra* to sea immediately. Then you're to go into hiding. Someplace remote, and tell no one where you are going. The council believes that even though the Americans know, they won't tell the Chinese out of fear that it would make the situation much worse. The Americans don't like the idea of significant Chinese casualties, but they abhor the thought of a massive retaliatory strike on India. They will remain silent."

"I see," the admiral replied skeptically.

"This was your idea, Badu," declared Thapar. "You're the one who volunteered to carry the load if things went awry."

Anger flashed through Dhankhar. "Don't presume you can lecture me, Ijay! I know what my duties are. You can tell the council that I'll carry them out to the fullest."

"I'm sorry, Badu," Thapar apologized. "I'll do what I can to slow down any legal proceedings, but it won't be a lot of time. Perhaps twenty-four hours at the most."

"Then I best get to work. Good-bye, Ijay."

"Good-bye, Badu. May the blessing of Rama go with you."

12

Plan B

Dhankhar had been in the yard since before five, pressing Mitra for anything that could speed *Chakra*'s sailing. The captain was competent enough, coping as well as could be expected with the sudden schedule change after the Kashmir incident. But Dhankhar and the Vajra plan were now on borrowed time. Fighting rising impatience, he chivvied and haggled with Mitra for ways to shave even minutes off the scheduled sailing time, regulations be damned. *Chakra*, with the weapons aboard, had to sail before the authorities arrived and put an end to everything.

The instant he'd learned of the Americans' briefing to the president, he knew it was only a matter of time before the government would act to seize the weapons and arrest everyone they could find. It was possible that he and some of the other members might be under surveillance, but given the warning he received last night from the deputy director of the premier law enforcement agency, that was unlikely, at least for now. His saving grace would be the bureaucratic inertia that was part and parcel of any Indian government agency. This "friction" would be exacerbated by discreet actions by other members; nonetheless, he couldn't count on that to give him more than a few hours. But for the moment, he was free to act.

A small voice had urged him to flee, or go into hiding to avoid arrest and imprisonment. But his disappearance would doom Vajra. That was unthinkable. After *Chakra* sailed, he'd go to a safe place, but not before.

Like the others, he had received the "execute" order late last night. But the majority of the Vajra members were unaware of the complete collapse in security. The four councilmen thought it a wiser course of action to use this deception; the prearranged actions for the execute order would initiate the elimination of any trace of the operation, without the risk of some of the members panicking.

If some of the conspirators were indeed under surveillance, then ignorance would prevent them from acting unwisely. Fear might make one of the group change his habits, or possibly bolt. Dhankhar didn't want to consider the possibility of one of them betraying the rest by running to the authorities.

And they still had a chance. The Americans had only warned his government about the attack on the Chinese ports. *Chakra*'s crucial role was only the first act of a much bigger plan. The army was readying itself for a spring offensive in the event that the peace talks were unsuccessful. This was a reasonable strategy, and expected. The likely date for that was still a few weeks off, but stockpiles of ammunition and fuel had been built up throughout the winter months. The Pakistanis wouldn't expect an early offensive in less-than-optimal weather.

Everything Dhankhar and his cohorts knew said China was on the brink of economic and social collapse. The sudden destruction of China's five largest port cities would wreak havoc throughout the country. *Chakra*'s attack would push them over the edge.

Officers that were part of Dhankhar's group would send orders launching a surprise offensive, well before the Pakistanis expected it and now without their Chinese protec-

tors. No Chinese AWACS aircraft flying just over the
border, warning of Indian aircraft. No more ordnance or
spares for the Chinese-made Pakistani fighters. India
would have air superiority.

No threat of Chinese troops tying up valuable units on
the flanks of the fighting. They'd need every soldier they
could to keep order in the cities. That would free up fresh
troops.

Because key people in the Indian armed forces were
ready for Vajra, they'd be able to take advantage of the
kind of shock and surprise that had been unintentionally
displayed in Kashmir. He expected Indian troops to break
through the Pakistani's static defenses and into the rear
within hours.

And again because of the Kashmir explosion, and
thanks to the Americans, the nuclear weapons could not
be directly linked to India. Yes, the Americans knew, but
they undoubtedly wouldn't say anything to China out of a
fear of causing even greater casualties—they'd take the
lesser of the two evils. Would the Indian government, when
presented with a fait accompli, pass up the chance to end
the Pakistani threat once and for all? India had gone to war
with that goal, and that victory would be his vindication
and redemption.

Dhankhar finally convinced himself that Mitra was doing all he could, and headed for the torpedo shop. He realized he'd been stalling, remaining in Mitra's office
because he didn't want to hear what the Russians would
tell him. But that was irresponsible. Whatever the problem,
he'd fix it somehow.

They'd worked through the night. Dhankhar was pleasantly
surprised; he'd half expected to find the place deserted,
the Russians fled to gods knew where. But the lure of the
money had been too great.

The door to the weapons vault was open, and all five
torpedoes were out. That gave Dhankhar a flash of hope,

but then he could see that two of the weapons were still in pieces, their warhead sections exposed. Kirichenko and Orlav were bent over one of them. The Russians were obviously not done.

Kirichenko stopped work as Dhankhar came into the shop. He'd found a pair of coveralls, and with a rag stuffed in a back pocket, looked more like a car mechanic than a former admiral. Actually, he looked like a tired and worried mechanic, the kind that has to give his customers bad news.

"We're not finished," Kirichenko announced. "We can't finish in time." He sounded matter-of-fact, as if he was going to tell Dhankhar the engine block was cracked and couldn't be repaired.

The Russian nodded toward three weapons neatly lined up near the door, resting in their cradles. "Those three are ready to be loaded. Final checks have been made." He gestured toward Orlav, still working. "The fourth device is in place, and we should be able to finish it in time for loading, but the fifth still needs to be installed. There's no way we can fit it, perform the necessary checks, assemble the complete weapon, and then make the rest of the checks."

Kirichenko shrugged. "I can give you four weapons. That's the best we can do." Again the same matter-of-fact tone, but Kirichenko was trying to pretend this wasn't a massive failure. It was clear he hoped Dhankhar would be satisfied with destroying four Chinese port cities.

"No. I want five," Dhankhar replied firmly. "Six was the original agreement. Four might not be enough. Five will barely deliver the body blow we need."

Kirichenko gestured helplessly. "I just told you. We can't finish in time."

"Actually," Dhankhar replied, "we've moved the sailing time up. *Chakra* leaves tonight."

"What?" Kirichenko's look of surprise almost made Dhankhar laugh. Then the Russian sighed, and rubbed his forehead. He was probably nursing a headache, not that

Dhankhar cared. "Then there's absolutely no time to even begin work on the fifth torpedo."

"Then you can finish the work under way, after *Chakra* sails. Just get the last two weapons assembled. You can make the final connections and tests aboard the submarine."

The Russian scratched his unshaven chin thoughtfully, then nodded. "All right. It means more of the crew will learn about the torpedoes," he warned.

"That can't be helped, and once *Chakra* sails, it won't matter," Dhankhar answered. "Jain and his men are up to the task."

Kirichenko brightened as he considered the possibilities. "You've got good weapons for the first three ports. With the transit, that gives us at least a week and a half, perhaps two, to finish the work on the last two torpedoes. We could both get some rest and still have time to finish. It's probably not a good idea to work nuclear weapons when you're short on sleep. I'll need you to put our payment into the account number I gave you before we leave, of course."

Dhankhar shook his head. "Absolutely not!"

"But we were to be paid before *Chakra* sails. I need that money!" Kirichenko was almost whining.

"You were to be paid when you deliver five armed torpedoes." Dhankhar tried not to sound too pleased. He found himself enjoying this. "I will tell Jain to send a message after the last weapon is launched and it is safe for him to transmit. Then, and only then, will I transfer the money to your account."

Kirichenko gestured helplessly. "What? You think we won't finish the work locked up on your submarine?"

"Were you going to use the money for something before you sailed?" replied Dhankhar. "There's nothing to spend it on here at the base, and I don't think you should go outside. Did I mention that the SVR knows all about your operation?"

"How?" Kirichenko was horrified.

"We know that part of a U.S. briefing given to the Indian government yesterday described a barge hidden off the coast of northern Russia, and your connection to it. Evidently the American and Russian governments have been working together."

Dhankhar watched the Russian's expression change from horror to fear, then something like resignation. "Fine. I must insist that we be paid today—in cash, preferably U.S. dollars."

"That's a lot of money, even if I wasn't in a hurry. Why should I?"

By now, Orlav had stopped work and had come over to listen as well. Kirichenko explained, "If the SVR is now looking for me, there's no guarantee that my offshore account is safe, or that my contacts are still trustworthy."

He paused, then added, "And can you arrange to have Captain Jain put us ashore near some neutral port after he has accomplished his mission? I can't go back to Russia, although that had been my intention."

Dhankhar scowled. "*Chakra* can't just pull into some Asian port and drop you two off. I'm sure you understand that it means surfacing and putting you—and your money—in a rubber raft and leaving you to make your own way to shore."

"Of course," Kirichenko answered, and looking over at Orlav, added, "Two rafts, please."

"Different destinations, as well?" sighed Dhankhar. "All right. I'll gather what cash I can, and Jain can hold on to it until he is satisfied. I'll also instruct Jain to put you off the boat at locations that meet with his approval, in return for you both completing the work aboard *Chakra*."

Both Russians nodded solemnly, and then Kirichenko stood up a little straighter. "Right, then. We'll get these two torpedoes assembled and then get organized. When do we board?"

"*Chakra* will sail at twenty-one hundred hours tonight.

Be ready to bring the weapons aboard at eighteen hundred."

"Understood. We will be ready."

Energized, the two quickly turned toward the workbench, but Dhankhar called after them. "Kirichenko, Orlav. If this were a movie, I'd order Jain to shoot you both the moment the mission was accomplished. I'm an honorable man, and I intend to keep my part of the bargain, but if there is any trouble, remember that Jain always has that option."

6 April 2017
0800 EST
White House Situation Room
Washington, D.C.

The situation room could hold twenty people comfortably. Patterson had seen thirty squeezed in, once, and nobody used their elbows or breathed deeply. It was just over half full now, with literally every person in the U.S. government who was aware of the Indian nuclear conspiracy.

The newest member of that elite group was preparing to brief the rest. Satisfied that his tablet and the screen were properly linked, he nodded nervously to Patterson and stepped behind the podium.

Patterson rose and the quiet conversation around the table stopped instantly. Her summons had been urgent. Nodding toward the briefer, she began, "Dr. Stan Tomasz is the senior economic analyst at the China desk in the State Department. In response to the president's question about the threat to China the Indian plot represented, I asked Stan—Dr. Tomasz, to estimate the consequences if the Indian conspirators are successful."

She started to sit down, but stopped, straightened, and added, "I should mention that Dr. Tomasz has been studying the Chinese economy since well before the Littoral

Alliance war, and during the war gave me frequent updates on its health, or lack thereof. When he told me of his findings last night, I immediately informed the president, and he told me to organize this briefing." She quickly sat down.

Dr. Tomasz was in his thirties, and fighting a losing battle with his hairline and midsection. Perhaps in compensation, he wore a neatly trimmed beard, which gave him a professorial appearance. He looked apprehensive, and tired.

He tapped a button on his tablet, and the flat-screen display behind him came to life. The title, "Chinese Economic Estimate," was deliberately vague, but the security markings said much more: "This briefing contains sensitive information and is classified Top Secret/Sensitive Compartmented Information."

"Dr. Patterson asked me to estimate the effects of five 150-kiloton nuclear weapons being detonated in major Chinese port cities. She gave me a list of ten cities that were potential targets."

He tapped his tablet and the screen changed to show a map of China, the coast dotted with small red disks. "These are the cities on the list she provided, and all are major ports with large civilian populations."

He gestured with a laser pointer, pointing out cities one after the other. "Hong Kong is a major economic center with a population over seven million people and nine separate harbors. Shanghai's population is over twenty-four million; it is also a major financial center, as well as the world's number-one container port with two large terminal facilities. Even smaller ports, like Ningbo or Xiamen, house over three million souls and are important shipping centers."

The image zoomed to show a close-up of Shanghai, sitting on the easternmost part of China's coast. Taiwan lay to the south, Japan directly east, and Korea to the northeast. It was easy to see why it was the world's busiest container port, the two large terminal facilities highlighted on the map. Tomasz shined his laser pointer on the seaward facility. Hangzhou Bay faced east, with the city on the northern side.

He waved the laser along a long structure that led to a pair of islands near the mouth of the bay. "Shanghai is a complex target set as the two facilities are far apart. The first, Yangshan Container Terminal, is built on two small islands and is connected to the mainland by the Donghai Bridge, which is just over twenty miles long. The Yangshan terminal moved just over twelve million twenty-foot equivalent units or TEUs last year."

He turned away from the harbor map to face his audience. "I consulted with CIA's subject matter experts about the effects of the weapons Dr. Patterson described. The most destructive way to use a torpedo with a 150-kiloton yield would be to set it shallow, so the detonation would be a surface burst." He pressed the tablet, and circles appeared, centered on a point just off the terminal.

"Yangshan's a deep-water port, so the torpedo could be sent well in, close to the islands the terminal was built on. This inner circle"—he pointed to a red circle that neatly surrounded the entire terminal—"is twelve kilometers in diameter, and represents the distance at which the blast would cause near-total destruction. This is only the initial effect. The damage from fires and secondary causes would likely finish off anything the blast left standing. Note the large petroleum refinery and storage facility to the east. This site was damaged during the Sino–Littoral Alliance War; a nuclear blast at the Yangshan terminal would level it." He pointed to orange and yellow circles farther out. "These represent the radii for moderate and light damage." While they extended much farther, neither reached the shoreline.

"The second port facility is the Waigaoqiao Free Trade Zone on the south bank of the Yangtze River, and it is home to four container terminals. Unlike Yangshan, the

Waigaoqiao facility is harder to reach, as it is twenty-four nautical miles upstream. However, based on the estimated weapon's characteristics, a nuclear-armed torpedo could theoretically reach this facility. A blast here would be more damaging."

Tomasz's next slide showed a lot of Shanghai proper within the twelve-kilometer-diameter destruction circle. "Civilian casualties would be on the order of a quarter of a million dead, and infrastructure damage would reach six to seven kilometers inland. Please note the Jiangnan Shipyard on Changxing Island, across the Yangtze's southern fork, is within this radius. The Jiangnan Shipyard is a major provider of modern warships to the PLAN as well as large civilian merchant ships.

"Between the Yangshan and Waigaoqiao port facilities, China moved about twenty million TEUs last year. Before the war, that number was just over thirty-four million. But considering the distances involved, the Indians would have to use two torpedoes to achieve the desired damage. Next, let's look at Hong Kong." Tomasz changed the screen and a new map appeared.

Victoria Harbor, the main port, lay between Kowloon to the north and Hong Kong Island to the south. He pressed his tablet and the same three circles reappeared. This time the red circle not only included the entire harbor, but extended well inland on both Kowloon and Hong Kong Island, including a large part of the downtown area.

"Everyone knows about how densely people are packed in over there. We estimate, with a fair degree of confidence, that about three hundred and fifty thousand people would be killed immediately, with almost another million injured."

Tomasz returned to the podium and checked his notes. "We don't know which ports are the actual targets. Assuming they're moderately competent, they've studied every name on the list, and then chosen, based on whatever their criteria were, and in fact, the others remain alternates if a primary target cannot be attacked." He looked over at Patterson, who was nodding. Geisler, the Secretary of Defense, also nodded approvingly.

"The two cities I showed you in detail are almost certainly on the target list, and we've run through different combinations of the others to create a range of results." He brought up a slide titled "Possible Combinations," but Patterson caught his eye.

"Just bring up the summary, please."

Tomasz nodded and quickly tapped the screen several times. Maps and tables flashed on the screen until he reached the summary page. The figures were stark, and almost everyone reacted with shock or disbelief. Patterson explained, "These are actually the refined results, based on guidance that I gave Dr. Tomasz last night."

"Anywhere between two and a quarter to four and a half million souls killed, and three times that injured," Tomasz remarked, reading the slide. "One bomb would be a catastrophe. Five would be apocalyptic. We did not calculate the effects of the fallout, tidal surges, or electromagnetic pulse both because of time constraints, and because, frankly, these initial effects are bad enough."

The economist explained, "The human cost and physical destruction are first-order effects. I needed these before I could begin my analysis of the true impact to China."

The next slide was titled "Economic Impact." He spoke confidently, explaining the figures. "China's gross domestic product was already suffering, down from seven point three trillion before the war to six point five last year. That doesn't sound like a lot, but to an economist, that's a strong recession and flirting with a depression. Foreign trade, exporting the manufactured goods the Chinese need to support their growing economy, was especially hard-hit. At a minimum, the destructive effects of the attack would knock at least a full trillion off of that, and probably closer to two trillion.

"That's not just a depression. A trillion gets you a nice,

solid depression, no question. But two trillion is real money. Not only would many, maybe most industries shut down, but the transportation and agricultural sectors, even basic government services, would be crippled as well. And that doesn't include the extraordinary burden of emergency relief. A lot of people will need medical care, food, water, and shelter for a considerable period of time."

He pressed a control and the screen shifted again, showing a map of the world with arrows linking China with the rest of the world. It was a simple enough diagram—the fatter the arrows, the more trade between the two nations.

"This graphic shows prewar trade levels." The fattest arrows were between China and the U.S., and China and the European Union. He pressed the tablet and the graphic shifted. All the arrows shrank; the ones to Asian nations almost disappeared. "This is postwar. Some of this is political, for example Vietnam's embargo, but most is due to China's reduced consumption and its reduced ability to provide goods for sale."

The screen changed again, with most arrows disappearing, and the remaining ones shrinking to mere threads. "And this is my estimate of the results of the Indian attack. China's exports drop to about fifteen percent of last year, while her need for all kinds of imports would grow substantially. Unfortunately, she likely doesn't have the cash reserves to pay for this increased need, let alone tackling the relief efforts.

"We're almost certain that her reserves were virtually eliminated during the Littoral Alliance war. She's got nothing to buy with."

Since Patterson had seen this before, she watched the president and the others. Their horrified expressions told her they understood not only the staggering cost in human life, but the impact this would have on the world economy. The U.S. was already suffering a mild recession, partly from direct effects of their trade with China, but aggravated by the more severe economic problems Japan and the other Asian nations were suffering.

Tomasz let them absorb the data for a few moments before adding, "This slide makes several assumptions that are out of my jurisdiction. Most relate to economic behavior and would change the overall values by five or ten percent. But the biggest variable, and one I can't predict, is the stability of the Chinese government and the maintenance of social order."

"A revolution," Secretary Lloyd remarked grimly.

"Anarchy," Tomasz responded. "A weak, discredited central government without the ability to rule; in essence, a failed state. Assuming a near-complete breakdown of authority and essential services, which will limit the ability of the Chinese Army to maintain order, chaos and massive civil unrest would almost certainly occur."

"You could have several revolutions," Myles added. "Tibet. The Uyghurs."

"And what happens when North Korea can't get its food from China anymore?"

Tomasz shrugged. "It's impossible to separate economics and politics, but I've learned the dangers of trying to predict events based on economic forecasts. I will say this: Based on this forecast, the Chinese would be *lucky* if they only suffered a severe depression, and the effects of that would be felt worldwide, including here. Just as the 1929 New York stock market crash triggered the Great Depression, China could drag the rest of the world down with it."

"We're too tightly connected, these days," Myles agreed. "Knock China down and we'll all fall over. What about India?"

"Economically, she'd be hurt as well. She doesn't have much trade with China these days, but she does with other countries that will be affected. It's a downward spiral for everyone."

"India's economic condition after the attack won't matter," Defense Secretary Geisler countered. "If China finds out who did this to them, they'll retaliate with their own nuclear weapons, and India will in turn shoot back. If that submarine launches those torpedoes, we'll have the first general nuclear exchange between the world's two largest and oldest nations."

"What's worse than an apocalypse?" Myles asked to nobody in particular. He then continued, "Thank you, Dr. Tomasz and Dr. Patterson. I am declaring that stopping this attack is in the vital interests of the United States." He took the time to look directly at Lloyd, Geisler, and Greg Alexander, Director of National Intelligence.

"Do we warn the Chinese?" Lloyd asked.

After a moment's pause, Myles replied. "Not yet. I can imagine the Chinese reacting in many different ways, all of them bad, and any hope of working with the Indians would be gone forever. As long as that sub hasn't sailed, it's only a plot, and the Indians should be able to deal with it themselves. That would look better to China, when the word does get out. But SECDEF," he turned to face Geisler, "start moving anything that would help toward the area, just in case."

6 April 2017
1810 Local Time
INS *Chakra*
Naval Shipyard
Visakhapatnam, India

Jain wondered if this was some sort of test, intended to find out exactly how much stress he could take. He'd considered asking Mitra, but the captain either was a very good actor or, for reasons still unexplained, was serious about having *Chakra* leave tonight.

Everyone else in the shipyard took it seriously. Workers were feverishly preparing the submarine for departure. The reactor was critical and the last checks in the engine room were being completed, and Mitra had assured him that two tugs would be standing by at 2100 to get him under way. Trucks with stores and foodstuffs were stacked five deep on the pier, and working parties from all over the yard had been drafted into getting the provisions aboard. In fact, supplies were coming aboard so quickly that his crew did not have time to store them properly.

And now this. In the midst of that chaos, five more torpedoes had arrived to be loaded, accompanied by two Russian civilians bearing a letter from Admiral Dhankhar. *Chakra*'s torpedomen had been helping the rest of the crew, and he'd had to pull them off working parties to rig the loading tray.

While Lieutenant Commander Rakash, his first officer, supervised the loading, Jain read the admiral's letter, then read it again. No information, just more confusion. "Treat your two visitors as VIPs, and come see me immediately."

At least there was no problem finding berths for them. Two of his officers and eight of the crew were off the boat, scheduled to return in time for the boat's originally planned sailing tomorrow.

But what were they going to do? "Weapons specialists" did not tell him anything useful, although it was obviously connected with *Chakra*'s sudden sailing.

Saluting the naval ensign at the fantail, Jain crossed the brow from the boat onto the pier. The warm evening was filled with the voices and the sounds of machinery, and Jain had to thread his way past sailors and yard workers and stacked boxes.

He saw his first officer near the bow. Rakash was acting as the safety observer as the torpedoes were winched over and lowered onto a horizontal tray that would guide them into the sub's torpedo room.

Rakash turned and saluted as Jain approached. "Everything's going smoothly here, sir. We should be done in about half an hour."

Jain forced himself to smile casually and returned the salute. "That's good to hear, Number One. If there's any part of this bedlam that should not dissolve into madness, it's loading those torpedoes."

Jain gestured down the pier. "I'm off then to see the admiral. Hopefully I'll find out what this is all about."

Rakash said, "The latest rumor, thanks to the arrival of those two Russian riders, is that we're bound for Russia to get a secret weapon to use against Pakistan."

"Replacing the one about the Pakistani spy that supposedly sabotaged the dry dock?" Jain shook his head.

The first officer shrugged, then nodded sagely. "I personally prefer the one about the secret Pakistani naval base best."

"I almost hoped that one was true," Jain replied. Taking a deep breath, he ordered, "Whip her into shape, Number One, and I'll be back, hopefully with our orders."

Jain strode quickly off into the darkness.

13

Sortie

April 2017
840 Local Time
NS *Circars*, Eastern Naval Command Headquarters
Visakhapatnam, India

The outer office was empty, and the door to the inner sanctum was open, although the opening was dark. Just inside the door, Jain hesitated. Where was the admiral's staff? It was late, but the admiral and his staff often worked late into the evening. The letter had said to come immediately. Jain assumed he was to report to Dhankhar's office, but could he have been mistaken? He reopened the letter to see if he had missed something. No, nothing.

Dhankhar saw the outer office door open, but didn't get up right away, and he left the lights in his office off. He was expecting Jain, but there could be others with him.

The admiral hadn't completely decided what he would do if the authorities showed up to arrest him. He was a loyal Indian officer, and he didn't want to shoot men only doing their duty, but Vajra was so close to success. All he had to do was give Jain his orders, and watch *Chakra* leave port. After that, his duty was done, and he had a hiding place so secret that he'd be perfectly safe until after Vajra was complete.

Dhankhar had no illusions about his chances if CBI sent

a SWAT team to arrest him. But what if it was just a few investigators, sent to check out "some wild conspiracy story"? He might—no, he'd probably use the pistol.

"Hello? Is anyone here? Admiral?" Jain called out.

Dhankhar could see that Jain was alone and rose from the corner chair. He put the pistol out of sight with one hand and turned the overhead light switch on with the other. "Captain Jain, come in, please."

Jain walked into the now fully lit office. "Sir, is everything all right?" *Chakra*'s captain looked worried and confused.

Everything is definitely not all right, but it will be soon, Dhankhar thought. He ignored Jain's question and gestured toward two chairs in a corner of the office. "Please sit."

As Jain sat down, Dhankhar took the other chair and asked casually, "How is the chaos at the dock?"

Jain laughed and answered, "We're coping, sir. The crew is performing wonderfully. We should be ready to sail by twenty-one hundred hours, maybe even a little earlier." The officer began to say something else, but then stopped himself.

"And you're wondering what the rush is all about, of course." Dhankhar smiled. " 'What are they thinking in headquarters? Are they all insane?' I've been there, Captain. But you've done your best to follow your orders without question, because you believed that it would all be revealed in the fullness of time."

Dhankhar stood and walked over to his desk and picked up a fat package, then turned and handed it to Jain. "This will answer all your questions. It has the nautical charts, codes, and everything else you will need for your mission."

Jain could see only one word on the outside: "Vajra." It didn't tell him much.

Dhankhar said formally, "As soon as you are able, leave Vizag and proceed to the waters off the People's Republic of China. Those five torpedoes that were just loaded on board your boat have nuclear warheads. You will fire them into the five ports listed in your sailing plan."

As Jain half rose out of his chair, the admiral held out one hand, forestalling any questions. "You see now why you were not told of this sooner." Jain nodded his understanding. "Security has been extraordinarily tight. Only the highest levels of our government are aware of Vajra, but even so, we believe some elements of a hostile intelligence arm may have gotten hints of our plans. Pakistani, Chinese, Russian? We're not sure.

"That's why we had to accelerate our schedule so suddenly. From my office, you will proceed directly back to your boat, speaking to no one else. Do not open this envelope until you're back aboard, and *Chakra* is safely under way."

Dhankhar watched Jain closely as he spoke. The admiral had rehearsed these orders dozens of times, because they had to be perfect, and Jain had to accept them wholeheartedly.

"The warheads are all set to detonate at the same time, in sixteen days. If you follow the sailing plan, you will be well away from the coast before they explode.

"The destruction of those five ports will throw China into economic and political upheaval, but more importantly, it will also signal the start of an early offensive by our army and air force into Pakistan. Surprised, and without Chinese support, the Pakistanis will crumble, and the war will be over in weeks. So your part in the operation is not just vital—it is the beginning of everything else, and with a little luck, will finally bring India the victory we have been working for."

Jain was absorbing the information, but appeared thunderstruck, wide-eyed.

Using a more relaxed manner, Dhankhar sat down again next to the submarine captain. "Operationally, it should be almost boring. The Chinese, we hope, have no idea of our plans, so it's just a matter of sailing from port to port, and at each of the firing positions described here," he tapped the package, "launching one of the specially modified torpe does into the harbor. It will settle to the bottom and wait for the appointed time. After you fire the fifth weapon, take a roundabout course back home. If things go as we expect by the time you return, the Paks will have surrendered and you can expect a hero's welcome. I dare say that you reputation will surpass that of your former commanding officer, Captain Samant." The admiral smiled encourag ingly.

Jain's eyes flicked with excitement, and when he finally spoke, his voice was calm. "I will do my best to remain covert, of course, but what if the Chinese do detect my presence, and evasion does not work?"

Dhankhar rejoiced inside. Jain had accepted the mis sion, and the story. "Engage only as an absolute last resort but your survival, and your mission, are paramount. Recent experience has showed us just how bad Chinese antisub marine warfare capabilities are. You should be able to press on, even if they have learned of our plan. Also, there are alternate targets in the package, if for any reason, you cannot attack one of the primaries."

Jain nodded his understanding, and the admiral added "And if you encounter Chinese-flagged vessels, naval o civilian, after the bombs have exploded, attack them a your discretion. The gloves are off, Captain. We'll finish our fight with China, as well as Pakistan."

The submariner grinned wolfishly. "Good. I had friends aboard *Arihant*."

"That's all, then. I'll be down there presently to watch you get under way."

As Jain stood, Dhankhar offered his hand. "Good luck Captain. Our country's future is going with you."

Jain took the admiral's hand, and as they shook Dhankhar could see a shadow pass across the captain's face. As Jain turned to leave, Dhankhar added, "It would be only natural to think about the many Chinese casual

es your attack will cause. Wiser men have already dis-
ussed and argued over this. China is the largest country
the world. Only a massive blow, something that inflicts
ue injury, will knock her out of the war. She's been using
he Paks as proxies for years to kill our people. This will
ing the war home to her, as well as ending it for us. No
cond thoughts. You have your orders."

Coming to attention, Jain put on his uniform cap and
luted crisply. "I won't disappoint you, sir."

April 2017
000 Local Time
quadron Fifteen Commander's Residence
aval Base Guam

---

he secure phone had a distinctive ring. It wasn't loud, but
s unique sound alerted Captain Simonis and brought him
pright out of the couch, his book fell to the ground as he
ished over and grabbed the phone. "Simonis."

"Sir, this is Lieutenant Keyes, the squadron watch of-
cer." He recognized her voice. "We've received an
perational-precedence message from CNO via SUBPAC.
hey want us to make all boats ready for sea."

Simonis knew the status of each of his boats intimately,
f course. So many men away on leave, machinery need-
g repairs, weapons aboard, and a dozen other things that
ad to be dealt with before a nuclear submarine could go
 sea. "Do they expect a reply?"

"Yes sir. They want to know the earliest time each boat
uld sail."

Simonis was already heading to the bedroom to change.
le looked over at his wife, Louise, as she worked on a
crapbook in the dining room; she glanced up, curious but
ot terribly concerned. Calls in the late evening were com-
ion, and she knew her husband would stay safely ashore.

"All right, have Captain Jacobs, Commander Walker,

and the three submarine COs report to squadron hea[d]
quarters ASAP. Is there any hint of what this is all about'

"No, sir, just orders to get ready."

"Very well. Have a car pick me up in fifteen minutes.

"Aye, aye, Commodore."

Simonis already had his uniform for tomorrow la[id]
out, so he quickly changed out of his civilian clothes. H[e]
always made it his business to be able to get out the do[or]
quickly, with a minimum of fuss. Even as he dressed, h[e]
was drafting his reply to SUBPAC. *Texas* was already ou[t]
returning from an exercise with the Philippine Navy. Sh[e]
had food and stores for several more weeks at sea. Que[s]
tion: Should he hold her on station in the area? Comin[g]
back to Guam could waste valuable time, depending o[n]
where the maddeningly unnamed crisis was happening.

It would take days to get *Oklahoma City* ready to sai[l]
One of her condensers was in pieces while they traced [a]
stubborn seawater leak. She'd been operating with th[e]
problem for a couple of weeks, and he'd finally allowed th[e]
boat's crew to try and find and fix it here in Guam. If the[y]
didn't, it might mean repairs back at Pearl, and he didn[']
want to lose a boat for an extended period.

He needed her skipper's best guess on how close the[y]
were to fixing it. Should they press on, or just slap it bac[k]
together so they could get under way quickly? It would b[e]
nice to know just how urgent the crisis was, not that they'[d]
told him.

North Dakota and *North Carolina* were in the be[st]
shape, although both had people off the boat for leave an[d]
training. He could send those two out by tomorrow, if th[e]
need was pressing.

The car was waiting for him in the cool darkness. I[n]
spite of the hour, it was still a little muggy. Early spring i[n]
Guam meant afternoon temperatures in the eighties.

The drive to squadron headquarters gave him time t[o]
ask himself the real question. What was the crisis? Wher[e]
were his boats needed? What was the timeline?

Operations had returned to almost peacetime levels following the Littoral Alliance war. To his knowledge, the region was quiet. Were the Chinese out for revenge? A land attack mission might require his subs to carry Tomahawk missiles. Those had to be prepped and loaded in port. The CNO knew that, of course, and would give him as much warning as security allowed.

Simonis and the Navy lived and breathed security and classification. The fleet had secrets that had to be protected. He understood that. But at times like this, an unspecified contingency limited his boats' ability to prepare for what could be a life-or-death situation.

He remembered Commander Mitchell, and the man's personal connection to the national security advisor. If Simonis asked him to, Mitchell could send a query to Washington. It was all back-channel stuff, and frankly distasteful, but the squadron commander balanced his need for information against the gravity of the offense: bypassing the chain of command.

By the time the car had arrived at squadron headquarters, he'd decided against using Mitchell to send a message—for the moment.

6 April 2017
2000 Local Time
Central Bureau of Investigation, Hyderabad Zone Office
Hyderabad, India

"I have just a few more questions about your timeline, Mr. Petrov."

"That's *Captain* Petrov, and you said we were finished working on that."

Agent Sushma Goyal was apologetic, but insistent. "I thought so, too, until I sent it to our headquarters in New Delhi. Special Director Thapar wanted to know more about your visit to the torpedo shop, and about the other Russian nationals you interviewed while you were attempting to gather more information on Mr. Orlav. He's especially interested in a Mr. Anton Kulik. Do you have any more information on him, and his interest in Indian nuclear weapons?"

While Petrov argued with Goyal, Samant stood and paced around the conference room, trying to walk off the frustration he felt. He'd watched the leaders of the Indian government receive the news that a conspiracy within the government and the navy was about to launch an attack on China that would likely trigger a nuclear war. They had photographic evidence of bootleg nuclear weapons present at the Vizag naval base, about to be loaded on a nuclear submarine. At the end of the teleconference, they'd heard President Handa assure President Myles and Ambassador Eldridge that CBI would take swift action to arrest the conspirators and confirm their control of *Chakra*.

After they broke the connection, Petrov and Samant had almost collapsed with exhaustion. More treatment for Petrov's injuries had been followed by an early meal and bed, Samant feeling completely safe for the first time in he couldn't remember how long.

Neither slept well. Petrov couldn't find a comfortable position, and Samant's dreams were troubled, full of him pleading to Gautama on the lake for wisdom or enlightenment, but always finding the statue of Buddha out of reach, facing away from him.

Shereen Massoud had awakened them at seven A.M., but she had no knowledge of events at the Vizag dockyard. Consul General Olson had joined them at breakfast, and informed them, with some puzzlement, that as far as he knew, no arrests had been made, and nothing had been done about *Chakra*. However, a CBI car was due to arrive at 0830 to pick them up. The local zone office wanted more details about Dhankhar and his associates, to help speed the investigation.

"They can come here," Petrov had insisted.

"It's to be a short meeting, and then they'll take you to the airport to get you back to Vizag. So, it does make some sense for them to come get you. However, even though we are a bit shorthanded," Olson replied, "I can spare a Marine to accompany you as your bodyguard should there be any trouble."

"You mean, if they try to arrest us," Samant added.

Olson shook his head sharply. "No. The head of the CBI told me personally this morning that all charges have been dropped. The Marine is going along just in case one of the conspirators tries something. CBI has even granted permission for him to be armed—that is extraordinarily unusual, gentlemen."

Petrov slumped. "I'd hoped we were done with that possibility."

"We will be, once the CBI rounds them up, which is why we need you to go over there and answer their questions. Now, neither of you are U.S. citizens, and I can't force you to go, but we'd be grateful if you did, and we'll do our best to protect you while you're doing it."

Olson had made a good case, and they'd agreed to go. The car had picked them up promptly. An officious but polite Agent Goyal and two husky-looking agents loaded Petrov, Samant, and a Marine corporal in civilian clothes named Matthews quickly into an SUV and headed to the Hyderabad Zone headquarters, in charge not just of Hyderabad, but the states of Andhra Pradesh and Karnataka.

Goyal's boss had met them, showed the three to a well-appointed conference room, offered them tea, and then left "to coordinate the investigation."

For the rest of the morning, Goyal and other agents had thoroughly debriefed the two submariners, with every answer written down, correlated, and examined for inconsistencies or inaccuracies. Repeated questions from the two about the status of *Chakra* and the conspirators were always met with the same answer: "It is all under control everything is being done properly." Neither Petrov nor Samant was reassured.

They broke for lunch, which was too spicy for Petrov, but while they were eating, Agent Goyal's boss, Joint Director Chaudhari, returned. "I understand you've been asking about the status of the submarine and Vice Admiral Dhankhar. I want to reassure you that we are moving with all possible speed to regain control of *Chakra* and apprehend the conspirators."

"Why the delay?" asked Petrov bluntly. "It should have happened this morning, or even last night."

Chaudhari disagreed. "True, there is a MARCOS unit stationed at the Vizag naval base." Samant was nodding agreement, and the joint director explained to Petrov, "It stands for Marine Commandos, like the Russian Spetsnaz troops or American SEALS. They could certainly perform the task, but given the concerns about the extent of the conspiracy, we were worried that using them would alert our targets. Special Director Thapar thought it best to use a unit that we could be virtually certain was reliable—not from this region, and not from the navy. An air force Garud commando unit is en route from Jodhpur. The Garud force is responsible for airbase security, and have extensive anti-terrorism training."

Samant exploded. "That's in Rajasthan, the other side of the country! Surely there was something closer."

"Special Director Thapar made the selection, based on the unit's readiness level," the joint director replied testily.

"And we're supposed to be there to provide technical support when the commandos take control of the submarine," Petrov added. "Why are we still here when you finished your questions this morning?"

"Relax," Chaudhari soothed. "An army helicopter is waiting to take you straight to Vizag as soon as we are finished here. It's a two-hour flight, but there's no rush. The

Garud force isn't scheduled to land until almost midnight. They'll begin preparations immediately, and we'll execute the raid at four or five o'clock tomorrow morning. We can get things tidied up here and then we will all go to the Visakhapatnam naval base together. I understand Consul General Olson himself will go with us, as an observer."

"But you've got Dhankhar identified as the leader, and Orlav as the technician. Just arrest those two. Without them, the plan falls apart."

Goyal shook his head, smiling, almost patronizing. "Their plan has already failed. That sub will never leave the pier. What we have to do now is arrest not just the leader and his henchman, but all the supporters of this conspiracy as well. We are watching the admiral and closely monitoring his communications. That will lead us to the other plotters. And we have eyes on the torpedo shop.

"Special Director Thapar has put some of his best men into the yard. They are watching everything. They report furious activity, but that the submarine won't be ready to sail until tomorrow morning, which matches your information, I might add."

"What if . . ." Petrov began, but Goyal interrupted him. "We also have people watching all the exits of the shipyard, and Dhankhar's house as well. There's a tracker on his car, and we've flagged his bank accounts and credit cards. He's helping us more by being temporarily free than if he was behind bars."

They'd started again after lunch, this time using the information from Petrov and Samant to construct a timeline of their own actions, and what they could reconstruct of the plot. "This will help us in our interrogation of the suspects, as well as suggesting places and times to concentrate our efforts."

Petrov kept glancing at his watch and mentally adding two hours to it. Samant seemed mesmerized by the wall clock. Corporal Matthews used his cell phone to make periodic reports to the consulate. He stayed in the room with his two charges, but well in the background.

Dinnertime came, and after another meal Goyal's questions about the timeline continued, fueled by a stream of messages from New Delhi. How were the two able to evade shipyard security?

Then they received a question from the captain leading the Garud detachment. How stable were the nuclear devices? Could the torpedoes be rigged with a suicide switch? After the bombs were secured, how should they be handled?

Those were really the kind of questions Orlav was qualified to answer, but Petrov did his best. No Indian nuclear expert could be contacted, Goyal explained, until after they'd been cleared of involvement in the plot. That might not be in time for the raid tomorrow morning.

Petrov began drawing up a checklist, based on what safety regulations he could remember from his own days in the navy. They were Russian weapons, after all. He still kept one eye on the clock. Earlier in the day, there had been talk of a nap for the still-fatigued pair before the flight to Vizag. That had been reduced to sleeping aboard the helicopter, and now that might have to be deferred if he couldn't finish the procedures . . .

The door burst open, surprising them all. Matthews, half dozing in the corner, was suddenly on his feet, weapon out in a shooter's stance. He quickly pointed the weapon up, though, when the first person through the door was a civilian, and unarmed.

Goyal leapt to his feet. "Director Kumar!" Surprise filled his exclamation, and he started to ask a question, but stopped, frozen in shock when President Handa followed the director into the room. Others, including Chaudhari, followed Handa into the room.

Matthews's weapon was out of sight even more quickly

than he'd drawn it, and the Marine had braced. Even Petrov had joined Samant in coming to attention. Handa nodded to them all, and motioned for them to relax.

Ignoring Goyal, the president walked over to Samant and offered his hand. "Captain Girish Samant, I wish to thank you personally for your courage and loyalty. You've already done our country a great service, and may have saved India from a horrible fate." After shaking hands with Samant, he turned to Petrov. "India is also grateful to you, Captain Petrov. How are your injuries?"

The Russian shrugged automatically, then winced. "I'm sorry, sir, but they're only a nuisance."

Shaking Petrov's hand, the president answered, "You risked your life in the service of my country. There will always be a place for you here in India." He looked over to Kumar and nodded.

The director of the CBI faced Agent Goyal, still dumbstruck. "Report!"

Almost stammering, the agent explained, "We have been drawing up safety procedures for the Garud force after they have secured the nuclear weapons . . ."

Kumar held up a hand, stopping Goyal in midword. "Plans have changed. The Garud force is going to be too late."

"What?" Samant wasn't sure if he'd said it first, or Goyal, or Petrov, but their exclamations were almost identical.

Handa said, "We should go," and turned to leave.

Kumar said, "Captain Petrov and Captain Samant, please come with us now." When Petrov gestured toward their escort, Kumar added, "And him, as well. Consul General Olson will join us at the airport."

They were already walking, with Handa in front and setting a fast pace. Workers in the corridors stopped, wide-eyed, and then got out of the way as the procession passed.

Kumar explained, "The president's jet is waiting for us.

Luckily we were already en route here. Once airborne, we should be in Vizag in about forty-five minutes, say midnight. By then the reaction force will be ready to move, but they won't wait for us."

Samant, keeping pace to one side of Kumar, was confused, and asked, "What about the Garud commandos? The raid tomorrow morning?"

"We can't wait," Kumar answered. "We have absolutely no idea what's going on at the shipyard. If they've been tipped off . . ."

They'd already hurried down two sets of stairs, and almost burst out of the front doors. A line of cars was waiting, an armored car at each end of the convoy. Kumar urged the three into one car, and followed them in.

As he belted in, Samant asked Kumar, "How? Who would do that? What about the agents . . ."

"You probably heard that Thapar had placed agents at the Vizag shipyard, that they had Dhankhar, Orlav, and the submarine under close surveillance."

"Yes."

Kumar scowled. He spat out, "Special Director Ijay Thapar is nowhere to be found." He paused a moment, then explained, "It was by pure luck that we discovered the facade. While we were en route here, I asked our communications officer to pipe in the radio circuit the agents were using to coordinate surveillance of the shipyard. Easier than jogging Thapar's elbow with constant demands for updates. Imagine our surprise when we couldn't find the circuit, and even more when the Vizag office said they knew nothing about any surveillance of the shipyard."

"Thapar lied," Petrov concluded.

"And fooled us into thinking we had the plotters in a bottle, ready to be scooped up at our leisure," Kumar continued. "Worse still, he's undoubtedly warned Dhankhar, and if we find any of them, or *Chakra*, still at the shipyard, it will be a miracle."

Sirens howling, the convoy had made good progress

through the streets of Hyderabad, and drove through the airport gates at nearly full speed.

"But what about the Garud force?" Samant asked.

Kumar held up his hand as the car came to a stop. Quickly unbuckling, they followed Handa and the others up the boarding ladder into the president's aircraft, a Boeing 737, engines idling.

They hurried up the stairs after the director, and saw Handa disappearing as he headed toward the front of the plane. "The president's private office is forward. We can sit back here." Kumar gestured toward a luxurious lounge, plush leather seats lining each side. A conference table farther aft was isolated by an etched-glass partition. Samant recognized the subject, depicting the three principal Hindu gods, Vishnu, Shiva, and Shakti, wielding celestial weapons against an army of demons.

Once they were settled, Kumar explained, "Just before we landed here, I ordered, on President Handa's authority, the Quick Reaction force from the Visakhapatnam Police to arrest Dhankhar and Orlav, and take control of *Chakra*. They're preparing right now. They have no experience with naval vessels, but then again, neither does the Garud force." Kumar made another face as he remembered Thapar's deception.

Samant glanced at his watch. It was 2250. Kumar said, "The team leader said they'd be ready to move a little after twenty-three forty-five. Our pilot's using full throttle, but there's no way we'll get to Vizag before they are ready to move, and I won't make them wait. We've lost too much time already."

"What do you want us to do?" Petrov said, gesturing to Samant and himself.

"We will need you to identify the devices, as well as your experience with submarine systems. Captain Samant, it's likely you will have to take command of *Chakra* again, since we will be taking Jain and his officers into custody."

Samant nodded sadly. He hadn't really thought much

about Jain's role, but he must be deeply involved. And *Chakra*'s reactor was certainly critical. Even if the conspirators did not sabotage the boat, somebody had to keep the plant running smoothly.

Together with Petrov, he began drawing up a new list.

6 April 2017
2230 Local Time
National Highway 39, Jeypore Road

There was a fair amount of traffic, but not enough to slow him down. Admiral Dhankhar checked his GPS. The next town was Chatuva, barely more than a cluster of buildings lining each side of the road. He didn't need to stop.

The old blue Outlander was running smoothly enough, and the weather was cooperating. His biggest worry wasn't the authorities. He was already a hundred kilometers northwest of Vizag, and the chance of them stopping a car registered to someone who didn't exist was virtually nil. What really concerned him was his fatigue. He'd planned to make it as far as Raipur tonight, but that would mean driving until about four in the morning.

He'd gotten a late start. Jain had shaken the admiral's hand for the last time at 2110, according to Dhankhar's watch, then hurried aboard *Chakra* as the shipyard workers waited to pull in the brow and take in the mooring lines. It had taken every bit of control Dhankhar possessed to appear calm and pleased to see the captain off. The authorities could show up at any second, but Jain could not know that this wasn't an officially sanctioned mission, approved by "the highest levels of the government," as Dhankhar had assured him.

The appearance of the authorities would not only end Vajra, but destroy Jain's trust in him, and that was suddenly a very important thing. He would somehow explain the deception when Jain returned. By then, the government would be celebrating the victory over Pakistan and it would all be moot.

He didn't have any special words for Jain, just the traditional "Good luck and good hunting." He hardly remembered what Jain had said in return, probably something about not letting him down.

Dhankhar had watched the sub leave the pier and fade into the darkness. In accordance with his orders, Jain would submerge the instant there was enough water under his keel and head off at high speed, about forty-five minutes from now, but that was out of the admiral's hands.

Leaving the pier, the admiral had walked a few blocks to where he'd left the car. He found it earlier, right where it was supposed to be, and put a few personal items inside.

Once inside the car, he changed into civilian clothes and packed his uniform and identification into a duffel bag. His new documents and driver's license described him as a retired army officer. The car was, of course, registered in the new name.

He drove out of the shipyard without incident, and headed northwest. It was a three-day drive to Amritsar, on the northwest border, but there was a bungalow reserved for him under another false name, and for the next three days, he'd be on the road.

As he drove, Dhankhar could feel the tension draining away. He'd done it—Vajra was under way. There was more than two weeks of waiting before it would be completed, but *Chakra* was on her way. He suddenly yawned, and realized how much he'd been depending on adrenaline to keep going. Fatigue was going to be an issue, but he'd brought a thermos of tea. He'd be fine.

14

Smoke and Mirrors

7 April 2017
0000 Local Time
INS *Circars*, Eastern Naval Command Headquarters
Visakhapatnam, India

The door burst open as six men in SWAT gear poured into the room, weapons at the ready. Their forced entry was unnecessary; the room was empty. The squad leader signaled for his men to disperse and make a thorough search. After the all-clear was given, a CBI agent entered, turned on the lights, and made his own inspection. The desk light was still on, as if the occupant had only stepped away for a moment. The desktop itself was immaculate, and the admiral's in-box was empty. All the paperwork had been moved neatly into the out-box. Disappointed, he sighed. The agent wasn't surprised that Dhankhar was gone; by all accounts the admiral was a very smart man. It just meant that his job was going to be a whole lot harder.

"This is Agent Devan," he said into his radio. "The suspect is not here. The office is empty. I'm about to begin an investigation of the office and will check the computer hard drive as well, but I'm not confident I'll find much. Please inform Director Kumar."

Devan turned to the SWAT team squad leader. "Begin a methodical search of the building. I doubt Admiral

Dhankhar is here, but we must know for certain. Check in every half hour."

The SWAT team departed, joining the rest of the law enforcement and military police personnel in securing and searching the Eastern Naval Command headquarters. The CBI agent knelt down next to the admiral's chair and examined the desk. All the drawers were unlocked. They contained nothing unusual, just mundane office supplies and documents that would be collected in due course. No thumb drives or external hard drives were present, nor were there any cell phones or other electronic devices. A check of the desk's structure showed there weren't any hidden compartments. The two filing cabinets were just like the desk: impeccably kept and full of routine paperwork and reports. There was nothing in the trash can.

Returning to the desk, Devan started up Dhankhar's computer and inserted a thumb drive in one of the USB ports. Moments later he had recovered the network access password and logged in. Checking the e-mail folder, he found it empty, no surprises there. But there weren't any files stored on Dhankhar's virtual drive or the hard drive either. Everything was gone. He used a quick recovery application to see if any files had been recently deleted, still nothing. Annoyed and frustrated, Devan removed the thumb drive and shut down the machine. The computer forensics team would have to tackle this one. The squawk of his radio pulled his attention away from his futile investigation; the SWAT team reported in that the perimeter was secure and that a room-to-room search of the building had begun.

The CBI agent acknowledged the report and left to supervise the search of the building. He was certain they'd find no trace of the admiral here. Silently, he hoped the other teams would have better luck. If not, India was a big country; it would take a long time to search just the cities and larger villages. And then there were the countless smaller villages near the borders, particularly with Pakistan, that national law enforcement rarely visited. If Dhankhar had decided to go to ground, they might never find him.

7 April 2017
0030 Local Time
Torpedo Shop 2
Naval Shipyard
Visakhapatnam, India

Samant and Petrov waited impatiently for the military police and explosive ordnance people to finish their detailed inspection of the torpedo shop. No one expected any booby traps, but Director Kumar wasn't taking any chances. None of them would be allowed into the workshop until the security detachment said it was safe. Exasperated by his forced inactivity, Samant wandered about the parking lot. His thoughts were racing, as he desperately tried to think of a way to save his former shipmates; his chest still ached from seeing the empty pier as they drove in. Now the whole world would be looking for *Chakra*, undoubtedly with orders to shoot to kill, and there was absolutely nothing he could do to help them. Samant couldn't recall a time when he felt more helpless.

"Gentlemen," shouted Kumar. "The workshop has been cleared for us to enter."

"Finally," Petrov grumbled, and headed quickly into the building. Samant followed close behind.

Petrov found it a little bizarre being back in the torpedo workshop, this time surrounded by civilian and military police officials. It looked much as it did the night he and Samant snuck in. Only this time, the secure vault doors were open and there wasn't a torpedo in sight. The disappointment felt by all was palpable.

"It would appear they left in good order," remarked Kumar scathingly. The worktables were littered with tools, but no documents were visible. The wooden shipping crates had been removed; even Orlav's makeshift bed was gone. "They obviously had sufficient opportunity to get rid of anything with forensic value. All that time we had, wasted! I'll personally make Thapar pay for his treachery!"

Turning to his agents, he ordered, "I want this building thoroughly searched! Every square centimeter is to be gone over—twice! Bring anything, however trivial, to the forensics team for examination."

Samant walked inside the vault. It was big enough to hold six torpedo trolleys and their payloads. Inspecting the floor, he saw nothing to indicate just how many weapons had been stored in the vault. They'd have to assume that five weapons had been moved to *Chakra*.

Wait! Naval personnel would have had to load the weapons onto the boat. Rushing over to Kumar, Samant exclaimed, "Director, have any of your people spoken to Captain Narahari Mitra? He's the shipyard commanding officer, he should be able to tell us how many weapons were loaded and when *Chakra* left port."

Kumar quickly raised his radio and passed on to the investigation team at the pier Samant's questions. While he waited for their response, the director ordered all teams to report in. The news was not encouraging. Dhankhar was nowhere to be found. His office and quarters were empty. The CBI agent in charge of each team said the same thing: Everything was neat and tidy. There was no indication that the admiral had been in any hurry when he departed. After several minutes, the pier team reported in.

"Captain Mitra has been questioned," Kumar told Samant and Petrov. "He confirms that five weapons were loaded early yesterday evening, and that *Chakra* set sail at about 2115—over three hours ago. He also said the deployment orders were delivered by Vice Admiral Dhankhar personally."

Samant shook his head. "Jain's undoubtedly gone deep and ordered a flank bell by now, putting as much distance between *Chakra* and Vizag as possible. At least, that's what I would do. Even if we alerted the patrol squadron at INS *Rajali* immediately, it would be another hour, maybe two, before they could even hope to have a maritime patrol aircraft in the rough vicinity. That puts her about two hundred miles out into the Bay of Bengal."

"That's a very large area for a single patrol plane to cover," remarked Petrov. "And if Jain is smart enough to drop down to a moderate tactical speed, he'll be very hard to find. Even for a new U.S. P-8 Poseidon aircraft."

"He's that smart. I trained him." Samant's face showed a mixture of pride and regret.

"We can sortie the fleet! Chase him down!" Kumar exclaimed.

Both Samant and Petrov smirked at the naive comment. "That wouldn't help. In fact, all that extra noise in the water would only make it easier for Jain to get away," Samant grunted. "No, the only assets we have that even have a chance of catching him right now are aircraft. But, as Aleks has already said, the odds are not good."

"What if Jain has been deceived? You've said he was impressionable, Girish. You could send out radio messages with the truth. Tell him about Dhankhar's lies, and order him to return to base," suggested Petrov.

Samant shrugged. "We certainly need to try that, Aleks. But I fear his orders will address that contingency. If he stays deep, and I suspect he will, only a VLF radio system can reach him, and the regular maintenance on the transmitter at INS *Kattabomman* hasn't been completed yet."

A deep scowl popped on Petrov's face. "I know about that project, there are several Russian technicians supporting it. That work should have been finished some time ago, who's in charge of that effort?" he grumbled in frustration.

Samant's expression was one of utter amazement. Petrov saw the "Duh" look on his friend's face, winced, and rubbed his brow. "Of course. Dhankhar. I knew that."

"Then the situation is hopeless!" Kumar moaned.

"Not hopeless, at least not yet," replied Samant with stern determination. "But we do need to ask for assistance. Aleks?"

Petrov nodded, took out his cell phone, and punched a few buttons. Raising the phone to his ear, he looked at the CBI director and explained, "It's times like this when one learns to appreciate friends in high places."

It took but a moment for the call to go through; the recipient answered quickly. "Dr. Patterson, this is Aleks Petrov. I have some bad news."

6 April 2017
1600 EST
The Oval Office, the White House
Washington, D.C.

Joanna Patterson didn't respond to Evangeline McDowell's greeting. It was questionable whether she even heard it. Marching deliberately, Patterson thrust her finger toward the door, and the Secret Service agent opened it without blinking. He'd been warned to admit the national security advisor without delay. Bursting into the Oval Office, she could see Secretary of State Lloyd speaking with the president. Joanna didn't care what they were talking about, and didn't even greet her boss.

"*Chakra*'s gone, and Dhankhar has escaped," she announced pointedly.

"WHAT!?" howled Lloyd. Myles let out a groan and cradled his face in his hands.

"How in God's name did the Indians botch it so badly? I thought we gave them plenty of warning!" Lloyd complained.

"Apparently the number-two man at the Indian Central Bureau of Investigation was in on the conspiracy. It looks like he warned Dhankhar and then stalled the investigation long enough for the admiral and the boat to disappear. *Chakra* set sail almost four hours ago with the five nuclear-armed torpedoes on board," answered Patterson.

"Joanna, who told you this?" asked a strained Myles.

"Alex Petrov just called me from the shipyard. They just executed the raid to seize the sub and arrest Dhankhar. Both were gone, Orlav as well. Petrov and Samant are at the torpedo workshop with the CBI director right now."

"I see. What do the Indians intend to do?"

"There really isn't much they can do, Mr. President. They'll scramble maritime patrol aircraft, but the odds aren't in their favor. Unless *Chakra*'s new captain does something stupid, an Akula-class boat has the advantage. And Samant has said he trained the man well, so we have to assume he won't do something stupid," replied Joanna grimly.

Myles rose and walked around his desk, struggling to come to grips with the nightmare unfolding before them, the nightmare they had tried so hard to prevent. Taking a deep breath and straightening himself, he laid the obvious next question on his advisors. "All right, what do we do now?"

"The cat's out of the bag, Mr. President. We have to tell the Chinese," sighed Lloyd.

Joanna nodded. "I concur with the secretary of state, Mr. President."

The president began pacing, considering his advisors' recommendation. There really wasn't a choice. "Agreed," he said finally. "And we'll have to inform the Russians as well. But isn't there something we can do to be more pro-active? I don't like the idea of warning the Chinese and then just watching."

"We should speak with the Littoral Alliance, get them involved. They have good ASW forces, and it would be in their interest to assist in hunting down *Chakra*," Lloyd suggested.

Myles nodded his head, thinking.

"The best platform to hunt down a submarine is another submarine, Mr. President," offered Joanna. "*We* have the most capable boats in theater at Guam."

"Squadron Fifteen," affirmed Myles.

"Yes, sir."

Lloyd was visibly unhappy with Patterson's idea and voiced his objection. "But Joanna, if *Chakra* is bent on attacking Chinese ports, then she'll be entering Chinese waters. Our boats would have to go into those same territorial waters to chase them. What makes you think the Chinese will tolerate the presence of our subs?"

"The Chinese know we have the best submarines, and they know what it's going to take to find and stop *Chakra*. They won't like it, not one bit, and they'll likely complain, but that doesn't change the fact that we substantially boost their chances of preventing a nuclear warhead from going off in one or more of their ports. Furthermore, if the Chinese do detect one of our subs, it doesn't sound like an Akula; you can tell the difference."

Myles paused; both Patterson and Lloyd had valid arguments. The president wasn't thrilled with the idea of putting U.S. military personnel directly on the firing line again, particularly the submarines of Squadron Fifteen that had borne the brunt of the war. Still, the odds of stopping the rogue Indian submarine were considerably better with the U.S. submarines involved. And offering to send America's best had political capital of its own. It didn't take long for Myles to come to a decision.

"All right, here's what we're going to do. Andy, I need you to get the Chinese ambassador here as soon as you can. It's my job to deliver the bad news, and make the pitch for our assistance, Joanna, you'll help me with that. Andy, then contact Foreign Secretary Jadeja and let him know what we're doing."

Lloyd opened his mouth to protest, but Myles cut him off.

"Yes, I know, this will be the second time we've gone around the Indian ambassador. It can't be helped . . . I'll personally apologize when this crisis is over, okay? Then I want you to contact the Russian ambassador and tell them what we're up to. We need to keep them in the loop. Finally, set up a meeting with the Littoral Alliance for Joanna, after she's helped me with the Chinese ambassador." Lloyd nodded tightly, acknowledging his orders.

Joanna sighed. "Up until now, the plot and everything connected with it has been kept secret, to avoid tipping our hand. Now, the conspirators in India appear to have been tipped off. At least two are on the run, and the Indian government is trying to recall the boat, and failing that, tracking it down and sinking it. Is there any more reason for strict secrecy?"

"You mean, like the massive embarrassment the Indian and Russian governments would suffer, and the possible panic and chaos it could trigger in China? Those reasons?" Myles was smiling, but it disappeared quickly. "If the Indians could have scooped up the conspirators before *Chakra* had sailed, the first time the world would have heard of the plot would have been when we issued a joint press release."

Myles continued. "The Chinese will keep this close, but we have to assume that telling the entire Littoral Alliance means news will eventually leak out, and then there will be hell to pay. All we can do is find and kill *Chakra* as quickly as possible. I'll send my communications people to your staff to get briefed, and they can get started on preparing our official response.

"Joanna, your first task is to run out of this room and call Simonis's staff. Set up a VTC for you to brief the commodore and his submarine captains, and tell them what they need to do. We've kept *most* of them in the dark long enough. You can brief the CNO after you've scheduled the videoconference."

"Yes, Mr. President."

"All right, then, let's get to it people! We have a wayward boat to catch."

7 April 2017
0430 Local Time
Squadron Fifteen Commander's Residence
Naval Base Guam

___

The nagging electronic buzz dragged him to consciousness. For the second time that night, the secure phone was ringing. Simonis got out of bed and slowly shuffled to the phone on the other side of the bedroom. Blinking sleep from his eyes, he picked up the handset. "Simonis," he yawned.

"Commodore, Ops, sorry to wake you, sir, but Dr. Patterson just called. She wants a secure VTC with you and the available sub skippers in one hour."

Simonis looked at his wristwatch and grunted. It hadn't been nine hours since COMSUBPAC issued the warning order. "Understood. Did she even give you a clue as to what this is about, Rich?"

"No, sir. She seemed to be in a big hurry and only said it was a high-priority mission that would involve sortieing the entire squadron. She promised a full explanation during the VTC."

"Very well. Call Mitchell, Dobson, and Nevens and have them report to the squadron conference room in forty-five minutes. Then send a flash precedence message to *Texas* to come to PD and link in; I want Pascovich in on this one," directed Simonis.

"Yes, sir. Do you want me to send a driver to pick you up?"

"No, I'll drive myself in. And make sure someone calls the CSO."

"He's next on my list, sir," replied Walker.

"Good. I'll be there in about twenty minutes."

Jerry hustled into the conference room only to find few people milling about. They were engaged in idle chatter, waiting for the VTC to begin. Taking a quick look around the room, Jerry was surprised not to see Simonis already in his seat. Dropping his cover and notebook onto one of the tables, Jerry made a beeline for the coffee mess. As he poured himself a cup, he caught the operations officer's eye. Jerry's facial expression silently asked the question, "What the hell is going on?"

Walker only shook his head and shrugged. He didn't know. *Great. I hope this doesn't have anything to do with my meeting with Samant,* thought Jerry. But his gut told him otherwise.

Sipping his coffee, Jerry kept an eye on the door. It wasn't long before Scott Nevens and Bruce Dobson walked in along with a number of Squadron Fifteen staff members. Jerry greeted his fellow captains and joined in a speculative discussion about the second summons—he didn't share what little he knew or suspected. After a few minutes, Captain Charles Simonis and his Chief Staff Officer, Captain Glenn Jacobs, entered the conference room. The commodore swiftly scanned the space, locked eyes with Jerry, and motioned for him to break away and come over. Jerry politely excused himself and approached Simonis. The commodore didn't look happy.

"Yes, sir?" solicited Jerry.

"Captain, if you have any insights into this upcoming confab, I'd appreciate hearing them." The commodore was visibly frustrated. "I don't like being kept in the dark, Captain. There's been no hint of a problem in our AOR; SUBPAC's warning order came out of the blue. Now, we have this zero dark thirty videoconference with the national security advisor . . ."

"I think it may have something to do with the information provided by Captain Samant," Jerry volunteered. "I can't think of anything else going on in our theater that could have Dr. Patterson so anxious."

"Do you really believe this Indian nuclear conspiracy theory?" asked Simonis. The tone of his voice betrayed his skepticism.

"I trust Alex Petrov, Commodore, implicitly. He's a good man, and a damn fine submariner. If he was sufficiently alarmed about this 'conspiracy theory' to contact us, covertly, then I think we should be worried."

"But what about this Indian captain?" Simonis challenged. "What evidence do we have that he's telling us the truth?"

Jerry glanced around the room and spoke with a lowered voice. "Sir, as I said when I got back from D.C., there *is* evidence to support Samant's claims, but I'm not at liberty to discuss it with you."

Simonis's jaw tightened. The commodore had been more than a little miffed when Jerry respectfully declined to discuss the evidence earlier, as it was in a special access program that Simonis wasn't cleared for. The commodore completely agreed with the concept of compartmenting sensitive information, but in this case, he believed he had a legitimate "need to know."

"But Captain Samant seemed genuinely concerned, sir," continued Jerry. "As for my impression of the man, he's a very good boat driver, and I can attest to the fact that he was a royal pain in the ass."

Simonis nodded. "Very well, Captain. I guess we'll just have to wait for Dr. Patterson to enlighten us."

"Commodore," called out Jacobs, interrupting the conversation. "We have *Texas* up on the secure video link."

Jerry looked up at the two large screens. On the left was Ian Pascovich, commanding officer of USS *Texas*. On the right was the White House Situation Room. An army lieutenant colonel suddenly came into view and hit the mike button. "Squadron Fifteen, stand by, Dr. Patterson will be here shortly."

"Everyone to your seats, but remain standing," barked Simonis. There was a brief but chaotic shuffle as the occupants quickly moved to their respective chairs, but soon all was quiet. As the national security advisor came into view, Simonis shouted, "Attention on deck!"

Patterson bowed slightly, acknowledging the honor. Jerry thought she looked a little ragged. "Please be seated," she said with a tired voice.

"Commodore, I must first apologize for the early wake-up," began Patterson. "But I'm afraid it couldn't be helped. We have a very serious situation on our hands."

"I have all four submarine commanding officers on line, Dr. Patterson. What do you need Squadron Fifteen to do?"

Joanna smiled faintly. "Let me get straight to the point, Captain Simonis. The Indian Akula SSN, *Chakra*, has gone rogue. She left port without authorization a little over four hours ago. She's armed with five modified torpedoes, each fitted with a one-hundred-fifty-kiloton nuclear weapon. Her mission is to fire those torpedoes into five of China's biggest and busiest ports. The apparent goal is to cripple China economically and politically. This operation is part of a high-level military conspiracy that has been initiated without the consent of the Indian government."

Patterson paused while the audience in Guam struggled with her message. Simonis was flabbergasted, his mouth hanging open in amazement. Everyone else, including Jerry, was just as shocked, if not more so. Not only was Samant's plot real, but it was in motion.

"We don't know exactly which ports are on the target list, but we do have some data that suggests no more than ten were considered. The intelligence community is currently working on a best estimate based on overall port capacity and the potential for collateral damage. We believe the desire of those running this conspiracy is to maximize both."

"Dr. Patterson," interrupted Simonis. "What are the Indians doing about this rogue submarine?"

Joanna shook her head. "They're doing everything they can, which unfortunately isn't much. The Indian government is trying to call her back, sending out radio messages over all available communication channels, but there is little hope this will do anything. *Chakra*'s too quiet and has too big a head start for the Indian fleet to do anything useful.

"Maritime patrol aircraft are being scrambled, but their best ASW squadron, the one with the P-8 aircraft, was placed in an unscheduled maintenance stand-down last week. Apparently, the Eastern Naval Commander was a key player of the conspiracy and he has severely degraded the ASW capability of his fleet. The best the Indian Navy can do is to get a couple of old Bear F patrol planes out into the Bay of Bengal in about an hour."

"How soon do you need me to sortie my boats, ma'am?"

"The president wants as many submarines out there as you can, as fast as you can," Joanna replied. "The one advantage we have is that you have less distance to cover, and if you can establish several patrol barriers near the most likely ports before she gets there, we have a reasonable chance of finding *Chakra*."

"And my orders?" asked Simonis hesitantly.

"You are to sink *Chakra*, Commodore. Preferably before she fires any nuclear-armed torpedoes."

Simonis seemed to relax a little. "I can get two subs out before the end of the day. *Texas* is currently at sea, and she'll reverse course as soon as we're done here."

Jerry glanced at the left-hand screen. Pascovich was already signaling his XO to bring her about.

"Unfortunately, it will be at least three days before we can complete the repairs to *Oklahoma City*," said Simonis.

"Then we should plan, at least initially, on only three patrol zones," Patterson concluded.

"Will I need to coordinate operations with any Littoral Alliance submarines?" Simonis looked wary.

Patterson shook her head vigorously. "No, I will be talking to the Littoral Alliance representatives within the next few hours. We will ask for surface ship and MPA support, but no submarines. There's too much ill will between China and the alliance and we can't risk their submarines getting in the way."

"That's good. We can work out a straightforward arrangement to keep their ships and aircraft away from my boats."

"You'll be doing the same with the PLAN," added Patterson.

Simonis stopped dead in his tracks. His expression was one of disbelief. He seemed unsure as to what he had heard. "Pardon me, Dr. Patterson. Did I hear you correctly; I need to coordinate operations with the Chinese Navy? Tell them where my boats are?"

"Yes, Commodore. The president already has an appointment with the Chinese ambassador and he will make a pitch for this course of action as the best way to stop *Chakra*. It's absolutely essential that we cooperate with them in this endeavor." Patterson's voice had taken on a stern tone.

"With all due respect, ma'am, that is insane! The Chinese are still trigger-happy from the war!" Simonis argued. "And even if you can work out some sort of arrangement, which I doubt, their performance during the war doesn't fill me with any confidence. They could very easily wander into one of our patrol areas, shoot any submarine contact they find first and maybe ask questions later!"

Jerry saw Joanna take a deep breath. There were deep furrows on her brow and her lips were tightly pursed. *Uh, oh,* he thought. He'd seen that look before.

"I understand your reservations, Commodore; in fact, the secretary of defense has voiced similar concerns. But the bigger picture requires us to work closely with the

PLAN. If we don't, and one or more Chinese ports gets wiped off the face of the earth, then we can look forward to *dozens* of nuclear explosions over China, India, and probably Pakistan. I don't think I need to explain what the implications of such a scenario are for the United States, do I?"

Patterson let her last point sink in before moving on. "Therefore, the president has decided that working with the Chinese is in our nation's best interest, and I suggest you act accordingly. Your squadron is the linchpin of our efforts to stop this insane plot. As such, your headquarters will be the primary command and control facility and you will have OPCON of any U.S. assets that may be assigned to this mission.

"Expect the intelligence estimate on the likely port targets and an analysis of *Chakra*'s probable avenue of approach within the hour. Please forward any personnel and technical support requirements up the chain of command. Rest assured you have the highest priority. Good luck, Commodore, and good hunting."

Before Simonis could say anything, Patterson got up and left the screen. Everyone in the Guam conference room was stunned. Pascovich's enlarged image on the left-hand screen echoed what everyone else was feeling—absolute astonishment. Silence fell on the conference room. No one at Squadron Fifteen dared to say a word.

15

Unpleasant News

6 April 2017
1730 Local Time
The White House
Washington, D.C.

It was 2:30 A.M. in New Delhi, but India's Foreign Secretary, Gopan Jadeja, was awake and in his office when Lloyd called, still digesting the news of the failed raid at Visakhapatnam. At first he was unhappy, even angry with the news that the U.S. intended to notify the Chinese of *Chakra*'s departure, but finally admitted that India's leadership was "distracted."

"President Handa has been trying to manage the news of the disastrous raid, as well as the investigation into the conspiracy. It's hard to know whom to trust. With the involvement of people like Vice Admiral Dankhar and Special Director Ijay Thapar, everyone in the government is now suspect. The president has acknowledged that we need to inform China, but wanted to wait. After all, it will take *Chakra* some time to get there."

"And every hour of delay increases the plot's chance of success," Lloyd countered.

"The navy has been mobilized." Jadeja bristled.

Lloyd was unimpressed. "It is unfortunate that there is so little they can do, in spite of their best efforts. *Chakra* is a very capable vessel. Because of the danger her mission puts us all in, the United States is using its naval ssets to find and stop *Chakra*, by whatever means necessary."

"What? Without coordinating with my government . . ."

"We are taking this action unilaterally," Lloyd said firmly. "Since *Chakra* has gone rogue, this is not an action against the Indian government, with whom the United States wishes to have the best possible relations."

Lloyd could hear the minister beginning to protest, but continued speaking. "In practicality, there is little the Indian Navy can do, especially once she enters the South China Sea. The only naval unit with the range to operate here is *Chakra* herself, and we both know her capabilities. If your P-8 aircraft can eventually be made operational, they would be welcome to join our own antisubmarine aircraft at Guam to help in the search."

Jadeja sighed. "You are correct, Mr. Secretary." After a short pause, he added sharply, "But, I'm afraid that's not good enough."

Lloyd, a little confused, replied, "The United States is willing to work with India in any way that facilitates stopping *Chakra*. We could rebroadcast the same message you are sending to the sub," he suggested.

"That's a good idea, but I had something else in mind," Jadeja answered. "We need a representative to be present."

Now perplexed, Secretary Lloyd said simply, "I don't understand."

"Most likely, someone, probably your navy, will have to sink *Chakra*. It is unlikely that everyone on the submarine is aware of the plot. Even as we agree that she must be stopped, we must also recognize that innocents will be killed, as well as the criminals that are carrying out the plan."

"It is unfortunate," Lloyd agreed.

"If this were an execution, there would be witnesses present. India requests that Captain Girish Samant be a witness to the events. As her former captain, he can provide valuable assitance, and should it become necessary to sink her, he can come back and tell us what happened."

"You make a strong case, Minister Jadeja," Lloyd admitted.

"I was an advocate for thirty-three years before I entered government service. Samant will have diplomatic status and plenipotentiary powers. There can be no question of his loyalty to India or his judgment."

"All right," Lloyd agreed. "The United States will allow Captain Girish Samant to act as India's liaison and representative during this crisis in matters relating to *Chakra*. The headquarters for the search is Guam."

"I will arrange transportation for the captain immediately, by the fastest possible means," Jadeja replied. "India is grateful for your agreement in this extremely difficult time. Captain Samant's presence will go far in assuaging any hard feelings that might arise between our countries."

"In that case, we will look forward to his arrival."

6 April 2017
1800 Local Time
The White House
Washington, D.C.

Ambassador Xi Ping didn't waste time contacting Beijing for instructions. A late-day summons to the White House without any warning, meant something unexpected, and probably bad news, not that he'd gotten any warning from back home.

Those turtles' sons back in Beijing were only interested in keeping their jobs. China's industry was in a shambles, her economy at a virtual standstill. People were hungry and dying of cold and disease, but the capital acted like the court of an ancient Chinese dynasty. Nothing but intrigue and backstabbing. They only knew what Xi told them, and if he didn't know what this new meeting was about, the Politburo would know even less.

Xi had been more than lucky to accept the posting as

China's new ambassador to America. It was his "reward" or faithful service in the intelligence arm during the Littoral Alliance war, which to him meant that the careerists nd sycophants wanted him well away from Beijing so he vouldn't pose a threat to their positions. He now realized ow fortunate he was to be clear of those toadies.

He'd reluctantly accepted, last November, and with just ix months in the post, was still getting used to the job. He'd net with President Myles several times, usually on business elating to the aftermath of the war or China's desperate rade situation. It was unsettling that the American president's Mandarin was better than Xi's English.

The trip from Cleveland Park through Washington usu-lly took fifteen minutes, but they were fighting rush-our congestion. Although there was no set time for the neeting, Xi was impatient. He wanted to find out what was mportant enough to summon him and the defense atta-hé with no notice and no explanation.

Milt Alvarez, the White House Chief of Staff, was wait-ng for them, and ushered the two to a conference room in he West Wing, then left to notify President Myles. Dr. Pat-erson, the National Security Advisor, was already there, vearing a serious expression. Americans liked to smile when hey greeted each other. It was almost a reflex. The best 'atterson could manage when she shook Xi's hand was rim and tight-lipped, and Xi began to worry.

She was well known for her work in addressing the mas-ive environmental cleanup under way in the South China ea. China didn't have a post equivalent to America's na-ional security advisor. With so many generals as mem-ers of the Politburo, there was no lack of military nowledge or experience in China's leadership. It said omething about the separation of the military and poli-ics in America that the president needed someone like that s his personal expert.

Patterson and the Chinese were still exchanging polite reetings when President Myles walked in, followed by a

U.S. Navy admiral. He was introduced to Xi as Admiral Hughes, the Chief of Naval Operations. So it was a military matter. That's why he'd been asked to bring Major General Yeng, the defense attaché. This was not going to be good.

Dr. Patterson walked over to the podium. "Mr. Ambassador, it is our unfortunate duty to inform China that an Indian nuclear attack submarine, INS *Chakra*, left the port of Visakhapatnam yesterday evening at twenty-one hundred their time, or noon today here." She was speaking carefully. Xi could tell she had rehearsed the speech. She was also speaking a little slowly, probably out of deference to his less-than-fluent English. She was watching him closely, and Xi nodded to her to continue.

She took a breath. "The Indian government, in cooperation with the United States and Russian Federation, discovered a conspiracy within the Indian military that was intent on attacking China because of its support to Pakistan. The Indian authorities tried to arrest the conspirators, but they escaped." She paused again, and Xi looked over to Major General Yeng, who looked worried, even alarmed.

Xi leaned close to Yeng and asked, "Is this *Chakra* the same nuclear submarine that India sent against us last year?" He spoke softly. There was at least two other Americans in the room that spoke Mandarin.

Yeng nodded. "She is a Russian-made Akula attack submarine, a very capable vessel. She sank more than her share of tankers and warships. She could hurt us, but I don't understand what the Indians think they could achieve with just a single submarine."

The Chinese ambassador turned back to face Dr. Patterson. "It is just this one submarine? Do you know their plan? What is their destination?"

Patterson swallowed hard and answered the ambassador. "They intend to approach five major Chinese ports and fire torpedoes fitted with nuclear warheads into each one."

Confused, Xi looked to Yeng again. The general's horrified expression told Xi he had understood Patterson's English.

glish correctly. Xi shook his head, as if to clear it, and looked at the other Americans. Myles sat grim-faced, and finally said, in Mandarin, "It is true, Mr. Ambassador."

Dr. Patterson said, "The Chinese ambassador to New Delhi will be briefed by India's President Handa and his top officials. That way, your nation's leaders will receive this extraordinary news from two different sources in two different countries."

Xi sat silently, still absorbing the news, and she continued, "The Indian plotters have fitted Russian one-hundred-and-fifty-kiloton nuclear warheads, obtained from an arms smuggler, to five torpedoes. The weapons will likely be set to go off at the same time, after all five have been fired into their target port. We have a list of potential targets that was uncovered during the investigation."

She handed Xi a single sheet of paper. It was a photocopy, and he could see the English names for ten ports, which were also some of China's largest cities. Hong Kong, Shanghai, Qingdao, others. His chest was tight. He found it hard to breathe. He had family in Shanghai. "And five of these ten cities will be attacked?"

"Yes, Mr. Ambassador." She seemed so calm, he noticed.

Yeng leaned toward him. "Can this be true?" he whispered.

The thought had not occurred to Xi. But what would the Americans gain by such an outrageous lie? *And the Indians are telling the same thing to our ambassador in New Delhi?* He shook his head again. "It's incredible. I don't want to believe this, but we will accept this as true, at least until we get more information."

Xi was starting to grasp the implications of the India plot. "Didn't the Indians understand that my country would retaliate after an attack like this?"

"If the conspirators' plan had remained secret, the first sign would have been the explosions. It is likely the submarine would have remained completely undetected. Nuclear forensics would show that the weapons were of Russian origin, exactly like the one that exploded in Kashmir."

Xi felt another shock, and confusion. "Kashmir was part of this plot?" he asked.

"Only accidentally," Patterson answered. "The schemers had acquired six weapons, but Kashmiri militants stole one, and accidentally set it off. Thanks to that accident the conspirators could blame Islamic terrorists for the nuclear attacks, and their Russian manufacture would clear India of any responsibility."

"How did the Indians get these bombs?"

Patterson explained what they had learned about the barge off the coast of Novaya Zemlya, showing Xi the same photographs the Russians had given them. She described her personal role, and how the analysis of the stolen warheads had allowed the U.S. to determine that the device that exploded, and by inference the others, was a Russian 150-kiloton missile warhead. "I'm sure your government sampled the debris cloud and made their own analysis."

Xi shrugged. "It's possible, but I would not expect to be shown such an analysis, if it existed."

"Ours was made public," she replied. "Hopefully comparing it with your own will help convince you that our warning is real."

She then described, without naming Petrov or Samant, how the Indian conspiracy had been suspected, then discovered, and finally confirmed. "President Myles informed the Indian government, including President Handa, of the plot two days ago. They acted to quash the plan, but failed to stop the submarine before it left port. We then discussed the situation and decided that we had to tell you immediately."

Xi did the math. "They knew about this for two days and they couldn't stop the submarine from leaving port? It doesn't sound like they were trying very hard."

"We don't have a complete picture of what happened be-

ween when we notified the Indian government and when
Chakra sailed," Patterson admitted.

Myles cut in. "The Indian *government*," he emphasized
the word, "was as horrified by the plotters' objective as we
were, as the Russians were when they learned of it, especially since their nationals were involved in smuggling the
weapons out of Russia and modifying them to fit in a Russian torpedo. Several high-level officials were undoubtedly involved, including an Indian Navy vice admiral, but
they operated outside of, and without the knowledge of, the
Indian government.

"Mr. Ambassador," Myles continued, "there's been
enough blood shed already. The United States, Russia, and
India all are willing to do all they can to stop this plan
from succeeding. It will likely take the submarine about a
week to reach Chinese waters. We can use that time."

Myles gestured toward the CNO. "Admiral Hughes is
ready to work with your navy and the Indian Navy to find
and stop *Chakra*, sinking her if need be. In a sense, the
conspirators have already failed, since their attack will no
longer be anonymous."

"Do the men on the submarine know that their plan has
been exposed?" Xi asked.

Myles looked over to Hughes, who answered. "We're
broadcasting messages to *Chakra* on frequencies the Indian Navy says they should be listening to, telling them
that the Chinese government has been warned and that
President Handa is ordering them to come back. We don't
know if they're listening, and if they are, if they will obey
the Indian president's order. But we're trying."

Xi Ping had been an army officer before accepting the
ambassador's post, but his intelligence background, as well
as the recent Littoral Alliance war, had given him a good
understanding of a submarine's strengths and weaknesses.
The ocean was vast, and if a submarine didn't want to be
found, then it was simple for it to avoid searching ships and
aircraft. The few hostile submarines China had sunk in the

recent war had been found and attacked after revealing themselves when they sank a Chinese ship.

This submarine would be attacking five of ten cities. Could the navy protect all ten? He wasn't sure the navy could protect five, or even one. The People's Liberation Army Navy had suffered many losses in combat with the Littoral Alliance countries. In the aftermath of the war, operating funds had been virtually eliminated. China needed the money to rebuild her industry, pay reparations, and buy desperately needed food and fuel.

And the admirals in charge had not been able to protest. After all, the navy had failed to protect China. Why should the country buy expensive replacement warships when the ones in service had failed to protect her vital merchant ships? The navy, stripped of funds and fuel, had essentially rotted at the pier for the last six months.

Xi realized that China would need to ask the Americans, and possibly even the Littoral Alliance navies, for help in finding and stopping this submarine. Even if China's navy was not in rags, the threat was so great that logic demanded they should ask for assistance from anyone able to help.

The Chinese ambassador turned his thoughts into carefully phrased English. "China is grateful for the American offer. I do not have the authority to answer for my government, but I believe they will accept your proposal. What type of assistance could you provide?"

"Maritime patrol aircraft searching along *Chakra*'s path, surface ships and submarines as well, although they will take longer to get in position," Hughes answered.

Ambassador Xi nodded his understanding, but turned to Yeng. The attaché replied to Hughes, "Then you will need to know the locations of our ships and submarines, and we'll need to know your units' positions, of course."

While Major General Yeng discussed details with Hughes, Xi tried to imagine the reaction back in Beijing. This was a much greater threat than losing the Littoral Alliance war, with the only possible help coming from enemies and rivals. There was nothing good in his message, and he could only hope his superiors wouldn't shoot the messenger. Inside, he cried for his country, already suffering. China's humiliation would be complete—and that was the best possible outcome, the one they would have to hope for.

6 April 2017
2000 Local Time
The White House
Washington, D.C.

There had obviously been no time for Patterson to actually travel to Manila, the new headquarters of the Littoral Alliance. The Philippine capital was centrally located for the member nations: Japan, Taiwan, Vietnam, Indonesia, Malaysia, South Korea, Singapore, and India. Only six months after the end of the war, it was still very much a military headquarters, but diplomats from all the member nations were in residence.

Manila was also twelve hours ahead of the U.S. East Coast, so the American request for a videoconference had reached the alliance headquarters at the start of the working day. Most of the representatives were just arriving, and were available in relatively short order. The videoconference had been set for 8:00 A.M. in Manila, or 8:00 P.M. in Washington, but it was a little after that when her deputy stood in the open door and knocked twice. "We've got a quorum. All the seats are filled."

Admiral Hughes was already in the room when Patterson arrived, and had been chatting with the different representatives as they logged in. The large flat-panel display showed the nine countries' civilian and military representatives in the main conference room. Ambassador Liao of Independent Taiwan had the rotating chairmanship, and introduced the civilian and military officers.

While her staffer transmitted photographs, diagrams, and maps that were displayed for the alliance officials, Patterson laid out the plot, the source of the bombs, and the status of the investigation in India. The last diagram was a nautical chart showing *Chakra*'s likely position in the Bay of Bengal, as well as arcs showing all possible positions at different speeds.

As soon as it was clear that she had finished, Ambassador Liao immediately asked, "Why are we finding out about this from the United States, instead of our own Indian representative?"

Indian ambassador Kanna was actually back in India, so his place had been taken by his deputy, who pleaded ignorance. Nobody believed he would be privy to such sensitive information. Still, this meant there was no way to corroborate Patterson's information.

Ambassador Suzuki, one of two diplomats speaking from their homes, said, "Dr. Patterson, we accept the information you present as true, but it's simply too much to take in all at once. Logic would demand that you wish us to assist in finding and possibly—no, probably sinking one of our own ally's submarines, to protect a country we recently fought. Destroying China's economy by attacking her commerce was part of our strategy," he reminded her.

"Not with nuclear weapons," Patterson countered. She gestured to her assistant, who displayed another image, a map of the Chinese coast. "These are the ten ports on the list we obtained." She nodded, and the aide pressed a key. "Here are the prevailing winds for late April in that region." Arrows appeared showing the general easterly wind patterns over Asia. She nodded again. "And here are the positions of the fallout from a one-hundred-and-fifty-kiloton surface burst at each of the ten locations." Elongated ovals stretched across the East China Sea, the Yellow Sea, and the South China Sea to the countries that lined China's coast.

"We can't know which of the ten ports the conspirators

have actually chosen, but the Philippines, Japan, Taiwan, and even South Korea would likely be in the path of the fallout. Some of it will certainly settle in the waters surrounding China, and you can imagine the effects on the fishing grounds. More environmental cleanup, and a lot of hungry people.

"Ignoring the effects of the attack on the Chinese economy, which would likely trigger a catastrophic worldwide depression, ignoring the humanitarian disaster of millions of Chinese injured and killed, some of your own citizens will suffer and die as a direct result of the attacks.

"And if any of you are reluctant to sink an 'allied' Indian submarine, remember that India is doing her level best to arrest the people who planned this, and that the plotters don't seem to be concerned about collateral damage to the other alliance members."

She could see nodding heads, and pressed home her point. "This is the alliance's problem as much as China's. When something this bad happens, everyone suffers."

Liao spoke again. "Normally, a matter like this would be discussed at length, with the senior military and civilian representative from each country speaking in turn. However, given the urgency, I will speak for the alliance without discussion and say that we will assist our Indian ally in finding, and if necessary, sinking this submarine. We welcome U.S. participation in this effort. Are there any objections?"

Each representative said "no," in turn, even the Indians, but the military representative quickly changed his vote to "abstain," sounding confused and unhappy. "I must believe this is actually happening, but my heart cannot let me vote yes."

The Taiwanese ambassador nodded sympathetically. "I understand, but your help will be vital in this."

The Indian's expression hardened. "You will have it, I promise."

Liao asked, "Doctor, do you have any recommendations?

You have been working with this for some time now and presumably have some thoughts."

"Our chief of naval operations will start sending your military staff what intelligence we have on *Chakra*, as well as any information on our own and Chinese ship, submarine, and aircraft movements. And although your countries have excellent submarines, we strongly recommend that you do not use them in the search. In fact, if you have any submarines operating in that area, you should recall them immediately. There is too much risk of a blue-on-blue incident."

The military officers were nodding agreement. The senior military officer was a Philippine Navy captain, and he said, "We concur, and will provide location data for any of our subs in *Chakra*'s path until they are all clear of the area. We will also share and coordinate our plans with our American friends." He paused, then added, "It might be best, if for the moment, that any information on Chinese movements came from you, rather than directly from Chinese sources."

Hughes nodded, smiling. "And we will, of course, inform the Chinese of Littoral Alliance movements, to make sure there is no duplication of effort."

Or unfriendly encounters, Patterson thought. Nerves were still raw, and this business didn't need any more complications.

6 April 2017
2100 Local Time
The Oval Office, the White House
Washington, D.C.

This time, Joanna Patterson waited to be announced and admitted before going into the Oval Office. Secretary Lloyd and the president were both waiting for her. "Done,

Mr. President," she announced with satisfaction. "They're not happy at having to find out from us, but they're even more unhappy about the problem. They've agreed to coordinate with us through Guam, and Admiral Hughes has gone back to the Pentagon to get it organized."

The two men looked disappointed, and Myles, looking at Lloyd, said, "It doesn't matter. We can reach him there."

Puzzled, Patterson asked, "Should I have kept him with me?"

Myles gave a small shake of his head. "No, Joanna, it's fine. He has a lot to do, and you couldn't have anticipated this. Nobody could."

Her heart started to sink. "What's happened?"

Myles quickly reassured her. "Nothing bad. It's just— unusual."

Lloyd said, "While you were in meetings with the Chinese and then the Littoral Alliance, I was informing the other governments of what we had decided." He paused for a moment, then declared, "The Indians want Girish Samant to take part in the hunt for *Chakra*, 'as a witness,' as they put it. They're making arrangements to fly him to Guam." He then reprised his conversation with the Indian foreign secretary.

By this time she'd sat down, and found herself agreeing with the Indians' logic. "It makes sense," she said, nodding. "If nothing else, they will be able to say it was a joint operation."

"Then I called the Russians," Lloyd reported, "to inform them that *Chakra* had sailed. They were not happy at the thought of their bootleg warheads actually being used. They want Alex Petrov there, as well." He saw her surprised expression, but didn't give her a chance to speak. "They also want to say they were involved in the 'search for and destruction of' the warheads."

"By sinking the sub they're carried on." She made a face.

"The Russians were not happy that the Indians had let *Chakra* leave, in spite of a two-day warning. They reminded me that Petrov has the best information on *Chakra*'s technical characteristics, since changes were made after Samant turned over command." Lloyd added, "I agreed, and the president has approved the request. I've already called the Hyderabad consulate and told them to load Petrov on the same plane as Samant. They'll be glad to have those two off their hands. What's left is to tell Admiral Hughes to expect two foreign observers at Guam for the duration of the operation. If nothing else, he has to find them a place to stay . . ."

"On the base, you mean." She interrupted. "On Guam." When he started to agree, she said firmly, "That won't work. They'll be treated as fifth wheels, and won't be able to help. Besides their information is more tactical; putting them at the headquarters doesn't make a lot of sense."

Lloyd shrugged. "That's where the operation will be run," he said. "Where else . . ." He paused, then frowned and shook his head. "No. Absolutely not."

"Put them aboard Jerry's sub," she insisted. "We know *North Dakota* is the best sub in Squadron Fifteen, and Simonis has already said he's going to place her off of Hong Kong—the most likely first target. She has the best chance of finding and killing *Chakra*."

"And I do not get a good feeling about putting an Indian and Russian aboard a sub that will probably have to fire on a Russian-built, Indian-crewed submarine."

"That is precisely why we need them aboard. Petrov knows the boat better than anyone else, and Samant knows the new skipper." She looked to President Myles, who was watching them both silently.

"And what if they attempt to interfere somehow?" Myles asked.

"I think there's little chance of that," she replied. "They've both showed, at considerable risk to themselves, that they aren't driven simply by national interests."

"One could suggest they've both acted in their higher national interests. Honorably," Myles concluded. After a short pause, he added, "The Navy won't be happy, they're allergic to this sort of thing, but I'll tell Simonis, through the chain, to put them aboard *North Dakota*. We get only one good crack at stopping *Chakra* before she launches a nuclear weapon. It needs to be our best shot."

16

En Route

8 April 2017
1800 Local Time
Andersen Air Force Base
Guam

The Indian Navy P-8 aircraft descended smoothly toward the tarmac, two short puffs of smoke marking when the tires touched the concrete. The aircraft rolled to the far end of runway 24R, passing by a half dozen B-52s parked in the center of the field, before turning left onto a taxiway that led to the air base terminal.

Glenn Jacobs paced impatiently by the car. He was anxious to collect his passengers, no, his guests, and get them to the pier as fast as he could. He wanted this bothersome evolution over and done with, preferably before his commodore suffered a severe stroke. Jacobs vividly recalled the video conversation Simonis had with his immediate boss, Rear Admiral Burroughs, yesterday evening. The chief staff officer had *never* seen that shade of purplish red on Simonis's face before, and if Jacobs had anything to do with it, he didn't want to ever see it again.

"Yes, sir, I get it that we have to work with India and Russia, truly," complained Simonis bitterly. "But that can easily be accommodated by having them observe the operation from my watch floor! Putting them on *North Da-*

kota is just a boondoggle, and a violation of every security safeguard we've ever put in place!"

"I'm sympathetic, Chuck, but those security regs were written for more 'normal times.' This current crisis is far from normal," Burroughs countered.

"Admiral, Dr. Patterson has gone too far by demanding we put two foreign senior naval officers, both qualified submarine commanders, onto our newest class of attack submarines! They'll be able to understand every single detail they see!"

"For the record, Chuck, she didn't demand. She made a recommendation to the president, who agreed with her argument—as did the CNO, and Pac Fleet, for that matter. Captain Samant knows *Chakra*'s current commanding officer intimately. He trained him and knows how he thinks. Captain Petrov personally supervised the modifications to the submarine's sonar system, and he's bringing a complete set of technical manuals with him. The information these men possess will be of tremendous value in finding and neutralizing the Akula, hopefully before it can deploy any nuclear weapons. And since *North Dakota* is our first line of defense, it made sense to put the two men on her."

"And the fact that both Samant and Petrov are on friendly terms with Patterson, and Mitchell, didn't influence this request at all?" grumbled Simonis sarcastically. "Sir, neither the CNO nor the Pacific Fleet commander are submariners, they don't fully understand why those regulations were created in the first place! To prevent our critical technological advantage from being compromised!"

Burroughs's expression hardened. He was visibly losing patience with Simonis.

"Commodore, if anyone doesn't understand this present situation, it's you. We are desperately trying to prevent an escalation of a conventional conflict into one that sees the wide-scale use of nuclear weapons. Can you not grasp that? How can the knowledge of these two individuals be of any help to Commander Mitchell when they are stuck in Guam and he's out searching for a very quiet boat that had just been updated, and is doing its damnedest not to be found. Is he going to spend his whole patrol at periscope depth just so he can call in at a moment's notice for tactical guidance?!

"The president has ordered our *full* cooperation with those nations who have offered assistance to stop this rogue boat. Let me repeat, *full* cooperation, and it was he who told the Navy to put the two captains on *North Dakota*. Given the circumstances, Commodore, are you that surprised the security manual just got tossed into the bilge? You can place whatever *reasonable* restrictions you believe are necessary to limit access to the more sensitive areas on *North Dakota*, but your orders are to get those men on board and Mitchell out to sea, expeditiously. I suggest you carry them out."

Jacobs had felt bad watching his boss get smacked by another senior official. Once was bad enough, but twice! In the same day—ouch!

Ironically, the CSO completely understood where Simonis was coming from. The commodore was a strictly "by the book" naval officer. He knew exactly what had to be done, and how to meet the incredible amount of bureaucratic bookkeeping required by a peacetime navy. The problem was, the squadron wasn't exactly operating in a peacetime mode right now, and one of Simonis's precious books had just been cast aside. And while the CNO's decision might have been influenced by political expediency, Admiral Hughes was an acknowledged "horse trader" within Washington circles. The truth of the matter was, it just made good sense, and the risk of compromise had been deemed acceptable by a competent authority.

Simonis's main problem was that he was risk-averse, and he wanted to play it safe. But Jacobs also knew that his commodore would follow his orders regardless of whether or not he liked them. The combination had made for interesting times at the squadron headquarters during the Sino–Littoral Alliance War, and now that round two was just getting started, there would be more to follow. The best thing Jacobs could do for his boss was to get Samant and Petrov on *North Dakota*, and have Mitchell get his butt to sea. Once all the three boats were on their way to their assigned patrol areas, the squadron headquarters could get into a steady routine—establishing a sustainable battle rhythm was high on Jacobs's list of things to do.

The aircraft slowly taxied to the parking apron, coming to a complete stop only when the marshaler crossed his batons. The airman then gave the hand signals for the pilot to cut the engines and for the ground crew to move in with the chocks for the landing gear wheels. Before the engines had even wound down, the forward fuselage door opened and a folding ladder was extended. As soon as the legs hit the ground, two men emerged from the aircraft and hustled down the ladder. Jacobs quickly moved forward to greet them.

"Captain Petrov, Captain Samant, I'm Glenn Jacobs, welcome to Guam. This way, please," he said hurriedly.

Two airmen grabbed the men's seabags from the Indian flight crew and tossed them into the car's trunk. The moment it was closed, the car sped off toward the submarine piers. A military police escort accompanied them, clearing the traffic ahead.

"My apologies for the abrupt welcome, but I have to get you two down to *North Dakota* immediately. We've held her for almost twenty-fours hours while we waited for you to get here, and I really need to get that boat to sea," explained Jacobs as the car took off. His words were polite, but his tone was stern.

"Completely understandable, Captain Jacobs," Petrov replied. "Although, I was very surprised that your government offered to allow us to go out on Jerry's boat. I'm certain my government didn't make that a condition for my assistance."

"They didn't, but the knowledge the two of you have argued strongly that you belong on *North Dakota*. Your relationship with the national security advisor didn't hurt, either. She's the one who came up with the idea." Jacobs was frowning as he spoke.

"I take it you're not entirely pleased with this arrangement," noted Samant bluntly.

Jacobs smiled thinly. "Whether or not I'm happy about this plan is irrelevant, Captain. Personally, I agree with Dr. Patterson's reasoning. My boss, however, does not, and he's the man I have to work for. I'm sure you can understand the complicated position I'm in. Nothing personal, but the sooner I get you two out of his hair, the better."

Petrov and Samant nodded; they'd both experienced similar situations sometime during their careers. "Any news on the patrol aircraft search?" asked Samant.

Jacobs shook his head. "Your navy has put up almost a dozen Bear F sorties so far, and they haven't found or heard a blessed thing. What I don't understand is why it's taking so long to get the P-8 Poseidon squadron involved in the hunt."

"The 312th Squadron is under the Eastern Naval Command, the same one that *Chakra* belongs to. The flag officer in charge, Vice Admiral Dhankhar, is the leader of this wretched plot and he ordered our brand-new P-8I squadron, the only one we have, to stand down." Samant glared with anger as he spoke.

"Most of the squadron's officers, including the pilots and mission commanders, were sent to an ASW training symposium in Mumbai. At the same time, many of the aircraft were scheduled for maintenance on their engines and acoustic systems. We're scrambling to get the planes up and running, but it will be at least two more days before the next one's ready to fly. All that was available for immediate service were six elderly Tu-142s with outdated sensors."

"How inconvenient for us," grumbled Jacobs. Samant shrugged apologetically; there wasn't anything he could say in response to the sarcastic remark. Suddenly, Jacobs's cell phone rang. He noted the caller's identity. "Excuse me while I take this call." Samant and Petrov nodded their consent.

"CSO," said Jacobs, answering the phone. After a short pause, he continued, "Yes, sir, I've picked up our guests and we are en route to the squadron piers. We should arrive in about fifteen minutes."

Jerry found it a bit strange scanning the road leading up to the wharf with his binoculars. Usually he would look for contacts at sea or in the air; concentrating his search landward was definitely not the norm. Then, in the distance, Jerry saw the flashing lights of a police car. Followed close behind by another vehicle. Leaning over the flying bridge, he raised the bullhorn and shouted down to Thigpen. "XO! Incoming!"

Thigpen signaled his response by waving his ball cap and sent two sailors quickly across the brow to help with their riders' gear. Turning to Lieutenant Covey, the officer of the deck, Jerry ordered, "Dave, get us under way the moment our guests are aboard." The junior officer acknowledged the order, and radioed the tug to stand by.

A minute later the two cars pulled up to Wharf B and came to a screeching stop just short of the small crane that was ready to remove the gangplank. Jerry saw the squadron CSO jump out, call over to the two sailors, and point to the opening trunk. As the men ran over to grab the seabags, Jerry saw Petrov and Samant getting out of the car. Thigpen rushed toward the two and rendered a smart salute. Gesturing toward the brow, he urged them to board. Jerry waved a quick greeting when they looked up at the sail. Once the two sailors with the seabags were clear of the gangplank, the small crane lifted it off the hull.

"On deck," announced Covey through the bullhorn. "Take in all lines!" As soon as the last line came over from the pier, a loud prolonged blast blared from the ship's horn: *North Dakota* was leaving port. The deep throbbing of a diesel engine abruptly roared to life as tug *Goliath* started to pull the submarine from the wharf. Down on the pier, Jacobs was walking along the edge, repeatedly motioning with his right arm for the sub to leave. Jerry tipped his cap in deference to the squadron's second-in-command, and then saluted. Jacobs returned the honor and waved goodbye. His face wore a broad smile of relief.

The squawk from the intercom on the bridge suitcase informed Jerry that his guests had dropped off their gear in the XO's stateroom and were making their way to control. They had requested permission to come up and pay their respects to the commanding officer. Jerry nodded his approval, and the OOD answered, "Permission granted."

A toot from the tug's whistle told Jerry and the OOD that *Goliath* had detached herself from *North Dakota*'s hull. As the submarine gradually started to get way on, the tug took up a supporting position astern. The concrete walls of the inner harbor channel passed by slowly, as if one were on a leisurely stroll. Just ahead of them was the exit into Apra Harbor proper, and beyond that, the open sea.

Moments later, Samant and Petrov emerged from the access trunk, squeezed past Covey and the pilot in the crammed cockpit, and climbed up to join Jerry and the lookout on the flying bridge. Each man sported a brandnew *North Dakota* ball cap, complete with scrambled eggs on the brim. Grabbing Petrov's right hand, Jerry gave him a brief pull to get him up and over the railing.

"Thank you, Jerry," grunted Petrov as he gained his footing. "My God, this is a *very* cramped bridge."

"Yeah, well, I suppose in comparison to a big Russian nuke boat this would be a little on the small side. But we like to keep things sleek and trim," Jerry replied a little defensively.

"Trim?" challenged Samant, trying to find some more space without bumping into the lookout. It was cozy up on the flying bridge with the four of them. "This is even more compact than what I had on my Kilo!"

Jerry shrugged; there was no way he was going to win this debate. Resigned, he politely changed the subject. "Once we clear the breakwater, we'll disembark the pilot and then crank her up to warp nine. We have to dogleg our way out of the harbor because of the numerous spots of shoal water." Jerry pointed to the large splotches of blue-green seawater dotted all around the boat.

"Is that the channel to our left?" Samant asked, pointing to a very slender band of darker water off the port bow. He had a slight frown on his face.

"That's it," responded Jerry. "It's wider than it looks from here. We have a good two hundred and fifty meters between the two reefs." The Indian nodded and seemed to relax. He then started a complete 360-degree visual sweep, looking around at the water, nearby landmarks, and the sub's position within the channel; exercising a well-rehearsed routine. Jerry then noticed the Indian dolphins on Samant's uniform. They were very similar to the U.S. Navy's submarine insignia. Except where the submarine conning tower was on the U.S. badge, the Indians had a pedestal with three lions arrayed back-to-back.

Samant's dolphins dragged Jerry back to his last conversation with Captain Simonis. The commodore had issued direct orders that neither foreign officer was to have access to the radio room or the engineering spaces. Simonis was less than happy at the very thought of two senior, submarine-command-qualified naval officers running around loose on one of his newest boats—and at sea!

He grumbled at first about Patterson's "casual disregard" of the security risk, but Simonis at least admitted she had some valid reasons for her recommendation. And she did use the chain of command this time. The only other guidance Jerry received was to put the pedal to the metal once he had submerged. *Chakra* had a two-day head start, and Simonis wanted all his subs on station well before the rogue Indian boat was expected to arrive in Chinese waters. Since *North Dakota* had the first patrol area near Hong Kong, she'd have to fly to make it in time.

Turning around, Jerry caught a glimpse of Petrov's face. His expression was a strange mixture of confusion, wonderment, and . . . uneasiness? Worried that something was wrong with his friend, Jerry asked, "Are you okay, Alex?"

Petrov immediately smiled, but his face took on a slight pinkish hue. "Oh, yes. I'm fine, Jerry. It's just that . . . well, I've never gone to sea in a short-sleeve shirt before."

Jerry bit down on his lower lip, while simultaneously taking in a slow, deep breath. He was trying very hard not to laugh at Petrov's awkward confession; his friend was already embarrassed enough as it was. Samant either didn't try, or failed utterly, as a hearty guffaw burst out. As soon as he was done laughing, he said, "Pay no attention to him, Captain Mitchell. Aleks has done nothing but complain about the fine Indian spring we were having."

Petrov ignored Samant's comment and tried to explain; his face had already transitioned to a deep red. "I've always had to wear at least a light jacket when I went out to sea, and oftentimes a heavy winter coat. It just seems very strange not to need one, that's all."

Feeling it was now safe, Jerry chuckled. "Well, Alex, a fifty-degree southerly shift in latitude will do that to you. You might as well enjoy it while you can, it won't take us long to reach the dive point, once we clear the harbor."

Fifteen minutes later, they passed the entrance to the breakwater and Jerry had the OOD slow while the pilot climbed down the rope ladder and hopped over to the tug.

After another quick toot, *Goliath* pulled away and *North Dakota* was free to accelerate to a higher speed.

Slowly, the boat's bow wave grew larger, expanding in both size and sound, becoming a loud wall of water slamming against the forward edge of the sail. Split by the unyielding metal, the frothing seawater tumbled down around the hull. Jerry always loved to be on the bridge when a submarine plowed its way through the ocean at high speed. Ever since that first time on *Memphis*, so many years ago, it never failed to fill him with excitement. Riding a boat on the surface with a flank bell on was just as addicting to him as flying a high-performance fighter. And he wasn't the only one.

Samant wore a pronounced grin as he leaned casually against the railing. He relished the wind whipping past his face, and the occasional drop of seawater thrown high into the air, striking him, only made him feel more alive. By comparison, Petrov appeared calm and tranquil. He leaned forward into the brisk wind, his hands grasping the railing tightly, his feet staggered to provide the best support on the vibrating deck.

Just as Jerry thought Petrov was enjoying the ride, he saw a pained or troubled look flash on the Russian's face. It then dawned on Jerry that his friend probably hadn't been to sea since the collision almost nine years earlier, and that this trip was likely opening up old wounds. For a brief second, Jerry thought he saw a tear creeping across Petrov's windswept face. Rather than encroach upon Petrov's private contemplation by speaking, Jerry left him alone to deal with the demons that were troubling him. Sometimes, even time couldn't heal all wounds—especially the really deep ones.

After about twenty minutes, Covey flagged Jerry's attention and pointed to the display screen. They'd reach the dive point in another thirty minutes, and the OOD still had some work to do topside before they could submerge. Jerry nodded and turned to his guests.

"As much as I hate to say it, gentlemen, we need to go below. We're getting close to the dive point and the OOD needs to take down the flying bridge. We can grab some fresh coffee before we submerge and you can observe the evolution from the control room."

Samant wasted no time in moving. He slid past Jerry and crawled down toward the access trunk. Petrov, on the other hand, continued to stare off toward the horizon, remaining motionless.

"Alex?" Jerry whispered.

Petrov sighed and bowed his head. "I'm coming," he replied with a tinge of weariness. Slowly, the Russian captain crept below. Jerry followed immediately after. At 1945 local time, *North Dakota* dove beneath the waves.

8 April 2017
2000 Local Time
USS *North Dakota*
Pacific Ocean

Dinner was really late that evening; usually the first seating was before 1800, so the watchstanders could eat before they went on duty. But with the late departure from Guam, Jerry had decided to delay dinner and make it a "welcome aboard" event for their two guests. Its execution had been a masterstroke of diplomacy by the supply officer. It certainly served its primary purpose as an icebreaker for the members of the wardroom and the two foreign naval officers who were, technically, senior to their captain.

Lieutenant Steven Westbrook, the supply officer, had his cooks dish up a traditional Southern fried chicken supper with all the fixings, to include buttermilk biscuits and pecan pie with vanilla bean ice cream for dessert. Petrov's nostrils flared at the aroma, and he dug into the hot chicken and mashed potatoes and gravy with gusto. Samant snickered as his friend chowed down on a thigh, and teased him about his lack of tolerance for spicy food. The Indian captain then went on to ask if U.S. submarines carried something with a little more "character" than Tabasco sauce.

Westbrook's left eyebrow cocked up in prideful defiance. But his facial expression echoed his unspoken feelings— "Challenge accepted, Captain." Excusing himself, the suppo went back into the pantry, and soon there was the sound of bottles being moved around. Jerry looked on with amusement—that is, until he saw his XO's face. Thigpen's eyes were as wide as saucers and he looked worried. Jerry's quizzical look caught Thigpen's attention, but all the XO could do was tightly shake his head no and very subtly tilt it in the direction of the pantry, as if he were trying to say, "Don't let him do it!"

Before Jerry could say or do anything, Westbrook appeared from the pantry and walked back over to Samant. With a hint of theatrics, the supply officer placed a small bottle in front of him and said, "Here you go, sir. I'm sure this will be more to your liking."

As the supply officer walked behind his skipper, Jerry heard him mutter indignantly, "Accuse my food of being bland, will you!"

Now Jerry was concerned, and he took a hard look at the bottle of orange-colored sauce in Samant's hands. The label had a grim reaper on it; the scythe blade was a small red chili—not a good omen.

Addressing Samant, Thigpen said warily, "Ah, Captain, you might want to use that stuff sparingly. It's pretty dang hot!"

Removing the cap, Samant took a sniff and replied, "Nonsense, Commander! It smells absolutely delightful." He then proceeded to liberally sprinkle it on a chicken leg. Thigpen winced when Samant bit down on a section of the leg with just two drops on it. Everyone at the table, including

Petrov, all watched intently to see Samant's reaction. Some of them knew exactly what kind of assault West-brook had just unleashed on the Indian's mouth.

Initially, Samant seemed to be enjoying the chili sauce. But then he started to chew more slowly and his eyes got bigger. After swallowing, he let out a quiet gasp, and to everyone's surprise Samant took another bite. Once he had finished the entire chicken leg, he waved his finger at West-brook, who had a wicked grin on his face. Samant grabbed the bottle, raised it, and asked in a raspy voice, "What is this, Lieutenant? It's quite wonderful! Very flavorful, and the heat!"

"That, sir, is a sauce made from the Carolina Reaper, the hottest chili on the planet," explained Westbrook with smug satisfaction. "There's more heat in that bottle than in the entire reactor core, I can assure you." At first, Sa-mant nodded his appreciation, and then applauded West-brook's boldness. Rising, he reached over to shake the supply officer's hand. The rest of the diners joined in and clapped as well.

After the meal, Jerry had those officers not on watch attend the mission overview and intelligence briefings. Before they left Guam, the squadron operations officer, Com-mander Walker, had condensed all the available informa-tion into a short presentation, with more detailed data and explanations in a written report. It was incomplete, but the information would be useful to the three Ameri-can submarines. Walker promised updates on *Chakra*'s position, as well as the location of Chinese and Littoral Alliance forces, as new information was received.

Lieutenant Commander Thigpen led off with the intel-ligence community's estimated target list. While the crum-pled-up piece of paper that Petrov and Samant found in the torpedo workshop had only ten ports on it, the actual number of possible targets was twelve. Both Hong Kong and Shanghai had two large port facilities. They were far enough apart that two separate weapons would be needed to take them both out.

"Fortunately for us, a number of the targets just aren't reachable by a submarine-launched torpedo: too far up a river, and a couple of the ports are way, way inside the Bo-hai Gulf, which is not exactly prime submarine water. So the list gets whittled down to the seven most likely: the two ports at Hong Kong, the two at Shanghai, Ningbo-Zhoushan, Qingdao, and Dalian.

"According to a joint State Department/CIA economic assessment, taking out five of these ports will result in the destruction of fifty to fifty-five percent of China's export capability, along with several large oil refineries, two major shipyards, and the two largest financial centers. Civilian casualties are estimated to be, *at a minimum*, four to five million from the blast, tidal surges, and radiation-induced illness. In short, China gets royally hosed if we don't find *Chakra* before she deploys her five packages of liquid sunshine," concluded Thigpen, sitting down.

The junior officers present just stared at the screen in stunned disbelief. The XO's overview was beyond scary—it was horrific!

The ship's engineer, Lieutenant Commander Philip So-becki, finally broke the shocked silence. He turned slowly to Samant. "This is for real, sir? I mean, your old boat has been given orders to do this?"

Samant sighed. He was getting used to the fact that when a rational person was first exposed to the plot, they simply couldn't comprehend that someone would actually attempt to murder millions. "I'm afraid so, Mr. Sobecki. And anything I could say would not answer your next question as to why. All you can do is accept what your first officer said and work with it."

"Okay, people," Jerry announced, "our squadron has been given this job because there isn't another U.S. boat that has a prayer of getting into position before *Chakra* could arrive. Based on the scrubbed target list, the commodore has decided to have our boat guard the waters around Hong Kong. *North Carolina* has Ningbo-Zhoushan to Shanghai, and *Texas* is covering Qingdao and points north. The going assumption is that Hong Kong is the first target, and that's why we're here. This represents a best guess, folks, nothing more. And while I accept the squadron's initial call, we can't afford to focus on just one avenue of approach. So we're going to have to develop our search plan with a lot of flexibility."

Jerry turned to Petrov and asked, "Captain Petrov, in general, what were the improvements to *Chakra*'s sonar during her refit?"

"All the improvements were to the towed array," began Petrov. "The new array is completely digital and the signal processing uses algorithms that were derived from the Irtysh-Amfora sonar suite that was on . . . on my old boat. Theoretically, you are looking at a potential four-to-five-decibel improvement in the signal-to-noise ratio."

"Damn! That's huge!" blurted Gaffney, *North Dakota*'s sonar officer.

Petrov smiled at the young officer's outburst. "Yes, indeed, Lieutenant. I'm afraid this will complicate your search planning considerably."

"Stuart, I want you to work with Captain Petrov to update *Chakra*'s sonar characteristics in our threat database. I need to know how much of our acoustic advantage we've just lost," ordered Jerry.

"Aye, aye, sir," replied Gaffney.

He then looked toward Thigpen and added, "XO, you and the nav will work with Captain Samant to figure out *Chakra*'s best avenues of approach and a list of potential firing positions. I want contingency options if she doesn't behave the way we think she will."

Standing, Jerry finished his instructions to his crew. "We have a little more than two days before we reach the coast of Hong Kong. I need to have all this work completed and double-checked before we assume our station. Since it's late, we'll start first thing in the morning. Sleep well tonight, it will probably start getting a little hectic tomorrow."

17

Confession

9 April 2017
1200 Local Time
Wardroom, USS *North Dakota*

Aleks Petrov had never had sloppy joes and sweet-potato fries before, but it turned out to be very good. He was pleasantly surprised at the Americans' culinary creativity, and it was a welcome break from the spicy Indian food he'd had to subsist on for months. For the first time in quite a while, Petrov felt safe and at ease—but there was an edginess that still nagged at him. Sure, he was on a submerged nuclear submarine, bound for a desperate battle with a dangerous opponent, but that was still a day away, at least, and he could use the time—in fact, he needed the time—to rest and heal. And think.

He'd remained quiet during the meal, seated with Samant at the head of the table on Jerry's left, while the officers treated them as honored guests. A lively conversation had sprung up during lunch as they reconstructed *Chakra*'s encounters with *North Dakota* during the Littoral Alliance war. Although the conversation had begun as a continuation of the morning's planning session, the discussion of an Akula-class's strengths and weaknesses in a sub-on-sub battle had turned into an animated exchange of war stories.

Petrov's left side still ached, from fatigue if nothing else.

Although they'd gotten some sleep during the twelve-hour flight from India to Guam, he and Samant had also talked extensively, trying to understand their place in a massive conspiracy. And Petrov's first night on board had been a restless one, with dreams of compartments flooding and men drowning. He'd awakened in a sweat, shaking as he tried to remember who the men were—he didn't recall them being members of his crew on *Severodvinsk*. But they seemed somehow familiar. Exhausted, he managed to make it through the morning's work with the help of lots of coffee.

Petrov had been unaware of the extent of Russia's role in this mess until he'd listened to the Americans warn the Indian leadership. He was especially ashamed that Orlav and Kirichenko, former Russian naval officers, were the main culprits behind this scheme. Petrov doubted very much that Dhankhar had gone looking for Russian nuclear weapons on his own—Kirichenko would have initiated the first contact.

He felt he'd atoned somewhat by sharing information on *Chakra*'s recent modifications with the Americans. Normally such sensitive data would be considered classified by both the Russian and Indian navies, but if they were successful, it would be a moot point. And if they failed, they would have larger problems than a simple breach of security.

Petrov had said little at lunch, and then only in response to direct questions. More than once he caught Jerry giving him sidelong looks now and then. Petrov was also watching Mitchell as well, seated at the head of the table on his boat. The Russian fondly recalled his own short time as a submarine captain, and he envied Jerry. Petrov had always been honest with himself about the loss of *Severodvinsk*. He still missed being her captain, and he missed the men he'd lost, but there was no helping that now.

Petrov hated his dark mood. Surrounded by friends and allies, in a place he understood, he couldn't shake the questions that plagued him. He really didn't want to pursue the answers, and that dread of what the answers might be also added to his ill humor.

When the meal finally ended, Petrov excused himself and headed to the XO's stateroom, which he and Samant had taken over while Thigpen moved in with Lieutenant Commander Sobecki and Lieutenant Iverson. His intention was to lie down and think, and hopefully lose himself in sleep, but Jerry followed him up the passageway, heading for his own quarters. The captain's stateroom was next to the XO's, of course, and on sudden impulse, Petrov approached him and asked, "Can I speak with you for a moment?"

Surprised, Jerry answered, "Of course," and gestured toward the door he'd just opened.

Marginally larger than a walk-in closet, Jerry's stateroom had the luxury of only one fold-down desk instead of two, and the extra floor space allowed room for a second chair. Petrov sat down, while Jerry dropped into the chair in front of the desk. It was similar enough to the captain's stateroom on a Russian boat to trigger another wave of memories, but Petrov refused to give in to nostalgia.

"I have some serious questions to ask you," Petrov announced.

Jerry Mitchell shrugged. "I'll tell you whatever I can, Alex. After all this, there aren't many secrets between us."

The Russian sighed. "I hope that is true. Jerry, I learned some disturbing things listening to your president and Dr. Patterson speaking with the Indians. She described how a large number of missile warheads had been diverted and hidden in a barge off the coast of Novaya Zemlya, and that she had been part of the mission that discovered those warheads. Is this correct?"

"Accidentally discovered," Jerry added, "as part of an environmental survey."

"A strange place to count whales," Petrov remarked. "But more importantly, she mentioned that she was aboard the submarine *Memphis* when they made the discovery."

"Yes, that's true." Jerry looked a little puzzled.

"And you were aboard that submarine as well, as a junior officer."

"Yes," Jerry admitted.

"I began fitting the pieces together aboard the plane. The Northern Fleet commander, Admiral Yuri Kirichenko, was court-martialed for an incident off the coast of Novaya Zemlya, which turns out to be where he'd actually hidden dozens of smuggled nuclear weapons."

Petrov drew a breath. "Kirichenko was dismissed from the service not because he sent the Northern Fleet on what turned out to be a wild-goose chase, but because our newest and best submarine, *Gepard*, with seventy-three men aboard, was lost in that operation. Her loss was a wound felt by every member of the navy, especially the submariners.

"I was a midgrade officer, a battle department commander on *Tigr*; *Gepard* was a squadron mate. I had competed with many others to be selected for her first crew. I knew most of her officers, some by reputation, and some very well, a few were close friends. I could have been aboard her when she was sunk."

Jerry was listening carefully, and Petrov could see that he knew more. The American had been surprised by the topic, but had listened like someone who knew what the speaker would say.

"Tell me how *Gepard* was lost," Petrov demanded. "You know, don't you?" There might have been more intensity in his words than he planned, but he didn't regret them.

Jerry took a deep breath. "Your navy found *Gepard*. The investigation determined that she had been sunk by one of her own torpedoes."

"Yes, but what was she firing torpedoes at?" pressed th
Russian. "Was Kirichenko chasing your sub when he ser
all those ships and planes out?"

Petrov was watching Jerry's face. He'd always believe
Mitchell was honest and fair-minded, but the America
seemed to be struggling.

Jerry sat for a moment, then another. He turned towar
the desk, as if looking for something; then he faced Petro
again. "It probably doesn't matter now, since the barge'
location was revealed to your government. Senator Hardy
my former skipper aboard *Memphis*, told me he briefed th
Russian ambassador about our mission, but it was whil
my government was investigating the Kashmir explosion
Nothing has been made public."

"There are many families that need to know how thei
loved ones died." Petrov stated it flatly, and he could see i
hit home with Mitchell. "My government will never tel
them, not when it involves a breach of Russian nuclea
safeguards."

"You're right," Jerry admitted. After taking a dee
breath, he started. "Dr. Patterson, and Emily, came aboar
to oversee a secret mission that involved conducting a sur
vey of radioactive waste disposal sites on the east side o
Novaya Zemlya . . ."

It took the American almost ten minutes to describ
Memphis's mission into the waters near the Russian coast
their inspection of several dump sites, and their discover
of something far more dangerous. They were pursued an
fired on by Russian naval forces. Damaged, they mad
good their escape, and had thought themselves safe whe
Gepard suddenly appeared and almost sank them. If no
for Jerry's Manta UUV, confusing and distracting the Rus
sian sub, *Memphis* would have been sunk. "But we neve
fired a weapon, Alex, we physically couldn't," Jerry in
sisted.

Petrov had remained silent, asking only an occasiona
question about positions and ranges, as one submarin

captain explained the engagement in terms the other understood completely. There was no uncertainty in the American's narration. No fuzzy memories or gaps in the timeline.

"For what it's worth, Alex, I'm very sorry about *Gepard*, and she's never been far from my memories. We did our level best to just get away, and it was really just luck that saved us."

Petrov scowled. "Did you intend to lure that last torpedo back toward *Gepard* with the Manta?"

Mitchell shook his head sharply. "No, absolutely not! I was trying to force *Gepard* to break off by running the Manta right at her. But she was violently maneuvering at the same time. She simply zigged when I had the Manta zag . . . both in the wrong direction. Before we knew it, one of the torpedoes had locked on to the Manta, and followed it in. The torpedo hit *Gepard* before I even had a chance to send a course-change order."

Petrov felt a weight lift off his chest. He'd feared Mitchell's answers, but they weren't what he'd expected, and his faith in his friend had been confirmed. But now his mind was whirling with the new facts, comparing and fitting together pieces that spanned more than ten years, perhaps much more than ten. How long ago had Kirichenko hidden those warheads?

"Another seventy-three lives to lay at Kirichenko's feet," Petrov finally observed.

"On his headstone would be better," Jerry added. "We can only hope, but first someone has to find him. *Gepard*, all the dead in Kashmir, and how many more could there be in China?" Jerry shuddered. "I'll do anything I can to stop *Chakra*, even if it means sinking her. This must be tearing Girish Samant apart."

The American paused for a moment, then added, "And now I'll ask you for a favor. If you're satisfied with my answers, please don't tell anyone, for just a little while longer. Please," he entreated.

"The families . . ." Petrov began, but trailed off.

"This won't be secret for much longer. Four governments are involved as major actors: the U.S., Russia, India, and China. Now the Littoral Alliance is joining in the hunt. If it doesn't leak out soon, the whole story will be revealed once *Chakra* is stopped. My country has no interest in keeping this secret once it's over. If you'd like, we can speak to Joanna about the best way to get the information out."

Petrov thought about it. Realistically, he couldn't tell anyone until *North Dakota* returned to port. After that, how would the Russian government react to him spreading this information? And concealing his source would be nearly impossible, which might cost Jerry his career. But Joanna Patterson was in a position of power to force the issue, backed by the U.S. president; perhaps she could finally get the truth out. "All right, you have my word," Petrov agreed.

In fact, how would the Russian government react when the entire episode became public? He asked Jerry that question, and the American just scratched his head. "The world's been going nuts over the Kashmir explosion and the idea that there really could be loose nukes. Now add a whole barge full of them, hidden in violation of an arms treaty, being used by an Indian conspiracy to severely cripple China. And we've got hard evidence to back up the story. Can you imagine the media feeding frenzy?"

In spite of himself, Petrov laughed. "It will be interesting watching the news shows for several weeks."

"And the best place for us may be on this submarine, at sea, and at depth," Jerry added, smiling, "at least until the smoke clears." He sat up straighter. "Migawd. I'll have to warn Emily, and my sister Clarice in Minnesota. Emily can stay on the base and away from the media, but Clarice may have to move into a convent to get any peace."

Petrov laughed again, remembering his own close family

members. He told a story about his older brother Yevgeny's experiment with propane in the family's tractor. Then Jerry told one involving the use of high-pressure air in cleaning a bilge, and Alex told one about how the Russian Navy had once tried to clear the snow in Murmansk—with a turboprop. They talked for hours, and only stopped when it was time for Jerry to make his next set of rounds.

Petrov napped that afternoon, and woke refreshed.

9 April 2017
1930 Local Time
Control Room, USS *North Dakota*

To Samant, it was more like a movie set than a submarine control room. He and *North Dakota*'s executive officer, Lieutenant Commander Bernie Thigpen, had decided after dinner to continue work on the search plan. Samant was tired, and a full stomach had him yawning, but his mind was still alive with questions about the search: How would the new towed sonar affect *Chakra*'s ability to detect other ships and subs? But towed arrays didn't work well in shallow water. Would Jain adjust his route to stay in deep water, even if it took longer?

As they worked, part of his mind cataloged the many differences between American and Indian submarines. The American sub's control room was more spacious than he was used to, which was surprising because *North Dakota* was three-quarters the size of *Chakra*. The layout was different, of course, but he understood what everything did. And it amazed and frightened him. The American sub had better sensors, including the UUVs, and a far superior combat system to use the data those sensors provided. To top it off, her enlisted men were better trained. American senior petty officers were doing the same jobs as lieutenants on his submarine.

Not his sub, Samant corrected himself. Not anymore. Not even part of the Indian Navy anymore. He'd spent all afternoon telling Jerry Mitchell and the other Americans secrets that under normal circumstances would have gotten him thrown in jail. Instead, he hoped it was enough to save his country and end this nightmare.

Samant had hardened his heart to the thought of what they were doing, turning the anger he felt toward Dhankhar and Kirichenko. Even if *Chakra* was . . . stopped, it would still be a tragedy—just not a catastrophe. It also helped if he didn't think about it too deeply, instead focusing on the here and now.

Using a spare display console, Thigpen had set up a series of encounters between *Chakra* and *North Dakota*, using different approach angles, depths, and acoustic conditions. According to the sonar simulation, the American boat still held an edge in good water. She was quieter, and her sensors were a little better. Another advantage that the computer couldn't model was that *North Dakota*'s crew was familiar with her systems, while Jain and his men would still be trying to understand their new sonar's capabilities.

Samant chided himself for thinking about *Chakra*'s new captain. He'd always been hard on his former first officer, but that was just his way of preparing the man for command—but not like this. He simply couldn't understand why Jain had been so easily duped by Dhankhar's plan. Samant took some small pleasure in knowing that the admiral had removed him from command because Dhankhar knew he couldn't count on Samant to be part of the plot.

Thigpen was looking for the best place to position *North Dakota* and her reconnaissance UUVs, asking Samant questions about *Chakra*'s standard operating procedures. What speed and depth would she transit at, depending on the water conditions? Samant, at the direction of the Indian government, answered all the questions as best he could. The information would be used to a good end.

Afterward, of course, the American navy would collect whatever he told them and share it with the rest of their fleet. *Chakra* was Russian-built, and there were other Improved Akula I–class submarines in the Russian fleet. He didn't feel any regrets about his information being used for that purpose. It was the price the Russians paid for hiding the bootleg warheads in the first place.

The hardest part of their job was to estimate the likely route that *Chakra* would take. If she hugged the Chinese coast as she moved north and east, she could hide in the noise generated by the hundreds of ships in the area, as well as the sounds made by the many life-forms that lived in coastal waters, and even the sound of waves on shore. But that made for a much longer trip and *Chakra*'s own sonar search capability would also be affected. Submariners didn't like shallow water. It limited their options.

Besides, *Chakra* had that new towed sonar, and she couldn't use it at all in shallow water. Samant tapped the chart near Hong Kong. It was not only the southernmost target on that list, but one of the biggest. Everyone had agreed with the U.S. intelligence community's assessment that it was likely *Chakra*'s first destination. "He will stay in deep water as long as possible, and approach directly. It's ten hours at fifteen knots from the deep water here until the water starts to shoal badly near the Wanshan Archipelago." Samant shifted his finger to the southwest and tapped the wide-open entrance to the Lema Channel; the water was just a little over thirty meters deep.

"Or less than eight hours if he pushes it to twenty knots," suggested Thigpen. "That reduces his time in shallow water leading up to the channel."

"If he doesn't think anyone's watching for him," replied Samant. "But I don't believe Jain would be so reckless. His predisposition is to follow established procedures whenever possible. That's just the way he is, and I reinforced this tendency through rigorous training. Jain will be cautious in his approach."

The American XO nodded agreement. "Well, it's the same waypoint regardless of his speed, or which of the two channels he takes. It's a place to start."

Having a location that *Chakra* was likely to pass through, Thigpen made some adjustments to the computer simulation to figure out what was the best search speed so their sonar would be able to detect the other sub but still cover the largest possible area. The trick was to find *Chakra* before she got to "Point X-ray."

Samant studied the two submarines at their respective locations, in deep water off the Chinese coast. "As an experiment," he asked, "can you change *Chakra* to her original configuration, before her towed array was upgraded?"

"Sure, no problem," Thigpen answered. He clicked on a side menu, lowered the array's performance, reset the simulation, and then ran the encounter again. This time, *North Dakota* detected the Indian submarine a full ten minutes earlier, with an increase in detection range of nearly four nautical miles.

Samant slowly dropped back into his chair; he'd expected an improvement, but the magnitude of the shift left him shocked. No, horrified. He asked Thigpen, "Is . . . is this what you remember? Was this what it was like when our submarines met before?"

Thigpen nodded soberly, but remained silent.

"I understood that the *Virginia* class were technically superior to the Akula I subs, but that much! No wonder your captain was able to beat us. With that much of an advantage, a monkey could have won."

The American XO was silent for a moment, but then spoke carefully. "Captain Mitchell is the smartest and most imaginative officer I've ever served under. You should be grateful that he never intended to sink your boat . . ."

"I quite agree," Samant interrupted. "It would have been a trivial exercise with this kind of superiority."

"You're selling my captain a little short, aren't you sir?" Thigpen said harshly.

"No, no," soothed Samant. "He's a good man, and I trust him, but with this *starship*"—he swept his arm, encompassing the control room—"against my old boat, he'd have been a fool to lose."

Thigpen's expression went through several changes, and Samant realized that *North Dakota*'s first officer was torn between defending his captain and disagreeing with a senior officer, even if he was from a different navy. Samant said, "Please, speak freely, Commander."

Permission to speak his mind seemed to calm the American naval officer slightly. Samant could have just as easily left him frustrated and silent. "Thank, you, sir." Thigpen drew a short breath, and explained, "Our orders were to interfere with your attacks, which was much more difficult than just firing a torpedo to sink you. Captain Mitchell's motives were always to prevent loss of life, and he was innovative and resourceful. Who do you think devised the operation that ended the war?"

"The nuclear blue-out was his idea?" Samant was surprised, but then vaguely recalled that Petrov had said something similar. In an attempt to stop the fighting, the Americans had taken drastic action, detonating eight nuclear weapons underwater in a pattern that had flooded the South and East China Seas with noise. The phenomenon, called "blue-out," had lasted for days. Ship and submarine sonars were blinded, and the combatants had retreated to port. Without causing any injuries, America had imposed a cease-fire.

Samant, commanding *Chakra*, had encountered *North Dakota* as the American sub was preparing to fire two of the nuclear-tipped torpedoes that were part of the plan. Without knowing the American's mission, Samant had done his level best to first drive off the U.S. sub, then to actually sink it. Mitchell's sub had not only avoided his weapons, but launched the torpedoes as planned and escaped. Samant had avoided damage from the blasts only by following the American sub's lead.

Jerry Mitchell had maneuvered his sub in a close-quarters melee that had almost resulted in a collision. Especially with what he'd learned since coming aboard *North Dakota*, he'd had to acknowledge that Mitchell had "won" that encounter.

Finally, Samant nodded and replied, "Your point is well taken. I may have given the technology too much credit." For Samant, it was an abject apology. He wasn't used to giving one, but he couldn't stand against Thigpen's loyalty to his captain. He wondered if Jain would have done the same thing under similar circumstances, and as soon as he thought of the question, he knew the answer was that Jain would not.

He'd never demanded or expected loyalty from Jain or any of his men, just immediate obedience, to the best of their ability. Samant knew that being a captain could not be a popularity contest, and he had always lumped loyalty into the same category.

Girish Samant would never command *Chakra* again, and would probably not command another submarine, but the president and defense minister had promised him a place in India's navy. He resolved to study Jerry Mitchell's methods. There was always something new to learn.

Samant spotted him at the same time as Lieutenant Iverson, the OOD, coming into control from forward. Iverson called, "Captain is in Control," but softly, per Jerry's standing orders. Anyone working wasn't supposed to come to attention, but Thigpen stood anyway, and reflexively Samant did as well. It was Jerry's boat, after all.

Thigpen briefed Jerry on the results of their planning. "Jain has two options in approaching the Hong Kong area, the larger Lema Channel to the southwest, or the much smaller Taitami Channel between the Dangan and Jiapeng island chains. Both are really shallow, barely one hundred feet deep, and both are busy shipping lanes. Taitami is more like a freeway in terms of shipping density, but it is the shortest route in."

Samant pointed to the narrow Taitami Channel on the chart. "The traffic separation scheme is very compressed here, the channel is only four nautical miles at its narrowest point. It would be a much more difficult path to navigate than the Lema Channel where Jain has adequate room to maneuver and there is a greater separation between the shipping lanes."

"But he spends more time in the really shallow water taking that route," Jerry protested.

"That's true, Captain, but any route Jain takes will require him to spend a lot of time in dangerously shallow water. The main advantage here is that there is a lot less traffic. You see, he has to fire from the center of Lema Channel, this is the best place given the fifty-kilometer range of the torpedo and the channel structure in the Wanshan Archipelago. By entering via the Lema Channel, Jain has to parallel this shipping lane for five miles, and only has to cross the two busiest. With Taitami, he has to run with the dense traffic for over twenty miles," argued Samant.

Jerry winced at the thought of having to play dodgeball with a bunch of very large merchant ships for twenty miles and then squeezing through a very narrow passage. "Okay, so the Lema Channel is our best bet. What's your recommendation for a search plan?"

Thigpen nodded and moved his finger to a dot on the chart labeled "X-ray." "Regardless of which channel Jain actually decides to use, Point X-ray is where he will likely begin his approach to Hong Kong. This is the closest point that deep water gets to the Chinese coast. If we park ourselves about ten miles out from this spot, we can look out into deeper water, while Jain has to look into shallower water. At twenty knots, we're quieter than *Chakra*, but we recommend we slow to fifteen knots—our optimum search speed. That maximizes our detection range and coverage."

Thigpen gestured to the south through southeast, showing the different routes they'd marked as possible routes for *Chakra*. "The greatest unknown is of course her current position. Captain Samant and I think these are the most likely avenues of approach, based on her standard transit rates, but which route she's using, and her progress, are just guesses. That's a lot to bet the farm on."

Samant watched Jerry listen to the briefing, then consider for a moment before asking, "What's the earliest time she could be at Point X-ray?"

The XO sighed. "If she takes the shortest route, and runs at the highest possible speed, which by the way makes her towed array useless, we still beat her to Point X-ray by almost a full day. Neither Captain Samant nor I think that's likely, because it makes them too detectable, and gives up their most valuable sensor. On the other hand, if she takes her time and tries to stay really covert, we get there about a week before *Chakra* does. Squadron Fifteen is going with a middle-of-the-road approach, but even so, she doesn't reach Hong Kong until fourteen or fifteen April."

"Why would Jain worry about being too detectable?" Jerry asked. "As far as he knows, this is a surprise attack. He's not expecting someone to be looking for him."

"We can't assume that, Captain," countered Samant. "Dhankhar was warned we were on to him before *Chakra* set sail, it's likely he gave Jain instructions to be careful without telling him explicitly what was going on. Besides, Jain would inherently become more cautious the closer he got to China."

"True, but if Jain thinks there's a chance he could be pursued, he could push at a higher speed to try and get to the targets as quickly as possible." Jerry straightened and turned to Samant. "Captain, how mission-oriented is Jain—compared to your average mission-oriented submariner, that is."

Samant answered, "That may be the wrong question, Jerry. I believe Jain will do everything in his power to accomplish his mission, but only if he believes it is a legal order. Jain is extremely respectful of authority. I'm afraid he may be too willing to obey orders, without examining them critically," the Indian admitted.

He continued, "If Jain were to hear a recall order, I believe—I want to believe—that he would obey it and return to Vizag. That's a happy ending for all of us. I also believe Dhankhar anticipated a recall. That's why he left our VLF station down for repairs. He's also probably told Jain to maintain radio silence, even turn his radio receivers off, until after he's accomplished his mission. So it's quite probable that he doesn't know he's been discovered, and will proceed at a higher transit speed. But I'm also convinced he'll slow as he approaches Hong Kong. He can't assume the Chinese will just sit in port."

Jerry frowned but nodded. "Thanks, Captain. That increases the chance he could get past us, which is not good." He paused, and his expression told Samant he was making a hard decision. He'd felt the same way himself.

"We're going to conduct our search closer to the Chinese coast," Jerry announced. "If we put ourselves right off the entrance to the Lema Channel, we cut our search area by more than half. We know where he's going, so let's take advantage of it. This also allows us to keep an eye on Taitami Channel, just in case our assumption is wrong."

"What?" Samant was incredulous. The shallower water and close proximity to numerous civilian merchant ships would negatively affect their detection range. Giving up the deeper water meant abandoning their greatest advantage over *Chakra*. Truth be told, he knew his old boat was tougher than *North Dakota*. Russian boats were designed to take a torpedo and survive. There was no question that one hit on the American submarine would be the end of them all. "You can't afford a close-quarters engagement," he protested.

"Bernie, what's the first thing you'd do before you went into really shallow water?" Jerry asked.

"Slow down, and reel in the towed array," the XO answered.

"And that's what we need, badly," Jerry explained. "If Jain slows down, that gives us more time to hear him as he gets closer. Yes, he'll be quieter, and the environment isn't as benign, but we still have an advantage, and this becomes even greater once he stows his towed array."

Thigpen started running the numbers. "With us sitting on the fifty-meter curve, against a slow Akula, we'd have an estimated detection range of ten, maybe twelve thousand yards depending on the local shipping noise."

"What about Napoleon and Bismarck?" asked Jerry.

"Hmph, I doubted they'd be even half that good. Give me a minute to check, sir," Thigpen grunted.

"Napoleon? Bismarck?" echoed Samant in confusion.

"Our UUVs. We named them after cities in the state of North Dakota," Jerry replied without taking his eyes off the display.

"You name them like pets?" demanded the Indian. *These Americans are a weird lot,* he thought.

"Sure, why not?" rebutted Thigpen. "We're actually quite attached to them. By the way, Captain, there are still some members of the crew that haven't forgiven you for running Minot over."

"I destroyed a city in North Dakota? Fortunes of war, Commander," Samant responded firmly, now convinced that the Americans were indeed crazy.

"Ah, here you go, Skipper," announced the XO. "Ooh, the UUVs' detection range is even shorter than I thought, about three thousand yards."

"Okay, Bernie, put the boat on a racetrack pattern roughly parallel to the Jiapeng Islands and the entrance to Lema Channel, speed fifteen knots. Then put Napoleon and Bismarck to the west and southwest, eight miles away from own ship. Use just barely overlapping five-mile race-tracks for both, speed five knots. How does that look?"

"Wait one, Skipper," Thigpen mumbled as his fingers rapped on the keyboard. It took a couple of minutes before he was ready to run the simulation. The results surprised him.

"Well, I'll be dipped in goo," he remarked. "The overall probability of detection actually is better, noticeably better. Nice call, Skipper."

"Thanks, XO. And I'm sure you and Captain Samant can refine the basic search pattern and eke out another percentage point or two." Jerry saw Samant lean forward, studying the simulation display. His head nodding slightly, a smile crept onto his face.

Although it went against his instincts, Samant was now convinced. He didn't know if he would make the same decision in Jerry's place, even if he'd thought of it. Mitchell was right, though. The approach Samant and Thigpen had originally planned had a lower calculated chance of finding *Chakra*.

Before departing, Jerry turned toward Samant and said, "Oh, Captain, I've got something else for you to do as well, if you're willing."

"Whatever I can do to help, of course."

"I'd like you to prerecord a message that we can play over the underwater telephone, just in case we can get close enough, without being shot at, of course. Even if they have shut down their communications, they can't ignore the sonar. If Jain and his crew hear the recall order from you, there's a chance they'll stop, and nobody has to die."

Samant felt a flash of hope, and he felt grateful to Jerry. The American was still doing his best to think of ways to end this peacefully. The underwater telephone had a range of only a few kilometers, and the chance of his crew actually recognizing his warbled voice was low, but he could certainly record a short message that would sound like it was coming from their old captain, and tell them to turn around.

They had to play every angle, and just hope for the best.

18

Pursuit

14 April 2017
1100 EST
White House Situation Room
Washington, D.C.

It had taken more time than she could afford to just get the videoconference organized. Although in theory, Submarine Squadron Fifteen was coordinating the military forces involved in the hunt for *Chakra*, the reality was far more complex.

China was insisting that any aircraft or ship employed in the operation be under their "positive control." They refused to say what that meant. They also refused to say what ships and aircraft from their own forces would take part in the search, or what their capabilities were. After three days of Chinese turndowns, delays, and evasions, Commodore Simonis had finally brought Joanna Patterson into the loop. She'd agreed that the issue was something that needed to be addressed at a higher level.

In spite of the urgency, the defense minister couldn't spare them any time until it was very late, Beijing time, and in Guam. When the teleconference was finally set up, General Shi We, the PRC's Minister of National Defense, was late, and appeared impatient, dividing his attention between the teleconference and someone off to one side and out of view. It was not a good start to the meeting.

Shi's image showed a man in his seventies, balding and thin. He was not sympathetic to Simonis's concerns. "We don't have time to deal with these requests. The Chinese government is currently concerned with mobilizing our forces to stop these criminals."

"That is unacceptable, General." Patterson's tone was harsh, almost angry. "Many nations have banded together to assist in your defense, and China seems reluctant, even unwilling, to accept that help."

"We might not need any assistance if our fleet had not been decimated by sneak attacks," he spat.

"General Shi, we have good information about the losses to your fleet during the recent conflict. While your commercial tankers suffered grievous losses, China only lost about a dozen major warships and even fewer submarines. Are these enough to prostrate China's navy?"

Shi looked ready to explode, then seemed to gather himself. He said carefully, "China is grateful for any assistance in this dangerous time." Patterson thought his English was very good, especially if he could use it when he was so upset. He'd obviously been ordered to play nicely, but also obviously didn't like doing it.

Commodore Simonis had been silent during this exchange, but Patterson had remained aware of his presence. He'd called her when he'd been unable to coordinate with the Chinese, and this meeting, arranged with such difficulty, confirmed his report. She was now as concerned as he was.

"General, Commodore Simonis reports he's been unable to properly organize aircraft patrols, because your navy refuses to abandon the initial barrier patrol off the coast of Vietnam. It's over three hundred miles from your base in Hainan, which means a lot of wasted time getting to and from the patrol line. He's recommended a zone closer to your coast, which will maximize the time your aircraft spend on station."

Shi nodded. "I am familiar with this issue."

"The commodore says he's been unable to get an explanation of the reasons for this, much less your navy's cooperation."

She nodded toward Simonis's image, and the commodore added, "I've promised to put a P-8 Poseidon in its place, the most capable aircraft we have, with far better sensors than the SH-5 or Y-8s you've been putting out there."

"It may be more capable," the general responded, "but is it true that the Indian Navy is also operating P-8 aircraft from your base in Guam?"

"Yes," Simonis replied. "They've provided four aircraft so far, all they have operational, and promise more within twenty-four hours."

"And they will be patrolling throughout the area?" Shi asked.

"Yes, all along *Chakra*'s possible transit routes, as part of the overall search plan." Simonis answered carefully, but Patterson could hear a question in his tone. Where was Shi going with this?

"Will there be American observers aboard the Indian planes, people other than the crews?"

Simonis's expression on the monitor showed his confusion. "No, why would there be?"

"To ensure that if they detect the criminal submarine, they actually report it." Patterson and Simonis both started to answer at the same time, and when they both paused, giving each other a chance to speak, Shi added, "We are amazed that the same country that owns the rogue submarine is sending aircraft to 'help' find it."

Patterson countered, "We have no reason to doubt the dedication of the Indian crews. Their government is doing its best to arrest the conspirators, and has actually sent a liaison officer to provide information on *Chakra*'s specifications and tactics."

"Very comforting. The Chinese government will be very surprised if an Indian aircraft reports the location of the Indian submarine, much less attacks and sinks it."

On her laptop computer, a text message from Simonis appeared. "I can put a parallel barrier just behind the Chinese zone. It's a waste of resources, but we can't make them trust the Indians." Shi couldn't see it, and she typed a quick "OK, thanks."

"Let's table that issue for a moment, General. Commodore Simonis is also concerned about receiving the hydrographic information near the target ports, and along the coast. He's requested the information several times, and the only answer he's received is that the information is being updated and isn't ready yet."

Simonis started to speak, but Shi cut him off. "I understand the importance of such information to antisubmarine searches," he said sharply. "Salinity, temperature gradients, ambient noise, and so on.

"Another important feature marked on the charts are wrecked ships. Patrol planes searching for submarines use magnetic detectors to look for the submarine's metal hull. A sunken ship could easily be mistaken for a submerged submarine, so even if the wreck is not a hazard to navigation, the location must still be marked on the chart."

By now, Patterson was texting Simonis offscreen. She typed a "???," to which the commodore responded, "Their ASW charts must be worse than ours."

Shi was still talking. "About six months ago, a large number of wrecks were added to those already present. If your pilots use the existing charts, they'll discover that China's coastal waters are full of submarines."

Patterson was still trying to think of what to text Simonis when a message appeared from him: "WAPOBS." She hadn't seen that acronym before. She wasn't sure what it meant, but it probably wasn't polite.

It turned out Shi was just getting started. "It is also vital that Commodore Simonis inform us of the flight plans and positions of all aircraft as they enter the South China Sea aircraft identification zone . . ."

Patterson had to stop herself from groaning out loud. Ever since the end of the war, the Chinese had "reestablished" the "air defense zone" to help support their territorial claim to the entire South China Sea. It was pure posturing, and accomplished nothing.

She cut Shi off in midsentence. "General Shi, is it possible that you do not understand the threat posed by this submarine to your country?"

"Do you mean the threat by the Indians to send nuclear torpedoes into five of our largest coastal cities, incinerating millions of Chinese citizens? That threat?"

Shi paused, then declared, "We have no intention of letting you turn the South China Sea into an American lake, or letting Littoral Alliance and American vessels operate freely in our waters. One reason why I'm meeting with you at this late hour is that the Central Military Commission just finished holding an emergency meeting. We are putting our nuclear forces on wartime alert. A message has been sent to the Indian government stating that if a nuclear weapon destroys a Chinese city, India will lose a city of the same size. Ports first, of course, but . . ."

"This is insane!" Patterson shouted. "The submarine has gone rogue. The Indians have been broadcasting recall messages nonstop."

"Maybe they haven't been trying hard enough," Shi replied in a condescending tone. "I know you're convinced it's gone rogue, and you're trying to stop it. But aren't you also taking advantage of a crisis created by the Indians to extend your influence in the region?

"Think about it, Dr. Patterson. The Littoral Alliance's goal in the recent war was to wreck our economy. They couldn't manage it then, so the Indians concocted this plot to finish the job. Because this will indeed wreck my nation, and if only millions died I'd think we were fortunate.

But if millions of Chinese do die, then India will suffer just as dearly."

"But they have no control over it!" Patterson insisted.

"That remains to be seen. A demarche was sent to the Indian government about an hour ago. Many of use believe the 'rogue' submarine will have a change of heart. They may even put the captain through some sort of show trial along with the rest of the 'conspirators.' Certainly a failed plan of this magnitude will require some housecleaning."

"And if *Chakra* doesn't turn around?"

"China will defend herself. If your ships and planes find and sink the Indian, that is good news and we will be genuinely grateful. But our navy commander has assured us that they are concentrating their defenses to protect our ports. Since those operations are happening inside our own territorial waters, there is no need to coordinate with your forces. As long as your ships and planes stay outside our territorial waters, you may do as you please."

15 April 2017
1100 Local Time
INS *Chakra*
Lema Channel, Wanshan Qundao
Hong Kong, China

"The navigation aid on Wenwei Zhou Island bears green zero nine one degrees, ten kilometers. We are on track, recommend turning to zero five five degrees in thirty seconds. That will take us between the two marked channels." Although Lieutenant Commander Kumar Rakash had taken over Jain's duties as first officer, before that he'd been *Chakra*'s navigator, and Jain had insisted that he take over his old job for the actual approach to the firing position.

"What's the distance to the wreck ahead of us?" Jain asked.

"Eight thousand, two hundred meters, bearing red zero

two five," Rakash responded instantly. "After the turn we will be opening the range. Mark the turn."

"Starboard fifteen, steer new course zero five five degrees." Now it began. Jain was nervous, and fought to keep his voice calm. Although they'd been warned to watch for signs of hostile activity, it appeared the Chinese were not expecting them. All he had to do was focus on the navigation. That was the only thing that could get him into trouble, but that was enough.

Hong Kong was a world-class deep-water port, but only for surface vessels. Thirty meters of water was more than enough for the largest supertanker, but *Chakra* needed eighteen meters just to submerge. Splitting the difference gave her only six meters over her sail and six between her keel and the bottom.

"Lieutenant Kota, report." Jain tried to speak softly, to project the calmness he wished he felt.

"There are five ships ahead of us in the Lema Channel, three heading northeast ahead of us, the other two approaching on southwest courses. Closing speeds on both approaching vessels are ten knots. All contacts show appropriate bearing drift."

Lieutenant Harish Kota, the usual navigator, had been assigned the sole task of tracking the heavy merchant traffic in the channel, using passive bearings from *Chakra*'s hull sonars.

"Drafts?" asked the captain.

"We've identified two, both container ships: *Xin Ning Bo*, nine meters, northeast at ten knots and *Wanhai 317*, eleven meters, southwest at ten knots. There's also a small tanker, and two even smaller vessels, all doing about ten knots."

That was the regulated speed in the channel, which was divided into two lanes, northeast toward the harbor and southwest toward the open sea. While it was theoretically possible to pass another ship in your lane in the channel, the authorities judged it unwise and required all vessels to maintain the same speed, as well as a healthy separation between each ship in the lane.

Jain was taking *Chakra*, submerged, up the two-thousand-meter-wide buffer between the inbound and outbound channels. Like a bicyclist pedaling on the median between opposing lanes of traffic, drifting too far to either side meant disaster.

But all he had to do was steer straight on course 055 degrees for eighteen and a half miles. At five knots, that would take almost four hours, but he didn't dare go any faster or *Chakra* would leave a V-shaped wake on the surface, pointing like an arrow to his exact position. Merchant sailors were not the most observant lot, but Jain was sure that with all the traffic up there, somebody would ask embarrassing questions.

And that would be a problem. From this point on, he was committed to a four-hour run to the northeast, to the firing point in the center of the channel. If he was spotted, he could not maneuver or dive deep to evade pursuit. Speeding up would be pointless.

"First Officer, keep us biased toward the outbound channel. It's the inbound channel I worry about."

"Only if they don't stay in the channel, sir."

"Exactly my concern. A merchant traveling at ten knots and us at five knots, and blind in our stern arc, with no way to see him coming? Do you trust civilian navigators to stay in the lane?"

"No, sir!"

Jain turned to Kota, working at the next console. "And any time there's a sizable gap in the outbound traffic, tell the first officer and me so we can slide *Chakra* over even farther to the left."

Jain saw the Russian Orlav enter the central post from forward. He waited for the captain to turn away from the chart table before reporting. "Prefiring checks are complete, Captain. The weapon is loaded in tube number one, as ordered." His navy reflexes had kicked in. He might as well have been one of the crew.

"Very well," Jain remarked automatically. He turned to look at Rakash, who without prompting reported, "Sixteen and a half miles, three hours and twenty minutes."

"Very well." Jain nodded, then asked Orlav, "Where is Kirichenko?" He didn't bother with the Russian's title. He might have been an admiral once, but he wasn't anymore, as far as Jain was concerned.

"In our stateroom," Orlav answered.

"Poring over maps, no doubt," Jain said, laughing. Orlav frowned at his tone, but said nothing.

Theoretically, Orlav didn't need to make any checks, but if there was a problem that prevented the torpedo from working as intended, he wouldn't get paid. The two Russians had actually finished their assembly work two days ago. In addition to installing the last two torpedo warheads, they had reset the timers on all five weapons to April 23, since they were leaving two weeks earlier than Operation Vajra had originally planned.

Kirichenko had complained nonstop about the lack of proper lighting, the lack of enough tools, and especially the cramped working conditions, but they had to work in the torpedo room. In addition to the five special weapons, *Chakra* carried thirty-three UGST-type torpedoes—a full load. Dhankhar had made sure that if they had to fight their way in or out, they had the wherewithal to do it.

So, although it had taken longer than expected, they had still finished with time to spare. The moment Jain had inspected their work, and announced that he was satisfied, Kirichenko turned over the code cards and asked for the money Dhankhar had promised them.

"Is there somewhere you plan to spend it?" Jain asked. He was smiling at the man's foolishness, even while he was repelled by the Russian's greed. Kirichenko started to protest, but Jain cut him off. "You will get your money as was agreed, once we are away and the weapons have exploded. As promised, we will then put you two off in rubber rafts with your money."

Knowing that there was nothing else to be done, Kirichenko had asked for a nautical chart and a port directory. Since then, he had appeared only for meals, which he ate silently, brooding.

Orlav had been more cooperative, or maybe Kirichenko wasn't the best company and he preferred the companionship of the crew. He'd borrowed a pair of coveralls and proceeded to thoroughly check over the firing circuits and all the other modifications that had been made.

"Sonar contact close aboard, starboard side aft!" The urgency of Kota's report almost made everyone glance over their shoulder. It was only a moment later that they actually heard a *thrum-thrum-thrum* through the hull.

"Bearing rate!" Jain demanded, which Kota acknowledged with a quick nod as he looked at the Omnibus display.

The navigator-turned-contact-coordinator held out a hand for a moment, then reported "Rapid left," meaning that the ship which had suddenly emerged from their blind arc aft was passing down their starboard side, as it was supposed to, and was not in danger of ramming into the submerged submarine.

Kota reported, "Contact evaluated as a medium-sized tanker."

"You could have fooled me," Jain replied, smiling.

Most of the crewmen in the central post laughed, and Jain with them.

"Let me guess: speed ten knots, headed northwest."

Kota nodded agreement.

"Tell the sonar operator well done."

There were five more overtakes in the next three hours, each as sudden as the first, and just as terrifying, until it could be confirmed that their bearing drift showed that they were passing along the sub's starboard side as they headed into port.

If the bearing had stayed constant, and knowing that the ship was likely five knots faster than his boat, Jain would have ordered a sudden zig out of the way. The problem was that ten-thousand-ton submarines didn't zig quickly. He'd actually had to consider the size of *Chakra*'s turning circle at five knots, which was huge, as well as the width of Lema Channel, which was not all that roomy. It would be a desperate, risky maneuver, but better than being ground down into the bottom under a merchant's keel.

Orlav had gone forward to the torpedo room. There was nothing else for him to do there, but it seemed the best place for him to wait.

"Firing point in six minutes," the first officer reported.

Jain acknowledged the report. He wouldn't use the periscope. They didn't need periscope bearings to launch the torpedo, not unless Stonecutters Bridge had shifted its position. The massive suspension bridge linking Stonecutters Island to southern Hong Kong was his aim point, and they couldn't see it anyway, not at twenty-plus miles away and with Lamma Island blocking the line of sight. Besides, the surface traffic was insane. He'd be lucky if someone only spotted the scope head, and didn't run him over.

"Tube one at action state," Rakash reported, now wearing his first officer hat. "Two thousand meters to firing point."

"Very well." Jain was watching the time and distance carefully, but launching the weapon was only the next step in a continuing process. Actually, he was already thinking about the turn, which would be just a little to the right. That would take them toward the northern exit from the channel, another five miles ahead.

"Confirm the settings," Jain ordered.

Kirit, the combat system officer, reported, "Turn to zero zero zero degrees, due north, for seventeen nautical miles, one waypoint with a turn to zero three two, then five point two miles. Constant depth of fifteen meters until the dive at the end."

Jain followed along on the chart as the combat system officer read off the torpedo's ordered course. It was all correct. The weapon could actually swim as far as twenty-seven nautical miles, and could turn more than once, but once was enough for this port. Not only did the torpedo's long range shorten the time he had to spend in a hostile location, but the harbor shallowed rapidly to the north, with depths of much less than thirty meters. Twenty meters was average, in some spots less than that. The torpedo could operate freely at fifteen meters, but *Chakra* would need wheels to stay submerged in water that shallow, if she could do it at all.

Jain walked over to the torpedo control console. Kirit had selected "Arming Code" on his display, and the cursor hovered over an empty box. A new keypad, part of *Chakra*'s modifications, sat on the upper left corner of the console, and Jain looked at the card he'd taken out of his shirt pocket. He slowly punched in the eight-digit code on the keypad, checking each number as he entered it, and as he typed the last digit, the numbers changed from white to red, and were then replaced with "Armed."

"Firing point in one minute."

Jain ordered, "Open bow cap on tube one." Operating the mechanism that opened the outer tube door would make some noise for a short time, called a "transient." In open water he might worry about a hostile sub hearing it, but in the bedlam of a harbor it was just one more hammer in a boiler factory.

"Bow cap open on tube number one," Kirit reported. "Standing by."

Jain watched Rakash, and Rakash watched the clock and the chart display. Jain could see him counting down, and the first officer said, "Fifteen seconds," and then, "Firing point."

"Firing sequence, tube one."

"Firing sequence tube one, aye," Kirit responded, then announced, "Torpedo is away."

Jain was ready. "Close bow cap on tube one, starboard fifteen, steady on new course zero three seven." He watched Rakash as he gave the order. The first officer nodded, confirming that the preplanned course was still good.

Five miles to the exit. He was tempted to increase speed, like a thief leaving the scene of a crime, but a wise thief would know to walk, and not run, lest he draw attention to himself.

Once they were steadied on their new course, and clear of any traffic using the northern part of the channel, Jain picked up the microphone for the general announcing system. "Attention, all hands, this is the Captain. You have all performed your different duties extremely well, without asking questions. That doesn't mean you don't have questions, and I can now tell you that our mission is to strike deep at the heart of Pakistan's patron and supplier, China. We have just launched a single torpedo which, about twenty minutes from now, will reach the heart of Hong Kong's Victoria Harbor and dive down, burying itself in the mud at the base of Stonecutters Bridge. In eight days, at exactly noon, the nuclear warhead the torpedo carries will detonate, destroying the heart of one of China's largest ports.

"We have four more such weapons, and will visit four more ports before we leave Chinese waters. We will be well out to sea by April twenty-third, when all five torpedoes explode at the same moment, crippling our old enemy and signaling the start of a new surprise offensive by our ground and air forces in Pakistan. Without the Chinese to prop them up, the Paks will turn tail and their lines will crumble. By the time we return home, China will be in ruins and the war will be over, with the Pakistanis in front of us on their knees!"

He hadn't intended to put that much emotion into the speech, but the thought of an end to not just the current war, but the decades-long struggle with Pakistan, had fired his mind since Vice Admiral Dhankhar had given him his orders. He'd do his utmost to knock out the support that had kept Pakistan fighting long after she should have given up.

Besides, he must have struck the right tone, because while the crewmen in the central post were quiet, he could hear cheering coming from the fore and aft passageways.

Although reaching the firing point and launching the weapon was a major accomplishment, the reality was anticlimactic. There was no explosion, and would not be for several days, thank goodness. For all the excitement they could have just as easily delivered a gallon of milk. He took some comfort in the fact that there were now only four nuclear weapons aboard his boat, instead of five.

Although the northern part of the Lema Channel was also divided into two lanes, there was considerably less traffic here, and it was a much shorter run, just five and a half miles to the turn point past Dangan Island on the southeast side. The greatest hazard was still navigational, and while they'd had to be careful around several submerged wrecks in the channel on the way in, the northern passage was littered with them, which might explain the lighter traffic. The biggest problem were three wrecks spaced like the posts of a picket fence, roughly one mile apart across the six-mile-wide exit. They were too deep for a merchant ship to worry about, but they lay square in his path.

Forty-five minutes after they had turned, and in accordance with the plan they'd worked out long before entering the harbor, Jain said, "Energize the Arfa sonar."

The Arfa was the exact opposite of *Chakra*'s main Skat-3 search sonar, which was a big, low-frequency set that lined the sub's flanks and filled the bow. Arfa was much smaller, and fit on the front of the sub's sail. It also operated at a much higher frequency, well above human hearing.

While it couldn't see more than a couple of miles or so out in front of the sub, it gave a clear image on the display, not quite an underwater camera but good enough to make out what was in front of them. Its earliest ancestors had guided submarines through minefields in World War II, and it could locate mines or obstructions, like wrecks, in a sub's path.

Although it sent out an active high-frequency ping, high-frequency sound didn't go as far as lower frequencies. An active pulse from the Skat-3 sonar transducer would carry dozens of miles. The Arfa's signal would weaken quickly. Besides, he wasn't going to leave it on all the time.

"No sign of obstructions," Rakash reported, or rather confirmed. Jain could see for himself that the Arfa's display was clear. "Recommend cease transmissions, next transmission in ten minutes."

"Very well," Jain acknowledged. They'd be fifteen hundred meters farther along, with a good chance of spotting the wrecks. He was beginning to feel impatient. His mind was already out past Dangan Island, wondering again if there was any way to shave more time off the trip to the next port.

"Tube one has been reloaded with a conventional UGST torpedo," Kirit reported.

"Very well." They would have to pull the weapon out when they reached the next target so they could load a nuclear-armed torpedo, but until then, he wanted all eight tubes ready for a fight.

Traffic was lighter in the channel, but there was still one ship approaching, and another almost out. The departing ship had been much closer when they turned, but with them still creeping at five knots, it had pulled steadily away.

"Recommend energizing Arfa sonar again."

"All right, First Officer, go ahead."

Thirty seconds later they studied a white-on-green image of the seabed and the objects ahead of them. It resembled a false-color television picture, but strangely shadowed unless you understood what it represented. Things that reflected sonar well were bright, while softer or porous materials were dimmer. Rocks and new metals were brightest, then sand and corroded metal were a little dimmer. Mud and masses of plant life showed as dark spots. There was enough resolution to not only see the three wrecks, but also their condition. One was little more than a skeleton, one an angular mass of metal, while the third was almost intact. Passing too close to any of them would risk damaging his boat.

A bearing readout across the bottom of the screen gave Jain exactly what he needed. "Starboard fifteen, steer zero three four."

The helmsman acknowledged the order, and Jain said, "Rakash, I intend to go to the left of the center wreck. The gap between left and center . . ."

"Torpedo propellers bearing green zero one four! Seeker is active!" shouted the sonar operator over the intercom. The acoustic intercept receiver, a device designed to listen for and warn them about hostile sonar transmissions, began beeping loudly just as sonar gave their report.

"Release countermeasure, release decoy!" Jain gave the order almost without thinking. "Rapid fire procedures, tubes one and two, torpedo course zero four six, zero five zero! Full speed, minimal enable run! Fire!"

Jain barely heard Kirit acknowledge the firing order. "Helmsman, increase speed to twenty knots, change depth to eighteen meters." His maneuvering orders were punctuated by two dull shocks he could feel through the deck as the torpedoes were fired.

He looked around the central post. The decoy and countermeasure were out there, hopefully muddying up the water, and he'd counterfired two weapons back down the bearing of the approaching torpedo. The deck was vibrating under their feet as the prop spun, churning the water

to froth as *Chakra* built up speed. For the moment, that
was all they could do. Was it enough?

"Sonar, report."

"Seeker is active, constant bearing."

Rakash was watching the sonar display next to Jain. They
were still heading for the gap between the wrecks, although *Chakra* seemed to be going slower, not speeding up.

The first officer observed, "Turning really isn't an
option here . . ."

"In the channel?" Jain observed. "Besides, that would
mean turning back the way we came. Open water and
safety is out ahead of us. Kirit, what about our torpedoes?"

"Both running at speed, their seekers are still searching."

Sonar reported, "Hostile torpedo has shifted from short
scale back to search! Steady bearing rate!"

"It's lost us?" Jain wondered hopefully.

"The countermeasure . . ." Rakash suggested.

"Hopefully the weapons we sent back will force our attacker to maneuver, breaking any guidance wire. And
then the weapon searches for us, it will hopefully home
in on either the decoy or maybe even one of the wrecks
we are rapidly closing on."

"Passing fifteen knots," the helmsman reported. Jain
knew that by looking at the Arfa's sonar display; the sonar didn't work well at high speed, and the image was blur-
ring and washing out.

He made one last adjustment. "Starboard ten, steer zero
three six."

The wrecks were just a few hundred meters ahead,
barely more than a boat length.

Jain announced, "After we're past the wrecks, I'm going to go active for one ping. Hopefully we will see him.
Stand by for sharp maneuvers and to fire another pair of
torpedoes. Open bow caps on tubes three and four."

Jain saw heads nodding. Both Rakash and Kirit said
"Understood" softly.

"Sonar, what about the torpedo?" he demanded.

"It's gone, Captain. Constant bearing all the way. It mu have passed directly under us. It's in the baffles now." H could almost hear the man's shrug over the intercom.

"One of our torpedoes has shifted to short scale!" Th sonarman's excited report was almost a shout.

They were past the line of wrecks by now. Part of hi wanted to slow down, but the more distance they put b tween them and the hostile torpedo, the better. It had be turning by now . . .

"Explosion!"

"Where away?" Jain demanded.

"Off our starboard bow. Solid hit." The sonar operato Chief Petty Officer Patil, had seen enough attacks on me chants during the war to know what one should soun like. But what about the weapon searching for them?

It came an eternity later, almost thirty seconds by th clock. "Sonar reports a low rumble, evaluated as reverbe ation from an explosion." Their enemy's weapon had foun something to home in on, and attacked it, all of it happen ing in their blind zone aft. Still, an echo was all the needed to hear.

"Rakash, can we turn now?"

The navigator only had to glance at the plot. "Yes, Cap tain! Recommend course one seven five, new depth twenty five meters. We can increase depth to forty meters in fiftee minutes—twenty minutes if we slow to fifteen knots, whic I strongly recommend."

Jain realized he was gripping the edge of the chart ta ble, hard, and told his hands to let go. They did, which wa a relief, and he realized he had fought and won his firs battle as *Chakra*'s captain.

He gave the helmsman the new course, speed, an depth, then turned back to the chart table. He studied th chart and did the math.

"He fired an active weapon, which meant he was clos

o more than five thousand meters. That's how I knew I
could fire active weapons back," Jain remarked to Rakash.

Jain then asked, "Sonar. Did you ever see more than one
orpedo fired at us? Did you identify the type?"

"Yes, Captain. Only one weapon was fired and it was a
TEST-71 on the high speed setting."

Jain nodded knowingly. The TEST-71 was a Russian-
made torpedo. *Chakra* had been equipped with similar
weapons in the past, but they'd been replaced a few years
ago with the newer UGST torpedoes, also Russian-made,
but a smarter, more dangerous weapon.

"And they only fired one torpedo," Jain observed. "That
means the shooter was one of their Kilo-class diesel boats.
They can only fire one wire-guided torpedo at a time."

Jain shook his head disparagingly. "He should have fired
two and just depended on the torpedo's seekers."

Rakash argued, "But the seekers wouldn't be able to tell
us apart from the wrecks."

"You're right," Jain agreed. "So he had to go for positive control and bet on a single shot being enough."

"But how did he hear us in the harbor? There were at
least two merchants between him and us, both as noisy as
cement mixers. And active sonar wouldn't help him search
with all that junk on the bottom."

"But it did," Jain countered, smiling. "Our own active
mine-hunting sonar, that is. When we used our Arfa to
search for the wrecks, he heard the pings, but not on his
passive search sonar."

Jain looked at the other officers. They were listening,
trying to understand. In fact, the central post was perfectly
silent. Everybody was listening.

"The Russian Kilo-class subs the Chinese bought are
fitted with the same Arfa collision-avoidance sonar we use.
Our first transmission, just for a short time, probably showed
up as a spike on their display. That warned them we were
out there. Then, we ran it continuously as we approached

the wrecks, it not only confirmed our presence, but gave him a beacon to line up his shot."

Jain admitted, "I made an assumption about the mine hunting sonar that almost killed us. I failed to ask a very important question about who or what might be searching for us. Well, we know they'll be searching for us now."

19

Flaming Datum

"CAPTAIN TO CONTROL," blared the 1MC, the ship's general announcing system. Jerry was in the torpedo room with Petrov when Thigpen's summons echoed throughout the ship. Dodging between the torpedo stowage racks and then up a ladder, Jerry moved at flank speed, with Petrov close behind. By the time they reached control, Samant was already beside Thigpen at the command workstation.

"It looks like she got past us," Thigpen stated grimly while handing his CO a message. "It's from the Squadron Fifteen OPCENTER."

Jerry took the piece of paper, glanced at it quickly, sighed, and read the message out loud. "Two large explosions reported by multiple civilian merchant ships in the vicinity of 22.11 north latitude, 114.20 east longitude at approximately sixteen hundred hotel time. No PLAN ships are listed as being in that area. Location of explosions is just north of Dangan Island in Dangan Shuido, which suggests *Chakra* was egressing from Hong Kong harbor area on an easterly course. Recommend you alter search area to the northeast in the direction of Ningbo-Zhoushan. PLAN has been notified of likely successful planting of nuclear-armed torpedo in Victoria Harbor and/or the Por of Shenzhen. *North Carolina* has been alerted."

He passed the message to Petrov, mumbling his frustration under his breath: "Damn it!" Spinning about, Jerr looked at the quartermaster of the watch and growled "Show me that location."

"Yessir," replied the petty officer hastily. It was rare fo the CO to be so pissed off. The chart display shifted and centered on the location, just outside Hong Kong. "Here is the reported position, Skipper, just to the right of the shipping channel." The young sailor pointed to the spot on the horizontal large-screen display.

Jerry nodded, and after a brief moment asked, "Where were we at sixteen hundred?" The quartermaster quickly entered in the time, and the pip marking *North Dakota's* location shifted twenty nautical miles back along her track By now Thigpen, Samant, and Petrov had gathered around the HLSD. A line of bearing extended from *North Dakota* ran right smack into the center of Dangan Island.

"No wonder we didn't hear the explosions," Jerry grumbled. "There's a fricking island in the way!"

"Murphy is working overtime today," lamented Thigpen

"Murphy? Who is Murphy?" asked Petrov, confused.

Thigpen smiled, then explained. "Murphy, as in Murphy's Laws. You know, if anything can go wrong, it will."

"Ah, I understand," Petrov responded. "The circumstances were not in our favor. So what do we do now? Head northeast in pursuit?"

"Why did Jain reveal his position by firing a weapon? What could he have been shooting at?" injected Samant. "The message made no mention of a ship being hit or sinking. Just two large explosions were observed."

"Another submarine," Jerry answered. "He got snapped up as he was exiting Dangan Shuido. A Chinese boat got lucky, found him, and fired first. Jain counterfired."

"Exactly!" exclaimed Samant. "He was forced to react,

and he did so in accordance with the tactical procedures that he was taught. I submit his evasion after the attack will follow along a similar line."

"And that means he probably won't be heading northeast, along the Chinese coast," concluded Jerry. "He'll head out to deeper water, give himself a little more maneuvering room."

"But he won't ignore his orders," Samant cautioned. "Jain will bias his evasion route toward the next target. Given that, the likely set of courses are between here and here." The Indian laid his hands down in a narrow pie wedge on the screen. The quartermaster made some adjustments on the screen, drawing two lines under Samant's hands, and quickly read off the bearings.

"It's between zero nine zero and one three zero, Skipper."

Jerry took over the controls and laid down two lines of bearing from *North Dakota*'s position toward the wedge. "Since we aren't hearing him now, he's almost certainly not at flank speed. Assuming a speed of, say, fifteen knots—" Jerry looked up at Samant, who nodded his agreement. "—*Chakra* is probably somewhere around here. Assuming we haven't totally messed things up."

"That's just thirty to forty miles behind us," said Thigpen.

"Correct, Commander. And that means we still have a chance of catching him," replied Samant; there was a tinge of regret in his voice.

"I'd like to note that we're making the explicit assumption *Chakra* wasn't hit in the encounter," noted Petrov. "And while I agree it's reasonable, someone should check and make sure it's valid."

Jerry looked at Petrov and nodded. "We can relay the request to Squadron Fifteen and they can ask the Chinese. It's way inside their territorial waters and I have no desire to test their acoustic classification ability. From what I've seen, their preferred method is to classify by ordnance. In the meantime, we have some things that need to be done before we can go chasing after *Chakra*.

"Bernie, recall Napoleon and Bismarck. I want them in their tubes in thirty minutes. Next, get us to periscope depth. We need to relay our questions and report our movements to Squadron Fifteen. Then we go hunting."

15 April 2017
1900 Local Time
Hong Kong Garrison Headquarters
People's Republic of China

Captain Zhang almost ran down the main corridor at the Hong Kong Garrison headquarters, hurrying to answer the urgent summons he'd just received from his superior's chief of staff. The day had started out on a chaotic note, and it had only gotten worse as it wore on. Besides coordinating the search for the Indian Akula, Zhang had been investigating the cause of the two large explosions reported by numerous ships in Dangan Shuido that afternoon. Moments earlier, he'd received the initial report from *Huizhou*, a Type 056 corvette assigned to the naval brigade at Hong Kong. *Huizhou*'s CO reported a large oil slick in the vicinity of the explosions, and that some debris had been recovered—debris that appeared to be of Chinese origin.

Then came the almost incomprehensible order from the South Sea Fleet headquarters in Zhanjiang to sortie the three minesweepers. When Zhang objected, saying the minesweepers would be of little use in searching for the Indian submarine, the agitated voice on the other end of the phone screamed, "Not the submarine, you fool! Sweep the harbor!" Before Zhang could even ask which one, the unidentified individual had slammed the receiver down. And now, Lieutenant General Tian wanted to see him immediately. If Zhang had any hair, it would've been on fire.

The chief of staff saw the captain coming and rushed

o open the door to the garrison commander's inner officer. Zhang nodded but said nothing. The door was shut almost before he'd passed through the jamb. He found
Lieutenant General Tian seated at his desk, both hands
cradling his head. At first, he seemed oblivious of the captain's presence; Tian's attention was focused on whatever
he was reading. Then slowly the general raised his head,
and Zhang saw his face—fear and dread were all over it.
Zhang suddenly felt a chill.

"Captain, I'm putting the entire garrison on a war footing. You're to have all ships in the naval brigade made
ready for sea immediately." Tian's voice was businesslike,
but there was a subtle shakiness to it as well.

"Of course, General. We are virtually ready now with
our patrol combatants currently out looking for the Indian
submarine. The minesweepers and the other auxiliaries
already have a full load of fuel and provisions and can deploy within the hour. Where am I to send the ships, sir?"

"What?" Tian mumbled. His expression seemed distant,
unfocused, and that's when Zhang realized the man was
in shock.

"General, what's wrong?" asked Zhang anxiously. He'd
never seen Tian so shaken before.

Tian raised the piece of paper in his hand, and offered
it to Zhang. The captain took it and started to read; he
didn't even get halfway through. "This . . . this can't be
true? It's unbelievable! Are we seriously going to accept
the Americans' word on something so . . . so fantastic?"

"The Central Military Commission has concluded the
Americans' warning is likely valid, and given the nature of
this emergency, we are hardly in the position to debate its
accuracy," replied Tian more firmly. "The question before
us, is what can we do about it?"

"Well, this explains the bizarre phone call I received
from the South Sea Fleet headquarters just before you
asked to see me. I was ordered to sortie the minesweepers, without any explanation," Zhang said as he glanced

again at the message. "I'll order the minesweepers out immediately and have them begin searching for the torpedo. But I still don't see which harbor they want us to search."

"You'll have to search both the Port of Shenzhen and Victoria Harbor, Captain, we don't have a choice."

"General, that is a lot of territory to cover with only three minesweepers," remarked Zhang cautiously. "We'd need at least twice that number to do the search properly. That and a lot of time."

Tian frowned; he was struggling to retain his composure, and the captain's pessimistic objections were causing him to lose his patience. "Aren't the crews adequately equipped and trained? We're talking about two relatively small areas, Captain."

"These are open-ocean minesweepers, General, they're designed to look for mines on the relatively clear ocean floor, not in the middle of a badly polluted port! The bottoms of Shenzhen and Victoria Harbor are littered with trash, and a lot of that trash will look very much like a torpedo. Each of those contacts will have to be visibly identified by a diver or an imaging sonar. With each port spread out over a hundred fifty square kilometers, that's a lot of area to cover, a lot of contacts that will have to be positively identified. This will take time."

The general didn't look happy. "What about the channel surveys the navy has conducted? How long did they take?"

Zhang shook his head. "Those surveys took weeks to complete and the most recent survey is nearly ten years old, and even then, that covers only a tiny fraction of the harbor floor. The rest of it hasn't been looked at in decades."

"We don't have weeks, Captain!" shouted Tian in frustration. "We may only have a few days! Perhaps even less!"

"I'm well aware of that, sir," Zhang shot back. "I'll deploy the minesweepers immediately and then request some civilian side-scan sonars be sent to equip the smaller auxiliaries. With a little luck I should be able to double the size of the mine-hunting force in the next twenty-four hours. When can I issue the Notice to Mariners that the ports of Shenzhen and Victoria Harbor are closed?"

Tian took a deep breath, and shook his head. "We aren't closing the harbors, Captain."

"What!?" exclaimed Zhang. "What bureaucratic fool made that decision!?"

"The Central Military Commission," Tian replied grimly. "Read the last paragraph of the message."

Zhang paused, and finished reading the message. He then looked up slowly and faced the general. Zhang couldn't believe his eyes. "We're not going to alert the civilian population? Do they not realize that if we fail, millions will die?"

"The CMC won't tolerate the political chaos that an evacuation announcement would create," explained Tian. "They're afraid that certain sections of the population would use this crisis to advance their political views."

"Do the commission members actually believe these people would stay in Hong Kong and hold demonstrations against the Communist Party rather than escape?" asked an astonished Zhang. "They aren't that stupid. They'd try to flee along with everyone else."

"No, Captain, the Central Military Commission isn't afraid they'll stay. The commission members are concerned they'll leave, and then hold their demonstrations in the shadow of a destroyed Hong Kong. It would be impossible for the Communist Party to refute that they had failed the people of China, once again.

"The CMC is aware of the risks, but they don't want photos and videos of massive traffic jams and panicking people appearing on the Internet or other social media, followed by a mushroom cloud climbing high into the sky. The CMC would appear to be totally helpless. They can't afford that," finished Tian. Sitting back down, he reached for the message. Zhang gave it back to him.

"Only high-level party members and their families are to be evacuated, and in total secrecy. The rest of the citizens of Hong Kong will have to unknowingly rely on your mine hunters' skills," said Tian.

Disheartened, Zhang nodded his head gently; he had his orders. "I'll do what I can, sir. But I make no promises."

"I understand, Captain."

Zhang turned to leave, took a couple of steps, stopped, and turned back around. "One request, General."

"Yes, Captain."

"When you provide your status report to the CMC, I would greatly appreciate it if you would be bluntly honest. If they want me to find this damn torpedo, they need to close the ports. Mine hunting is a difficult enough task to do without having to worry about being run over by a massive container ship. If they don't close the ports, the search will take longer and it will not be as accurate as it could be."

"I will include your exact concerns in my report, Captain, I assure you. Is there anything else I should ask for?"

"Yes, General. Help. We need more ships to scan the bottom, preferably with high-resolution imaging sonars. And frankly, I don't care where they find them."

15 April 2017
0900 EST
White House Situation Room
Washington, D.C.

An irritated Joanna Patterson strode into the room; she was still tired from the late night and had just started her second cup of coffee before being dragged down by an urgent message from one of the watchstanders. A Chinese vice chairman of the CMC demanded to speak with her on the video teleconferencing system. She really didn't want to have another conversation with General Shi; the last one had been painful enough with his constant posturing and threats. Braced for a rude greeting, Patterson was surprised to see a People's Liberation Army Navy admiral on the screen. As she sat down within view of the camera, the Chinese admiral welcomed her.

"Dr. Patterson, good morning. I am Admiral Jing Fei, Commander of the People's Liberation Army Navy and a member of the Central Military Commission."

"Good evening, Admiral Jing," Patterson responded carefully. "I don't mean to be impolite, Admiral, but I was under the impression that General Shi was my liaison with the CMC."

"Unfortunately, General Shi is occupied with other duties this evening," explained Jing. Joanna didn't detect any change in the admiral's facial features as he spoke; his expression remained neutral—a perfect poker face. "And since the reason for the call deals with a naval issue, it was thought that I would be a more appropriate representative."

"I see," replied Patterson. *Shi got canned,* she thought. *They must want something from us.* "So, Admiral, what can I do for you this evening?"

"Per our agreement, I'm to report that our investigation of the explosions this afternoon in Dangan Shuido were caused by torpedoes. We also agree with the analysis by your Squadron Fifteen commodore, that *Chakra* was likely leaving the Hong Kong area. The Indian submarine torpedoed and sank one of our Project 636M Kilo submarines."

Patterson took a sharp breath, suddenly worried about the Chinese crew. "Were there any survivors?"

"That is unknown at the moment. None of the crew has escaped the stricken boat thus far. And even though the Kilo is in shallow water, she is lying on her port side and this may be complicating the situation."

"What can we do to help with the rescue effort?"

"While I appreciate your offer, Dr. Patterson, we have more important matters to discuss. We are in urgent need of assistance to help locate the torpedo, or torpedoes, that

Chakra has undoubtedly fired into our ports. Anything the United States can provide to aid our search will be greatly welcomed."

Finally, thought Patterson. The Chinese government had at last come to their senses and was now asking for help. She was certain the decision was unpopular, and had caused more than a few bruised egos, but better that than a radioactive hole in Hong Kong. While she rejoiced on the inside, her outside voice remained businesslike.

"I'm not sure what resources we have nearby, but I'll find out and will send the information to Commodore Simonis at Guam," she promised. "Please have your staff work directly with him to get the equipment to Hong Kong."

"Thank you, Doctor. I'll have the commander of the Hong Kong Garrison establish communications with Squadron Fifteen." Jing looked like he was getting ready to leave when Patterson pressed him.

"Admiral, I again offer our assistance with rescuing your crew." She leaned forward, emphasizing her point. "Don't abandon them."

The admiral's face finally cracked a little; a flash of regret briefly appeared. He then let out a deep sigh. "Doctor, I'm not confident there is anyone alive to rescue. Divers went down and rapped on the hull, there was no response. We will try again in the morning, but the odds are not particularly good."

"You're a submariner, aren't you?" queried Patterson.

Jing looked a little surprised, then slowly smiled. "Yes, Doctor, I am."

Grinning, Patterson answered his unasked question. "It shows. Now, if you'll excuse me, I need to speak with our CNO and get things moving. Your people in Hong Kong will hear from Commodore Simonis shortly."

Patterson walked as fast as she could back to her office and telephoned Admiral Hughes. After a brief conversation, she took off for the Oval Office and for the umpteenth time resolved to start wearing flats to work. The president was with Milt Alvarez going over the afternoon's schedule when he saw his grim-faced national security advisor stride into the office.

"You've got that look, Joanna. What disaster has befallen us this time?"

"I just spoke with the PLAN commander, Admiral Jing, they've basically confirmed what we thought; *Chakra* has almost certainly mined Hong Kong harbor. And she sank a Chinese submarine on her way out."

Myles closed his eyes and rubbed his forehead; disappointment and frustration filled his face. "I had high hopes that Commander Mitchell would have caught *Chakra* before she could have launched any of the torpedoes. This unfortunate turn of events makes the situation considerably worse."

"No one is more disappointed than Jerry, Mr. President. And if I know him, he's already trying to pick up the trail, which leads me to what I need to discuss with you."

The president looked perplexed. "What do you mean?"

"Sir, the Chinese have formally asked for our help in searching the two port facilities in Hong Kong. They need high-resolution, imaging-sonar-equipped platforms, and they need them now. I just talked to Admiral Hughes; the best he said we can do is to fly out side-scan sonar teams to Hong Kong, but this will take about twenty-four hours. And even after the teams arrive, it will take another six to twelve hours to get their gear rigged for operations aboard a Chinese ship.

"Thirty-six hours is too damn long, Mr. President. Once all the preps are completed, it's still going to take days to properly scour both harbors. They aren't small and the bottoms are undoubtedly strewn with all sorts of junk. We need to move faster," stressed Patterson.

"What's this got to do with Mitchell, Joanna? He certainly

can't rummage around looking for the torpedo with his submarine," protested Myles.

"No, he can't. But his UUVs can."

Myles's expression changed instantly to one of curiosity. Joanna had his attention.

"Jerry is carrying underwater remotes equipped with imaging side-scan sonars specifically designed for mine hunting. The resolution on those sonars is incredible, down to a couple of inches. They'll have little problem identifying a torpedo, even if it's buried in the mud. If we send him to Hong Kong, he can deploy his UUVs and monitor the search remotely from outside Chinese territorial waters."

The president caught the implication immediately. "But that means pulling Mitchell off the hunt for *Chakra*."

Patterson gave a resigned shrug; she wasn't thrilled about the idea either. "Yes, Mr. President, but *North Dakota* is the only asset we have that can begin looking for the torpedo, or torpedoes, within hours instead of days."

Myles leaned back in his chair, carefully considering Joanna's recommendation. After a brief moment, he took a deep breath and shook his head slightly; there was a weary grin on his face. "He won't be happy."

"No, sir, I expect Jerry will be thoroughly pissed off. No submariner worth his salt is going to like being pulled off a hot pursuit, but that doesn't change the fact that doing so is in the best interests of the United States. Jerry's a smart guy, and a professional, he'll recognize the right answer when told."

"All right, Joanna, issue the order for *North Dakota* to return to Hong Kong and begin searching the port facilities for any sign of a torpedo. You'd better send it via the chain of command. Captain Mitchell doesn't have to know this was your idea."

Patterson shook her head ruefully. "I'm afraid that will be unavoidable, Mr. President."

15 April 2017
2145 Local Time
USS *North Dakota*
25 NM South of Dangan Island
South China Sea

"Excuse me, sir, they want me to do *what*!?" Jerry couldn't believe what his commodore had just told him.

Simonis was completely sympathetic with Mitchell's disbelief. He'd had to have the order repeated to him twice as well. "You're to disengage from pursuing *Chakra* and proceed to Hong Kong at best possible speed. Once in position you'll deploy your UUVs and commence surveying the bottoms of the port facilities at Shenzhen and Victoria Harbor. Since the concentration of false targets is expected to be very high, direct human monitoring is required to expedite the search for the nuclear-armed torpedoes."

"Commodore, does SUBPAC realize I'm just a few hours behind *Chakra*? We're in a position to overtake her within the next six hours. We can stop her from launching any more torpedoes."

"Can you guarantee that, Captain?" demanded Simonis.

Jerry paused to let himself calm down; he knew he couldn't. "No, sir, I can't. But the odds are in our favor. We know where *Chakra* was about six hours ago and we know she's not moving at high speed. This gives us a much better chance of catching her."

"I completely agree, Captain, flaming datums have a habit of doing that. But the president is far more concerned with the threat of nuclear torpedoes being lodged in the mud inside two of China's busiest ports. The Chinese government has formally asked for assistance in locating the torpedoes and your UUVs are the best and quickest way for us to help."

Simonis's tone was sympathetic. "I don't like it either,

Captain, but it's his call to make and it does make sense. We'll just have to let *North Carolina* deal with *Chakra*."

"Sir, no disrespect to Scott Nevens and *North Carolina*, but he has a lot more area to cover and he doesn't have anything other than her organic sensors—and her towed arrays aren't as good as mine!" Jerry pleaded.

Simonis took a deep sigh; he was experiencing a bad case of déjà vu. Mitchell's argument was essentially the exact same one he'd used with SUBPAC. But Admiral Burroughs was adamant; the UUVs had to get to Hong Kong as fast as possible. "You're preaching to the choir, Captain," replied Simonis. "The bottom line is we have our orders and we are expected to carry them out. Besides, you and I both know where this plan came from, don't we?"

The smug look on the commodore's face confirmed what Jerry had suspected. "Yes, sir, I'm sure this was Dr. Patterson's idea. It sounds like something she'd come up with."

"Then there's nothing left to discuss then, is there? You're to get the UUVs to Hong Kong ASAP and conduct a thorough search of both harbors. The Chinese are going to provide detailed hydrographic information, as well as any previous bottom surveys to assist you in planning your surveys. I'll have the data sent to you as soon as we get it." Simonis saw Jerry nod his acknowledgment. His face was crestfallen. Deep inside, the commodore felt bad for the young captain; he could sense Mitchell's disappointment. The commodore decided a short pep talk was in order.

"If it's any consolation, Jerry, you and your crew have the best chance of finding these nukes before they cause untold damage and millions of casualties. That's not exactly a weak FITREP bullet, Captain."

Jerry's eyes lit up, and a slight grin popped on his face. "Commodore, I have one question."

"And that would be?"

"Do you believe the assumption that my crew is the best

qualified for this mission played a key role in Dr. Patterson's suggestion to the president?"

"Undoubtedly. Why?" Simonis asked. Mitchell's question perplexed him.

"Then I would argue, sir, that the assumption is incorrect."

Simonis was now completely baffled. "What are you talking about, Captain!? Your crew has more experience with the ISR UUVs than anyone else in the fleet!"

"Yes, sir, I completely agree. But only in regard to the ASW search mode. We've hardly used the mine-hunting function at all. In fact, the last time we used it was during workup training."

Simonis was getting more and more annoyed with Jerry's line of reasoning. It was obvious that Mitchell had something in mind, it just wasn't very clear and the commodore's patience was waning. "Captain, if you have a point, would you please make it!"

"Sir, I would argue that you have the most qualified operators for this mission. Your training staff has more time using the mine-hunting mode than anyone in the Navy. They should be the ones to run the port surveys," argued Jerry strenuously.

"Ridiculous!" yelped Simonis. "We don't have an appropriate facility to run a remote search like this. The trainer lacks the necessary communications gear."

Jerry smiled broadly. "With all due respect, sir, yes, you do—*Oklahoma City*."

Simonis's eyes grew wide as soon as Jerry mentioned the stranded submarine.

"Dobson's boat has the necessary comms and some UYQ-70 workstations on board. The UUV control and display software can be downloaded into them and your training staff can run the entire op from *Oklahoma City*'s control room," stressed Jerry.

Simonis was clearly intrigued by the suggestion, but altering an order flew in the face of everything he believed in. "Are you suggesting that I intentionally ignore a direct order, mister?"

"No, sir. What I'm suggesting is that as a squadron commodore, you have some leeway to make the best use of your resources to maximize the success of both missions. I'll bust my butt to get the UUVs to Hong Kong as fast as I can, but your staff runs the mine-hunting operation while I go after *Chakra*. Besides, this gets some of Bruce's guys into the fight."

Simonis's scowl slowly melted into a devious smirk. "Captain, why do I get the distinct impression you're trying to goad me into going around one of your close friend's pet schemes?"

Grinning, Jerry shrugged and admitted his guilt. "Because maybe that's exactly what I'm trying to do."

Simonis shook his head, but there was a smile on his face. "All right, Jerry, I'll go with your recommendation. It makes good sense, and I like the idea of getting Dobson's boat involved. And I find the idea of tweaking Dr. Patterson very appealing. It would be nice to win at least one argument with that woman! However, since I'll be putting *both* our butts in a sling, you'd better get that Indian *Akula*."

"We will, sir."

20

Evasion

The videoconference image was blurry, and angled upward. It looked like something taken by a handheld cell phone rather than a mounted camera, but the picture quality was really irrelevant. The audio was perfectly clear, even if the situation wasn't.

Commodore Simonis was first introduced to Hong Kong's garrison commander, a gray-haired general named Tian. Thin and distinguished-looking, Tian spoke not a word of English, so a thirtyish army lieutenant named Li translated. Li had explained that translating was not his primary occupation, but he was doing a creditable job.

"When will the devices arrive?" Tian asked through the translator.

Simonis replied, "*North Dakota* is launching them as we speak, and they should take about three hours to reach Victoria Harbor and four to Shenzhen Harbor. I'll give you a definite arrival time once her captain sends me the information."

"How will we know where they are?" The general's expression showed some confusion, as if he was still trying to understand how the UUVs operated.

"They don't really need to be tracked, General. They have accurate navigation systems that use GPS updates, so they don't require human assistance to reach their destinations. But they are equipped with a sonar transponder, which can be heard by any sonar operating at the proper frequency."

That prompted a short sidebar with Lieutenant Li, as the lieutenant searched for the correct Chinese word for "transponder." Li was still explaining it to the general when another senior officer, wearing a naval captain's rank, hurried in. He bowed quickly to Tian and reported in rapid-fire Mandarin. The general nodded and then stood, indicating that the captain should take the seat in front of the camera.

As the new arrival sat down, Tian took a chair in the background, but remained visible. Li explained, "This is Captain Zhang, Commander of the Hong Kong Garrison Naval Brigade." Squat and weather-beaten, Zhang looked like he belonged on a ship's bridge. To Simonis's eyes, he also looked a little wall-eyed, as if he couldn't quite grasp the situation. The translator was more matter-of-fact. Zhang didn't speak any English, either.

He explained through Li. "I have just closed the harbors to incoming traffic and ordered all ships in the harbor to either leave immediately or remain stationary until they are given permission to move." He shook his head, as if to clear it. "This is more than what we do for typhoons."

"That's very good," Simonis responded. "The UUVs need the harbor to be as clear as possible."

Through Li, Zhang asked, "How will we control them?"

"You don't have to," Simonis answered. "They are completely autonomous—think of them as underwater robots. When they reach the harbor, they will extend a satellite antenna and ask for new instructions. My staff is preparing a search plan for each vehicle. One will search

Shenzhen Harbor while the other looks in Victoria Harbor."

This triggered an extended exchange between Zhang and his interpreter. When Li spoke to him again, he asked, "But how will your submarine, *North Dakota*, send them to the robots? Isn't she submerged, pursuing the Indian rogue submarine?"

"We will direct the UUVs from here, Captain." Simonis had to keep remembering that although Li was doing the talking, his audience was Zhang and his boss, the general. "Although *North Dakota* carried the two UUVs, any submarine can take over control, once they've loaded the software into its combat system. Any American submarine," he added.

"A submarine in my squadron, *Oklahoma City*, was unable to take part in the search for *Chakra* because of a fault in her propulsion plant. She will monitor the search and transmit instructions to the UUVs by satellite. They're downloading the software right now, and will be ready to send commands to the vehicles in plenty of time."

Li asked, "Wouldn't it be simpler to transmit the instructions from here? We have some very good computers."

Simonis noted that Li asked the question without prompting from Zhang. Was he just curious, or did he have something he wanted to suggest to his boss?

"That's not possible," Simonis said truthfully. "The software is designed to operate with a display console in our submarines' control room. It won't work on a standard computer." Simonis had no illusions about what would happen if the Chinese got their hands on that code.

Having deflected the inquiry, Simonis got back to business. "My immediate need is for the best information you have on obstructions and wrecks in the two harbors, Captain. Although the vehicles can avoid objects they encounter on their own, larger or more complex obstacles can confuse them, and certainly slow them down. It's best if obstructions are entered in their navigation systems ahead of time. It will also help to reduce the number of false alarms."

The commodore added, smiling, "I can't even begin to imagine the amount of junk that's accumulated on the floor of the two harbors."

The three Chinese officers spoke together for several minutes; then the general addressed someone out of view of the camera. Li said, "We have surveys of different parts of both harbor bottoms taken over the years. None are complete."

Zhang asked through Li, "What is the resolution of the vehicle's sonar?"

"In area search mode, a foot. Excuse me, thirty centimeters. In high-resolution mode, it's a little over three centimeters. The vehicles will be searching for an object only fifty-three centimeters in diameter and about seven meters long. If it sees something that matches this basic description, it will switch its sonar to high-resolution mode, go lower, and take sonar images of the object from several different angles. Then it will come to shallow depth and transmit them to us, along with the object's location."

Simonis waited while Li translated, and Captain Zhang asked, "Can the vehicle also retrieve the torpedo? Does it have a claw or other handing tools?"

"No, you will have to use divers, but the UUV will be able to tell them the object's location within centimeters of its true position. I'm sure visibility near the bottom is terrible, but they won't have to waste time searching."

Li nodded his understanding, and relayed the information to Zhang, who also nodded, and answered affirmatively.

"You are welcome to anything that will speed the search. We will send the bottom information to you, but, in truth, your survey will be more detailed than anything we have."

General Tian spoke up in the back. He sounded impatient, and Li relayed, "Do you have any more information on how long we have to search? When will the warheads explode?"

Simonis scowled. "That's the big question. If we assume that the bombs are all supposed to go off at the same time, then we may have several days. It's likely that Hong Kong was the first port on their target list. It's our good luck that *Chakra* was discovered so soon after placing her torpedo, and we can begin searching so quickly."

Li scowled and shook his head. So did Zhang, as soon as Li passed on Simonis's words. "It's hard to talk about 'good luck' when there is a nuclear bomb buried somewhere in your harbor, and that the good luck came at the expense of a submarine and her crew."

"I'm a submariner, Captain, and I've lost a boat myself. I understand exactly how you feel. We all want to stop these criminals before any more blood is shed. My staff is calling on experts from all over my country to make the search as efficient and swift as possible. For instance, we know the weapon used was a Russian UGST-M torpedo, so we know its range. We know *Chakra* can't go into very shallow water. That allows us to rule out some parts of both harbors."

Zhang listened through Li, and asked, "Can one of my staff participate in the search planning?"

"Yes, of course," Simonis answered immediately. He felt a small twinge of hope. After seeing and hearing Patterson getting the door slammed in her face earlier, he hadn't expected the Chinese to be civil, much less willing to collaborate.

A side console flashed a text message from Patterson. "Good job, Commodore." He knew she been listening in from Washington, but that was the first time she said anything.

Li said, "Can you please send us complete information on these UUVs? It will help our staff understand their capabilities." Neither Tian nor Zhang had asked that question.

Simonis answered immediately, "Of course, I'll have my staff send you the relevant information." He hoped the Chinese wouldn't object to only getting the "relevant" data. He could see Jacobs off to one side, taking notes.

Again unprompted, Li asked, "How often must the vehicles be recharged?"

"At their normal search speed, they have three days' endurance—seventy-two hours, minus the time they spend reaching the harbors. Hopefully we'll find the torpedo before it becomes an issue."

Zhang fired a string of Mandarin at Li that sounded like an impatient question, and then Tian joined the conversation. There seemed to be a dispute between the two senior officers and the lieutenant.

While the three spoke with each other, a new text appeared from Patterson. "Lieutenant Li is actually a major, appears to be from intelligence—POTUS."

There were two important facts included in that text. One explained why Li was so interested in anything to do with the UUV. The other was that not just the national security advisor, but the president himself, was monitoring his conversation with these Chinese officials.

It said something about the urgent nature of the meeting that the Chinese either hadn't considered that they could be overheard, or just didn't care. And, it was more than a little creepy to know that the commander-in-chief was "looking over his shoulder" in cyberspace. *No pressure,* thought Simonis.

Another text appeared. "They're telling Li to focus on the problem, and not go into business for himself."

Simonis had to read that one as Li was speaking again. "So all we have to do is sit and wait while the vehicles search our harbor, and hopefully when one finds the torpedo, we send divers down to recover it."

"Well, we do have to work together on the search plan, but yes, once the vehicles begin their search, all we can do is monitor their progress and wait."

Li relayed Simonis's response, listened to Zhang, then said, "The captain wants to know if a minesweeper can hear the sonar transponder. That way he can follow the vehicles with divers standing by on board. That will save some time."

Simonis frowned, but nodded. "Tell Captain Zhang that depending on the frequency of their system, yes, they should be able to detect the pinger. And his plan is fine as long as the minesweeper stays at least a hundred meters away from the UUV's position. When it's rising to make a report, if there's a surface craft nearby, it will move that far away before transmitting. So staying too close will just slow it down."

Li began to relay Simonis's explanation, but then the commodore added, "Above all, we don't want the minesweeper accidentally colliding with the UUV, or even just bumping into it. And if it becomes disabled in some way, don't attempt to recover or repair it. The UUVs are equipped with anti-tamper circuits that will fry the electronics and wipe the software if the correct handling procedures aren't followed."

That got Li's attention. Hopefully it would reduce the chance of the vehicle meeting with some sort of "accident" after the torpedo had been found. Both Tian and Zhang asked more questions as Li explained, but evidently Zhang was satisfied. "The captain says he will keep the craft much farther away than one hundred meters. What are we to do with the UUVs after the torpedo is found?"

"We are sending a surface ship to the area. It will wait outside the harbor until the weapon is found and the harbors are cleared, then come in and recover the two vehicles. What are your plans for the torpedo?" Finding the weapon was just one part of the problem, the part they'd spent the most time on. Simonis was equally concerned about what to do after the weapon had been located.

"There has been a great deal of discussion about this. There is great anxiety that the torpedoes also have an anti-tampering feature—how do you say it . . . a booby trap. We decided that we will make no attempt to disarm it; we can't risk it detonating when a technician tries to open an access plate. We plan to load it on a helicopter, manned with a volunteer crew. They will fly at maximum speed to a point about two hundred miles off the coast and discard it there. It is past the continental shelf, and the water depth is over one thousand fathoms. Captain Zhang's staff is preparing a notice to airmen and mariners right now that will warn all craft to remain clear of the area."

"Very well, please tell Captain Zhang to have his staff contact Captain Jacobs in my watch center, he's coordinating the search planning. We'll put whoever he assigns to good use."

Li interpreted Simonis's comment; Zhang nodded and smiled. He then spoke briefly and Li relayed the message. "Captain Zhang thanks you and wishes you good luck."

"Good luck to us all," Simonis answered. The screen suddenly went blank as the VTC link was terminated. Sitting back in his chair, Simonis let out a deep sigh of relief. The videoconference with the Chinese had gone better than he had expected. He was about to give Jacobs an order when the commodore noted another text from Patterson on the screen. "POTUS left—very impressed with your performance. Oh, BTW, Touché."

Simonis grunted smugly after reading her message. He'd finally won an argument.

16 April 2017
1000 Local Time
INS *Chakra*
South China Sea

"Captain."

"Captain Jain."

"CAPTAIN JAIN!"

Jain came awake with a start, sitting upright in his bunk and looking around with alarm. A petty officer was standing over him, looking very guilty.

As he took in his surroundings, he could feel the smooth vibration of the sub's engines, the sound of the ventilation system. Everything seemed normal. He asked, "The boat—is it all right? It felt like a collision."

"That was me, sir, I'm sorry, but I had to shake you hard to wake you. The first officer has been trying to reach you, but you weren't answering."

His head still clearing, Jain said, "I'm awake now. Thank you." He turned to the phone on the bulkhead next to his bed. It was buzzing loudly, not a foot from where his head had been. The display next to the phone showed *Chakra*'s speed, depth, and current location, southwest of Taiwan. The clock said he' been asleep for five hours, give or take.

He picked up the handset. "Jain here."

"Captain, we have a problem with our route." It was Rakash's voice. He didn't sound happy. "You need to see what sonar has detected."

Jain turned and nodded to the petty officer, who quickly departed. "Understood. I'll be there in a moment."

Lieutenant Commander Rakash looked apologetic when Jain came into the central post a few minutes later. "I tried to let you sleep a little longer, sir, but we must decide now." He gestured toward one of the displays. "Please, sir, look at the plot." His voice still held the same worried tone.

The map display showed *Chakra* headed almost straight for Taiwan. They'd been on the same course for the last twelve hours, according to the clock, as planned.

The first officer had finally convinced his captain to rest thirteen hours after their battle with the Chinese diesel boat. They'd headed directly away from the Chinese coast for six hours, which had put them in deeper water, and then they'd turned east by north, toward Taiwan's west cost. Seven hours after that, with no sign of Chinese pursuit, the first officer was finally able to persuade his captain to lie down.

The revelation that the Chinese were waiting for *Chakra* had thrown most of their voyage planning into the rubbish bin. Vajra was supposed to be a surprise attack. Jain and Rakash had laid out their route using the simplest, most direct route between each of the target ports, but that wouldn't work if the Chinese navy had been alerted.

As they had hurried away from Hong Kong and the scene of their battle, Jain, Rakash, and the other officers had debated whether or not the encounter with the Chinese Kilo was an accident, a coincidence, or a deliberate confrontation. It had been a short discussion. There were no PLA Navy submarine bases near Hong Kong, and there were few operations that a submarine could be performing in such a spot. It was very shallow water, not the kind of place a submariner liked to be. And if it was some sort of exercise, a practice run sneaking into an enemy port, where was the other side, the defenders?

Besides, the Kilo had fired on them, based only on their active sonar signal. Peacetime rules of engagement would require more positive identification before launching a weapon. For the Chinese sub to have fired with only the information it had, the target would have to be "presumed hostile."

And by sinking the Kilo, they'd confirmed their presence. They had to assume that every subsequent port would now be heavily guarded, complicating an already difficult task.

But why were the Chinese looking for anything in the first place? Dhankhar had said he was worried about foreign intelligence learning of the plan. It looked like his concerns were justified. If that was the case, how much did they know?

Chakra's next destination was Ningbo, on the eastern-most tip of the Chinese coast. It was the fourth-busiest port in China, and by far the most difficult target on their list. The approach to Ningbo-Zhoushan was treacherous, and even shallower than Hong Kong. It would have taken them less than two days at their earlier twenty-knot transit speed, but Jain had to assume that they were being actively hunted, and they'd had to slow to twelve knots so that their towed array would give them some warning of an enemy's approach. That turned a forty-hour transit into sixty-five hours, and Jain worried about losing so much of their time margin.

And the Taiwan Strait was an excellent place to set up a barrier of escort vessels. The approach to the strait was largely blocked by the Taiwan Banks, an incredibly shal-low patch of water, and patrol ships could be placed to block the deep areas that *Chakra* would have to use. The Chinese had Type 054 frigates and Type 056 corvettes fitted with passive towed sonar arrays. Patrolling at five knots, the PLA Navy could layer two lines of escorts across the entire strait—more if they were smart about it. Jain couldn't hope to get through a robust barrier like that.

Blasting a hole in the line wasn't even an option. Sub-marines used concealment and guile to stay alive. The last thing he wanted to do was signal his position again with another wreck. His orders explicitly forbade him from looking for naval targets until after the nuclear-armed tor-pedoes had been laid. Business before pleasure.

That's why he had planned to get so close to Taiwan, through the Penghu Channel. The Chinese might be searching for him, but they wouldn't enter newly indepen-dent Taiwan's territorial waters. By hugging the coast, he planned to go around one end of the PLAN sonar fence.

And the waters of the Penghu Channel were relatively deep, on the order of one hundred meters. He might even be able to increase speed while he was there, and he was sure *Chakra* was safe from PLAN searchers.

The display showed surface contacts that had been detected by *Chakra*'s passive sonar. Ahead and to the left was the Taiwan Strait, one of the most heavily traveled water passages in the world. He could see a dozen ships headed north and south between the Chinese coast to the west and Taiwan to the east. That had been his original plan—just sail due north into the strait, then turn northeast. Adjusting the course to the east to hug the west coast of Taiwan cost him a little distance, but it was definitely safer.

Or had been. Rakash was pointing to several bright lines that marked powerful active sonars. They were all coming from warships ahead of them, along Taiwan's coast.

"Sonar's evaluated them all as American low-frequency sets. SQS-26 and SQS-53 sonars," Rakash reported.

Jain shrugged. "That fits. The Taiwanese navy uses surplus American destroyers and frigates."

"I tracked them for a while before waking you, sir. I thought after twenty-plus hours in the central post, you should get some rest. A captain at sea may be all-powerful, but he's not invulnerable."

"No harm done, Rakash. Plotting their movements is the first thing I would have ordered, and I probably did need the sleep," Jain admitted.

Rakash sighed. "It's very unusual. They've got four ships patrolling the west coast of the island. They're staying within their territorial waters and they're blasting away with active sonar. We can hear them sixty or even ninety miles out, thanks to the convergence zones."

Jain concluded, "Effectively blocking our passage through Taiwan's coastal waters."

Rakash pointed out how the four patrol zones neatly

covered most of Taiwan's west coast. "They're looking for us. But why?"

Jain pleaded ignorance. "I'm sure they've heard about the sub being sunk in Hong Kong. That will be big news everywhere in Asia. But why would they feel threatened? That doesn't make sense. And I can't imagine them cooperating with the mainland Chinese."

Jain calculated the odds of somehow getting through, in spite of the active searchers. Without understanding why they were looking, it would be hard to guess how they'd act if they found him, but he was pretty sure it wouldn't be to his benefit. It was too much to risk.

The first officer could see his captain considering, calculating. Rakash suggested, "The Chinese towed arrays aren't that good. If we stick close under a merchant ship it will mask our noise."

"No. Too obvious. They'll be delousing with active sonar. It doesn't take very long. They have enough corvettes to check each merchant as it passes. It doesn't matter how quiet we are. Besides, we are very limited by the Taiwan Banks. It won't bother a merchant ship, but we'd have to go around and the Chinese aren't stupid. They know where the choke points are." Jain tapped the chart. "We have to go around."

"Around Taiwan?" Rakash couldn't hide his surprise. "That will take too long."

"Not at twenty knots. We'll be in open ocean and much harder to find. And I'm going to look at the target list again. The admiral gave me some discretion about the targets, if necessary. Now I wish I'd put a second torpedo into Shenzhen Harbor. It was right next to Victoria Harbor, it was on the list, and then we'd only have three weapons to deploy."

Jain turned toward the helmsman. "Starboard fifteen, new course one one five degrees. Once we're away from the strait, Rakash, we'll increase speed to twenty knots and go deep."

16 April 2017
1030 Local Time
Republic of China Submarine *Hai Lung*
South China Sea

"Contact has turned to starboard. New course is shiftin
to east-southeast. Speed is still fifteen knots."

Captain Zhu Heng leaned over the display. "That cours
will take him south of the island entirely. Sheng, what'
his closest point of approach?"

"Sixty-five hundred meters," the executive officer re
ported, "at bearing one eight zero. If we want to maintai
contact after he passes us, we should reverse course an
head west ourselves, and increase speed above thre
knots."

Zhu shook his head sharply. "Absolutely not. We wil
do nothing that increases the chance of him detecting us
Our orders were to stay completely hidden and report, an
I intend to do just that. Keep the boat at ultra quiet an
watch this fellow like a hawk. If he continues to head to
ward the east, then we will break contact and transmit."

16 April 2017
1600 Local Time
Republic of China P-3C Orion
35NM South of Taiwan, Luzon Strait

Petty Officer Wang rubbed his eyes and tried hard to fo
cus on his screen; they'd been out looking for the Indian
Akula for the last four hours and they hadn't seen anything
other than fishing boats and whales. They had just finishe
laying their second passive sonobuoy field, and the acous
tic data was starting to show up on the processor display
At first, there was nothing. Then a weak line appeared or
the waterfall display. After staring at it for a minute, h
made the call.

"TACCO, Sensor One. I have a weak fifty-hertz line on buoy fifty-one."

"Sensor One, TACCO. Contact on buoy fifty-one, aye. Let me take a look."

The tactical coordinator pulled up the acoustic display and looked at the picture as it formed. The TACCO was impressed. It was a very weak narrowband line, but it was there. Wang had caught it just right. Frankly, the coordinator hadn't had great expectations for this mission. His sensor operators were used to looking for Chinese nukes that sounded like freight trains. Looking for a much quieter Akula was in a whole other league.

"All Stations, TACCO. Possub contact on buoy fifty-one. Sensor Two, stand by to drop a localization pattern south of our buoy field. Sensor Three, keep your eyes open for a MAD contact."

The Orion banked hard left and flew to the far southern corner of the sonobuoy field. Five more sonobuoys dropped from the aircraft's underside and parachuted down to the water.

"TACCO, Sensor Three. No MAD contact."

Figures, thought the tactical coordinator. Russian boats were all fitted with degaussing gear and had really low magnetic signatures. They'd have to fly within a thousand meters before they'd even have a chance of picking the Akula up.

"TACCO, Sensor Two. Localization field up, no contacts."

"TACCO, Sensor One. Narrowband line is fading. Contact is showing down Doppler, target is moving away from the buoy."

Shit, swore the officer, *we're losing him!* He needed to do something fast if they were going to keep this sub.

"Sensor Two, TACCO: Stand by to drop a DICASS buoy. Set depth selection to deep."

Once again the aircraft turned and proceeded back toward the southern corner. As it was just about to fly over sonobuoy fifty-one another silver canister was dropped from her belly. The DICASS buoy splashed into the water, and immediately released the transducer subsection from its float. Unwinding rapidly, the transducer dropped to a depth of 136 meters, well below the seasonal thermocline, or layer. Seconds later, a sharp high-frequency ping began scanning the water.

INS *Chakra*

The acoustic intercept receiver chirped madly. The estimated sound level indicated the active sonar was close.

"Helmsman, slow ahead. Make your depth three hundred meters," barked Jain. "First Officer, report!"

"Active sonobuoy bears red one seven eight. It's almost directly behind us."

"Set ultra quiet condition throughout the ship," Jain ordered. "Now we have to act just like a water molecule."

"Captain, frequency and pulse pattern indicates it's an American SSQ-62 active, directional sonobuoy. I can't believe that the Americans are looking for us!"

"I don't think they are, Number One. It's probably a Taiwanese P-3."

"Sir, something is very wrong here. Why are our allies looking for us, and so aggressively I might add?"

"I don't have a clue, Number One. But we're on a good course to get out of range of the buoy, and between the anechoic coating and our narrow aspect, I think we'll get out of this with our hides intact."

"Captain, our speed is five knots and ultra quiet is set," reported Rakash.

"Very well. Given the circumstances, we may want to rethink that twenty-knot speed idea." Jain wasn't thrilled with slowing down, but he had little choice. He pulled out the target list again and started looking real hard at his options. He'd have to get the time back somehow.

16 April 2017
1800 Local Time
USS *North Dakota*
40 NM West of Taiwan
South China Sea

Samant and Petrov hovered over the digital chart of the waters around Taiwan. It had been twenty-two hours since they'd left Hong Kong, after sending the two UUVs on their way to begin searching the harbors. Mitchell had wasted little time, and turned his boat toward the northeast and ran off at high speed. After six hours, he slowed to get a good look around, and then alternated between a sprint and what Thigpen had called "a fast walk." They hadn't seen any signs of the Indian Akula yet, but by Samant and Petrov's estimate they were still sixty-some-odd miles behind. Nevertheless, the lack of even the slightest contact was disheartening.

Poring over the available data, the two struggled to guess where *Chakra* would go next. That the first target would be Hong Kong was intuitively obvious. Figuring out the second one was far more difficult. The multiple commercial facilities at Ningbo-Zhoushan and Shanghai placed both in the top five busiest ports, with the Shanghai International Port on the edge of the Yangtze River being number one. And while a submerged submarine could approach all of the ports, some were considerably easier than others.

Jerry and his executive officer were in the radio room talking with their superior at Squadron Fifteen. They'd received an urgent message a quarter of an hour earlier for the submarine to come up to periscope depth and make contact. Since Petrov and Samant were barred from that part of the ship, they hung out in control and watched as the crew expertly handled their boat. Both were still in awe of the sheer processing power that a *Virginia*-class submarine possessed.

Still, Samant felt uneasy, out of sorts, there was something wrong with this picture. Then it struck him; there were too many pictures. Everywhere he looked there were multiple display screens. The two vertical flat-screen panels forward were simply enormous. The starboard display had the output from one of the BVS-1 optronics masts on it. Samant sighed and shook his head.

"I'm still not comfortable with this central post configuration, Aleks. It doesn't feel right to not have a periscope!" he grumbled.

"I understand how you feel, Girish, but this is the future. The newest Russian submarines are going down this path for the same reasons the Americans have, to make more information available to the commanding officer."

"Not all progress is necessarily a good thing," Samant shot back. "There's a feeling of control, of being in *command*, when one stares at his adversary through an eyepiece. This is like watching a video game!"

Petrov chuckled. "You're sounding like a hopeless romantic, Girish. You have to remember that these 'children' grew up with video games. We just have to accept that how we did things is behind the times, old-fashioned, obsolete."

Samant turned to Petrov, a crushed expression on his face. "Thank you for making me feel ancient, Aleks."

"You're welcome, my friend," Petrov laughed. He was definitely feeling more like himself, and he enjoyed being able to poke fun at his Indian comrade. Samant just growled in frustration.

"Well, we finally got a break," Jerry declared as he and Thigpen came out of the radio room. "A Taiwanese submarine got a solid contact and reported in. Please plot these positions," he said to the quartermaster, handing him a piece of paper.

"Aye, aye, sir," replied the petty officer.

The four officers gazed at the chart as two dots popped

up. "The sub reported contact here, and about six hours later a Taiwan P-3C got a weak hit here. This puts them on a course to the southeast. Jain's going around the east side of Taiwan," explained Jerry.

"Any indication Jain knows he'd been picked up?" questioned Samant with excitement.

"I think that's a given, Captain. The P-3 dropped a DICASS bouy when they tried to maintain contact. They failed, but Jain would've had to be completely deaf not to hear it."

Thigpen smiled and said, "Talk about a prompt jump in the pucker factor. An active sonobuoy coming from out of nowhere, those boys probably had to change their britches!"

Samant nodded; he too was encouraged by the news. "This also means Jain had to slow down. Since he knows he's being hunted, he'll have to reduce speed to try and stay undetected. This will make it easier for us to catch him." The Indian then measured the distance between the P-3's reported position and *North Dakota*'s at the same time. The two locations were only seventy-two miles apart. "At our present speed we can make up the distance in ten hours, perhaps less."

"Or we could get out ahead of him," Petrov observed, pointing to the Penghu Channel on the chart.

"I was thinking the same thing, Alex," agreed Jerry. "Since Jain has slowed down, and probably gone to ultra quiet, our detection range will also be reduced. And if we maintain our current speed, he could pick us up first and evade. But, if we go around the west side of Taiwan, we have a shorter distance to travel and we can fly through without having to worry about being heard."

"An old-fashioned end-around, eh, Skipper?" remarked Thigpen.

Jerry nodded. "Basically."

"So it's your intention to set up another ambush?" asked Samant.

"Yes, Captain. But the question that still needs to be answered is, where do we go?"

"We're still working on that problem, Jerry," said Petrov. Then, pointing to himself, Samant, and Thigpen, he added, "Give us a few more hours and we'll have a recommendation for you."

"Very well. In the meantime, XO, change course for Penghu Channel."

21

Approaches

Jacobs met him at his office with a fresh mug of coffee. It seemed to Commodore Simonis that he had taken up residence in the watch center lately, and while he was grateful for a change of scene, he didn't know if a videoconference with Captain Jerry Mitchell would qualify as a break.

To transmit a video signal, a submarine had to come to shallow depth and raise an antenna, or surface completely. Either way, he'd have to slow down, and Mitchell wouldn't do that now unless it was important. *And probably bad news,* thought Simonis.

Jacobs had already set up the link, and the commodore could see Mitchell waiting on the display. He didn't waste Jerry's time on pleasantries. "Report, Captain Mitchell."

"Sir, it's our firm belief that *Chakra* is going to bypass Ningbo harbor altogether," Jerry announced. "I need a new patrol box, toward the north, covering Dachu and Dahuanglong Islands."

That got Simonis's attention. "Explain."

"I know you've looked at the approaches to Ningbo. It's an incredibly difficult shot even for an experienced submariner. It's very shallow water, the torpedo has to make more than one turn around islands to get to the port facility, and there's a ton of shipping in the area, including fishing boats and now patrols. There are very few spots where he actually has water deep enough to make an approach and still be in torpedo range."

Simonis nodded. "Concur, that's why we've got you guarding the southern approach. It's the best of *Chakra*'s several unattractive choices."

"I agree, sir. It's where I'd make the shot from, and Captain Samant thinks that was Jain's original plan. But the situation has changed. Jain knows he's being hunted. He wouldn't go around Taiwan otherwise," replied Jerry as he gestured to someone offscreen.

Samant came into view and sat next to Jerry. Simonis saw the Indian and his nostrils flared. Jerry knew his commodore wouldn't be pleased and preempted him. "Yes, sir, I know, he's in radio, but we really don't have time for that. You need to hear his argument from him."

"Very well, we'll discuss this later. Captain Samant, would you please explain."

"Captain Simonis, Jain wouldn't skip Ningbo if he thought the Chinese were still ignorant of his presence. But he knows the Chinese can saturate those few spots where it's even possible for him to take a shot with ASW assets. With an alerted defender, the risk becomes too great—indeed, it's suicidal. *I* would not make the attempt."

Simonis had just been looking at the chart of Ningbo harbor. He agreed it was a mess, but reading Jain's intentions was a lot harder than reading a nautical chart.

"I respect your evaluation, Captain Samant, but we've got *North Dakota*'s two UUVs searching Hong Kong now, and if Jain gets by us and plants one in Ningbo . . ."

"Add this to the equation," Samant replied. "He's lost at least one day, perhaps more, because of his unexpected detour around the east coast of Taiwan. He's behind schedule, and even though we don't know exactly what that schedule is, it's still there because he launched the torpedo into Hong Kong. Add to that the fact that he's being hunted, means he can't just rush up to the firing point. He'll have to slow way down and thread his way through heavy shipping traffic in thirty meters of water, all the while trying to stay covert with an alerted adversary out looking for him. Even if he could do it, it's going to take him a lot of time, much more than they probably planned for originally."

Jerry continued, "Look at Shanghai, just to the north on the other side of Hangzhou Bay. The geography's more amenable for making an approach, and there are actually two targets fairly close to each other. There's the Shanghai International Port, at the mouth of the Yangtze, and the Yangshan deep-water terminal that sticks out into the bay. Shanghai International is at the top of the list due to its huge capacity, but Yangshan's is just a little below Ningbo's. Either one is worthy of a nuke, according to that list."

Simonis was nodding. "All right, you've convinced me. He trades one high-risk, time-consuming target for one that's not only easier to attack, but doesn't add any time to his schedule. I'll tell the staff to shift your patrol zone. And if Jain actually does try to attack Ningbo, the Chinese units there will have a decent chance of catching him, even without *North Dakota*. There are eight Yuan- and Song-class submarines at Daxie Dao alone, they will make for a rude welcoming committee."

Jerry looked satisfied, but Samant just looked grim. Every time he used his expertise to help the Americans, he put another nail in *Chakra*'s coffin.

"Do you have a good ambush position in mind? *North Carolina*'s already up there, so I'll make sure that your patrol zones don't conflict."

"Yes, sir, we do. There's a lovely patch of water along the fifty-meter curve where we can look out into deeper water. It's right alongside the best approach route to Yangshan. And *Chakra* will have to come in with her towed array stowed, which gives us a significant acoustic advantage."

"When do you expect to be on station?" demanded Simonis.

"In about four hours, Commodore. Oh, and sir, can you please make sure the Chinese have all their submarines out of there? I don't think you could call it a 'blue-on-blue' attack, but whether we shoot or they do, it wouldn't be good."

Simonis smiled. "Concur. I'll make sure they're clear." He leaned a little closer to the screen. "And I'm giving you the hot spot, Captain."

"Yessir, I understand. We won't let you down," Jerry answered resolutely.

"I'm not worried about that, Captain Mitchell, but I would appreciate it if you'd stop making my life so complicated."

17 April 2017
1800 Local Time
USS *Oklahoma City*
Apra Harbor, Guam

"Squadron Fifteen, arriving!"

Habit overcame urgency as Commodore Simonis paused just long enough to salute the ensign fluttering at the stern of the sub and then return the OOD's salute. Lieutenant Commander Gill Adams, *Oke City*'s XO, was waiting, but was careful to keep out of the commodore's way.

Adams started talking as soon as Simonis returned his salute, and continued his rapid-fire briefing as Simonis took the ladder in the amidships escape trunk down into the boat, then headed forward toward control. "Bismarck reported the object eleven minutes ago. We called you as soon as we saw the images. It can't be anything but a torpedo."

Simonis was moving fast. Sailors either ducked into doorways or flattened themselves against the bulkhead.

"What about the Chinese?" the commodore asked over his shoulder.

"The skipper was calling the Chinese liaison when I left."

Commander Bruce Dobson, *Oke City*'s commanding officer, was the only one who came to attention when the commodore burst into the control room, and then only momentarily. More to the point, he immediately offered Simonis a sheet of paper. "This is the best image so far. It has to be the Russian weapon."

It was a false-color sonar picture, but the torpedo's shape was immediately obvious—angled down and apparently embedded in the harbor bottom. The front of the weapon was fuzzy and possibly misshapen, although it was hard to tell.

Dobson reported, "We were lucky that the torpedo went in nose-first. We've got clean pictures of the back end, and the fins and pumpjet are completely consistent with a Russian UGST torpedo."

Simonis asked, "Just in case this was not the correct torpedo?" He almost laughed.

Dodson shrugged. "It could happen. And wouldn't we all be very embarrassed?"

"What about the front end?" Simonis asked, pointing to the printout.

"There's stuff in the mud that is likely messing up the return, and the weapon may have struck something hard when it angled over and into the bottom. It doesn't look like the damage goes back as far as the warhead section. We should be so lucky. We will warn the divers, of course."

A display on the bulkhead changed from a map of Hong Kong to an image of "Lieutenant" Li, who had either volunteered or been picked as the liaison with the Americans. He was visibly excited. "We have the images and the position you sent us! Captain Zhang has left to alert the helicopter crew. The minesweeper is almost on top of the location and the divers are preparing to enter the water.

I'm going to connect us with the captain on the mine-sweeper now."

Li typed on his keyboard, and the screen split and a second image appeared, even fuzzier and more badly angled than the first one. Simonis imagined it coming from a cell phone propped up on, or more likely taped to, some fitting on the bridge. They could make out pale gray bulkheads crowded with boxes and fittings, but there was nobody in the picture. After about twenty seconds, which seemed more like an hour, a crew-cut man in a dappled-blue camouflage shirt popped in from the side. He fired a string of Mandarin that hardly sounded like words to Simonis.

Li reported, "He says he sees the UUV's strobe light, and has marked the location." Minesweepers were very good at navigation. They had to be, considering their line of work. Simonis wasn't worried about them losing the position.

Dobson replied, "Good. Tell him we're moving the UUV away now. He should be able to watch it back away from his bridge."

Although Bismarck's sonar made it a vital part of the search, once it found and marked the position of the object, there was nothing it could do to help the divers. Both the Chinese and American planners had tried to find some way that the divers could attach a line to the UUV, and then follow it down, but the external casing was perfectly smooth. With the Chinese divers on station, the best place for the vehicle was out of the way.

Simonis watched as the petty officer on *Oke City* controlling the vehicle reported in a voice loud enough to be heard over the microphone, "Bismarck is moving two hundred yards to the south, speed three knots, sonar is *off*." He emphasized the last word, and Simonis, Dobson, and Li on the screen all nodded approvingly.

Although short-ranged, the vehicle's sonar was still powerful enough to be painful to anyone caught in its beam. During the planning for the search, and then again while the vehicles searched for the device, all hands had been briefed on the hazards associated with operating close to the UUV.

The minesweeper's captain, whose name was Min, listened to Li's translation, nodded, and shouted something over his shoulder.

Dobson then told Li about the possible damage to the front of the torpedo. "The forward part may be crumpled, but it doesn't extend very far aft."

Li spoke quickly to Captain Min, who answered, then reached toward the camera, his hand blotting out the image.

"They're using a standard torpedo collar, the same kind we use to recover expended exercise torpedoes; the damaged nose shouldn't be a problem. And the captain says that the next model of your UUV should have a pad eye on it."

The image was shaking and flashing, and Li said something in Chinese, but there was no immediate reply. A moment later the screen was flooded with light, and everyone could see the stern deck of the minesweeper, cluttered with diving gear and men, as well as the booms and winches used to handle the ship's sweep gear.

Li translated Captain Min's explanation. "He's taped the camera to a fitting so we should be able to see what happens. There are two divers already in the water, and two more standing by if they are needed. The water temperature is good, twenty-three degrees Celsius, and the depth is only seventeen meters here, so they won't even need to decompress."

Simonis could see two divers, already in wet suits, surrounded by other crewmen and helpers. One of the divers was wearing a headset.

Dobson asked Li, "What's the current like?"

Li answered quickly, without even passing the question to Min. "The tidal range near Stonecutters Island is only a meter or so. The tide is going out, but it shouldn't be more than a knot. The biggest problem will be visibility. They are both wearing lights, and one of the divers has a hand-held sonar, but they're literally searching in the dark."

All they could do was wait. The camera image jiggled and moved constantly, either from the motion of the ship or vibrations as equipment was used or from someone walking nearby. Simonis could see lines draped over the railing by the stern, starboard side. He knew one led to the collar, and another a communications line.

Five minutes into the search, the diver on the headset called out something, and Li translated. "Visibility isn't good, but they've seen worse. They're starting on a third circle, centered on the anchor."

Simonis was a submariner, so naturally he tried to do the math. With two divers swimming abreast, searching with flashlights and sonar, they could sweep a section maybe two meters wide. They'd tie a line to the anchor, and hold it while they swam in a two-meter circle. Then they'd move out to four meters from the anchor and go around again. Then six meters, but it was a larger circle now. How far do you go out before you worry about having missed the torpedo? He wondered how good their hand-held sonar was. On the inner or outer diver? Outer, he thought.

The diver with the headset said something, and Li re-layed, "Fourth circle."

That one would take longer still. How long did it take to swim twelve and a half meters in a circle? In really rotten visibility? By rights, the torpedo would be hard to miss. Even with the front third stuck in the mud, it would still stick out fifteen feet or so.

Li reported, "Fifth circle." What if the torpedo was cov-ered by mud? A thin layer would not even show up on the UUV's sonar, but would make the weapon invisible to a visual search, and might block the handheld sonar. And even if they found it, then they'd have to dig the thingie out of the bottom so they could attach the collar.

"Sixth circle." Simonis knew he was a worrywart, but it came with the job. If this went on too much longer, he could offer to use the UUV somehow to mark the torpedo's position. Bismarck knew its location within inches, but had lousy verbal skills.

He could ask the divers to go shallow, then send the UUV back in. When it was directly over the torpedo, they could turn the sonar off and set the speed to zero. But then they'd have to find the vehicle first.

They all saw it in the control room before Li translated the excited shouts. The diver with the headset yelled something, and suddenly everyone on the stern was moving purposefully. Li reported, "They found it, and the midsection is clear of the bottom! They are attaching the collar."

Li called to someone offscreen, and then told the Americans, "The helicopter will be airborne in moments." He repeated the same thing to Captain Min in Mandarin.

Sailors on the stern were taking the line that was attached to the torpedo collar and passing it through the block on a boom. As soon as they were finished, the boom swung out to starboard and up, ready to take a strain.

Simonis half expected to see the line jerk or straighten like a fish on a hook, but they were leaving in a lot of slack, so the divers were free to work. How long would it take to attach the collar to the torpedo? He didn't know exactly how the Chinese model worked, but if it was anything like the U.S. version, it was pretty simple. After all, it was designed to be used on a weapon that was floating in the water. Clamping it on one that was stationary should be even easier.

The diver with the headset called out and they watched the boom swing out a little farther. The line became taut.

Simonis started praying. This was the moment of greatest danger. There had been extensive discussions about the chance that the warhead had been fitted with anti-tamper devices, such as a sensor to detect movement. Such a device would activate once the torpedo had reached its destination.

After that, any attempt to remove it would trigger the warhead.

It was impossible to defuse or disable the torpedo in place. Trying to do it on the deck of the minesweeper would take a long time, and then there was still the concern that the access panels had all been wired somehow. Both the Chinese and American planners had studied the photos from the torpedo shop that showed the weapon's mechanism, looking for clues as to whether anti-movement devices had been fitted, but finding nothing.

In the end, they'd had to fall back on logic and hope. The installation had been improvised, and while anything involving nuclear weapons could not be described as "crude," it was simple. And while booby-trapping the access panels was within the technician's ability, a motion sensor seemed a bit much. In the end, all they could do was hope for the best.

If the warhead was fitted with any kind of anti-movement device, pulling it out of the mud would be more than enough to set it off. Of course, Simonis and *Oke City*'s crew were safe in Guam, but the crew of the minesweeper, and Li, and the population of Hong Kong were about to find out if their logic had been correct.

The boom operator was working the controls, but everyone else on the stern had paused. There was little to do now, which probably gave them more time than they wanted to think about what was happening on the bottom of the harbor. Li was staring at the screen intently.

The line to the torpedo collar was still taut, and vibrated a little with tension, but only for a moment, then moved a little back and forth. Li hardly had to translate the diver's report that the weapon was free of the bottom. Sailors clapped and patted each other's backs. Simonis could see money changing hands, and wondered what that bet had been about.

The boom operator was bringing it up steadily, and other crewmen on the stern were getting ready to receive it. It finally broke water, followed by the two divers. The other members of the dive team helped them back aboard, while a sailor played a fire hose on the weapon, rinsing off the mud and giving them a clear look at the nose.

The front was badly crumpled, one side almost caved in, but that section held the torpedo's acoustic seeker, not the warhead. Most of the dark green cylinder was undamaged.

They swung the torpedo over the stern gently, while everyone stayed well clear. This was not because the warhead was sensitive to movement, but because the torpedo weighed well over a ton, even with its fuel expended. Getting caught by either end as it swung past would be good for a broken bone.

A photographer to one side was taking pictures of everything, and a petty officer passed what looked like a radiation sensor down one side of the torpedo and back up the other before signaling all clear.

Everyone was moving quickly, and it was clear they had drilled ahead of time. Within a minute, the torpedo was poised over a cradle that had been waiting on the stern. They slipped a lifting harness over each end and then lowered it into the cradle. Simonis noticed that unless a Chinese sailor was actually working on the torpedo in some way, they tended to congregate at the far end of the stern, as far away from the weapon as they could get.

Simonis couldn't see the helicopter's arrival, but he could tell it was overhead by the noise and the sudden swirling wind, as well as most of the crewmen looking up and waving. A hook appeared in the top of the frame and came down until one of the Chinese sailors grabbed it and put it through a loop on the lifting harness. He signaled it was ready, and the line became taut, and lifted the torpedo up and out of the frame.

Simonis could hear the helicopter's engines become louder as the pilot opened the throttle. Nobody was sure whether the warhead was set to detonate in minutes, hours, or even days, but the pilot was doing his best to not be part of the fireball.

Smiling, Captain Min said something into the camera; then the image tumbled and steadied, and centered on the gray-painted helicopter, rapidly vanishing to the east and south.

Captain Dodson said, "It's just over twenty miles to Dangan Island, and another ten miles to get everyone outside the blast. A Kamov Helix can do about a hundred forty knots flat-out—and you can bet they're redlining those engines, so everyone except the helo crew will be in the clear in fifteen minutes for sure."

"And a little over an hour after that, they'll be over the drop point," Simonis added. "But we've got work to do. Get Bismarck headed over to Shenzhen Harbor and have it help out Napoleon. The sooner we're done looking that harbor over, the better."

18 April 2017
2000 Local Time
INS *Chakra*
Approach to Hangzhou Bay

They'd lost more time than even the new schedule allowed. Jain cursed himself for watching the clock so closely. Tactics shouldn't be tied to a schedule, but he kept remembering Dhankhar's briefing. *Chakra*'s strike was going to signal the start of a surprise and hopefully final offensive against Pakistan. *Chakra*'s captain thought of thousands of troops and mountains of supplies being moved through horrible weather, staying hidden until they could launch an unexpected early spring offensive.

Was it any wonder that he looked at the clock, and cursed the physics of sound that made him choose either speed or stealth?

They had to slow, both to reduce their own noise and

improve the performance of their sensors, but that came at a price in time. Swinging wide around Taiwan, then having to slow to tactical speeds, had added too much distance. Skipping Ningbo in favor of a second attack at Shanghai put him almost back on schedule.

He'd come up the eastern side of Taiwan as fast as he'd dared. From there the Chinese coast was dead ahead almost due north. There had been no sign of naval forces since the encounter with the active sonobuoy, but that changed as he neared Santiao Chiao, on the northeast coast of Taiwan. There were more Taiwanese warships, arranged in an east-west line abreast, banging away with active sonar as they steamed back and forth almost randomly. Jain lost time tracking their movements until he'd determined they actually were random, and then more time going still farther east to avoid the search group.

Jain and his officers had debated and speculated on the possible reasons for Taiwan's actions. Dhankhar's concern about a spy could explain why a Chinese diesel boat had been lurking outside Hong Kong, but not why what seemed like Taiwan's entire navy was on the lookout for submarines.

Everyone in *Chakra*'s wardroom agreed that Taiwan would not cooperate with Communist China without some compelling reason. Had China shared the spy's information with their newly independent cousins? Would that have been enough? Did the sinking of the Chinese diesel boat have anything to do with the activity off Taiwan's coast? Nothing made sense, and that worried Jain. What was he missing? A submarine on patrol has no friends, but it usually knows who its enemies are.

Crossing the East China Sea was a trial in patience. Lines of active sonobuoys thirty, even forty miles long lay across his path, forcing more detours, and more questions.

Typically, a patrol aircraft might carry a hundred sonobuoys, but most were passive. Usually a patrol plane would lay out a barrier of passive sonobuoys. The buoys were silent, listening only, and a passing submarine could not hear a plane unless it flew very low. It had the endurance to watch and listen for six or eight hours, and some sonobuoys could last even longer, for as much as a day, allowing a relief plane to pick up the barrier without losing a step.

If a sonobuoy heard a submarine, the aircraft would usually lay a tighter localization pattern to confirm the submarine's presence and find out its course and speed. Armed with this information, the sub hunter would then drop an active buoy that marked their target's actual position. The active pinging would alert the submarine, of course, but by then it would be too late. The submarine would likely be exposed and located and, on the next pass, the patrol plane would drop a homing torpedo. Jain was sure that only luck had allowed them to escape from the encounter earlier.

Patrol planes practiced their craft constantly. Practicing against their own navy's subs while they practiced evading the planes, or tracking an unfriendly nation's boat, they could perform the entire process, except for dropping the torpedo. Jain had practiced against Indian Navy aircraft in exercises, and he'd dodged Chinese patrol planes during the recent war.

But he'd never heard of laying a barrier of active buoys of that size. Had the Chinese given up on hearing *Chakra* with passive buoys? True, she was quiet, but the schoolbook answer was to place the buoys closer together. This new tactic made no sense, and went into the bucket he'd created with all the other puzzles.

An active buoy might detect *Chakra* at one mile, but she could hear them five or even ten miles away. He would of course turn away from the barrier, but then he had to figure out which end was closer, and then go miles off course to get past it.

Over the twenty-plus hours it took *Chakra* to cross the

East China Sea, her captain had watched the clock closely, and watched their earliest arrival time slip farther and farther behind. He'd regained most of the lost time by deciding to skip Ningbo, but didn't know if he could do that again. In his stateroom, where Rakash insisted he sleep, he studied the target folders, comparing different combinations of targets, not for their effect on the Chinese economy, but to see how quickly he could launch the rest of his torpedoes without getting his boat killed in the process.

The clock, positioned right next to his head, now loomed over him. He wasn't worried about the timers, already set and running inside the torpedoes. He could order the Russians to reset them to any time he liked. But he'd rejected that choice earlier. Not only was one weapon already ticking away at the bottom of Victoria Harbor, but the troops waiting at the front lines couldn't wait forever. He and Dhankhar had together confirmed the detonation time. Everything else flowed from that.

The panel next to his head buzzed. "CAPTAIN TO CENTRAL POST." This time he was still awake, and was there in moments. "Time to the next turn?" he queried, walking up to the navigation plot.

Rakash didn't even look at the clock. "Twenty-three minutes."

"The Russians?" Jain asked.

"Still making checks forward. They haven't reported any problems. Should I call them?" Jain thought about it, then shook his head no. There were two torpedoes to check this time. Orlav had even managed to get Kirichenko to help.

"We can wait a little longer. I don't like jogging a man's elbow when he's working with nuclear warheads. What about the surface traffic?"

Rakash sighed, but reported, "The wall of fishing boats has hardly shifted, but you were right; they're thinning out, so the planned turn point looks good." *Chakra* had to actually go north, beyond the clustered fishing boats and their presumed fishing banks.

Jain stepped over to the door to the sonar space. "Sonar, do you hold anything that sounds like a warship?"

Patil, the senior sonarman, said, "Yes, sir. Several active sonars, SJD-7 medium-frequency sets off to the north, but nothing close by that could be a warship. Lots of small diesels and single-props moving at low speed." He then shrugged apologetically. "There's too much traffic in the main channel to tell anything." He pointed to the display, which showed a broad, fuzzy band on those bearings.

"I'm not worried about the channel. It's too shallow for subs, and warships in the channel can't maneuver. And their sonar will be even more confused by the shipping than ours is. Watch the seaward exits closely."

Patil nodded. "Watch the port exits. Aye, aye sir."

"If there aren't any warships here right now, we're lucky, but they could come roaring out of the harbor at any moment—" Jain made a face. "—and probably will."

Orlav and Kirichenko were waiting next to the nav plot when Jain stepped out of the sonar space.

Kirichenko leaned against a nearby bulkhead and remained silent, but Orlav reported, "Both torpedoes and all the firing circuits have been checked. No faults."

"And since we have two torpedoes this time, what have you done to reduce the chance of pressing the wrong button?" joked Jain, but only slightly.

Orlav confirmed, "Are you still planning to attack the deep-water terminal first, then Shanghai International?"

Jain nodded solemnly. "Yes. That's the plan."

"Then tube one has the weapon programmed for a straight-in approach. It will bury itself in the shoals near the Yangshan container terminal. The other weapon, in tube two, is programmed for a five-mile run, a turn to starboard to three four zero, and then straight up the Yangtze to the harbor. The enable switches for tube two are tagged open, and won't be closed until after the torpedo in tube one is fired."

"Very well," Jain said approvingly.

Orlav excused himself, saying something about getting something to eat, but Kirichenko asked permission to stay. Jain could have easily booted him out of central post, but had no reason to, and he was frankly curious to see what the ex-admiral wanted.

There was still ten minutes to the first turn, with no close threatening contacts to worry about, and all preparations completed, when the Russian approached Jain. "I've decided where I'd like to go ashore," he said cautiously.

Getting the Russian off his boat was such a pleasant prospect that Jain almost smiled. "What is your choice?"

"Bali," Kirichenko answered. Jain thought it was a good choice. The island sat on the western side of the Lombok Strait, the passage that *Chakra* planned to use on their return trip. Dropping off this Russian would be simple. He might even let Kirichenko have a raft.

"It is acceptable," Jain said. "Do you know if Orlav has decided?"

"I think he wants to enlist in the Indian Navy," Kirichenko grumbled.

"That's not going to happen," Jain answered sternly. Orlav had redeemed himself somewhat by his labors aboard *Chakra*, but Jain would never forget that the man was a traitor, someone who sold his nation's secrets for money without conscience. *He might have just as easily been working for the Chinese, or anyone with coin to fill his pockets . . .*

The quartermaster announced, "Time for the turn, sir."

Rakash was checking the chart against the sonar display. "Two eight zero is still good, Captain."

"Port fifteen, then. Steer course two eight zero."

The helmsman repeated the order, and Rakash marked

the chart. "Forty-two minutes until the firing point at this speed, Captain."

Jain leaned over to study the chart. After the first weapon was fired, *Chakra* had a short six-hour run to the second firing point. Plenty of time to close the enable switches on tube two.

As he was double-checking the distance, he looked to his left and saw Kirichenko examining the route as well. The Russian was almost mimicking Jain's posture. *Must be the old reflexes,* thought Jain.

"Mind your depth, Number One. Hopefully it matches the charts, but we won't have much under us when we fire."

"Mind my depth, aye, sir," Rakash answered, and gestured to the quartermaster. They'd both keep their eye on the fathometer. They were firing in twenty-nine meters of water. It was enough, but barely.

Jain shifted his gaze back to the chart. Everything was going according to plan, and yet he still felt edgy. Something wasn't right. What was he missing?

"It's an easier harbor than Ningbo," commented Kirichenko. "Much easier, and you have sufficient water depth right up to the firing point."

The Indian skipper bristled at Kirichenko's comments. He was, of course, correct. But that didn't soothe Jain's growing anxiety.

Yes, the approach to the firing point had water depths deeper than Ningbo, or even Hong Kong. But in looking at the chart, Jain saw wrecks and obstructions that reduced the water depth to less than twenty meters to the north and south of him. He felt like he was sailing into a box canyon. And the complete lack of Chinese patrols didn't encourage him. Surely the Chinese had to know this was one of only a few approaches to Yangshan, and yet not a single PLAN vessel was in sight. It was almost as if the Chinese were intentionally avoiding the area. Sweat began to form on his brow—*were they walking into a trap?*

Jain hurriedly pressed an intercom switch. "Torpedo

oom, confirm that tubes one, three, and eight are at action state, ready to fire, and tube two is *not* ready."

"Central post, tubes one, three, and eight are at action state. Tube two is secure."

"Very well. Is Orlav there?"

"No, sir."

"Well, send someone to find him. I want him in the bomb shop before . . ."

"Captain! Torpedoes in the water bearing green one four five!" Patil's voice rang throughout the space like an alarm bell. "Two weapons! They've gone active! Captain, they're American Mark 48s!"

22

Endgame

18 April 2017
2030 Local Time
USS *North Dakota*
20 NM Southeast of Dahuanglong Island
East China Sea

"Captain, own ship's units have enabled," reported Thigpen.

"Very well, XO," Jerry replied. The ambush had been perfectly executed. *Chakra* had remained oblivious until *North Dakota*'s weapons had gone active. He'd initially doglegged them to the south at slow speed, and after a four-thousand-yard separation from his boat, he turned the torpedoes to their intercept course and sped up to forty knots. *Chakra* knew where the torpedoes were, but she would still be clueless about the whereabouts of her assailant. And that was fine with Jerry, although he took little pleasure in the flawless attack. He could almost hear Samant's teeth grinding next to him.

Petrov had watched the skilled torpedo attack with admiration. Mitchell's crew operated like a well-oiled machine, a tribute to Jerry's leadership. Feeling confident, he leaned over and whispered, "I'm sure you're aware that this will be the *third* Russian submarine you've had a hand in sinking."

Sighing, Jerry turned to his friend and grumbled, "Yes, I know. And I really didn't need to be reminded, Alex. It's

ot something I'm proud of. Besides, this battle isn't over.
et's not count our chickens just yet."

"Captain!" called out the sonar supervisor. "Possible
arget zig by Sierra eight seven."

NS *Chakra*

"Countermeasures! Launch decoy! Counterfire tube three!
Torpedo course zero six zero, high speed, minimal enable
un!" shouted Jain as he shoved Kirichenko aside. The Rus-
ian staggered back, thrown against the engineering con-
ole, shocked by the unexpected attack.

"Helmsman, port twenty, steer course one eight zero.
Half ahead, make one hundred seventy-five revs," Jain
arked. "Number One, what's the position of the wreck to
he south?"

"Sir?" Rakash replied, dazed.

"Snap out of it, Number One. How far to the damn
wreck!?"

"Ah, three thousand two hundred meters, bearing red
zero one zero, sir."

"Helmsman, continue left to one seven zero," commanded Jain. Then, hitting the intercom button, "Sonar,
any contact on our attacker?"

"Negative, sir. We only hold the torpedoes bearing
green one four five, zero bearing rate!"

Jain swore. He had no idea where the attacking submarine was. He'd been jumped completely unawares—the
mark of a professional. He didn't have time to wonder who
the American was that was attacking him, or even why. He
needed to get his boat out of this birdcage and into deeper
water; to flee if he could, or to maneuver if he couldn't.

Joining his first officer at the chart table, Jain stabbed
at the wreck symbol. "I'm going to get as close to the wreck
as I can and then turn east. Get on the Arfa sonar and stand
by to go active."

As Rakash jumped to the mine-hunting sonar console, Jain ordered, "Helmsman, make your depth forty meters and be quick about it!" He was getting as close to the bottom as he dared.

USS *North Dakota*

"Torpedo in the water! Bearing two zero eight, it's moving away from us, drawing rapidly to the left!" reported the sonar supervisor.

Jerry smiled slightly and whispered, "I'm not there, Captain."

"Skipper, new contact bearing two one eight, drawing right. Sierra eight seven is heading south."

"Very well, sonar supervisor." Jerry saw the new trace show up on the command workstation display; then, looking up at the starboard VLSD, he saw that the target was moving northwest at fifteen knots.

"That's a decoy, Captain," advised Samant. "Jain is following our evasion doctrine perfectly. The countermeasures are to obscure his movements while he counterfires, launches a decoy, and turns away from the attacker." There was a hint of pride in his voice.

Jerry nodded his approval. "It's unfortunate for him that I still have my thin-line towed array out. The acoustic countermeasures can't affect it. And that decoy isn't very convincing."

"It's an older MG-84 mobile decoy, Jerry," Petrov volunteered. "It's more effective against ships, submarine hull arrays, and . . ."

Suddenly, Thigpen burst out, "Detect. Detect. Detect. Homing. Torpedo number one is homing! Wait a second, it's turning to the right. Shit, it's locked on to the decoy!"

". . . and torpedoes," finished a smug Petrov. Jerry countered with an irritated look.

Before he could order the torpedo turned back to the correct target, Thigpen let out a loud groan. "Loss of fire continuity on torpedo number one. The wire must have broken when the weapon turned sharply to the right. We still have the wire on torpedo number two."

Frustrated, Jerry took a deep breath. That was why he fired a salvo instead of a single weapon. "XO, command torpedo number two to turn fifty degrees to port."

While Thigpen turned and ordered the fire control operator to make the course change, Jerry looked at the position of the Indian UGST torpedo. It was well past them, screaming out toward the northeast. He could safely turn. Turning toward Lieutenant Junior Grade Quela Lymburn, the battle stations OOD, Jerry instructed, "Q, bring us to the left. New course two zero zero, and increase speed to twenty knots."

"Come to new course two zero zero, and increase speed to twenty knots, aye, sir," acknowledged Lymburn. "Pilot, left full rudder, come to course two zero zero. All ahead standard."

NS *Chakra*

"Captain, one of the attacking torpedoes appears to have turned away. It may have been confused by the countermeasures and decoy," reported Lieutenant Kirit from the Omnibus combat system consoles.

"Very well, but that still leaves one on our tail," responded Jain. "Number One, activate the Arfa. Report bearing and range to the wreck."

"Aye, aye, sir." The first officer hit the transmit button, and after what seemed like an inordinately long time said, "Captain, the wreck bears red zero zero one. Range nine hundred meters."

"Central post, Mark 48 torpedo has begun range gating! It's got us!" cried Patil.

"Helmsman, full ahead! Stand by countermeasures!" Jain roared. "Number One, report range!"

"Range to the wreck is seven hundred fifty meters."

Jain began a silent countdown; he needed to time his next move just right. Struggling to remain composed, the young captain glanced at the Omnibus display. The torpedo was just over three thousand meters away and closing rapidly. This was going to be close.

"Range?" he asked calmly.

"Range to the wreck is five hundred meters!" Rakas bawled.

"Steady yourself, Number One!" chastised Jain. He counted about twenty seconds, then, turning to Lieutenant Kota, commanded, "Deploy countermeasures!"

Jain quietly mumbled a fifteen-second count, then ordered, "Helmsman, port thirty! Steer east! All hands brace for shock!"

With the rudder over hard, and speed creeping past twenty-three knots, *Chakra* banked markedly into the turn. Jain clung to one of the periscopes for support while Kirichenko fought to keep his footing by the engineering consoles. The deck vibrated intensely as the speed increased and the sub heeled over in a stiff bank. Jain kept staring at the heading repeater, counting the seconds quietly, urging his boat to move faster.

After a tense minute, he yelled out, "Any moment now!"

Confused by the sudden appearance of the two countermeasures, the Mark 48 torpedo momentarily lost track of its target. Before it could begin a reattack search pattern, it blew past the stationary noisemakers and quickly reacquired a target dead ahead. But while the echo return was strong, the target wasn't moving; the torpedo's acoustic seeker detected no Doppler shift. The homing logic judged the target as invalid and began to turn the weapon to port, but it was too close now. The torpedo plowed

to the sunken wreck and the high-explosive warhead
detonated, sending strong shock waves out in all direc-
ons.

SS *North Dakota*

Loud explosion bearing two zero zero!" sang out the so-
ar supervisor. The control room erupted in a cheer. Jerry
aw his crew congratulating each other. To his right, Sa-
ant stood rigidly, his fists clenched, hardly breathing.

"Quiet in control!" bellowed Jerry. The celebratory
clamor dropped instantly. Looking over at his exec, he in-
uired, "XO, status?"

"Torpedo number two has detonated in close proximity
Sierra eight seven's location, sir. It looks like a hit."

Jerry nodded his acknowledgment, turned, and stepped
ver to the sonar displays. "Senior chief, what do you hear?"

Senior Chief Halleck held up a finger, meaning, "Wait
me." After a long ten seconds, he shook his head and said,
I still have stable propulsion plant tonals, sir. I don't
ink . . . Hold on! There's a strong broadband contact on
he hull array, drawing left."

Leaning over the sonar supervisor's shoulder, Jerry
poke softly. "Is it *Chakra*?"

Halleck nodded. "Confirmed, sir. Sierra eight seven is
moving eastward at high speed, bearing rate is left five de-
rees per minute."

"Range?"

"Maybe eight or nine thousand yards, Skipper, but that's
n educated guess. She's in the WAA's baffles."

Straightening up, Jerry announced, "Attention in con-
ol. It appears that we missed. Sierra eight seven is still
live and kicking. I want a new firing solution ASAP."

"Skipper, if we missed *Chakra*, what the hell did the
orpedo detonate on?" complained Thigpen.

Jerry motioned for his XO to look at the HLSD ar pointed to the wreck symbol on the chart near *Chakra* track. Thigpen was incredulous. "We sank a wreck!?"

"Technically, XO, it was already sunk," noted Jerry wi a grin. He couldn't tell if he was disappointed or relieve that the attack had failed.

Samant stared at the chart; his expression was ui questionably one of relief. "Bravo, Maahir, bravo!" I whispered softly.

"You trained that young man well, Girish," compl mented Petrov, just as impressed with Jain's well-execute maneuver as the rest.

"I used to flog him relentlessly about not being as awa of his environment as he could've been. He always seeme to miss a critical detail that could have been used to h advantage." Samant's voice and face showed his pride. Th kind of pride a headmaster has when a struggling stude finally understands a difficult lesson.

"Well, it would appear that Jain did listen to you afte all, Captain," Jerry remarked. "Which means, unfortu nately, that this fight will be more difficult than I'd like.

Samant opened his mouth to speak, then thought bette of it and just shrugged.

"Possible target zig, Sierra eight seven," said Hallec "Target has turned away or slowed down."

Jerry looked up at the VLSD and saw the range of po sible vectors. Facing Lymburn, he instructed, "Q, bring to one one zero. Let's see if we can't figure out where he going."

INS *Chakra*

The jolt was tremendous. Loose items were thrown all ov in central post; several of the occupants were also flun colliding with each other or unforgiving consoles. Whi the lights did flicker several times, they stayed on.

"Damage report, all compartments," Jain thundered. Reaching down, he helped Kirichenko get up off the deck. The Russian had a nasty bruise forming on his left cheek.

"Nicely done, Captain," grunted Kirichenko as he regained his footing.

Jain ignored the man and hit the intercom button. "Sonar, any sign of that bastard?"

"Central post, no, sir, we're going too fast. I can't hear a thing," replied a shaken Patil.

The report was exactly what Jain expected. He'd successfully evaded the ambush, but if he stayed at full speed, he'd be blind. If he slowed down, however, he'd become more vulnerable to another attack. Either way, the hidden adversary would have the advantage—at least temporarily. "Number One," he beckoned, motioning for his first officer to join him at the navigation plot. But Jain wasn't going to wait; he had to keep the enemy off balance. Since he didn't have contact, all he could do right now was throw off the fire control solution with frequent course and speed changes.

"Helmsman, right fifteen, course one three zero. Half ahead, one hundred forty revs."

Rakash limped over and reported, "Captain, minimal damage in compartments one, three, and six. Nothing critical, we retain full combat capability. The medical officer reports mostly minor injuries, although one crew member may have suffered a concussion."

"Very well, Number One." Jain then smiled wearily. "That was close."

"A little *too* close for my liking, Captain. What do we do now?"

Jain sighed. "We certainly can't proceed with the attack on Yangshan. I'd like to get out to deeper water so we can either lose this chap or gain some room to maneuver." Pointing to the chart, he outlined their escape routes. "If we head in an easterly direction, we should be able to reach the eighty meter curve fairly quickly. Mark depth under the keel."

Rakash looked at the fathometer. "There's nine meters beneath us, Captain. That puts us in water forty-eight meters deep."

"Very good. Number One, deploy the towed array as soon as we slow to twenty-five knots."

"But, Captain, it's not recommended to deploy the towed array at speeds over twenty knots."

Jain stiffened, irritated by Rakash's reminder. The speed limitation was a peacetime specification made by the Russian manufacturer—it didn't apply to the current situation. "I realize that, Number One, but we don't have the luxury of mindlessly following the manual right now. Get the array deployed, I have to know where this fellow is if we are going to fight him. Also, load the new mobile decoy in tube eight and bring it to action state immediately."

USS *North Dakota*

"Captain, Sierra eight seven has steadied up, estimated course one three five, but its speed continues to decrease. Current speed is twenty-two knots," stated Thigpen. The report sounded definitive, but Jerry heard the slight indecision in his voice.

"Understood, XO. Is it good enough to shoot on?" It had been only a few minutes since both submarines had last maneuvered and the target motion analysis solution had only just started firming up.

"Sir, I'd like another minute of data. I feel okay about the range, but I'd like to refine the course and speed a little more."

"Very well, XO, one more minute." Jerry looked at the current solution on his display. *Chakra* was to his south at eight thousand two hundred yards, slowly opening. Pivoting to Samant, he asked, "Captain, why is he slowing down? I would have kept on running."

"I think he believes he needs to fight. Perhaps his mission orders don't allow him to just walk away from a target, so he has to engage, either to sink us, or make us retreat. But he can't fight without a sensor, and in this very shallow water the Skat-3 main hull sonar will be limited."

"You think Jain is trying to deploy his towed array?" wondered Petrov. "He's going a little fast for that; he could snap the cable."

"True, but he really doesn't have much of a choice now, does he?" Samant responded.

"How long does it take to deploy the array?" asked Jerry.

"Just a few minutes. It depends on the ship's speed," Petrov answered.

"XO! We're running out of time. I need that solution now!"

INS *Chakra*

"Central post, new towed array contact bearing red one three zero," Patil announced over the speaker.

Jain lunged for the intercom box and punched the button. "Sonar, you're sure of the single bearing?" He was puzzled by the report, as towed array bearings always came in pairs, requiring another course change to resolve the ambiguity.

"Yes, sir. The other bearing points toward the mud, the ten-meter curve. The contact has to be to the north. It looks like an American *Virginia*-class attack submarine."

The sonar chief's report caused the color to drain from both Jain's and Rakash's faces. For a brief moment, they looked at each other with hushed anxiety. Finally, the first officer broke the awkward silence. "Could it be the American we fought during the war?"

"The *North Dakota*?" Jain replied cautiously. He remembered the letter that Samant had received from the American right after the Sino–Littoral Alliance War asking for a draw. His old captain was initially furious, but then, after he had calmed down, took the letter as a sign of respect. Regardless, the man had bested Samant twice, and this sent shivers down Jain's spine. Given the complete surprise of the ambush, and the tactical skills needed to pull that off, Jain could come to no other conclusion. "I'm afraid our nemesis has returned. We won't be able to run away from this fellow, Number One."

"You're not seriously thinking of engaging a frontline fourth-generation American attack submarine, are you?" whined Kirichenko. "That's sheer madness!"

"Shut up!" fired Jain. "I don't recall asking for your opinion, *Mister* Kirichenko! One more word out of you and I'll have you confined to your quarters!" Pivoting back to his first officer, Jain belted out a rapid series of orders.

"Number One, deploy countermeasures! Bring tubes four and five to action state. Launch decoy, course zero five zero! Helmsman, left twenty-five, steer north! Half ahead, one hundred five revs!"

USS *North Dakota*

"Possible target zig, Sierra eight seven," said the sonar supervisor. And then almost immediately: "Countermeasures! Bearing one nine three!"

"Damn it!" snarled Jerry. "Snapshot, Sierra eight seven, tube four!"

"Solution ready," Thigpen called out.

"Weapon ready," followed the weapons officer.

"Ship ready," Lymburn exclaimed.

"Shoot!" barked the fire control technician as he hit the

button, followed by, "Normal launch. Torpedo course one eight five, speed five five knots!"

"Pilot, left full rudder. Steady course zero six zero," Jerry commanded.

"Skipper, we'll lose . . ." warned Thigpen.

"Understood!" Jerry shot back forcefully. He was well aware that a turn at this speed would almost certainly break the wire with the torpedo.

Sure enough, seconds later Thigpen reported, "Loss of wire continuity."

"Close the outer door on tube four. Make tube three ready in all respects," instructed Jerry.

"Captain!" yelled Halleck. "There are two contacts emerging from the countermeasures. One bears two zero seven, the other one nine seven. They look identical!"

Jerry quickly leaned over the supervisor's shoulder and looked at the two contacts. Their narrowband profiles were indistinguishable, acoustic twins. Checking their speed, he saw that both contacts were at fifteen knots; there was no clear way to tell *Chakra* from the decoy she'd just launched. Surprised, Jerry turned to Samant and Petrov, who'd joined him at the sonar displays. Both men examined the side-by-side display of the two signatures. Neither one could tell them apart.

"It's a perfect replicate," said Samant, astonished.

"Looks like a later-model decoy, either an MG-104 or MG-114," concluded Petrov. Turning to Samant, he remarked, "I didn't know we had sold these to the Indian Navy."

"I had two during the war. Never got a chance to use one, though. The signature simulation is simply amazing!"

"Senior Chief," interrupted Jerry. "Make sure you're recording the data. We'll examine it more closely later."

"Skipper," called Thigpen. "Own ship's unit has enabled. Slowing to forty knots. It's searching."

INS *Chakra*

"Incoming torpedo has gone active!" squawked the intercom. Chief Petty Officer Patil's voice was strained. The acoustic intercept receiver echoed the dire report.

"Bearing drift!?" demanded Jain.

"Nearly zero!" Patil yelled.

"Number One, deploy countermeasures!" Jain then counted to ten and barked out more orders. "Helmsman, starboard twenty, steer zero four zero, full ahead. Sonar stand by to go active on the main hull array."

Two more cylinders popped out from *Chakra*'s hull, and as soon as the seawater-activated batteries were brought up to power, the devices began shrieking like banshees. The Mark 48 torpedo had initially been in a quandary. It had two valid targets, one to the left, and the other to the right. Which one to home in on? Suddenly, the right-hand target disappeared behind a wall of sound. Seeing only one valid target, the torpedo veered left and began range gating, homing in on the decoy.

USS *North Dakota*

"More countermeasures, Skipper. Sierra eight seven is the contact to the left, bearing two one zero," announced the sonar supervisor.

Jerry looked down at the command display and then up at the starboard VLSD; the countermeasure symbol was blinking near *Chakra*'s last reported position. He also saw the torpedo begin tacking to the left, toward the decoy. They'd missed again.

"This is starting to get old," he grumbled. The hull array was completely blinded by the noise from the acoustic jammers, but the towed array still had a tenuous lock. The jammer didn't have a lot of power at the lower frequencies. He'd just switched back to the narrowband display on the command workstation when Senior Chief Halleck shouted out, "Possible target zig, Sierra eight seven. Contact has turned toward us and is increasing speed."

Jerry wasn't quite as fast as his leading sonarman, and it took him a few more seconds to verify that *Chakra* had indeed maneuvered again. Still, Jain's maneuvers showed he wasn't confident about his estimates of *North Dakota*'s position. That meant Jerry still held the advantage. An advantage he intended to exploit. "XO, get me a new firing solution, pronto!"

"Aye, aye, sir," replied Thigpen, watching one of the displays. It was clear the Indian Akula was changing course and speed. That she was turning toward them was beyond question, but what would her final course and speed be? Recalling Jerry's admonition, he gave the operator an initial "best guesstimate" for the computer to chew on. "Put in course zero five zero, speed thirty-three knots and see if the machine barfs."

After a minute of data, it was apparent that the solution was off. With a few adjustments for a more northerly course, and a slightly higher speed the TMA solution seemed to hang together. The contact was closing; the range was down to about seven thousand yards.

"Skipper, I have an initial firing solution. It's up on the starboard VLSD," said Thigpen.

In looking at the fruits of Thigpen's labors, Jerry became more and more perplexed. *Chakra* was pointed, more or less, in the right direction and was ramping up to high speed. "What is he doing?" whispered Jerry. Then, looking at Samant, he added, "He's going too fast, and we're in the towed array's forward end fire beam. He won't be able to track us at all!"

Samant shook his head. Jain was either impatient or afraid; he was trying to force the issue. "He's attempting to charge into a position so he can use his active sonar to get a good solution. He doesn't feel confident firing on the sparse towed-array data."

"But in this water, a Skat-3 sonar will sound like a kettledrum in an empty closet. The reverberation will be horrendous," Jerry observed.

"Agreed, Captain, but if he can get close enough, it could still work."

Jerry pulled up the line-of-sight diagram and looked at the range rate. *Chakra* was closing, but slowly, about 330 yards every minute. Facing Samant, he pointed to the diagram and said, "Jain's guessing. He's not sure where we are."

"I concur, Captain. I believe he's trying to run down the bearing from your last torpedo, but I don't think he's factored in the effects of the decoy on the torpedo's course—his estimate will be off." Samant looked pained as he spoke; then he began to fidget. It looked like he was mentally arguing with himself. Finally, he just spit the words out. "Captain, I request that you transmit the recording I made."

Astonished by the appeal, Jerry looked Samant straight in the eyes. "Captain, we've exchanged weapons fire. Do you seriously believe he'll respond positively to your message? Assuming of course he can even hear it."

"Honestly, I do not know. But it's something we haven't tried yet. You have his complete and undivided attention, and a little time before you have to shoot another weapon. I'm just asking that you try." Samant's face and voice were strained with emotion. He desperately wanted to try anything that could save his crew. Glancing over at Petrov, Jerry saw him nod in agreement.

Rubbing his eyes and taking a deep breath, Jerry weighed Samant's plea. He was right, they had a little time, but it also meant transmitting—putting a string of strong acoustic pulses into the water. But even if the Indian crew couldn't understand what was being said, they'd sure as hell get a good bearing. Jerry would be voluntarily giving up his advantage. Sighing loudly, he turned his head toward the sonar watchstanders and said, "Senior Chief, transmit Captain Samant's message over the main active array. Point it directly at *Chakra*."

The sonar supervisor initially balked as he struggled to comprehend the order. But a quick look at his CO's face removed any doubt. "Aye, aye, sir. Transmit Captain Samant's message." Halleck's fingers worked hesitantly over the keyboard, and after a brief moment, he hit the last one and reported, "Transmitting."

Jerry saw Thigpen's disbelieving expression and raised his hand, signaling his XO to wait. Thigpen turned back toward the fire control consoles, whispering softly, "This will get interesting."

INS *Chakra*

"Central post. I'm picking up what sounds like a UWC transmission, bearing red zero one zero. It's in the direction of the American submarine," Patil declared, not quite convinced that he had heard correctly.

Jain and Rakash looked at each other with utter bewilderment. Why would the American be trying to contact them? He'd already fired three torpedoes at them, what purpose could there be in attempting to communicate? Before Jain could respond, Patil's voice came over the intercom again.

"Central post. The transmission is in Hindi!"

Now Jain was really curious. He acknowledged the bizarre report and then went to the sonar shack; he had to hear this transmission for himself.

Patil was waiting with a set of headphones in his right hand. "It appears to be a recorded message, sir, as it is being repeated."

Jain put on the headphones and listened. The reception was extremely poor, owing to *Chakra*'s high speed and the shallow water, but the voice was most definitely speaking in Hindi. He couldn't understand much of the transmission, it warbled and broke up often, but he did make out the words "Dhankhar," "illegal," and "return." The voice also sounded strangely familiar, but the distortion made it difficult to pin down.

The Indian captain pulled the headset off and handed it back to the sonar chief. He struggled to understand the message and its meaning. Then Jain remembered Vice Admiral Dhankhar warning him that several foreign governments had discovered the plan. Could the United States be one of them? Were they trying to deceive him now, as they seemed unable to sink him? Then Jain recalled his orders; the attack on the Chinese ports was the first act in an elaborate strategy by the Indian military to defeat Pakistan once and for all. *Chakra*'s pivotal role in the plan stiffened his resolve.

While Jain was trying to make heads or tails of the transmission, Patil hit him with an unthinkable question: "Sir, didn't that voice sound like Captain Samant's?"

Anger suddenly flooded Jain. The very thought of their former captain cooperating with India's enemies was blasphemous. "Mind your bearing, Chief! I will not tolerate any insult of our old CO. Lash that bearing with the main hull array and get me something to shoot on!"

Still seething, Jain returned to central post. Rakash could see something was dreadfully wrong, but before he could even ask the speaker squawked again. "Central post, weak return bearing red zero zero six, range five thousand two hundred meters."

"Stand by for torpedo attack. Open bow caps on tubes four and five," thundered Jain. Rakash moved quickly to follow his captain's orders.

Leaning over Lieutenant Kirit's shoulders, Jain blurted, "We'll bracket the bearing! Set tube four to course zero two five, and tube five to zero four zero! High speed, minimal enable run!"

"Bow caps on tubes four and five are open, sir," cried Rakash.

"Torpedo course set," Kirit called out.

Jain stood with an unwavering air, paused for a few seconds, and then shouted, "Fire!"

USS *North Dakota*

The WLY-1 acoustic intercept receiver's chirping beat Senior Chief Halleck's warning by a second or two. "Sierra eight seven has gone active. Skat-3 transmissions bearing two one five."

"Secure transmissions," Jerry ordered. Then, looking at Samant, he said, "I'm sorry, Captain. Jain's made his choice." The Indian's face was burdened with pain, his only response a slight nod.

"Torpedoes in the water!" yelled Halleck. "Same bearing as Sierra eight seven!"

"Execute starburst maneuver to starboard," snapped Jerry.

"Starburst to starboard, aye, sir," Thigpen responded. "Countermeasure station, deploy starburst pattern!"

As soon as countermeasure symbols started popping up on the starboard VLSD, Jerry commanded, "Pilot, right full rudder, steady course one three zero!"

The countermeasure pods near *North Dakota*'s stern launched two stationary sonar jammers just before she started to turn. Now, two mobile jammers were kicked out, heading away from the submarine on reciprocal courses, building a wall of intense sound—essentially a barrier, opaque to any acoustic sensor. Finally, a mobile decoy was deployed and it continued down the course *North Dakota* had just turned away from—a maneuver that had been completely hidden from the onrushing *Chakra*.

INS *Chakra*

"Central post, contact has deployed countermeasures, I've lost contact," shouted Patil.

Jain had expected as much. The commander of *North Dakota* had demonstrated that he was no fool. "What was the last good bearing and range?" he demanded.

"Bearing red zero zero five, range, four thousand eight hundred meters. He was still on course zero six zero at last contact."

Looking at the Omnibus display, Jain saw that the American was running away from the countermeasure barrier. *Excellent,* he thought proudly. *The salvo should catch him.* "Steady on course!" he cried out, smiling.

USS *North Dakota*

Two minutes after making the run, Jerry deployed another stationary ADC Mark 5 countermeasure. Between this new addition and the mobile jammer, there was another wall of sound hiding *North Dakota* from the oncoming UGST torpedoes. The only legitimate target in their field of view would be the mobile decoy that was now running away from the scene at twenty knots.

"Skipper, one of the torpedoes has begun range gating! It's past CPA and opening, it's locked on to the decoy!" said Halleck with noticeable relief.

"Gotcha," Jerry whispered, followed immediately by, "Firing point procedures, Sierra eight seven . . ."

"Wait, Captain!" howled Samant.

Jerry turned, taken aback by the Indian's sudden interruption. He looked at the man's face and saw the tears welling in his eyes.

"Please, Captain, Jerry, allow me to issue the order to fire," choked Samant. Both Jerry and Petrov looked at him with amazement.

"I appreciate the offer, Captain," replied Jerry. "But you wouldn't be able to live with yourself if you gave the order."

Samant gave a cynical chuckle, then responded, "I won't be able to live with myself now as it is, Jerry. But if my crew has to die, then I prefer it be at my hands. An Indian started this nightmare, it's only proper that an Indian end it."

Jerry paused, considering Samant's emotional appeal, then nodded. Turning forward, he announced loudly, "Attention in control, Captain Girish Samant has the conn, Lieutenant Lymburn retains the deck."

All the stations acknowledged Jerry's pronouncement and then watched as Samant stepped over to the fire control consoles.

"Which control launches the torpedo?" he asked the fire control technician quietly.

The petty officer looked toward his XO. Thigpen gave a curt nod signaling it was okay. "This one, sir," answered the young sailor.

Straightening himself, Samant gave the order. His voice was firm and professional. "Stand by torpedo attack, target, INS *Chakra*, tube three." Reaching over, he pushed the button and thundered, "Fire!"

"Normal launch, torpedo course, two seven zero, speed four zero knots," reported the petty officer. He was looking at Samant when he spoke.

The torpedo ran straight out from tube number three to clear itself and the guidance wire from the submarine. It then began a wide turn to the right, its movement screened by the mobile sonar jammer. By the time it had passed in front of the countermeasure field it had already gone active. And once it was past the intense sound barrier, its seeker was pointed straight at *Chakra*, barely fifteen hundred yards away. The torpedo locked on and began accelerating.

INS *Chakra*

"Torpedo alert! Starboard side!" screeched Patil.

Jain's head spun as he looked at the Omnibus display. The incoming weapon was very close. "Deploy countermeasures!" he screamed.

It was too late. Before the countermeasures were ejected from the Akula, the Mark 48 torpedo's warhead detonated, devastating compartment three and violating the bulkhead with compartment two. The submarine heeled sharply over to port and pitched downward. At thirty-four knots she slammed into the shallow bottom with tremendous force, crushing some of the torpedo tubes and the weapons loading hatch. Water began gushing into the torpedo room.

The submarine's momentum carried it forward, lifting its stern clear of the water as it rotated about its shattered bow. Slamming back down into the water, the boat jumped a bit and then settled quickly. The aft part of the boat came crashing down onto the ocean floor; the harsh impact caused the shaft seals to fail, and water began pouring into yet another compartment. Skidding to a stop, *Chakra* lay still, bleeding to death.

USS *North Dakota*

"Loud explosion bearing two six zero! There's breaking-up noise, loss of propulsion plant tonals!" reported the sonar supervisor. But unlike the last time, there were no cheers, no congratulatory backslapping. Just silence.

Thigpen finally broke the stillness. "It looks like we got her, sir."

Jerry nodded and sighed; he felt relief and sadness at the same time. A lot of brave men had just been killed, betrayed by their fleet commander, and executed by their former skipper—the irony couldn't have been more tragic.

Jerry watched as Samant walked slowly out of control, spots of water appearing on the deck as he headed aft.

Petrov had started to move toward him when Jerry grabbed his arm. "Let him go, Alex. He needs some time alone. He has to deal with this on his own terms. It's what he wanted."

The Russian fought initially, then stopped, heeding Jerry's counsel. Petrov knew exactly how Samant felt; he'd lost a boat and some of his men as well. He knew that his friend would never get over this day. Sometimes doing the right thing can be personally devastating.

Facing Jerry, Petrov remarked quietly, "That was the most courageous act I've ever witnessed. I don't know if I could do what he had to."

Jerry shook his head, struggling with his own emotions. "I know I couldn't."

INS *Chakra*

The pounding of his head dragged Kirichenko to a state of semiconsciousness. He tried to move, but found he was pinned under a console. The central post was dimly lit by the battle lanterns; wisps of smoke floated through the beams. No one moved.

Off to his right, Kirichenko saw Jain's body draped over the navigation plotting table, his neck at an unnatural angle. The Russian felt his eardrums pop and he heard the noise of rushing water. He could feel the cold liquid as it crawled up his legs.

Unable to completely understand what was going on, Kirichenko did realize that *Chakra* was dead, and that he would be soon enough. Weary and racked with pain, he couldn't summon the strength to try and move the console off of him. Then he saw a shadow move, or thought he did.

At first, he couldn't make it out. But then it looked like men slowly making their way toward him. He tried calling out to them, but all he could manage was a faint gurgle. As the nebulous figures got closer, Kirichenko thought they looked odd. They didn't seem to be Indian. Then two of them moved into the light. They were pale, vague images, dressed in Russian naval uniforms. Straining to focus his eyes, he finally caught sight of the billet patch on the closest individual; it was in Russian, and it read COMMANDER.

Panic gripped Kirichenko as the muddy seawater lapped upon his face. More and more of the wraithlike images huddled around him, waiting patiently. Soon the seawater covered his mouth and he struggled to breathe through his nose. The apparitions were now all smiling, and began reaching out to him. And just before the murky water covered his eyes, he saw the commissioning pin on the commander's uniform—the name on the pin was *Gepard*.

23

Cleanup

20 April 2017
0800 EST
White House Situation Room
Washington, D.C.

"The water depth is only fifty-two meters, Dr. Patterson. What do your experts tell you?" The Chinese minister of national defense sounded impatient, like he'd already had this discussion, perhaps more than once.

Patterson tried to sound positive. "My experts tell me we likely have a few days, General. They want to use some of that time to find out if there is a way to use conventional explosives. They think they can adapt one of our air force's Massive Ordnance Penetrators for the task. They're running simulations now to see how the bomb behaves in an underwater explosion. The tamping effect . . ."

General Shi interrupted, "We've considered that as well. The problem is that no matter how big a conventional device is used, there is no guarantee that the devices in the remaining nuclear torpedoes will be destroyed. It might simply shred and scatter the wreck, leaving the torpedo warheads intact. Even one or two one-hundred-fifty-kiloton bombs detonating off our coast could do tremendous damage.

"And what if a conventional explosion merely damages the devices so they fail to detonate? The wreck is not in deep water. It is conceivable that some organization could search the wreck and recover them." The general's voice hardened. "We have been threatened with rogue nuclear weapons once. We will not let it happen again."

Patterson argued, "Our engineers are optimistic they can come up with a nonnuclear way to destroy the torpedoes in *Chakra*'s wreck."

"So are ours," Shi countered, "but can they do it in time? We know the torpedoes were not fitted with any kind of deadman switch, or they would have exploded already. But we don't know the Indians' timetable. How far north were they going to go? The list of targets your source discovered goes all the way to Qingdao and Dalian. Do we have days, or hours? And your people have suggested that the Indian captain had the ability to change targets, skipping one port to save time."

"That's true," Patterson conceded.

"Then they could probably reset the timers, as well," Shi continued. "In truth, the hulk of that submarine could explode with the equivalent of a six-hundred-kiloton nuclear bomb at any moment. We've issued the standard notice to airmen and mariners, and our navy is doing its best to keep the area clear, but when those bombs go off, people are going to die, and more will die later from the fallout. The only certain way to completely destroy everything inside the submarine's hull is with another nuclear device—much smaller than the one-hundred-fifty-kiloton weapons on board, but big enough."

Patterson recognized that Shi's argument was based on hyperbole. It would be virtually impossible for all four timers to hold the exact same time, within nanoseconds of each, and at best two weapons might detonate simultaneously—the other weapons destroyed in the blast before their fuze mechanisms could get them started. But still, that meant a three-hundred-kiloton explosion. On the whole, the general's reasoning was sound. "All right," she conceded. "The U.S. will support your decision. How big a bomb will you use?" she asked.

"I don't think that's important, as long . . ."

"We'll be able to measure the size of the blast as soon as you detonate it," she pointed out.

Shi nodded. "Of course. My country, like yours, has a store of nuclear depth bombs designed for use against hostile submarines. They can be set for different yields. Our minesweepers have already verified the location of the wrecked submarine and placed a buoy over it. *North Dakota*'s initial position report was most accurate and due to her assistance, we were able to quickly assess the situation. Our aviators say they can place the depth bomb within half a meter of the wreck, perhaps directly on it, by helicopter. After listening to our best scientists, the Central Military Commission decided on a ten-kiloton yield."

I'll bet the experts said five would be sufficient, she thought. Still, in a case like this, overkill might be the best course.

"When will this happen?"

"Tomorrow morning at zero six hundred hours, just after dawn local time," Shi answered. "We will be ready sometime later tonight, but we will wait until it is light and we can be sure that all ships and aircraft are out of the area. Because it is a much smaller explosion, we only have to clear an area a few kilometers square. The fireball will be less than four hundred meters in diameter, with no damage three kilometers from the center. Even the fallout from the explosion will only extend a few tens of kilometers to the northeast, all over open water. If the four torpedoes were allowed to detonate, the fallout cloud would reach all the way to the Korean peninsula."

"Is there anything we can do to assist you?" Patterson asked. She tried to sound helpful.

"China is taking this action unilaterally, and does not require the permission or assistance of any nation or organization to protect its citizens." Shi paused, then scowled. "But we would ask for America's support in the Western media that this deliberate, peaceful detonation of a nuclear device is intended to save lives and reduce damage."

Patterson thought about all the back-and-forth the U.S. and the PRC had engaged in, for so many years. They were still rivals, but that didn't mean the two countries had to act like jerks all the time. "Ending this incident quickly and safely is in everyone's interest. You can count on the U.S. administration releasing a statement in support of your operation. We have no interest in furthering tension or mistrust in the region. And General, I would submit that the more information the People's Republic of China releases about this operation, the better."

General Shi sighed and suddenly looked very tired. "China is grateful for America's continuing assistance, and we will consider your advice carefully."

21 April 2017
1100 Local Time
Amritsar, India

The local police had set up a checkpoint a block away from the address. Senior inspector Narendra Bhati had to thread his way through a crowd of locals to reach the barrier, but after seeing his badge, the officers guarding it quickly saluted and moved aside to let him past. A Sikh police corporal offered to guide him to the lieutenant who was the on-scene commander.

The crime scene was a mass of flashing lights and dozens of people milling about. Most were firemen or police, with a sprinkling of other emergency workers. The corporal led him past a line of idling fire engines to a van labeled "Amritsar District Police." The doors were open and Bhati could see a very busy police lieutenant, also a Sikh, trying to speak on the radio and to a fireman at the same time. He noticed the corporal, with Bhati in tow, and held up one hand while he signed off the radio, then quickly finished with the sergeant.

He also saluted when Bhati flashed his CBI credentials, then said happily, "I am more than pleased to turn over jurisdiction of this matter to the Central Bureau of Investigation."

"Not so fast, Lieutenant," Bahti said. "Just what are you trying to give me?"

"They didn't tell you?"

Bhati shook his head and replied with an irritated voice. "The office just gave me this address and said it was likely a CBI matter."

The lieutenant laughed. " 'Likely' is one word for it. That makes sense. Security." He took out a small notebook, and took a breath.

"The fire brigade was called at nine eleven this morning, after they received a report of black smoke rising at an address on Canal Bank Road." He tilted his head toward the bungalow behind him. "Emergency services received a call at nine twenty-five of gunshots at the same address. Two cars were dispatched and the fire brigade company en route was warned to wait for the police before entering the structure.

"The fire brigade arrived at nine twenty-seven, the police two minutes later. They effected entry through the front door, which was unlocked, and declared the building cleared five minutes later. They discovered one individual, deceased, inside the house. As per standard procedure, a lieutenant and an ambulance were dispatched. I arrived while the fire brigade extinguished what appeared to be a trash fire in the backyard. They said it had been intentionally set.

"I took charge of the scene, which was an apparent suicide of an elderly male. I immediately recognized the individual as someone wanted by the CBI. I notified headquarters, and they summoned you."

The lieutenant's briefing, while efficient, was also entirely uninformative. "Who is it?" Bhati demanded with impatience. The lieutenant just put his finger to his lips, smiled, and motioned for the inspector to follow him. The fire brigade was still rolling up hoses, but they made room for the two men to pass.

The yard was small and the landscaping was not particularly impressive. It was enclosed by a low iron fence, and a paved walkway led up to a modest house that was practical and well kept. The lieutenant explained, "It's a rental property used mostly by tourists. The landlord is on his way here. He said the current occupant had rented it for two weeks."

The front door was open, leading into a well-furnished living room. An easy chair in one corner held the corpse of an older man. A spatter of blood and gray matter on the wall behind him told Bhati the manner of death, and an automatic pistol in his lap seemingly confirmed the method. He was sure the medical examiner would find the bullet hole and powder burns on the roof of his mouth.

It wasn't until then that he paused in his examination to look at the face of the corpse. It was untouched by the bullet. A shock of recognition and excitement flashed through Bhati's body. Vice Admiral Badu Singh Dhankhar was the most wanted man in India, but he'd decided to make himself unavailable.

Bhati gathered himself. The news media in India and indeed, throughout the world, had been in an uproar for two days. That was when the population had learned of a frightening plot that had been stopped by the destruction of the nuclear submarine, *Chakra*, and its crew of seventy-three. The submarine was destroyed by Indian naval assets after it had gone renegade and evidently intent on starting a nuclear war with China. Vice Admiral Dhankhar, a famous and respected naval officer, had been named as the ringleader, and his image was plastered all over India.

The CBI had actually received orders to find Dhankhar

two weeks earlier, for reasons then unexplained. News of the conspiracy had let Bhati and the rest of the special crime branch at the regional headquarters in Chandigarh put the pieces together.

It was a miracle that the two police officers that cleared the house had not recognized him.

"What about the fire?" Bhati asked, already suspecting the answer.

"Mostly paper, but other objects as well. Pieces of plastic, and what looks like a melted cell phone, perhaps other personal electronics." The lieutenant pointed to a bedroom. "There's a laptop computer in there with several bullet holes through it."

The senior inspector organized his thoughts. "Bring in more men to fully secure the area, and your best forensics team. Tell the fire brigade not to touch the remains of that fire, but don't let them leave yet. Have your people go over the entire house with a fine comb, and don't let the two officers who found the body talk to anyone until I've spoken with them."

The lieutenant was writing rapidly as Bhati spat out orders. When he paused, Bhati realized he'd run out of urgent tasks. That was enough to get started. "You've done well, Lieutenant. Get your people busy. I have to make a call."

Bhati stepped outside to phone his superiors. As busy as this place was now, it was going to get a whole lot busier.

23 April 2017
0700 Local Time
CNN

"This is Sam Markham with breaking news: The nuclear weapon originally intended for Victoria Harbor in Hong Kong finally detonated at noon local time today. Initial reports confirm it was a larger weapon—much, much larger than the ten-kiloton nuclear depth bomb used two days ago to destroy the wreck of the rogue Indian submarine *Chakra* and its deadly cargo."

An inset showed a flat ocean horizon suddenly rising up in an angry white ball, ringed with fire. "That relatively small explosion was in water less than two hundred feet deep. Luckily, this much larger weapon had been dropped into water over four thousand feet deep.

"As far as can be determined, there was no loss of life or property damage. The explosion did not break the surface of the water, although the site was kept clear as a safety precaution. Scientific teams have moved in to determine the radiation levels at the site of the explosion and when it will be safe for fishing vessels to return to the area. Commercial traffic, which was severely disrupted by the exclusion zone, will resume normal operations immediately.

"Although the Indians are credited with the destruction of their renegade submarine, apparently American naval forces were heavily involved, and the full story of the hunt and sinking of *Chakra* will depend on the willingness of those involved to share what was a battle hidden under the surface of a distant ocean.

"The Indian government has declared a state of emergency while the hunt continues for the plotters of what we now know was called 'Operation Vajra.' The destruction of the rogue submarine and the suicide of the ringleader have not dampened the Indian authorities' investigation completely, and what has been learned comes from several high-ranking government officials now facing charges of treason and terrorism.

"News of the scandal forced the Indian delegation in Geneva to abandon the dormant Indo-Pak peace talks, literally disappearing in the middle of the night. Indian troops have been withdrawing to their original starting lines inside India for several days, and experts believe hat the once-temporary cease-fire will now be extended ndefinitely, even if an official peace treaty is never signed.

"Upon receiving news of the final torpedo's detonaion, President Myles's staff released a prepared statenent. 'This thankfully harmless explosion is the coda to he Littoral Alliance war, which has claimed more lives in ecent days, but could have exploded into a worldwide lisaster. Its successful resolution required the courageous fforts of both individuals and nations who were more interested in peace than power. Let their actions be an exmple to us all.' "

29 April 2017
USS *North Dakota*
Wharf B, U.S. Naval Base Guam

The commodore had the base's band at the pier, playing "Victory at Sea" as *North Dakota* pulled in. Jerry had one of his more junior officers make the approach, with only a minor bobble, due to a wind setting them off the pier.

Simonis and the rest of his staff were drawn up in welcome, but the families were absent. That had been scheduled for the evening, after Jerry, his officers, and senior enlisted had been debriefed, and instructed on what they could and couldn't say.

Once the lines were over and the inport watch set, the three sub captains came ashore. Jerry, Samant, and Petrov received four bells each, and the 1MC announcing system blared, "*North Dakota*, departing," then "Captain, Indian Navy, departing," and finally "Captain, Russian Navy, retired, departing."

Both Samant and Petrov were still wearing their *North Dakota* ball caps, but Samant replaced his with his Indian Navy uniform cover once he was on the pier. Commodore Simonis, with a larger smile than Jerry remembered, greeted each at the foot of the brow, and joked, "There were so many bells I thought you were on fire."

Most of *North Dakota*'s wardroom followed the three senior officers off the ship, and along with the staff, piled

nto vans bound for the squadron headquarters and the debriefing.

Simonis offered them a ride in his official car, but said,
"Jerry, you usually like to stretch your legs when you come
ashore." To Jerry's guests, he explained, "It's a ten-minute
walk from here." They were all agreeable.

The four officers started out, and Simonis immediately
said, "Dr. Patterson sends her apologies to all of you. She
had hoped to be here to welcome you back herself, but
managing the aftermath of the situation is demanding
more of her time than the crisis itself. She also mentioned
something about 'not embarrassing Jerry any further.'"

That earned Jerry curious looks from both Samant and
Petrov, but he just answered, "I'll explain later," and kept
walking.

Simonis adjusted his stride to walk alongside Captain
Samant. "I have the honor of relaying messages to you
from two presidents. Our President Myles sends his deepest condolences over the loss of *Chakra*, and wishes he
could award you a medal for your courage both during and
at the end of this crisis.

"On the other hand, President Handa appears ready to
award you several medals, and broadly hinted that when
you return, you should visit a uniform shop for admirals' rank insignia. He wants you back ASAP, and there
has been negotiation at the highest levels of our governments regarding when that will be. As far as we are concerned, that's whenever you want."

Next he turned to Petrov. "My instructions are to offer
you our deepest thanks, and to ask if there is anything the
United States can offer you in appreciation."

Petrov shrugged. "We three talked during the trip back.
I don't think I can get my old job back, and I don't know
if I'd even be welcome in Russia. I've been instrumental
in embarrassing my government, and I've been party to the
loss of another Russian submarine." The Russian intentionally bumped into Jerry as he finished his statement.

Jerry's hands flew up in frustration, and he all bu[t] pleaded, "Alex, will you give it a rest! Please!" Saman[t] chuckled, having been informed of the inside joke, while Simonis looked on with confusion.

"Well, I can guarantee that the U.S. would welcome you, Captain Petrov," Simonis said, and Jerry nodded firmly.

The Russian smiled but shook his head. "Thank you, bu[t] President Handa said that I'd 'always have a home in India,' which is about the nicest thing anyone's ever said to me, and Girish has made the point that the Indian Navy will need technical experts like me for a long time yet."

Samant appeared totally surprised and said, "But . . . but you're always complaining about the heat, and the spicy food!"

Petrov shrugged with a broad grin. "I'll cope. Besides, I'm starting to like cricket."

As they were finishing their walk, Simonis was re minded of a message he had to pass on. He began with the four most feared words.

"Oh, by the way, Jerry, in addition to a well-deserved 'well done,' from the entire chain of command, I have to warn you: Dr. Patterson's been finalizing plans with Emily for a house-hunting expedition to Washington, D.C. You don't rotate out for a while yet, but Emily wants to find a new home now, before the baby comes. Besides, real estate transactions can take longer to arrive than a baby."

Simonis smiled wolfishly. "You'll *love* the Pentagon."